Lucky

To Be Alive?

ALICE
CROMIE

SIMON AND SCHUSTER *New York*

Copyright © 1978 by Alice Cromie
and Pamela Painter Skeen
All rights reserved
including the right of reproduction
in whole or in part in any form
Published by Simon and Schuster
A Division of Gulf & Western Corporation
Simon & Schuster Building
Rockefeller Center
1230 Avenue of the Americas
New York, New York 10020
Designed by Jill Weber
Manufactured in the United States of America

1 2 3 4 5 6 7 8 9 10

Library of Congress Cataloging in Publication Data

Cromie, Alice Hamilton.
  Lucky to be alive?

  I. Title.
PZ4.C944Lu   [PS3553.R538]   813'.5'4   78-12483

ISBN 0-671-24081-1

The author wishes to thank:
  Alfred A. Knopf, Inc., for permission to reprint
lines from "A Farewell to a Friend" by Li Po,
from *The Jade Mountain: A Chinese Anthology*,
translated by Witter Bynner from the texts of
Kiang Kang-Hu, copyright 1929, renewed 1957 by
Alfred A. Knopf, Inc.;
  Holt, Rinehart and Winston, Publishers, for
permission to reprint "I promise nothing: friends
will part" from *The Collected Poems of A. E.
Housman*, copyright 1936 by Barclays Bank Ltd.,
copyright © 1964 by Robert E. Symons.

to Bob

1.

"*How tall* are you?" he asked.

"One and a half feet," I said, and then added, "Sorry."

I was saying sorry a lot these days, accidentally bumping people, asking hurrying passengers to please hold elevator doors, apologizing to impatient drivers when I couldn't cross a street all the way on the green, but it was getting better. I was moving at a reasonable speed and had abandoned my cane. I was trying to monitor my tongue, too, when I was nervous and tired, and tended to snap at curious strangers.

This man was a stranger, but he was here to ask questions. And it wasn't his fault I was lame. He wasn't the one who had come out of the night on the wrong side of the road and wiped out my family. My mother, father, and Sam, my kid brother, and part of my left foot, as it turned out. All gone. Eighteen months ago, and I could think about it without going blank. Almost without a shiver, but not without my foot hurting.

"I'm five-six. Without heels, as they say on the weight charts. One eighteen pounds. Why does it matter? Would she want me to wear a uniform? What kind of uniform does a tutor wear?"

He tried to smile at me. His amber eyes were apologetic. "I know this is tiring, but it's so important to get the right person."

His lids dropped, he had sandy lashes. He was getting ready to lie, I was sure. Whatever for? A year in a hospital, if nothing else, makes you an expert on liars, especially well-meant, kindly ones. "Alison was an executive secretary for Clinton before they were married. She's one of the most organized persons I've ever met and I believe you'll find her easy to work for." There it was—the last part. He wasn't at all sure this Alison Clinton was an easy person to work for. "She really *needs* the help this summer."

I said, "I really want the job. And I need it." Doctor's orders, for one thing. "Tutoring a nine-year-old sounds fine to me." "Therapy," my doctor had said, "but don't tell a prospective employer that. Don't worry him. You can handle it."

"You wouldn't mind being tied down? And quite a long way from Chicago? Even from Lakeview, as a matter of fact, the house is remote, but there are plenty of cars. Can you drive? Good. However that's another thing. The hours are long though the work is light. You'll need to be with the boy most of the time."

"I don't mind." I studied his hands. He had long, thin, but strong-looking fingers. He might have been a surgeon, but he was only an interviewer. Randolph Paul, trying to hire the best tutor for Colin Clinton, the younger son of Jonathan Clinton, internationally known artist, and none of them had anything to do with trauma centers, hospitals, or rehab clinics. Colin had missed school this past spring because of a rou-

8

tine appendectomy. I would be leaving the rubber-tired life behind and getting back to a normal world.

"The house is spectacular. There's a beach for walking, rock hunting, though not for swimming. No one else lives in. Not really. Savannah, the cook, goes home to Evanston nights —she has her own family."

"I've been—sort of institutionalized, call it that. Hospital, rehab—I'll enjoy being on my own, I'm sure of it."

"Miles and Stella Burton live in an apartment over the garages. But their nights are their own, unless there's an emergency. Stella is head housekeeper. Miles supervises the gardeners, fills in as chauffeur, he's a sort of jack-of-all-trades, even to playing chess all night with Jonathan if the master is restless." This time his hazel eyes smiled along with his lips. "Jonathan's other son uses a cabin on the property some of the time, but it's a considerable distance from the house. You probably wouldn't see him. Jonathan's studio is separate, too. Colin would be your only responsibility."

My responsibility? Not the boy's parents'?

"The Clintons will be away this summer?"

"Not *away*, exactly, but extremely busy. There's to be a major fall exhibition."

"Okay," I said quickly, intent on the right answers and not the details. "I'll be glad to stay quiet and probably go to bed as early as Colin. I've never had a real job before, mostly baby-sitting. I'll need to keep in shape." Then I shut up. I wanted to be hired, but I wouldn't beg.

Randolph Paul suddenly leaned across the desk and took my hand in his. "Miss Ames, we've had a lot of response to the ad, but you are the first one who seems right for the job. We've had other art majors, some much more advanced than you, but they weren't interested in the hours required. We've had suitable tutors for math or English who couldn't tell a Calder from a windmill or a Clinton from a Jasper Johns.

9

You are just twenty-two, which is young, perhaps, but will make you a better companion in Colin's eyes, I'm sure." Again he paused, and then said hesitantly, "As for your—"

"Deformity," I said swiftly.

"Your injury," he corrected gently, keeping his gaze steady now. "I can see how aware you must be—but I confess if you hadn't been totally honest on the application, I wouldn't have guessed. As I recall, you didn't even limp when you came in. In any case, I don't see how it could affect your qualifications. Colin's going on ten and able to do nearly everything for himself. We—Alison Clinton and I—felt that someone who'd studied art and cared about it would fit the household best. Colin's own mother was an architect. She—died a few years ago. Most of the family friends are in the arts. Even Colin's brother is a sculptor. You do see it's important you have some knowledge of the world these people live in and talk about? Colin's been accustomed to artists all his life."

He talked on, but I heard only that he was accepting me. For a moment I thought I might burst into tears. But I hadn't wept in eighteen months and I didn't now.

"There's just one thing to be settled," he said, "you understand the job is for the entire summer?"

"I know."

"And you wouldn't run away if Jonathan should get one of his famous tantrums at the sight of you?"

"I can't run," I said. But famous tantrums? At the sight of me?

"You see we've rented this office for interviews—if we give it up and dismiss the other applicants, I'd like to have your word that you won't change your mind."

"I can put it in writing if you like."

"No!" His response was immediate, then he laughed. "That's not at all necessary. Miss Ames, could you be in Lakeview by Monday afternoon or is that rushing you?"

10

"No trouble at all. I'll be there." I travel light, I could have added, and no one to say good-bye to. Because how would it sound to mention an aunt, my father's sister and my only living relative, who hadn't even heard about the accident? Aunt Lynne travels and writes books but I wouldn't want to bother her publishers. The travel writers' organization has an office in Washington, and I'd left a message there. I could leave the Clintons' number and another message.

Randolph Paul was beaming at me, giving me directions, telling me the chauffeur might meet me, but if not there was a gabby taxi-driver, better not encourage him. "Give him one word and he'll talk an arm or a leg off. Oh, I *am* sorry!"

"Don't be. Happens all the time. I do it myself."

His smile flashed. He had perfect teeth. "I'm sure you'll cope and I'm looking forward to seeing you again."

"Do you work there, too, Mr. Paul?"

Now why did he look flushed?

"I'm an art dealer, Miss Ames, with my father. Paul Galleries."

I said, "I should've remembered the name. You're on Michigan Avenue, or just around the corner? Your place looks elegant."

"My father had a heart attack in March but he's improving. We're having a Clinton exhibition in September—he'll have to be well then. He and Jonathan are old friends. Alison —Mrs. Clinton—and I are working very hard on the preparations. So she won't have time to help Colin just now."

I nodded, wanting to ask a question. Why would Clinton throw a tantrum at the sight of a tutor? But I let it go. I concentrated on leaving without limping.

As usual I was worrying about the wrong thing.

11

2.

Several other passengers were getting off at Lakeview. Three women carried packages. I read the labels—Marshall Field's, I. Magnin, Saks, and one Lane Bryant. Something for the maid, no doubt. The woman who carried it was a size 5. I stared through the filthy windows. All the women across the tracks waiting for the southbound train were black. Some were thin, others heavy, but all looked hot and tired. Then I couldn't delay any longer. I moved awkwardly in my haste to leave before the train moved on toward Milwaukee.

Here in a hot, dusty, and strange suburb I was soon alone except for a wilted old man leaning against his cab, picking what looked to be his last three teeth. Five cars had slashed past and were gone. A Mercedes, an Alfa Romeo, one beat-up old Triumph, then two Ford station wagons. Whatever car the Clintons' man drove, it wasn't one of these. Nor was it still parked, though I looked hopefully at the lot. The cabdriver shoved his cap back, scratched his perspiring brow and finally asked, "You Miss Ames?"

I nodded.

"You was supposed to be here an hour ago."

"I missed the two-forty." I hadn't reckoned the time that carrying even a light bag would cost me.

"You're pretty young, ain't you?" But he opened the back door, watched me half fall into the seat, and put my bag beside him in the front of the cab.

"Depends. Some days, maybe."

"You a relative?"

"No, and can we get going please? I'm late already."

"Suits me, your highness." We pulled away from the curb at a pace that scarcely disturbed the dust. "So you're no relation. You one of them models?"

"I'm the purple highlight in the foreground," I said recklessly. "How did you recognize me?"

He muttered something about smartass kids. How could even a cabdriver live in a town with a genius and not know Jonathan Clinton's abstract canvases? Surely the local paper carried stories on their resident celebrity?

"These dames they come and go," he said. "Not so many now as used to be." We passed a high school with a wide, sloping lawn and pebbled walks. And a piece of sculpture that might be a Henry Moore. Too far away to tell, even at twenty miles an hour.

"I never see much a' the Clintons anymore. Only Miles. Lord knows, anyone hangs out at Griff's Tavern sees all they want of Miles."

I stayed silent, but he darted frequent looks at me in the rearview mirror. "You just visiting for the day?"

"Um."

"Ever been here before? Ever seen that house?"

I shrugged. He was watching with keen interest.

13

"Looks like whatchacallit—a maw-*sole*-eum."

"Mausoleum," I murmured and shivered, though my mother and father and Sam lay in no stately tomb.

"Guess you're alive anyway. I can see your lips moving."

We passed tennis courts and a golf course and came into a shopping area. One poster propped against a piece of driftwood, anchored in sand, decorated the window of a travel agency, and I thought of my aunt, Lynne Babcock, travel writer these days, once a foreign correspondent. Actually a war correspondent, but I thought foreign sounded more glamorous. Trench coat, belted, hat pulled low over the eyes, and a curl of cigarette smoke—Lauren Bacall of years ago.

Cancun-Ixtapa the poster advertised. *Follow the sun to Mexico's golden beaches.* How do you walk the golden beaches with a prosthesis strapped to your heel? All golden boys must run away, when Tyler hobbles out to play. "Oh, boy, oh, boy," I said, pulling back from the easy mire of self-pity.

"You all right, miss? I can turn the blower down if it's too cold."

"I'm okay. Are you sure we're going in the right direction? Mr. Paul said the house was outside of town, we seem to be in town—" Too late I bit my lip.

"It's the other side, way the hell and gone the other side. You work for the Pauls, huh?"

I shook my head. "All I said was the house is in the country, and right on the lake."

"We're getting there, little lady. Take it easy." He tapped a silent tune on the steering wheel with a veined old hand as he waited at a stoplight. "I see Paul, the young one, now and again. Not the old fellow lately. Young Paul takes a cab every time he has a snootful, up at the house."

"You make it sound as if everyone out here has a drinking problem!"

14

"Not a-tall. Not Paul anyway. He's just mighty careful. Miles—that's somethin' else." He fell into silence at last as we moved forward across some more railroad tracks into middle-of-town traffic, and eventually turned down a curving residential street. The houses were set in landscaped lawns and were rambling frame-structures, flanked by deep porches, upper stories with wrought-iron or picket-railed balconies, and here and there a widow's walk, though not even the tallest widow could have seen anything but trees. Stately houses, full of grace, to a person who had grown up in Independence, Missouri, home of Victoriana.

"This used to be called Packing-House Row." The driver winked at me in the mirror. "All them ham and pork barons."

I was silent but I smiled back at him. Maybe these imposing mansions set comfortably distant from each other on wooded lots were "out in the country" to Randolph Paul, city boy. I could easily walk to town from here. Colin and I could explore in all directions, taking our time about it. The lake must be just beyond some of these trees. Maybe Jonathan Clinton would be stately, too, and full of grace despite the violence of his paintings.

Forgetting possible tantrums, hoping for the best of all possible worlds as optimistically as Candide's tutor, I shut my eyes and drifted. The prescribed pain-killer I had swallowed reluctantly at the last minute before the train pulled into Lakeview was finally taking effect. When I sat up again we had reached a wooded road with thick underbrush, tall, windswept but untrimmed trees, no traffic and no houses. I saw the driver's tired shoulders as he maneuvered turns on the bumpy, potholed road. He was an old man and I had been rude. I said, "I'm here to tutor Colin Clinton for the summer. I've never been in this part of the country before." I meant economically more than geographically. My roots and all of my family lay in Missouri, not a continent away.

15

"Well, let me tell you, little lady—" He was off on a mono-logue again. That the Clintons were pretty much ree-clooses since all the trouble was his opener, but I tuned him out, having translated ree-clooses to recluses and conquering my curiosity about "all the trouble"; another major mistake, but how was I to know that on an innocent June day? Eventually the road smoothed and we turned between massive stone posts up a winding driveway and stopped at the steps of a well-tended terrace which led to a stark-white building shaped rather like a lozenge.

"Well, we made it," the driver announced. "Ever see any-thing like it?"

"Once," I said. "The Solomon R. Guggenheim Museum, but it was smaller, I think."

"How's that, miss?"

"A real maw-*sole*-eum, all right." Then I was ashamed of myself and said, "A modern art gallery." And worked on getting out without falling forward.

"Here's my card, miss," he offered surprisingly. "It's got two numbers you can call. Anybody young and pretty as you ain't going to be cooped up way out here all summer, right?"

I smiled my thanks and tucked the tattered card in my jacket pocket. "It's so quiet," I said. "Not even bird sounds."

"Yeah," he agreed. "Birds got better sense than hang around here." We gazed at the silent house. The old taxi was noisy, but no one had stirred from within. The driver's cigar bobbed up and down. "You want me to try to raise someone? Carry your bag inside?"

"I can handle it, thanks." I searched for my coin purse but he waved me off. "That's been taken care of, miss. They got a charge."

I shook hands. "Thanks for the lift then. See you around."

He set my bag on the top step and finally departed, looking disappointed that no human being, nor even a family pet, showed up to welcome me. More likely a lizard than a

16

friendly dog, I thought, looking at the expanse of white curving wall. There were no windows. The house seemed almost to shimmer in heat waves. The large oiled-wood, carved, Spanish-style doors had a heavy knocker shaped like a gauntlet. Imagine Jonathan Clinton, abstract expressionist, choosing an entrance fit for Hernando Cortes. I lifted the bronze glove again and let it fall resoundingly, but no one came.

My leg ached. I leaned on the door for support and it slowly swung inward and I stepped inside, leaving my bag on the bricks of the entrance.

No one was in the hall, but the air stirred as if something had moved swiftly and vanished. I held still, listening, holding my breath. I was alone in a vast and deadly quiet hallway, but the door could have been opened by a remote switch. Like garage doors. No big deal.

The hall was lined with doors, set at angles, making it impossible to see into any rooms they led to. Its walls were dazzling white and bare, but rich Oriental runners lay on Carrara marble tiles. The heat was stifling. Surely the wealthy had air conditioning?

I felt faint and limped toward a door, picking the second one for no reason, and found myself in an L-shaped room with one long glass wall. Beyond it the lake glimmered dimly. It seemed as if I floated across thick carpeting, making no sound, yearning toward the cool view.

Waves washed against rocks which were beneath my feet. The house—at least this enormous room—was cantilevered above a cliff, perhaps. No beach was visible, no grass, nor water's edge. Rocks. Heat and straining to keep my balance dizzied me, and I looked for a chair.

Then something sighed. Something stirred just at the edge of my vision and I faltered. I'd been caught limping and glared fiercely in the direction of the sound, the slight movement.

But his back was turned. He was hunched over, elbows on

jean-clad knees, leaning forward, studying the painting which filled the end of the L. The canvas was only partially covered with the vivid colors Jonathan Clinton favored, but it was overwhelming even in this unfinished stage. Dear God! I had blundered upon the master himself at a moment of intense concentration.

His shaggy, gray-frosted hair fell in an uneven line against the collar of a yellow smock. He was tall—even seated that was obvious—and thinner than I had expected. Why had I looked for a modern Rembrandt with a velvet hat and plump Dutch cheeks? Painters come in all shapes and sizes; even a freshman art major knows that. At least he wore a smock that could have been Rembrandt's, I decided. And laughed. I hadn't laughed in eighteen months. The sound startled both of us.

His blue eyes flashed with irritation. "Who in hell are you? Never mind, just get out of here." He rose abruptly and strode past me to a door at the opposite end of the room. Without knocking, he thrust it open and said, "Alison, have Miles take it back to the studio. If you can find the bastard."

He slammed the door, met my stare with a disinterested scowl, asked, "Have you taken root?" And left the room.

I rested on a padded bench. Beyond the slammed door— Alison Clinton. The one who hired me by proxy. I glanced again at the painting, finding no great comfort there. Flame reds, thick blues, a streak of violet swirling across canvas while veils of green and yellow misted the foreground. One famous critic lately had called Clinton a bold invader of inner spaces. This canvas—not even completed—seemed almost to strike me a blow.

Better Alison, I thought, and walked slowly toward her door.

He was half kneeling, half standing in the dark, with the can and the brush at his left hand. On the top step and the lid

18

lightly on the can, but tight enough not to come off too soon. He checked it again with the pencil beam of the flashlight. His fingers were trembling.

It wasn't that he hated the dark. He liked the dark. It was the damned walls closing in. And the smell of this place. It must have been closed for eight, ten years, maybe more, until this week. And there'd been no chance to air it. Maybe no way either.

You weren't supposed to wait around in secret stairways. Not unless you were a ghost, and he was no ghost. Not that he wasn't, when you thought about it, in the ghost business. In a way. It was funny—but he didn't feel like smiling. He was getting a cramp in his leg but he had to be ready. Like a fool Olympic runner, waiting for the signal. No, he wasn't a runner. First he had to get the signal and then he had to wait and keep an eye on his watch, and count, too, might as well. Keep the filthy walls back. This was worse than a priest's hidey-hole. He'd been in one. In Mexico. He hadn't liked it then and he didn't like it now. But there wasn't any other way to bring this thing off. And it had to work.

He was never without a handkerchief, a fresh, white handkerchief, but not now. Sweat ran in his mouth. He licked his lips and reached for the tail of his shirt to wipe his face. Wouldn't you know? Wouldn't this be the time? God, how he hated dirt. If only he could use his right hand to carry the bucket, but he needed his best hand to open the door. It would open. It had opened two days ago. Twice in a dozen years maybe. Unless that kid, always sneaking around, had found it. But if the brat knew about the stairs he'd have made a racetrack out of them, for sure. And there was too much dust, cobwebs, mice droppings.

It would be more like a sack race, potato relay, maybe. One of those idiot games people played on picnics. He didn't have his feet in a gunnysack or a paper bag over his head, but he was carrying a hot potato, you could say that. The paint was green and he couldn't let it drip until the right moment, then it could gush like hell. Make that splash. Gush sounded more like blood. He hated blood—that's why he wouldn't use red, or purple. Sure it would've been a shocker, but green would do the job.

He was glad he'd thought about the air conditioner. Breaking the belt had done the trick. And giving the service joker the wrong directions had been very clever indeed. God! he couldn't hear his watch. He shook his wrist. The watch was all right. It was his pulse racing in his ear that made the roar. Nobody else could hear it. Maybe the mice. Spiders. He put his ear to the door. Clinton was talking to someone, *or talking to himself; just get the hell out of there. The pencil beam lighted the watch face. He had a few minutes to go.*

3.

"*Your résumé* interests me," Alison Clinton said. "Such a lot of trouble for a young woman, but it looks as if—even if you're all alone in the world—well, you're lucky to be alive."

Sooner or later, I could have told her, everyone says it. Lucky to be alive. Standard salve for a survivor's wound. And about as helpful, in my case, as a Band-Aid. Randolph Paul had promised to say nothing to the staff, only to my employers. I wondered if this included the two boys.

I had looked up Clintons in *Who's Who*. Jonathan's first wife had been Agatha Dornblaser, architect. She had died six years ago, when Colin was three. The older son, Dornblaser, was already a young man, Paul had told me. Jonathan Clinton had married Alison Dent less than a year after his first wife's death. "Compliment to his first wife," be damned. No matter if Randolph Paul saw it that way. I wondered if my father would have tried to ease his pain with another woman so soon. For the first time I thought maybe it was better

21

they'd gone together. They'd been childhood sweethearts and best friends. And my Aunt Lynne had once said that was the reason she so seldom came around. "You two are the only couple in the world who make me feel unhappily unmarried," she'd confessed, being a great lady for getting the facts right.

"Miss Ames, you're very quiet!" Alison Clinton spoke tartly, but her green eyes glistened with interest, and she added, "We do appreciate quiet here." I nodded, and she added more gently, "Randy—Mr. Paul—explained about your wanting not to speak of your handicap. I'll leave it to you, my dear. It isn't important to your duties, or to us, though you have my sympathy."

I said thanks just as a small green light blinked on her telephone. When she picked the receiver up, the light went out. She said, "Yes, Jonathan, I'll see to it now." Her voice dropped to a murmur, but mostly she listened. She had crisp dark hair and a deep tan. Her lips and nails matched in glossiness a shade that might be called cinnamon, and could have been created just for her. How many women, even such beauties, get away with brownish lipstick? The wet look. Highly kissable. Jonathan Clinton as a lover might be as violent as his brushstrokes, or as soft as the wisps of dawn colors that sometimes trailed across a stark parallelogram. He'd reminded me of someone. I decided it was the late Peter Finch. And Finch's wife had been exotic, too. I must have made a grimace—reading movie magazines was a hospital pastime.

"I'm sorry for the interruption, Miss Ames." Alison apparently mistook my turned-down mouth for irritation at the delay. "When the green lights blinks Jonathan is calling. When it's red, no one calls *him*. No one. If it's a steady green we may call if we like. There's another light in the kitchen. You do understand? It isn't likely you'd ever have occasion to call him, but Colin might try."

"I'll keep an eye on him," I promised, and wiped my forehead.

"Sorry about the heat. The air-conditioning man promised to be here by now but they're all alike." She rolled back a silken cuff and glanced at her bracelet watch. "You are late, too. We've been expecting you for an hour."

Who would have guessed it? "I missed connections. I won't be late again, Mrs. Clinton."

This time she said, "Excuse me, I must tell Randy you got here." She tapped out the numbers and spoke into the phone. Then she covered the mouthpiece with her hand. "This may take a moment, dear; Randy and I have so much business. Will you excuse me, dear?"

I wanted to protest, Don't call me dear. Nurses called everyone dear! But I was a hired hand here. I looked for a place to get lost but there was nowhere to go out of earshot. I moved to the end of the room and stood before a wall of books. The titles ran together. I twirled a Replogle globe. I could save all the money she was going to pay me while she was calling me dear and get away from here come September. Maybe go find my aunt and have a relative like everyone else. Even if she couldn't be counted on to stay in one place.

The spinning globe sent a flash of light across a polished steel obelisk on a jet base. I leaned toward the sculpture and could see my brown eyes, tinier than life, an enormous clown mouth. Not fair. My mouth was a little too large anyway. The light made my hair almost as cornsilk fine as I could want. I had supposed that sitting on a hospital sun deck dried up the hair as fast as the soul.

Alison's lashes were thick and dark, concealing her thoughts as she looked down at the phone and spoke softly. If they were fake lashes, they were expertly applied, like her nail lacquer. When she cradled the phone again, she reached for a leather portfolio. Its embossed initials—ADC—were antique gold.

"Let me see—Ames—Tyler—isn't that a rather unusual name for—Missouri? Independence, Missouri?"

"Only one in town, Mrs. Clinton."

"Alison," she amended. She moved her calendar a millimeter to the left, moved it back, examined her cinnamon polish, and waited. For what? For me to explain my name?

"My parents were both professors. Small college. They once thought they'd like to buy a yacht and go breezing about the ports of call, that's how they put it. Anyway they got a canoe, from somebody, and they went breezing up and down the Missouri River—the year I was born. My dad—he was a teacher, you see, American history and literature—anyway he said he had Tippy-canoe and Tyler, too."

He'd said it once and that had been more than enough, but whose business? I hadn't talked this much about the past since the accident. Alison Clinton's kind smile was hard to take.

"Actually it was my mother's maiden name," I said, and a man's laugh rang out from the doorway. The newcomer approached Alison's desk, moving lightly, enviably, jointless like a superjock in jeans and sneakers. He wore a sweat shirt with the sleeves cut out and his brown forearms were developed like a sculptor's.

He extended a hand to me. "I'm Blase, rhymes with days or haze. The best I could do with my mother's name, Dornblaser. Now I find in old English it means 'livid' or 'one who lisps and stammers.' Isn't that rotten?" His handshake was firm.

I couldn't help smiling back at him. "I've never covered any buildings with tiles. I looked mine up, too."

Alison said, "Tyler is Colin's tutor. Randy found her for us. Aren't we lucky?"

Her light, pleasant words had an odd effect. He dropped my hand as if it were a dead thing.

"How is Randy?" he asked me flatly.

24

"He's fine," Alison answered swiftly. "I've just been talking with him. What do you want, Blase?"

"Boxes. I ran out. Cartons, paper bags, an old pillowcase, anything— And what happened to the air conditioning?" His question was for Alison, but his dark blue eyes gave me a direct gaze and then he added softly, "Are you a friend of Randy's or an employee?"

I said, "I answered the ad." He sent a questioning look toward his stepmother, but the telephone was ringing again and she answered it.

"You shouldn't have to stand in all this heat, Miss Ames." Blase Clinton pushed a chair forward and held it for me. I sank into it with a lump of bitterness in my throat. Paul hadn't kept his word. This son knew and probably Colin, too. I stared at my hands and my ten fingers and almost missed his next casual remark, "Do you play tennis, Miss Ames? There are plenty of courts at the club. Ours have gone to grass lately. Anybody playing games around here bothers the master. If you like to sail, or just get out and ride the waves, Jonathan has a two-boat fleet—a cabin cruiser and a Q boat . . . sounds like a German sub, but it's a sailboat."

"Swimming?" I asked, thanking God I'd been wrong; Blase didn't know about my foot. His navy eyes seemed to darken almost to black. "Plenty of pools we can get you to," he said. "Here it's, ah—off limits. There's a drop-off."

Alison had put down the phone. "Too deep and too dirty," she added. "I thought Randy would have mentioned that." She looked concerned. "Do you need to swim?" she asked, making it an innocuous query, for which I thanked her silently while I shook my head no, I didn't need to swim.

"You look pale," Blase commented. "Can I get you a cold drink?"

"I'm fine, thanks."

Alison said, "Miss Ames—Tyler—is from Missouri. I'm

25

sure she's used to hot weather. It's a shame this house wasn't built for regular changes of season. That's about the only thing Agatha didn't think of."

"One among others," Blase said remotely, and Alison flushed. She fanned her face with her hand. "Ask Savannah for boxes, or Miles— Good heavens, I nearly forgot. Jonathan wants Miles to move the painting back to the studio."

"I can do it, don't bother Miles." He was moving toward the door, but Alison jumped up. "No! Wait, please, Blase!" She brushed a damp strand of hair from her forehead. "Just get your packing done. We want to have Tyler settled as soon as possible."

I said, "Hey, am I putting anyone out? Excuse me, but I don't need much space—isn't there another room?"

Alison told me to shush and beckoned for me to follow her to the gallery. I watched Blase, departing by the door he had come in. "That's the way to the library," Alison told me. "You'll see the entire house later. Blase is taking his books, I suppose."

"But I—" Again she shushed me. "You're not putting him out of his room. He moves to the cabin every summer. Oh, oh—my God!"

We both came to a standstill at the sight in the gallery. The painting at the end of the L had been splashed with green, wildly, recklessly, with globules still dripping to the marble floor, not carpeted at this one end of the vast room. Luckily not carpeted. Rivulets of green ran across yellow triangles blurring them into neon shapes. Alison stepped forward like a sleepwalker until her fingers touched the wetness as if to confirm the wreckage.

"Stella! Savannah! Miles! Come here at once! Hurry!"

Even sharing her shock I wondered why she didn't call out for Blase who was only a room away. There was an open can of paint on the floor. House paint! A brush had been dropped beside it. I bent awkwardly and picked up the brush by its messy handle and tried to wipe excess paint on the inner rim of the can. But where was the lid?

A woman's voice rose in dismay. The redhead who rushed in from the hall stared first at the canvas and then at me and the brush in my hand. A look of relief slid across her face and vanished. Alison said crisply, "Stella, this is Tyler Ames, the tutor we've hired for Colin. Where is Miles?"

"Who knows? Out back maybe. I'll look for him."

"Wait a minute. Where's Colin? Have you seen him?"

Stella shook her head. Her gray eyes were angry. "I was downstairs fixing the room. Blase said—"

"Blase is in the library," Alison cut her off. "He's busy packing—don't say anything to him. Get Miles and Savannah to look for Colin. You can try to clean this up—the floor anyway. Don't touch the canvas."

Stella looked scornful, I thought, as if she knew better than to touch the canvas, but she left without speaking again. Alison said, "The only way into the library is through my office. Blase has been there for several hours—or maybe it only seems hours—I'm too upset to think. When the house was built, both the office and library were meant for my husband's first wife. Now, it's not very convenient, but too late to change— Oh, what does it matter? I just pray Colin had nothing to do with this. Years ago he pulled a little boy's prank. Smeared watercolors on a valuable book—and some other things. He's a strange child—but quiet—"

I looked at the size of the canvas and the reach of the green house paint. As a stranger I should keep out of the problem, but how could a child do so much damage in such little time at such heights well above his head and wide, even for a boy's arms extended by a brush?

I spoke hesitantly. "Please forgive me, Mrs. Clinton, but your husband and I were both here just a short while ago—

27

maybe thirty minutes, however long it's been since I came in your office. The painting was all right then. I don't see how—"

"You saw Jonathan?" Her eyes went wide, then narrowed, as if she were counting time in her head. "He was still here when you arrived? Did he speak to you?"

"Not really. He was in a dreadful hurry." And mood, but I wouldn't add that. She was already too distraught.

Another female voice rose in a shriek. "Oh, Lord, Lord, it's happen again!"

The tall, thin black woman who came in was drying her hands on an apron. Her mouth drew down at the corners. She looked at Alison as if ready to do battle. "Don't you blame that boy!"

Watercolors in a book was not to be compared to this vandalism. I wondered why everyone seemed to assume the boy was guilty. Stella's look of relief at seeing a stranger with a paintbrush could have been a momentary hope that I was a crazy person who had wandered in to wreck the place, I decided. But she must have realized at once, even before Alison introduced me, that someone else was to blame. She must have feared for the boy, I thought. At least I hoped. If Colin was indeed a problem child, the more allies he had the better. We could all work together. I realized that while I was musing, Alison had been trying to introduce the cook, Savannah, who wanted to take the brush from my hand.

Savannah said, "Colin was out in the front drive waiting for you, hour ago. I guess he gave up." She wrinkled her long nose. "Wish we could open some windows. We ought to get rid of this paint stink. When's that fool air man coming? Likely Colin's off in the woods trying to keep cool. I been watering my tomato vines out back. Didn't see him last hour anyway."

Alison sighed heavily. "I'd better tell Jonathan. Stella is

28

bringing some cleaning materials. You look for Colin, Savannah."

"The light is on," said Savannah darkly.

"I know." Alison was grim. "I'll have to take my chances. Tyler, will you wait for me here, please?"

I nodded and slid into a Barcelona chair, leaning back against the heavenly soft leather, shutting my eyes. All too soon footsteps came back. Stella had lost no time, I thought, and then someone whistled. A hoarse voice said, " 'Ah, alone I did it.' "

I sat up and stared at the stranger. His breath told me this was probably the missing Miles. He attempted a bow but nearly pitched headlong. "Ah, ma'am—thousand pardons. Miles Burton. At your service."

His curly dark hair was threaded with gray and so was his beard. Sweat glistened on the hairs of his forearms, and little wonder. He wore a plaid flannel shirt with its long sleeves rolled back just below the elbows. And a bandanna scarf knotted at his neck.

"Where's the lid?" I asked bluntly and not much to the point. The culprit was more important than the evidence, but I was bone weary.

"What are we talking about?" he asked, not unkindly. "If anything at all that is. You recall the fabled Lewis Carroll— 'if there's no meaning in it, that saves a world of trouble, quoth the White Queen,' or something to that effect."

"I said, "Well, the paint can lid was missing, but so's the can now. I mean, Savannah took it away."

"Our boy Colin is missing, too, is he not?"

"But you just admitted—"

He struck his brow dramatically with the palm of his hand. A perfectly clean hand, I noticed. No paint on it. No paint on his clothes.

" 'Alone I did it'? You don't recognize Shakespeare, the

29

immortal bard? And you supposed to be a schoolmarm? *Coriolanus*, Mistress Ignorance, or perhaps Mistress Innocence is more like it, forgive me. The 'I' in this instance will probably prove to be the young Master Colin, boy brat. Wait and see."

Pain stabbed my heel and leg. Even my knee hurt. Stella was back with a rolling cart which held wire baskets of cleaning supplies. She was pulling rubber gloves over her freckled but manicured hands. Her white uniform must have been custom-made to fit a small waist, rounded hips, and a bosom that surely took a C-cup bra.

"Miles, get a move on," Stella ordered. "Miss Ames, where's your luggage?"

"One bag. It's just outside the front door. I can manage it."

She ignored the offer. "Miles, take it down to Blase's room. Then get the dolly and take this thing out of here. Better ask Alison where she wants it. Maybe he better not see it today."

Everyone on a first-name basis around here. I liked that. Miles saluted Stella behind her back, silently clicking the heels of his worn sneakers. Then he winked at me and departed humming. His shoes were old and so were the paint and grass stains on them. He could have changed clothes, of course, but his cheerful humming didn't sound like a guilty man's.

Stella said, "Please don't pay any attention to Miles, Miss Ames, especially when he's like this. He talks a lot of nonsense." She had removed the worst of the spots with cleaner and was trying another one of the stubborn parts, wrinkling her nose at the smell of paint and cleaning fluid. "Colin has been acting up lately, the way boys do. But he didn't have anything to do with this. Don't let anyone convince you of that. He's enormously shy and has strange ways, but any loner does."

30

"I'm looking forward to seeing him," I said.

Alison came back slightly out of breath, as if she had been running to rejoin us. "Well, let's get you moved in, Tyler. Follow me, please."

Stella called after her. "How did he take it, Alison?"

"Later, later," came the vague response. "Come along, Tyler."

We went down a free-hanging spiral staircase which looked more like a steel sculpture than a functional part of the house.

"I wonder what Thomas Jefferson would have done with steel," I said, to make a change of subject, small talk, whatever.

"It is beautiful, isn't it?" she agreed. "Jonathan commissioned it. The stairs as such were not a part of Agatha Clinton's original plan. My husband's first wife was the architect —but you must have gathered that."

We reached the lower hallway and entered a large room with one glass wall, like the gallery, but this was a lived-in area and at last I saw signs that a child inhabited the house. Miniature cars were lined up in race formation on a low table and a pile of library books was stacked on a low wooden chair.

Here the walls were brightened with watercolors and oils. In one small painting, the light played on a pale, fair-haired woman reading a book to a boy who had golden red curls. Both were sitting on a grassy hill in summertime. I asked, "A Renoir? One of the Impressionists?" It was a distance away.

"An early Dornblaser Clinton," Alison said, dismissing it. "Will this room do for lessons?"

Large leather chairs flanked the fireplace. Music came softly from a concealed stereo. "Muskrat Ramble." Not a piece you heard in elevators equipped with Muzak. There was a wall of bookshelves. Empty now except for a row of

Dickens in what looked to be a well-used set and a twelve-volume lot of a popular encyclopedia for children, looking untouched. I said, "I wish I hadn't left Jane Austen behind," and belatedly added, "It's a lovely room."

She nodded and led the way down another hallway to a smaller sitting room. "Colin is moody, Tyler. He'll come out of hiding when he feels ready. He may have thought your lateness was a form of rejection."

I had a shocking thought. "He wouldn't have been angry enough to—" and broke off, as Alison shook her head in understanding.

"No, I don't think so. This is your suite—sorry it's a bit masculine. We won't have time to redecorate."

I leaned against the doorjamb. "It's far grander than any I've ever occupied." Beyond doubt a man's room, but wonderfully inviting with a sturdy desk and padded swivel chair. A good lamp beside the desk and another equally good for reading beside an easy chair. More bookshelves. Solid tables. One low chair, which faced the glass wall and the lake, looked the most used of all.

Alison said, "Your bedroom is more of the same. If it bothers you to have the lake so close, you can draw the curtains anytime. I often do. I'm on the third floor, or second, depending where you begin counting, and so is Colin. But if he has an upset—or a nightmare—and wants to be nearer to you, one of the divans in the family room is a pullout bed." She went on, vaguely explaining the layout of the house, until a voice interrupted from the bedroom doorway.

"Stepmama, I think I've got the last of my gear, but considering the new tenant"—Blase was carrying golf clubs and an expensive-looking camera case—"I'm not at all sure I want to leave. Maybe I should bunk in the family room."

"Blase, please." Alison sounded patient but tired. "Did Stella bring clean linens?"

"She did." He bowed, and he tossed the camera case on the soft chair seat. "It's a Minolta, Tyler. It's got a good lens and maybe you can have some fun with it. I've just treated myself to a new Nikon. Welcome, Tyler Ames. Welcome to my bed." Then he was gone.

4.

Within a few minutes I was moved in. My face still felt hot, more from the searching look Blase had given me as he departed than from his words. I stowed my few books, all paperbacks because I'd had to carry them, on the shelves of a night table, my toothbrush in the luxurious bathroom, and my underwear in a small pile in a pine-scented drawer. To make the summer dresses, tops, slacks, shorts, and a raincoat seem a larger collection in the wall of closets, I hung my sweater and a shawl on separate hangers. Probably Blase Clinton's wardrobe had filled the entire space, although his outfit today had been casual enough.

The lake side of the bedroom had heavy linen draperies and a sliding glass door to the balcony, which was redwood and narrow but looked solid with a waist-high railing. This part of the house was south of the gallery section, and when I stepped outside I could see the water's edge with sand instead of rocks directly below. The balcony ran past my sitting room and the lounge to steps which could lead to the beach or perhaps the back driveway. Both my bedroom and parlor had access to the outdoors, but only the latter opened on the inside hall leading to the room we would use for Colin's lessons. All doors had locks, I noticed. Hospital rooms do not.

A lone sail, far out on Lake Michigan, made the water and sky seem wider, deeper, even more endless than if there'd been no break in the horizon. I found myself sighing repeatedly and then snapped my fingers with annoyance.

For months I'd been easing into a kind of melancholy at twilight as an older woman, perhaps, would have slipped into a comforting shawl. Tonight it was heavy and oppressive.

I stared at my shoes, resenting them, though only an expert would know they were orthopedic. A careful observer might notice that the left shoe was somewhat larger than the right. The soft green leather covered a steel shield. My doctor had said, "We called these safety shoes in World War Two when I worked in a defense plant. I suppose that's what they're called now. Everyone wore them. Steelworkers, anyone in dangerous areas, probably wears them today."

"Not to dances, though."

"A lot of us don't dance, Tyler."

"That's the least of my worries, anyway," I'd said. True enough, then. Now, somewhere in this Guggenheim Museum house or in a cabin nearby was a man who danced, or played tennis, or made love with flawless grace, I suspected.

A pebble lay on the redwood flooring of the balcony. I picked it up and threw it over the railing. I could toss my heart away just as simply, if I were very foolish, but I hadn't better. I couldn't follow my secret heart, if it came to that. Cole Porter—or maybe Noel Coward—had put those lovely words together. But I *wouldn't* follow a secret heart my whole life through, however the lyrics went. Ridiculous. I went indoors and sank into the armchair and thought of leather brown arms encircling me instead of upholstery.

35

Oh, damn, damn, where was that Colin anyway? Why would he hide from me, not even say hello? Had Colin let me in and run away at the sight of me, wilting on the doorstep? Limping inside?

And what about dinner? Was I supposed to dress up? Or would I be expected to eat in the kitchen? Or here on a tray?

In all the excitement, Alison had forgotten to mention meal procedure. Maybe a bell would ring. I could at least get cleaned up and look for the kitchen.

The shower had a nozzle which could be adjusted to four speeds like the ones in commercials where a series of idiots carried on indoors and out as if heaven were a needle spray hard enough to knock you over. A year or so ago I'd been too uncaring to switch channels or turn the set off when actors showered giggling, or, as little men, went boating in toilet tanks, or as housewives, sniffed their garbage cans for mold. Now I almost enjoyed the challenge of the spray which had been installed for Blase Clinton. It could have been disastrous, but I held firm to a chrome bar with one hand and to the soap with the other.

Other handicapped patients had warned me not to trust just any towel rack or handhold. You could make a crash landing still hanging to the rack, an a good chunk of the wallboard or tiles behind it, in many places, particularly motels. But this house was built solidly, with the best fixtures. And the towels were fit for giants.

I buried my face in one of them and went to black for a moment as an intern who had been a television floor director used to say. It helped to clear my head of fancies. Then I dried my hair and put on my second-best dress, apple green with a soft full skirt. The rooms were still warm but I kept the outer doors locked. Better too hot than to be caught by surprise.

My only piece of jewelry was a bracelet of linked silver

rectangles on which the head of the serpent of Teotihuacán was represented in a stylized design. My parents had bought it on a long-ago and never-surpassed trip to Mexico. And I should have bought a safety chain long ago but hadn't. The bracelet, though, also had survived the accident. I checked its catch, as always, nearly too absorbed in memories to hear the tapping on a door. It sounded faint, I soon discovered, because it was the balcony door of the lounge just down the hall.

A thin boy stared soberly at me when I opened the way for him. His hair was red and his skin so pale the dusting of freckles seemed minor stains that could be washed away. He was fingering a sandy stone.

"You want this old rock?" He offered it through the open doorway but did not enter.

I said, "Thanks, it looks like a good find." The stone was still damp as if he had just picked it up on the beach. "Come on in," I invited casually and took one of the chairs near the fireplace. "Do you like to polish rocks?"

He advanced slowly, shaking his head.

I said, "My brother Sam got a polisher for his last—for his birthday. Maybe we could get one for you."

"Ask Blase," he said indifferently. "He'll get me anything —nearly." His eyes darted toward every corner of the room as if he were looking for enemies or checking to see if all exits were clear.

I studied the stone as if it were the Star of India—wanting to ask if he had opened the front door when I arrived. But he was perched on the very edge of a love seat. Any sudden query would probably send him running for cover. He was shockingly thin. Randolph Paul had said the boy was slow to recover from his appendectomy though it had gone well, purely routine surgery. I doubted that any hospital experience could be routine for a nine-year-old whose mother was dead, but I hadn't argued the statement.

"Tomorrow we'll make a schedule for lessons. What do you do just for fun around here, Colin?"

He hunched his shoulders and hugged his bony knees with thin, freckled arms. "I don't know. Not much."

"Neither do I. Lately," I said, and for the first time he looked at me unguardedly.

"I saw your taxi drive up. You were late."

"I didn't see you." I was certain no windows overlooked the front drive. A peephole in that massive front door would have been a desecration. "I missed my train, but I'll try to be on time from now on. Sorry." *Hey, Colin, did you let me in and then run away?*

"You couldn't see me." He was mildly triumphant. "Nobody ever does, unless I want them to."

"I wish I knew your secret," I said carelessly, having lately yearned for invisibility at awkward moments. The remark brought a deep flush to his cheeks. Now what had I done? "You were in the maze Mr. Paul told me about?" This was an even worse mistake. Too late I remembered that in my queries about the house I'd asked if there were a gazebo and Paul had said no, but there was a boxwood maze and Colin hated it.

The boy's scornful eyes turned away from me. His tennis shoes were old and laced with different ties, a thin, faded blue and a fat argyle. His khaki shorts were torn at the pockets. His plaid cotton shirt was new. But he could have been cast for an orphan too old for adoption. Had Alison adopted the boy? I wondered abstractedly. Randolph Paul hadn't said.

"There must be a lot of things we can find for our spare time. Have you got a bike, Colin?"

"Not anymore."

I must have showed my surprise.

"I ran away once or twice," he volunteered after a pause.

38

"Has the doctor said it's okay to get outdoors and exercise again?" I winced thinking of exercise as a therapy word.

"Guess so." He had hunched his shoulders into a continuing shrug. Sitting still and looking forlorn had never been Sam's style. Getting this child to cheer up and move around might be the biggest part of my job, other than catching up the lessons missed.

"I guess you swim a lot."

He shook his head. "We can't use the beach. It's deep by the rocks and some of it's too dirty. That's what she said."

"She" would be Alison, I gathered.

"I've been to Isle Royale once. We got a big old house there. My great-great-grandfather or somebody like that built it. My dad likes it in the wilderness. She don't."

"Doesn't," I said, not stressing it. I watched his fingers feeling the fabric of the couch. "Do you want to be a sculptor or a painter, too? Or haven't you decided yet, Colin?"

"I don't—haven't decided." He looked pleased with my choice of words.

"Should we find out what your mother's plans are for dinner?"

"She's not my mother! Didn't they tell you *anything?*"

"I forgot," I said. "Sorry."

He was looking at the small painting which I had mistaken at a distance for a Renoir. "That's my mother, and me. Blase drew us. Usually he sculpts stuff, but sometimes he draws. Used to, anyway."

"He's lucky to be so talented. It's lovely."

He jumped up with a look of some excitement and said, "You wait here for just a coupla minutes, Miss Ames. I'll be right back."

I could hear his light feet bounding up the stairs. He was gone no more than five minutes. Then he returned carrying a small wooden sculpture.

39

"Blase gave me this. He calls it *Headstrong*. That's kind of crazy, isn't it? He's always horsing around."

The wood was dark and gleaming. The figure was that of a woman with full bosom and hips, narrow waist, and lovely legs, but above the polished breasts the sculpture ended in rough, unfinished wood. No head, as such. Colin was watching for my reaction, but I didn't know what to say. It seemed a queer gift for a young boy, even the son of an artist and the brother of a sculptor. But, most of all, I didn't know what I thought of it. Obviously Colin treasured it as another child might have cherished a favorite toy.

"Have you met Jonathan yet?" he asked.

I was beginning not to be startled by everyone's using first names but Colin's casual "Jonathan" was mildly upsetting. "Met him in passing, wasn't introduced," I said. Colin's eyes were lighter than his brother's, less vivid than his father's, but equally hard to read.

At last he asked bluntly, "Miss Ames, did you see that messed-up painting?" He waited for my nod, then studied his sneakers. "I did something dumb like that once. They probably told you. I was just a kid."

"Colin, did you open the door for me?"

He made one quick nod. "But I didn't wreck that painting."

"Maybe it was someone who was—let's say temporarily out of control. Drunk perhaps." Might as well say it.

He shook his head. "I don't think Miles would ever want to hurt my father. They're friends."

"Well, you know him and I don't. Savannah certainly seems to be on your team. Stella, too. And I'm sure Alison—" I hesitated, not at all sure Alison didn't feel Colin could have wrecked the painting. "Savannah looks like a good person to have for an ally."

"She's my best friend," he said solemnly.

The family cook in her forties a best friend for a nine-year-old? "Hasn't she got any boys your age?" I ventured.

He grinned. "Beebee, he's ten. But they don't let him come out since I been sick. Alison says we make too much noise."

"I'll ask about it," I said. "Maybe we can take ourselves and Beebee somewhere else, some of the time. Once we get started on our work."

"Oh, golly, Miss Ames! You won't forget? Promise?"

"I promise. Now what about dinner?"

His grin remained easy. "I forgot. Savannah fixed us something. We're supposed to eat on the patio. They're all gone, I guess."

His manner indicated he saw nothing unusual in being left behind to share a cold meal with a stranger he hadn't even been introduced to, expected or not. "Colin, do you mean they all go off without checking to see if you're here and not alone?"

"*You're* here, and probably Jonathan's in his studio."

"But, my God, Colin, people don't just—" I swallowed the rest of it. "All right, let's go to supper."

He asked as we headed for the hall, "Do you think we can go exploring sometimes like Blase and me used to?"

"You bet your sneakers."

"But we won't tell her—Alison, I mean."

"Whyever not?"

"She doesn't want me to go up north toward the rocks anymore."

"Well, that makes sense. You could slip."

"She doesn't want me to remember all that stuff."

All that stuff was probably twin to the cabdriver's *all the trouble*, but I hadn't quizzed a taximan and I wouldn't ask a child. Tomorrow I'd ask Alison.

"I remember though," Colin said, as we began to climb the echoing stairs.

41

5.

After breakfast next morning, Colin showed me his school-books in the lounge and explained the stereo system. He said I could use any of his belongings anytime, and I decided we'd come a long way already without too many words. He knew that I limped often but he hadn't asked why and I hadn't explained. I would soon, but it could wait.

We went up the stairs again. I heard the sound of his chattering, the resonance within the stairwell, and realized that his voice seemed to come from above or below, or bounce all around. If you weren't near the person speaking, you couldn't tell where he might be in relation to yourself. It was fun-show stuff and could be pleasantly spooky. I could use it to entertain Colin and Beebee, if first I could get Bee-bee's entrance permit from the boss lady. *Whoa again, Tyler.* Not fair to criticize a woman protecting her genius husband's need for quiet.

We reached the main floor just as Alison came from the gallery, smiling a greeting. "So you've found each other."

I smiled in return. Colin had just squeezed my hand as if it were a secret signal, and I squeezed back. Maybe she'd already learned that easy does it with the elusive boy.

Her smile dimmed as she said, "Colin, we must have a talk this morning."

"I didn't do it." His hands were now shoved into his torn pockets. He stood apart from us—balanced on his feet like a small featherweight ready to dodge the punch. "Miles said you'd probably blame me."

"Colin, I'm *not* blaming you—or accusing anyone. We have to settle a lot of things, including your summer schedule, but run along now while I talk to Miss Ames."

"I was showing her my stuff. She wants to see my room," he protested, improvising.

I shot a glance at him. Sam had always protected his room from strangers. Only the chosen few were ever invited. Would Colin have actually taken me to his own quarters?

Alison sighed. "I'll call you when I have time for our talk. Run along now. Scat." She tried to make a joke of her dismissal, but the boy departed with his shoulders slumped again. His stepmother, watching him leave, erased a frown with her fingertips. It looked to be an automatic gesture, but she managed to smile at me.

"I wish I could convince myself that Colin had nothing to do with what happened yesterday. He's a secretive boy. He slips in and out of rooms, I must warn you."

"Childhood is a time for secrets, don't you think? And trying to be mysterious, playing roles. If he had a friend to keep him busy outdoors—"

But Alison wasn't buying the distraction at the moment. She said, "Let's go see if Savannah has some iced tea or lemonade. The air-conditioner man has actually arrived, Miles tells me, and today will be in the nineties."

We were passing a formal dining room which had bare white walls, though random smudges seemed to indicate that

43

paintings had once hung here. "Are any of Mr. Clinton's works in the house?" I asked. Maybe the "trouble" the cabby referred to had been a robbery.

"It must seem bleak," she said. "Jonathan's private collection is part of a traveling exhibit at the moment." Her smile widened. "I guess that takes away the privacy. Some works are already at the gallery for the September showing. Some are stored for safekeeping until then. And I am taking this opportunity to have the walls redone in the fall when it's cooler. So nothing will be hanging here, I'm afraid, until later, except what he wants to put up and study—as unfortunately he did yesterday." Her green eyes slid across my listening face. "He wasn't well and had a long layoff but he's back at work now. Did you hear about the Modern Art incident?"

"No, I don't believe so. I went to the Art Institute Sunday to see as much as I could, but I haven't had a chance to really study his works as I hope to do."

"It doesn't matter. I'll tell you about the museum happening when we have more time."

I knew a little, but not enough, about saving damaged artworks. I'd read a book called *The Waters of November* in which Howard Greenfeld told about art rescue teams in Florence after the disastrous flooding of the Arno. There had even been a sort of hospital for priceless artworks. My Aunt Lynne had been there, too, but I hadn't mentioned her and this didn't seem to be the moment for it. "Can yesterday's damage be repaired?" I asked. "I can understand how worried you must be."

"Jonathan's state of mind worries us more," Alison said. "There are times like this when we all walk on tiptoe around him. I'm sure you can appreciate that, Tyler, since you've studied about artists."

What I appreciated most was her forgetting my lameness.

44

She was thinking only of her husband's problems, not mine, and my spirits soared. I was invisible at last.

The kitchen was another pleasant surprise. Color vibrated on all sides. Natural wood and red brick were set off by wallpaper which had matching curtains in a tiny flower print. Comfortable chairs and a low table were here, too, near a wide fireplace which at present had a row of potted red geraniums instead of fire tools and a log basket but which looked as if it were well used in wintertime. Wrought-iron fixtures on one wall held an amazing assortment of pots, pans, and cooking tools. There was a sort of bar peninsula, with padded stools, for serving quick meals. A red light gleamed steadily over the door to the rear.

Savannah was assembling ingredients for a cake. "How many for dinner?" she asked.

"I doubt that Blase will be here," Alison answered, "and certainly not Jonathan unless his attitude changes radically. But Randy Paul will be coming—not his father."

"What about—" Savannah inclined her head toward me.

"Yes, Tyler and Colin will be dining with us. Is there any iced tea, Savannah?"

"All you want." Savannah brought a frosted glass pitcher from the refrigerator, poured two tall glasses, and topped them with mint and lemon slices which she took from separate plastic bags. Savannah could match the mistress for organization. We sat on the barstools and sipped in silence, watching the cook continue her baking preparations. Then Alison stood up, told me to take my time, and departed by the back door.

Savannah winked at me. "That's the way it is. Now you see 'em, now you don't. Just don't hold your breath between times. Can I get you a slice of my lemon chiffon?"

I shook my head. "Thanks, but it's only ten o'clock."

"Ten in the morning or ten at night, you're too thin, Miss Ames."

"Please make it Tyler. Please."

"If you try my pie."

"I don't want to gain weight, Savannah. I know I'm a bean pole, but I don't think I can balance any more pounds."

"Now what do that mean, girl?"

The gentle but determined tone undid me. I talked for the next half hour. When we both had wet eyes and had used paper towels for tissues, having already emptied the Kleenex box, we ate lemon chiffon pie.

"Don't worry about eating any extra," Savannah suddenly spoke in an impersonal manner, "Colin'll run your legs off."

I glanced up in dismay and surprise, and then saw that Colin had arrived quietly and was trying not to look at my shoes. Savannah ordered him to run out back and fetch her some fresh mint if he wanted any pie for himself and also to take a look at her tomato vines, see if they needed water.

"I hope he quits that sneaking around soon," she said, when he had gone. "He don't mean anything by it. Kid stuff, but he's got nothing else to do. You're going to fix that anyway."

I said, "I've been thinking about it. First I want Beebee to come back. We can get out of earshot, have picnics in the woods, away from the house and the studio. See some movies? All right with you?"

She nodded thoughtfully. "Just be careful which way you wander."

"This is the nicest part of the house," I volunteered. An assortment of skillets hung from an overhead rack. Spoons, spatulas, whisks, strainers, and oddments stood in baskets, looking sorted, ready for instant use.

She beamed at me. "When I first came here, nine, going on ten, years ago, just behind Colin as it was, I told them I couldn't work in no half-assed kitchen. I was willing to put

46

up with a lot—and I do put up with a lot—" Her roving glance took in a stack of trays, and then the handsome dark eyes considered me at length again. "Lately I got another rule. Come night, I'm gone. You lock your door nights, hear me?"

I laughed at her solemn manner. "Don't tell me a modern house has ghosts?"

"Maybe this particular ghost ain't so old," Savannah said, then she switched the subject. "Mr. Clinton put up a squawk about buying a lot of French potware but he kind of likes it all the same. I think he'd a' been a cook, a first-class one, if he hadn't got hold of a paintbrush first."

"You go home every night after dinner?"

"Every night except when things is way off schedule. Lot of running back and forth when he's eating in like now." She bent her head toward the outdoors, and I realized she meant Jonathan Clinton took his meals in his studio. "But that's the way it is. Ruby does some of it, days she's here."

Ruby was a friend of Savannah's who came from Waukegan for cleaning four days a week, and extra for parties. Not that there'd been much partying around here lately. Stella managed to keep the place in fine running order the rest of the time. Even Miles did his job all right when he was sober. He could drive anything that had wheels, and he managed to keep two elderly locals happy as outdoor help when needed.

"Does the family have many callers? Just regular friends, I mean. And I know it's none of my business, except it seems to me that Colin would be less lonely with people coming and going. Not just hired help, kids his own age—are there any?"

Savannah shook her head. "Not these days." She looked ready to say more, but after a hesitant moment she stepped to the door and peered out, asking instead, "Where do you suppose that child got to? I hope he didn't take it into his head to wander up by the studio. This ain't the morning for it."

47

"I'll look for him. Which way is the tomato patch?"

She pointed to a flagstone walk beyond the redwood deck, which was wide at this part of the house and furnished with expensive-looking wrought-iron chairs, tables, and a canopied swing. A couple of extra canvas chairs were folded against a rail. "And you might take a look out front if he ain't in the garden. Might be Blase's leaving and Colin'll be hanging around him, if that's the case."

"I'll try the garden first," I said, hoping I looked and sounded calm.

6.

The path was edged with sweet alyssum and four-o'clocks. An herb garden was planted in a circle. Pole beans, cherry tomatoes, and morning glory vines were carefully staked and tied. Perennials and small flowering shrubs backed the low beds of petunias and deep purple pansies. A homelike garden for such an oddly formal house. It went with the kitchen, not the gallery, in any case. And Colin was not there.

By the time I found my way to the front driveway, Blase Clinton was opening the trunk of a dark red Alfa Romeo. Two or three pieces of canvas luggage were heaped on the pavement. He fitted them above the spare tire and slammed the lid shut while I tried to ease back out of sight, but Colin, skipping around the hood of the car, yelled, "Hey, Tyler, come meet my brother!"

I moved forward reluctantly.

"Why can't you stay?" Colin was asking Blase. His fingers were clasping the handle of the car door, holding it shut, I thought, rather than trying to open it.

"Because I can't. I've got business in town."

"This is Tyler," Colin said, but the corners of his mouth were still turned down in disappointment.

Blase nodded indifferently and I murmured, "Hello," without smiling. Colin was too intent on his own feelings to look at either of us. He leaned forward and studied his reflection in the shining hood.

"You'll be back though? You ain't going to Spain again, Blase, promise?" Colin's young body looked like stretched elastic; even his voice was taut with anxiety.

"I'm not even going to Gary," Blase answered. "I'll be back and forth all summer, before you get those ain'ts out of your vocabulary." He looked at me. "Don't blame Savannah for Colin's grammar; blame the tube. No more *Baretta* reruns until he shapes up, okay?"

"I hope we won't have time for them. We've been making plans—" Something small and fast brushed my unsteady leg in passing. I pitched forward and Blase caught me in his arms, then set me firmly on my feet. I reddened as he gazed at me curiously. Colin was tugging at his brother's hand and trying to whisper.

I said, "It's all right, Colin. Time everyone knew—I've got a bum foot. I'm sorry I fell on you." I stood stiff as a cardboard cutout, an outraged paper doll, I must have seemed.

"Match you for ailments," Blase said. "I've got a tennis elbow and hay fever."

Go to hell with your hay fever! Damn your elbow! I wanted to scream, but I kept my lips closed tight. After a moment he turned away, looking obscurely disappointed. Then he bent swiftly, scooped up the dog and dropped him into the back seat.

"Picasso, make your apologies to the lady," he ordered.

The mutt yipped. He was obviously king of the road in the Alfa.

"Picasso?" I echoed, feeling idiotic.

"I found him on the highway after a hit-and-run bastard had changed his noble image. All his best features were on one side of his head until we got him patched up at the vet's. Now he's quite presentable, don't you think?"

"He's beautiful," I said. Sam would have loved him instantly.

Blase glanced at his watch. I looked at the blond hairs glistening on his strong wrist. He said, "Colin, will you dash in and see what's keeping Stella?"

He was waiting for the housekeeper? Well, why not? I decided nothing would surprise me in this weird ménage. Stella Burton was lushly beautiful like a cabbage rose or a peony in full bloom. I thought of her red hair and delicate skin and then I thought of *Headstrong*, the sculpture Blase had given his brother. Had Stella been the model? Had the perfect housekeeper in the immaculate white uniform ever been headstrong? In this house? Maybe. In Blase's rooms. My rooms now.

"Either you're getting ready for sunstroke, Miss Ames," Blase said, "or you're having some very interesting thoughts. Color becomes you. Where did you learn the art of maidenly confusion? I thought it died with Sweet Alice Ben Bolt." He was leaning back against the car, arms crossed, watching me, laughing silently. "So you're here to baby-sit this summer? Teach Colin a few sums— Only that and nothing more?"

"Plenty more!" I snapped.

He said, "Ah, in temper *veritas*," as if my outburst had been a confession. Something was very wrong, but how could I hope to put it straight unless I knew why he shifted constantly from indifference, to friendliness, to suspicion, almost accusation? From warmth to a chilling hostility, and back again without warning?

"Colin is not a baby," I said, sounding tutor-snappish, even to myself. No wonder Blase Clinton looked at me so oddly.

"He could use a *little* supervision, however. As long as you're here, make it more than an excuse."

I wasn't sure I'd heard him correctly. His words made no sense. I said, "I'm certain Colin had nothing to do with the vandalism."

"You sound so positive for a stranger, Miss Ames, or have you known some of us longer than a day?"

What in the name of God was he driving at? But there was no time to ask him to explain; Colin and Stella were coming out of the house. She carried a small overnight case and wore a bright primrose shift instead of the white uniform. It made her look totally different. *Loose, and cool, and easy,* the first words that came to mind. Younger, prettier. No bra, I decided, that's why such silly thoughts popped into my already muddled head.

Blase said, "Stella is on loan to make me safe in Old Town. She's the official cockroach chaser. She won't believe that a building put up in 1890 isn't infested with generations of vermin. Did you pack enough bug spray, Stella?"

"Oh, shut up, Blase. It's too hot to breathe. Miss Ames, you look pale. Don't get sunstroke, for heaven's sake."

In other words, get back indoors, I thought, unappreciative of her concern. Colin was yelping in dismay, "Blase, you ain't—aren't—moving away all summer!"

"Just a friend's place for whenever I need it, *amigo*."

I said, "I hope it isn't because of me. I don't need much space. I could stay anywhere. I don't need a suite." *And stop babbling,* I told myself in chagrin.

"If that's an offer, I'll move back in." Blase Clinton's

laughing-again dark blue eyes held mine, then he took Stella's suitcase and dropped it beside Picasso in the back seat. Stella went around the car and got in beside the driver's place. Blase said, "Colin, study hard and I'll take you sailing. That's a promise."

I pulled Colin close to me as they departed. Stella lifted her hand in a wan farewell wave but neither looked back. Tires squealed on baked pavement as they passed through the gates. Picasso's ears flattened in the breeze. They were gone.

An overnight case implied overnight, and a nightgown, and a lot of things that were none of my business.

"Let's go eat," Colin said and I slowly and reluctantly followed him into the house. It was cool. The repairman had been and gone. That was something, but it wasn't much.

We lunched mostly in silence with only a huge, old-fashioned clock breaking the stillness in the kitchen. Somewhere a lawn mower roared into action, but here it was restful. Peaceful as a graveyard, I decided. Colin sat at the bar swinging gently on the stool as he ate. I lounged in a chair by the fireplace and remarked that I hadn't heard a clock ticking in years. Most mealtimes at our house you couldn't have heard Big Ben striking midnight. "Sam had so many of his gang in and out—" I stopped. I could have bitten my tongue and shot a guilty glance at Savannah.

"Well, maybe you can get Beebee back," she said easily. "He and Colin are a gang all by themselves. Beebee can come when he ain't working, if Alison says it's all right. This time of year he mows lawns besides his paper route. Winters he shovels snow. You know how it is. Guess you had snow in Missouri."

"We had snow and we had President Truman. Both were front-page news." The awkward moment was over.

Colin said, "I hope it rains all week so Beebee'll get here."

"Well, here comes trouble anyway," Savannah announced,

53

as Miles came in the back door. "Stella was lookin' for you to say g'bye."

"That'll be the day," Miles said. He wore a crooked smile. He moved as easily as Blase, I noticed, though he was much older. "Savannah, my own true love, you're never going to make it into choir singer's heaven telling whoppers like that. Stella comes and goes and never says hello *or* good-bye. You know that. You trying to make Miss Ames think we're all pretty normal folks around here? Hey, Colin, how's the ten o'clock scholar? Going to bend over the math now you got a pretty teacher all your own?" He sent me a glance. "This kid could outread a Rhodes scholar if he really wanted to, but he hates math."

Colin wrinkled his nose but didn't deny the statement. Burton's long-sleeved wrinkled shirt again was soaked with sweat under the arms and in the middle of the back, but the sleeves were only partly rolled up. He washed his hands at the sink, though Savannah told him to use the lavatory and get out of her way. "Ain't it time you took your yearly bath, Miles?" she added.

"Ah, Savannah, Savannah, why didn't we meet when I was young and not so gay?" Again he threw me a curious glance. "Got anything against gay, schoolmarm?"

I shook my head. Savannah told him to be sure all the paint upstairs was cleaned up. "Lessen you fixin' to slap some more around?" Her dark eyes stared at his bloodshot ones, and he said:

"Don't give me any of that put-on, down-home darky talk either. You are some woman, baby, but you got the wrong pig by the tail this time. I didn't come anywhere near that house-paint job—and I'll tell you something else—when I find out who *did*, I'll deal with him. Or her."

He slammed the screen door in leaving.

"Good riddance," Savannah said. "Colin, ain't it time for your program? Past time even."

54

I said, "Alison wanted to talk to him, and to me; I guess she forgot."

"Well, I told you. That's the way it is. Don't hold your breath. Colin, go on, make tracks."

He took off down the hall and I started to leave, too, but Savannah waved me back into the chair and poured fresh lemonade for both of us. Then she slumped in the chair opposite mine and kicked off her shoes. "Anything I can tell you about this place that might help you, honey, just ask," she offered astonishingly.

I was too surprised to think of the most important questions. "Everyone's on such a first-name basis," I mentioned. "I don't think that's usual; granted I don't know much about big houses and their staffs, but Miles certainly seems to be free and easy—"

"Oh, Miles." She paused to take a long sip of lemonade. "He and Mr. Clinton are old war buddies. Mr. Clinton did some paintings of battles, real sensible stuff for one of them New York magazines. People was people in them, and mostly dead. And dead horses. You could tell what you were looking at anyway." She made a small grimace which could have been intended for the battle art or for today's abstract expressionism. I didn't want her to get sidetracked and asked hastily,

"But what war could that be? Miles is too young for World War Two and too old for Vietnam, isn't he?" And when was the last war that used horses?

Savannah seemed to take offense at my doubting expression. "I disremember egg-zactly," she exaggerated to let me know her feelings. "They brought home a sign that says Press Tent from one of them jungles. I guess Miles typed and Mr. Clinton drew. Don't ask me, if you don't want to know."

I said, "It doesn't matter. They were wartime buddies anyway and now Miles works here." A thought struck me. "Was Miles hurt in the war? Is that why he doesn't have a

55

better job and why he drinks?" Miles—who always seemed to be carrying a book—and who could quote Shakespeare.

"He drinks because it's Tuesday or because his corns hurt or the mail ain't come yet." Savannah dismissed Miles and his thirst. "Mr. Clinton got a photograph of all of 'em taken overseas somewheres. Now when he's layin' off work, Clinton, I mean, he and Miles play chess all night or drink, or both. The Burtons got a nice place over the garages. Stella— she started making herself useful around the house a long time back, just about the time I got here. Colin was a baby then, but she wouldn't have no part of baby-tending. She liked to clean. She's a worker and then some, but she never did like looking after kids."

"What was Colin's mother like?"

"Sick all the time I knew her. A real nice lady. Mrs. Agatha was older. Older than him." She pointed toward the red light over the rear door so there wouldn't be any doubt who was being discussed. "She gave up her own work mostly after Colin came and spent as much time with him as she had strength for. Not too long, as it turned out. I found it pitiful. She was a real good lady." Then she grinned at me. "I think you put me in mind of her. You're prettier though and a whole lot younger."

"Well, thanks!" I said just as the intercom sounded. It was Alison, ready at last for our conference. I found her again at the orderly desk, looking controlled and businesslike, but apologizing for having departed so abruptly this morning. She added:

"I decided I had to see Jonathan—I couldn't put it off any longer."

My eyes must have widened, for she hurried on: "It's not easy to explain my husband to someone who doesn't know him." She was fingering a silver pencil. "Sometimes Jonathan lives as if he were packed in cotton batting and takes almost a

56

hypochondriac's care of himself. Other times he seems to court danger, almost challenges the elements to strike him down, sails in the worst weather, walks on the beach in lightning storms, just asking for trouble."

I could see King Lear in tennis sneakers striding lakeside, against a malevolent sky, but the Lear image was too old. Peter Finch, again, crazed by jungle fever, or whatever. A tall, thin man with frosted shaggy hair and a hawklike profile taking long steps beside the churning waves, under the blackened sky with scudding clouds. *Hold on again, I had to warn myself. No time for romance. Pay attention.*

While I had sailed off on that tangent, Alison had been talking about her husband's health, I realized belatedly.

"Last fall it got so bad he even saw a doctor. Apparently he was right on the verge of malnutrition. Can you imagine that! Starving to death in the midst of plenty—partially because of a bug he picked up in Africa when he and Miles took a short vacation, a weekend really, after an exhibition in Rome."

She sighed and tapped the pencil against the red light on her phone. "Partly it was because he neglected himself for his work, never stopped to eat. Sent his trays back untouched, though Savannah outdid herself trying to tempt his appetite with his favorite food. Can you understand such a man?" Her green eyes studied me intently.

"I don't know," I answered honestly. "I think people are lucky to find work that totally absorbs them. Maybe not to the extent that it endangers their health. But to have a talent worth pursuing—well, I envy that."

"Thank you, Tyler. I appreciate your frankness. And I don't need to worry that our crazy schedules here will upset you, right?"

"Right. Except that—"

Immediately she was on guard. Her teeth caught her lower

lip as she waited for my next words. I smiled to reassure her. "It's only that he's my employer and I'd like to meet him. Just once, at least."

"*I* am your employer, Tyler. I doubt if Jonathan is aware that you are here—he stays totally out of household matters. You may see him this summer, but again you may not. Occasionally he decides to favor us with his presence at dinner. Usually not. Not when he's working. Dinner tonight is at seven, and you wear whatever you like—that is, a short dress or a long one. Randy Paul will be here, too."

"I'll be glad to see him again," I said. Now what? My polite remark had struck sparks in the watchful eyes, but all she said was, "We'll tackle the schedule for lessons tomorrow. See you at seven."

7.

The dinner table was set with fresh flowers which had arrived by air-cooled florist truck this afternoon. Alison, in a flamingo silk caftan, sat at the foot of the table. The bare walls, the furniture of brushed aluminum, glass, and white leather, and the gleaming silver and crystal of the service—even the candles in crystal holders were white—all were store-displayed perfect, with only Alison and the centerpiece providing splashes of vivid color. By chance I had selected a white sleeveless sheath and Colin wore a white shirt and dark jacket.

The master's place was fully laid, but his chair remained empty as the ice slowly melted in the Waterford goblet, and the white wine disappeared steadily and was replaced in Alison's tulip-shaped glass. She sat with her fingers on the stem of it even when she was looking into space.

I hadn't thought my own careful sipping of the wine had got to me until I suddenly said, "White rum. We ought to be drinking rum martinis. You know those ads? Only it's always a couple dressed in white, in a white room—" My voice trailed into the awesome silence. No couples here. Colin giggled and then we were silent again.

"You want rum, Tyler?" Alison's hand was reaching for the silver bell, which tinkled pleasantly, but the sound must have carried well. Ruby shot in from the service pantry with bowls of gazpacho on a silver tray. I shook my head to the rum offer and Alison ordered another bottle of wine. I said I'd never met Liza Minnelli and Colin said he hadn't either.

"What in the name of heaven are you talking about?" Alison looked cross. I explained that Liza Minnelli might introduce her to white rum—it was an old ad and not very believable. "There was this couple said they met Miss Minnelli and—"

"Oh, please," Alison interrupted. She leaned forward and plucked a blue-dyed carnation from the centerpiece. Holding it like a plume, she walked to her husband's empty place and laid the flower on his service plate. She had returned to her chair when Randolph Paul arrived.

He was a tan man tonight. The hazel eyes, sandy lashes, sandy hair, buff-colored sports coat, oyster-toned shirt, pale tie, all full of apologies, I thought. *Pale ties I loved—beside the Shalimar. Cut off the wine.*

Apologies over, Paul asked if I would please call him Randy. "We're all family, more or less."

"More or less," Alison echoed dimly, and he glanced sharply at her wineglass. Chicken breasts in wine sauce replaced the gazpacho and hearts of palm salad appeared almost magically it seemed as I recited a Clarence Day verse about a tradesman who used to hop completely nude around his shop, waving a blue linoleum rose.

Alison said, "Really, Tyler."

"It was the blue-dyed carnation that set me off," I said.

Paul smoothly changed the subject. "I meant to tell you, Tyler, whenever you need something from town I'm your errand boy."

"Miles is the errand boy," Alison said very slowly and distinctly.

"When is your father coming back?" Colin asked Paul. "I want him to meet Tyler."

How about *your* father? I longed to ask the boy as Randy assured him Mr. Paul would soon be well enough to visit again and warned, "He's been practicing backgammon with the nurse, Colin. You'll have to be at your best. But I agree— he should meet Tyler. He'll be delighted to see you've got a new friend."

"We're all delighted," Alison said, still speaking in Japanese no-accent style. I thought of the cabdriver. He'd list Alison as one of his bottle problems. An elegant wino, and me not far behind.

"I haven't seen Jonathan Clinton yet," I said, not meaning to speak at all.

Randy and Alison exchanged glances. Then she stood up to leave, and I felt that his eyes were warning me to be quiet, but all he said was a casual, "Ah, that's a problem, Tyler, one for us all. We'd all like to see Jonathan, but it's not easy. His work comes first. Try to be patient, honey. You may get lucky."

Alison, at the door, gazed back at me solemnly. "If you want dessert, or you'd like to take a snack to your room for later, just ask Savannah or Ruby. Randy, please hurry. You haven't heard what happened yesterday."

News travels slowly around here, I thought. Jonathan Clinton hadn't been told about his green-daubed painting for nearly twenty-four hours. Now the Pauls, who obviously

61

expected to have the canvas in their exhibition, had not been advised of the delay.

Colin said, "Can't *you* play any games, Tyler?"

"Used to play 'em all," I said crabbily, feeling moody. "Hand me that bottle, please. Alison left half an inch in it. At least."

Colin said, "I like old Mr. Paul. He never lets me win. Randy does, all the time."

"How about your precious brother? He let you win?"

"Are you *kidding?*"

Gloomily I persevered: "He probably wins everything he tries. The old Robert Redford syndrome, right?"

"Robert Redford, yechhh!"

I stared at him. "You are probably the *only* human being in the whole wide world who would say 'Robert Redford, yechhh!' I'm beginning to have second thoughts about your intelligence. Excuse me." I hiccuped, then recited a bit of doggerel from the long ago—something about " 'Brigitte Bardot, and a big ho-hum—she's not the sex I am opposite from.' Sounds like something my Aunt Lynne wrote," I said.

Colin said, "Alison thinks Blase *looks* like Robert Redford. That's about the only nice thing she ever said about him. I *guess* she meant it to be nice, anyway." And he added, "You got an aunt, Tyler?"

"Right. So what games have you got? You'll probably beat me even if I try. I'm out of touch."

"And you're a girl."

"Thanks for reminding me," I said. "I almost forgot."

Before bedtime he won four out of six games played, though we switched from backgammon to checkers to cribbage. I called it a night. "But it's like algebra and roller skating," I cautioned him. "It'll come back. Just watch out in the future, boy-o."

"I really truly like you, Tyler." He was leaving the room

with the widest grin he'd worn yet. I called after him, "Better watch that teeth display, too. You could wind up looking like Redford, yourself."

"You're really crazy, you know that?" His parting shot.

Long after midnight—on a sudden impulse—I put on my robe and protective slippers and went stealthily to the gallery to see if any new painting hung in the L end of the room. The strategic placing of small, round floor projectors cast shadows of the sculptures on the blank walls and glistening reflections on the polished marble floor of the L. There was no painting, however, only the towering shadow figures.

Hurrying back to my own room I realized that the halls, stairway, and even the rooms I passed were softly lit, indirectly but keeping the night beyond the shining black glass windows. *Somebody hates the dark*, I thought. Or perhaps it was a safety measure.

Back in bed, with the draperies tightly closed, and my own lights doused, I pulled the summer blanket up to my chin and lay awake. Tomorrow I would try to see the whole house. It would be sensible to know where other people were supposed to be if an emergency should arise in the night. Only common sense. What if Colin needed me? I hadn't set foot on the top floor of this maw-*sole*-eum.

The man who watched the house, the studio, the path to the cabin, and the garages sat cross-legged in a tree house, nothing but a platform now, but sturdy enough for his weight. He had reinforced it himself. He was silent, smoking, sipping from his Thermos, keeping alert.

The first weeks of his vigil had been hard. He'd dozed off at times. Not now. Not since he'd found the opening to the sealed-off cellar and what was going on there.

Tonight he saw the girl go upstairs to the gallery. Figured

*her return. Saw her lights go out. She hadn't spoken at all.
He could have heard, if she had. The gallery and most of the
rooms were clear channels; no static in his ear tonight.*

*No lights flickered from the bluff where the cabin stood
behind the pines. If Blase was up and using even the tiniest
lamp, a glimmer would slip through, the tree dweller knew
from experience. Even the rays of a flashlight could be de-
tected from here.*

*The house of Clinton was now silent as the tomb it looked
to be. The studio was silent except for the lion's snoring. Let
him sleep—he'd need it. Time was running out.*

*No use checking the apartment again. All quiet there. He
yawned and began to stir gently, then leaped catlike to the
ground, landing lightly on the balls of his feet. Soundlessly.
It would be dawn soon . . .*

At breakfast I learned that Alison had gone back to the city
with Randy, leaving word to plan my own schedule for
Colin's lessons. Savannah, delivering the news, shrugged and
rolled her eyes. "What I tell you? Now you see 'em, now you
don't."

"Do the Clintons keep an apartment in Chicago?"

"Yep. And she's the only one that uses it." Another signifi-
cant drawing up of the bony shoulders. "Like they say, makes
me no never mind, girl. And you best look at it that way,
too."

"But—" I began and stopped.

"You might as well spit it out, girl."

"Well, is that where Blase is staying? I mean, that was what
I was going to ask—but he said 'a friend's apartment'—so I
guess it's somewhere else. . . ." I must have looked as foolish
as I sounded.

Savannah looked ready to comment, but changed her mind
as Colin arrived late for his meal and she began to harangue
him about cold eggs and bacon.

By nine o'clock we had set up our schoolroom in the lounge and had started on his worst subject, math. I selected easy lessons to begin with. When Ruby came to clean at ten, I left Colin with pages of work to complete and followed her from door to door, getting the general layout of the upper floor.

The master bedroom was above the gallery and nearly as large. Colin's smaller room was across the hall and down a short distance, but I didn't invade either place, even behind Ruby's vacuum and cleaning cart. I peered into a sort of storeroom directly opposite the main bedroom. It was orderly but filled with odds and ends of equipment that looked as if they had been out of use for a long time.

"I don't bother to dust in there more'n twice a year," Ruby said. "Nobody uses any of that stuff these days." I saw a sewing machine and cabinet, a slide projector and rolled-up screen, badminton rackets and a baseball bat and mitt which must have been Blase's in the past. They seemed too large, too long unused, for Colin.

"Take a peek into the guest bedroom down to the other end of the hall," Ruby suggested. "It's really something."

She was right. There was a canopied bed, and also a glaze-chintz-upholstered chaise longue. Louis XV, if I remembered a college course right. The House of Clinton held no end of surprises in decorating moods. Here the carpet had a raised design with a grass-green background. The walls were white, but the bed and window curtains were vividly piped with tangerine. Two velvet upholstered chairs were a matching color, but the swan banquette at the foot of the bed was an astonishing turquoise. Elegance and femininity. Didn't the Clintons ever have male overnight guests? But I hadn't seen all of the establishment, probably not even half of it. Ruby invited me to look at Alison's bath and dressing room and I guiltily peered inside. It was carpeted in kelly green, with mirrored walls and ceiling and vermeil cups for toothbrushes

65

and bunches of fresh flowers on a gold metal stand which held towels and on the dressing table.

"I feel too much like a snooper," I confessed to Ruby. "You've got business here but I'm just being nosy. See you," and hurried back downstairs as fast as I could manage.

Stella Burton's office as housekeeper was just off the kitchen. Beyond it was a bed-sitting room, with a television, bookshelves, bathroom. The bed-divan had a beige upholstery. Fat pillows had Inca designs. Savannah told me later, "When I got to stay overnight, I stay in that Indian room. Thanks to you and Lord be praised I can get out of here come sundown or not too much later. Most nights at least. I don't reckon there'll be too much entertaining till winter." She leveled a look at me. "You locking your doors nights?"

I nodded.

"You keep on doing that even if Blase gets back. He's too far away to hear any ruckus down here and the mister wouldn't pay no attention."

I wanted to ask what kind of ruckus she feared, but Colin had joined us and the opportune moment slid past.

June remained hot and dry. We followed our work-and-rest schedule and found time to explore. Sometimes we walked on the beach, or found a cool spot for reading, but we never went near the maze, the rocks, or the studio. We developed our own companionable silences. I wished Colin had his own copy of *The Golden Age*, with illustrations by Arthur Rackham. My father had sent me one from England and it was in storage now with most of my clothes and the belongings I had wanted to keep.

Some Saturdays Miles drove us to the train and we visited Chicago sights. When I got too tired at the Museum of Science and Industry and Colin still wanted to see the coal mine, I realized I had better buy another cane. I prayed Blase would never catch me using it. After brooding about this, I almost convinced myself that I wasn't being infatuated. He represented a world I'd lost for now. Maybe next year, maybe never, I'd try to go back. Right now nine-year-olds were the most I could handle. Beebee was ten, but life and his mother had already made him a grown-up. I had managed twice to get permission for him to accompany us. He was an expert at keeping up with and even beyond Colin, and I could rest nearby with a book when he was in charge.

But I wished Blase Clinton would come back for just a few days so that I could study the flaws in him. Let him be a fathead or an egotistical bore. Let him be vain and totally self-centered. Let him be a lot of undesirable things. But I never quite wished let him be married, or even engaged to the girl of his choice.

At lunch one noisy day in the busy cafeteria of the Art Institute, I asked Colin, "Does your brother have a lot of girlfriends?" and jabbed a fork into a tomato, hoping my face didn't match the fruit.

"Are you kidding?" His stock answer to foolish queries.

"Any special one?"

"I don't know. I don't think so. Can I use your cane?"

I had bought an acrylic cane which was colorless, see-through, and forgettable. I was always hooking it over the backs of chairs and sending Colin to fetch it for me. He never minded. He liked to limp exaggeratedly on the return journey, leaning hard on the handle which almost reached his chin.

July blew in with a thunderstorm and brought Beebee for a full weekend. Jonathan Clinton had not come into the house when I was there, but no one seemed to find this extraordinary. I heard from Savannah that he'd been sailing a few times and often took walks on the beach at night and fre-

67

quently played chess till dawn with Miles. Savannah was getting tired of planning trays to tempt his appetite.

"Look at these chicken tracks. Can you figure them out?" She handed me a note on yellow scratch paper.

"I think he wants the toast burnt and the coffee thicker. Is that possible?" I gave it back.

"Sounds like him. He and Miles been boozing." She looked slightly abashed as Alison came into the kitchen with a list of menus. "Well, they got to let off steam, I guess," she added, in a placating tone, not her usual grumble.

"You ought to keep his notes, Savannah," I suggested. "They're the hand script of a very important man and someday may be worth real money to an autograph collector."

"His autograph ain't on them," Savannah said, but her interest was caught. So was Alison's. She dropped the list she'd brought as if it had burst into flames and grabbed for the note Savannah still held. "Give me that at once! From now on give me every note he writes you, *do* you understand?"

"I'd be deaf if I didn't," Savannah said stonily, pronouncing it "deef," probably for pure orneriness.

Spots of color stained Alison's tanned cheeks. "Tyler, I'm surprised at you. This house is not to be dissected and carried away piece by piece for souvenir hunters. We've had enough of that, God knows, in the past. I assumed you understood when you took residence here our privacy is not to be invaded." She ranted on as Savannah and I exchanged glances and stayed silent in mutual surprise at the attack.

Colin's arrival cut off her words, but he took one look at us and departed as swiftly as he had come in. Alison breathed hard, simmering down, and eventually apologized. "Sorry I lost my temper. But I simply cannot bear for Jonathan to be criticized in any way—even the slightest—and his handwriting is poor, I'll grant you that. Shaky, but he's been ill. You

68

know that. But bring all the notes directly to me, Savannah, from now on, and we'll say no more about it. All right?" She tried to smile. "I'll be happy to translate them for you, if necessary."

"Oh, boy!" Savannah walked back to the sink where she rattled some pans to ease her feelings.

Alison looked at me for understanding. "It may seem silly but I want to protect my husband and help him as much as I can." She still looked troubled. "Shall we take a moment to sit on the deck and talk? We haven't really had a chat since you've been here."

Amen to that. I went along willingly, full of questions if the chance came.

She took a lounge chair in the full sunlight and lit a cigarette she had fitted into a jade holder. "I probably should try to fill you in on family history—so much as I know anyway. Agatha was rather old to have the boy, but she adored him. I wasn't here then, though I came soon after. She wanted to delegate as much of her work as she could, to spend time with him. Eventually I took over Jonathan's correspondence and other business details. Old Mr. Paul is his good friend and actually his business manager. Though I do what I can. He's also named as guardian of Colin. I meant to adopt the boy when we were married, but it never got done. It might have made us closer—and perhaps I'll get to it—when Jonathan has time for family matters. Blase is an adult, of course, no problem; I never saw much of him. He was in school or off to Spain and Italy; France, too, but he loves the Latin countries." She took a long drag on her cigarette and I slipped in a question.

"Don't Blase and his father spend any time together?"

At her direct look, I felt defensive. "I've never seen either one of them all summer."

"Why on earth should you, Tyler?" No answer, to be sure,

so I said, "What about the Modern Art incident you mentioned?"

"Oh, Jonathan and Miles on a tear—Jonathan decided to take down one of his own paintings and they hauled him away until Mr. Paul took care of the matter and brought them safely home."

She threw her cigarette over the railing instead of using the ceramic ashtray at hand. The gesture reminded me that I wanted to ask about her own background, but I didn't quite dare. She said, "No charges were brought. Jonathan very generously donated another painting for the trouble he'd caused. But it got in the papers. Some of the locals decided he was a madman."

"Is that why you have so few visitors?" I ventured cautiously.

She studied me for an uncomfortable pause and then said, "Partly, I suppose. Artists can't afford to be gregarious. Jonathan once cut out a quotation from someone—Christopher Morley, I think it was—and pasted it on the studio wall. Something about having time only for your own work. Energy is not endless. Otherwise evade, elude, recede, lie if necessary, but keep your own hours—and counsel."

"I can understand that," I said, not sure whether I was relieved or vaguely disappointed that "the trouble" had been no more than a drunken prank, or whim.

Alison resumed her self-chosen task of filling me in. "Blase and his father have a curious relationship. I'm sure many families are the same. They are a lot alike and they don't get along well with each other." She lit another cigarette and smoked in silence for a time. "Colin and Agatha were inseparable until she—was gone. He was lost, of course. Everyone tried to find extra time for him. Even Stella. Stella likes boys all right, but not toddlers, or prepuberty, let's say. She and Blase are good friends. And my husband won't let anyone

70

else touch the studio. She's been here so long she knows how particular he is. If Stella ever left I don't know how we'd manage. I don't know anyone else outside the family who would ever put up with Jonathan's demands."

"Savannah does," I reminded her softly.

"Yes, Savannah's a good sport, but even she cannot enter the magic kingdom without an invitation."

"But she delivers meals there three times a day!"

"She delivers meals to an outside contraption, a dumbwaiter, which Jonathan raises and lowers when he's ready. Good and ready. Savannah often has to tote back the same tray she delivered—untouched." Alison looked thoughtful, then she shook her head like a swimmer coming out of a dive. "He used to make an effort to fit Colin into his day, but he's forgetful—has been more so since his illness, and at the moment he really doesn't have the time. Once when he was in a spell of work like this, Colin tried to get his attention by using his own watercolors on one of Jonathan's books. I forgot—I mentioned that earlier. Well, it got him plenty of attention, you can bet. But the boy has behaved much better since then—on the whole. He still sneaks around, though. You must have noticed."

"Some," I admitted. "Is that little-boy prank why everyone thought he was guilty this time?"

"Who knows, Tyler?" Alison stood up and brushed ashes from her skirt. "Randy thinks that Jonathan—oh, I don't want to talk about it— If you'd like to take Colin to the library or a movie, ask Miles for one of the cars. I'm sorry I haven't even thought about your getting out on your own." Miles had driven us to the station or to the village or we'd taken a taxi all month, and I'd assumed it was the way Alison wanted it. But driving ourselves would give us much more freedom. She added, "You can drive all right? And you have a license?"

71

"Yes, and I can manage a stick shift, if necessary. I think."

"Well, it's not necessary. There are plenty of cars available. Help yourself if Miles is not around. If he is around, and in a state of sobriety, you probably had better ask him."

"Of course, and thanks," I said. It was a blue and gold Tiepolo sky. The heat was breathtaking and no birds sang. Nothing disturbed the brilliant midsummer day. No bolts of lightning struck. No thunderclaps sounded. *So much for guardian angels*, I would think long later, looking back on that hour when Colin and I were given freedom to come and go as we pleased.

8.

The village library was a vine-covered brick building, set in a green lawn and landscaped so that shrubbery protected the aging foundation as a dowager's pearl or diamond choker hides a sagging neck. Colin headed directly for his favorite section.

I followed after him and looked at books on string art, tincraft, how to whittle and carve, and said at last, "I don't suppose they'd issue me a card when I'm only a visitor."

"You can use mine, Tyler. There's no limit. We can take all we can carry."

"I'll be back," I said. "Symmography may appeal to you but I like chillers. I wonder where they keep the Teys, Lyalls, and Cliffords."

"The what?"

"Josephine Tey, Gavin Lyall, Francis Clifford—some of Britain's best story-tellers."

"What's symmography?" he asked. "I never heard of it."

"Nor did I till now." I pointed. "It seems to be string art." Then I remembered that his mother had been an architect and he must have a natural inclination for building things, or thought it brought her nearer perhaps. "How about *String and Nail Projects*? If we get stuck maybe Miles—or your brother—could help us." Almost giggling to think what Blase Clinton would say if asked to construct a ballerina or a snail in string and nails.

"I already did that one," Colin said, and I went away to look for mysteries and romantic adventure shelves. A half hour later when we both had selected as many books as we could carry, we approached the check-out counter. A large woman peered at us over Benjamin Franklin half-glasses. Colin whispered, "She's new."

"I'm Mrs. White," she said, as she studied Colin's card. She gave him a startled look and asked sharply, "You're Jonathan Clinton's son? I thought you were older."

"I'm the other one," he said so patiently I was sure it couldn't be the first time he'd been asked. I nudged the pile of books toward the woman, but she wasn't ready to check them yet. "You're that housekeeper?" Still in a tentative tone. Why *that* housekeeper?

"Would you stamp the cards, please, Mrs. White?"

She asked me to wait a minute and went to confer with another librarian who was filing cards. They held a brief conference, then the second woman also came to the desk. "I'm Eleanor Murkell. Hello, Colin." She had an overbite and brown interested eyes. "You're the tutor? Well, I'm sure Colin's happy to have a young person." She was feeding the numbered cards into a stamping machine. "Mrs. White is just learning the ropes here," she explained her co-worker. "Would you like your own card, Miss ———?"

"Tyler Ames, and I don't think it will be necessary if there's no limit."

"You're just temporary?" The bright eyes were curious but not unfriendly.

"Yes." Mrs. White was listening with her lips parted. Maybe all communities with a famous person in residence took an interest in his household matters. Eleanor Murkell looked as if she longed to ask more but thought better of it.

I said, "We'll be back soon. We read fast," and took haste to leave.

I felt an urge to put my arms around the child, like a shield, but we were both laden with books and I had never been a toucher in my life. I realized with surprise that often lately I'd wanted to hug him. I said, "Let's dump our loot in the car and head for the ice-cream cones, okay?"

"They got about six hundred flavors now," he announced.

"You can try two and no more." I had better add wash-and-wipes to my gear. Tutoring was only the tip of the iceberg. It was more like total take-over, and Randy Paul had tried to make that clear so I had no cause for complaint. I didn't have to cook or mend or do his laundry. What I had to do, and soon, was try to figure out how to prepare him for the real world again. Having been in the hospital and then with his family, the family friends, few as they were, the hired help, and Beebee—all protectors more or less, he would be raw again in a curious or uncaring school. If librarians were this interested in his oddball celebrity family, maybe his teachers were, too. And who could count on his making friends among his peers if they never were invited to come home with him?

Even with our fresh load of books, Colin was restless when we got back to the house. "Can't we take a hike or something, Tyler? You ain't even seen the studio."

"And ain't about to!"

He giggled, "Blase's cabin? He's not there."

"Are you sure?"

75

"You don't see his Alfa, do you?"

I gave up. "Lead on, but take it a little easy?"

We reached a rise of ground just before the woods began, and I turned to look back at the house and its outbuildings and the expanse of perfectly trimmed lawn. One of the gardeners had told me it was special grass, and cut with an English mower. You could trim a shag rug with it. The house shimmered in the summer heat, but inside now it was cold and quiet. I tried to picture kids racing up the drive to knock at the massive door—lifting the bronze gauntlet, if they could reach it, and asking if Colin could come out to play. Beebee had been here several times, arriving and leaving with his mother, on rainy days, but we'd made the most of them. Playing parlor games, board games, in the lounge. No other boys had called.

My roving look took in the maze and I ventured to say, "I saw the movie *Sleuth*. Oliver had a topiary labyrinth—I've always wanted to see a real one. Can't we wander in?"

"It's dumb!" Colin said fiercely. "I thought we were going to the cabin."

"All right, all right, to the cabin."

The path led upward through the trees, narrow and twisting, so we walked Indian file with Colin leading. He chattered contentedly. "Blase is going to use me for a model again sometime. Maybe he'll use you, too, Tyler."

So Blase was the one who used models. Now I understood the taximan's reference. "Does he like to paint or sculpt best?" I asked. And would he want a half-footed Venus with arms?

"Sculpt, I think."

"Maybe because your father is so great."

"Yeah, but once I heard him tell Savannah that if Randy Paul could beat him, he wanted to try something else. Even blackjack dealing. What's blackjack, Tyler?"

76

"I'm surprised you don't know and aren't a whiz at it. I didn't realize that Randy is a painter, too."

"He's what he calls a weekend painter. You're pretty, Tyler. I bet you're even beautiful. Like my mom. Blase said she was really beautiful. Sometimes I can't remember."

"I'm sure she was, Colin." The lie was easy. Any mother is beautiful to her sons, or should be. Agatha Dornblaser Clinton had been lovely in the oil painting Blase had made, but in a reference book her photograph had showed a long upper lip and bony jawline, a nose rather like Ethel Barrymore's or my aunt Lynne's, an intelligent face, handsome, not a beauty. The uphill climb was exhausting me.

"Let's sit for a minute, Colin. I'm bushed."

We found a fallen log and rested. Sunlight dappled the path between the tall trees. I said, "I like it here. I'm glad we came."

"We almost moved away once," he confided. "Right after the accident. People trampled all over everything. Jonathan had to hire guards and stuff. Once when I was down there—where—where it happened, a man started taking my picture and Blase came running and busted his camera. He was sure mad."

"The photographer? Well, he had a right to be maybe."

"Jonathan bought him another camera," Colin said defensively, then added, "Everybody was mad. Didn't you read about it?"

I said, "Colin, I came here from Missouri and I never paid much attention to—" Well, I wouldn't, couldn't, say gossip sheets when it concerned his mother. "Don't talk about it—if it hurts too much." But sometimes talk is therapy. "Let it hang out," I said, "but only if you feel like it."

He felt like it. He told me his mother had fallen from a scaffolding put up for a studio she was planning. It was to have been Blase's own place to work, instead of the cabin,

77

which wasn't really suited for a serious sculptor. "Any accident brings a crowd," I thought aloud. "But why so many people tramping around?"

"It was on all the TV," he said remotely. "Somebody way off on a sailboat said she wasn't alone, but nobody was with her, nobody ever said. Maybe if it hadn't been so deep there—" His small, sorrowful face stabbed at me. I had my own memories, still agonizing, and I said briskly, "Colin, it's getting late. We'd better move along." I would look up the newspaper stories someday at a library if I ever wanted to know more. Alison was right to keep the boy away from the areas that would remind him of the tragedy.

"Okay." He lent a hand to help me stand. "They all think I don't know somebody killed my mother on purpose. She didn't just fall and drown."

The small freckled face was pale. "Tyler, will you help me? Please, will you help me find who killed my mother?"

9.

Twigs were crunching and someone was whistling on the path above us. Colin stood, blinking back tears, and I was silent with the terrifying feeling that I had no idea what to say to him.

For once I was glad to see Miles Burton swaggering into view. He swung one hand at the bushes, narrowing the already almost thready path through the trees. He was wearing his plaid flannel shirt, and a golf cap, jeans, and tennis shoes.

I leaned on Colin's frail shoulder. "Sorry, I thought I was slipping." I put my arm around him and clung to him for lack of words to comfort.

Miles said, "You can grab me anytime, Teach." He licked his lips in an exaggerated leer. The wolf that ate Little Red Ridinghood's grandmother. A sardonic, George C. Scott mannerism, quick and amusing. And Colin began to smile again. I wondered if Miles had accidentally overheard the boy's desperate plea for help and was hoping to change the atmosphere.

We made way for Miles to step around us. Colin said in a still urgent, but low, tone, "Tyler, my mom was a good swimmer. And she could walk on scaffolds easy—she did all the time."

I hugged him again and told him my Aunt Lynne had tried to swim the Hellespont once because some male writer had done it, and she had almost drowned. Even the best swimmers had accidents. He said, "Oh, Tyler!" sounding more cheerful and managing a smile.

I said, "Let's go back to the house, Colin. I'm much more tired than I thought. We'll go walking tomorrow, right?"

His grin vanished and he hesitated. Miles already had gone past us down the path. "Tyler, it's only a little way to something I want to show you special. And you can sit down all you want."

"You mean the cabin?"

"No, my place. It's a secret. I never showed anybody before."

"In that case, how could I refuse?" I said lightly. "Lead on, MacClinton."

I was garbling Shakespeare in my effort to be casual, but if I had taken time to remember the lines right: "Lay on, Macduff, / And damn'd be him that first cries 'Hold, enough!'" I'd have held and gone the other way down the rising path. I would never have followed Colin into his secret hiding place, his watchtower, his front-row balcony seat, as it turned out, for a mystifying performance.

Hold, enough! indeed. The path upward curved and diverged. One fork led almost straight ahead, the other went slightly to the left. Colin said, "That way goes to Blase's place." We went the other way and climbed only an easy rise to a point where he pulled aside some honeysuckle bushes long gone wild and woody. He waited, bent over, holding back the branches as I stepped into a clearing on the crest of the hill and saw Jonathan Clinton's studio for the first time.

It was frame but as magnificent in its design as the main house. Planned to fit its setting of deep woods with a view of the lake from its farther side. Nestled against a curve of the bluff. A chimney identified the fireplace wall. A large window, nearly filling the A-frame on this side of the rambling structure, could be seen from the clearing when the bushes were parted as Colin held them now. If his father came to this end of the room, the son could easily observe him. At the moment the stage was empty.

I whispered, "Colin, does he know you come here?"

"Nobody knows. I made it. It's my own place."

"You don't think it's—maybe a little sneaky?" My voice was anxious. My face must have matched, but he seemed to know I was more concerned than condemning.

"I don't bother him," he said and hunched his shoulders. "Tyler, why don't you sit down?" He let the bushes fall back into place and I sat on the rock he indicated. It was smooth and warm although the bower was shady. I decided the sun must reach the clearing earlier. It was probably a good thing that Colin was willing to share his hideout. Maybe soon he would outgrow it. But a long summer lay ahead and now looked treacherous. I shivered, but Colin was kneeling on the cleared space and was gazing in the direction of the studio again.

As I studied his quiet face with its worried blue eyes, I was certain the job was too big for me. I shouldn't have accepted it, thinking only of myself and not of the boy who would look to me for guidance. Sam, at his worst moments, sneaking smokes with a buddy, getting caught trying to attend a rock concert or a ball game without paying, had never known the deep-set fears that plagued Colin. I damned myself for in-

81

adequacy. Did I dare ask someone what to do? Alison? Savannah? Blase—if he returned?

Colin said, "Jonathan is working too hard again, but I don't think he wants to. Maybe he'll stop soon."

"Oh, Colin, I don't think artists can work if they really don't want to. Writers, maybe. I know a lot of authors who worked on when they were sick—Sir Walter Scott, Scott Fitzgerald . . ." My argument died as I remembered Toulouse-Lautrec and his paralytic stroke from syphilis, Van Gogh and his slashed-off ear, and Goya who was seriously ill, or mad, when he turned out the fourteen murals called *The Black Paintings*.

Colin said, "I think it's because we need the money."

I must have looked astonished, for he added, "I think he already sold everything. He's got to make more."

This at least I could explain. "The paintings which were in the house are in a traveling exhibit—not sold, Colin. Your father is preparing for the exhibition this fall. Naturally that means a lot of work. And Alison says he is much better now. He did see a doctor—and he's probably eating most of his meals. In any case I'm sure he has someone to manage his business affairs and he wouldn't want you to worry about him."

"Mr. Paul does, but he's sick now." Colin sat on the ground with his knees drawn up to his chin. He picked up a stick and drew figures in the dirt.

"And Mr. Paul is on the mend, too," I reminded him. "You heard what Randy said the other night."

"I think we'd better get back—" I was adding, when my words were drowned by a crash of symphonic music. Sibelius. *Finlandia*. Soaring majestically into the clearing where we sat. Then Jonathan Clinton appeared at the tall window with a brush in his hand. Before I could turn away, I saw the brush leaving sweeping parabolas of crimson paint, circles, overlapping squares, squiggles—all gigantic and eventually obscuring the man in the bright yellow smock as the glass was filled with an immense design. *Finlandia in Red.* "Oh, my God!" I whispered. When the music stopped, the paintbrush was withdrawn.

Colin had jumped to his feet and stood trembling before me. "He's not crazy, Tyler! He's not! He paints the window a lot—when he wants to. It washes off!"

"He's magnificent," I murmured, but the boy had already bolted down the path, missing my words and my meaning.

I lost my balance trying to scramble to my feet. Then I tried to run. Thorns caught at my skirt. Low branches snagged my flying hair. My ankle wobbled and gave way. I pitched forward, taking a belly flop onto the path. It was a knockout punch. Seconds or minutes later I sat up. *Let tears be your tranquilizers,* someone had advised eighteen months ago when there was plenty of time. There was no time now. Colin must be found and made to understand.

Dirt and tears streaked my hands as I scratched and dug for purchase. I looked behind me for something to grab hold of and saw that a stripped branch lay across the path, carefully anchored between rocks on either side of the lane. A hurdle only a few inches high, but blending into the shadows. Easy enough for a hurrying boy to skip over. But not for me. And it hadn't been there when we climbed Indian file, step by step.

The man hunkered down in the shade and lit a cigarette. He had a lot of thinking to do. Fast. There were too many players in the field now. He couldn't keep an eye on all of them all the time. Not even if he had help.

It was hot. His brains were shrinking faster than his chances were. Though he wouldn't lay odds either way. He had to figure out a better setup. How to be half a dozen places at once, now that he had to watch the girl all the time. She knew about the balcony seat for the studio. That was one he hadn't seen coming. The kid had never taken anyone there before. No one. Not even— But it was a waste of precious time to worry about that one-foot girl and what she knew or didn't know yet. He had to think, really think, for a change.

He sat down and stretched his long legs in front of him on the bumpy ground and leaned his head back against the tree trunk.

10.

I had never been invited to visit the Burtons' apartment, nor expected to be, but it was Stella's day off. If she was at home surely she would help me find Colin. I could walk only with pain—running would be an impossibility now.

The garage building had space for four cars and a two-story section for the storing of canvases and tall equipment. The Burtons must have plenty of room. The outdoor stair-case overlooked a small, thriftily planned, and carefully tended vegetable and flower garden. I had plenty of time to admire it as I climbed, stop and start like a balky elevator. There were trees at the back in a cleared spot where Miles had hung a hammock for reading or napping. It was empty now.

I had observed that the garage doors were closed and the blinds of the windows above were drawn, but I banged hard and called out for "Stella!" The door opened quickly, but only a short way, and she peered at me silently.

"I must find Colin," I said. "Can—"

"He's not here," before I could finish.

Her feet were bare. She held a lit cigarette in one hand while the other served as a clasp to close her robe. Her hair was damp as if she had just come from the shower. Bright tendrils curled on her flushed cheeks. A beauty, I thought, or would be if she'd try to look pleasant. Then remembered that pouting, sultry women seemed to be the favorite models for artists and commercial photographers these days.

But something was wrong about Stella's appearance. Something didn't fit, but I couldn't bring it into focus. "Please help me look for him?" I asked.

"I can't imagine how you lost him," she snapped back. "You're never out of eye- or earshot." A calico cat suddenly darted past her legs and she yelled, "Grab him! I don't want him out!"

I caught the cat only because he had stopped to rub against my leg, scooped it up, and handed it back through the still half-opened doorway. To my amazement, Stella cradled the animal in her arms and crooned to it, but when she looked at me her eyes were as bleak as ever. "It's quite possible Colin would like to be on his own for a change, isn't it?"

"He misunderstood something I said."

She took a closer look at me, but without opening the door to invite me inside. "What happened to you? Your face is all dirty."

"I know. I fell down, but that doesn't matter. I'm worried about Colin."

For a moment I thought I had won my plea. She put the cat down, but after that she merely narrowed the door opening to a slit. And continued to stare at me dubiously.

"I'm not dressed and Miles isn't here."

I turned away but her voice stopped me, "You worry too much, Tyler. If you'd ever had any kids of your own, you'd know they are tougher than they look. Colin won't stay mad at you for long—whatever you did."

"Thanks heaps," I said, and limped back down the stairs. *How many kids have you got?* I wanted to yell at the closed door but luckily refrained. I wouldn't have put it past her to shove me down the remaining steps. Her red hair was real, not a dye job.

At the foot of the stairway I saw that my bracelet was gone. Add one small disaster, but it was probably in the path where I had fallen and could be recovered later. The main thing was to find Colin and set matters straight. It took nearly half an hour for me to search the house. It was empty except for Savannah, napping in the back room. I headed for the beach and for the first time walked north toward the forbidden rocks. Either here or the maze, I decided. He might have deliberately chosen the two places I wasn't likely to look for him.

He sat in the shadow of the cliff, with his bare feet in the narrow stretch of sand left by the water's edge. I fell in a heap beside him and said nothing. I worked off my shoes and pushed my good foot into the sand and breathed deeply.

Eventually Colin asked, "Can I see that up close? Is it okay, Tyler?"

He meant my prosthesis. I said, "Sure. I owe you one. Look away." And minutes later added, "I wasn't swearing at your father. I was what you call awestruck, stricken, whatever. Let's forget it, okay?"

Okay all around. But I thought about my bracelet, one of few tangible links to my parents, and as the shadows lengthened I grew depressed and felt weighted with unshed tears. I would not leave my most precious possession lying in the dirt all night.

"See you in a little while, Colin," I said, and headed back for the woods. I tried not to look at the Burtons' windows as I crossed the driveway. Maybe the shades were still pulled, or perhaps Stella and her calico cat were watching my clumsy progress. I came to a momentary halt when I saw that Blase's red Alfa Romeo stood in the parking space for delivery vans. Was he in the house or somewhere else—his cabin, or even behind those closed shades? It didn't matter. My bracelet mattered.

The woods were cooler and dim now. I seemed more to creep than to climb as I moved slowly upward, keeping my head bent for a glint of silver, and reached the spot where I had fallen. I searched carefully, pushing aside branches and foliage, fruitlessly. I went on to the clearing, keeping a sharp watch all the way.

The studio window was still *Finlandia in Red*, but the artist had gone. The music was somewhat quieter. And totally different. I didn't recognize the composition; then it flashed into memory—"Take the A-Train." Another Ellington fan in the household. Was it the same one who had put "Muskrat Ramble" on the stereo in the family room my first day? Blase?

For a moment I knelt in the soft pine needles at the side of Colin's clearing and felt for my bracelet. But all I found was an unused packet of matches with a brilliant purple satiny cover. I dropped them into my skirt pocket. Someone might want them back. And then a giant WHO? moved across the screen of my mind. Colin did not carry matches. I was sure that he didn't try to sneak smokes, especially in his hideaway, precious to him for his father's nearness. Nor would he light a fire here and bring attention.

I shivered and rubbed my upper arms. The sun had lowered considerably since I'd last noticed. Gray clouds moved eastward over the lake. It would be better to give up the search until tomorrow and pray that it would be a fair day. I went downhill seemingly inch by inch, gritting my teeth with each jarring step. A shadow of a man lay across the bottom of the path, startling me into a quavering, "Who's there?" followed by a nervous but less shaky, "Damn it, who's there?"

"That's my question," he said.

I tried to turn too fast, thinking wildly I might go back to the hiding place, and I fell at Blase Clinton's feet. He lifted me, held me straight, and his disbelieving eyes took in my tangled hair, streaked face, torn skirt, dirty hands, and badly swollen ankle. Something subtly altered his expression. I prayed God it wasn't sympathy.

"I lost my bracelet," I said. Wind blew hair in my face. I pushed it back. A strand of hair stuck to my lips. He gently lifted it and tucked it behind my ear, as if I were a woebegone child. The hell with it. "Colin and I were walking. I must have dropped it."

"Into an old well? And dived in after it?"

"Whatever you say." I would not give away Colin's secret. Nor my own. Whoever had laid the branch for me to fall over was waiting to see my reaction—or to see if I had survived.

Blase blocked my path to the house. "Exactly where were you?"

"I don't know. It doesn't matter, does it?"

"Did you see anyone? Anyone at all."

"No, but—" I remembered the matches and handed them to him. "These are yours, no doubt."

He barely glanced at the packet. "I don't smoke. Are you sure you're all right? Where's Colin?"

"On the beach—we were walking earlier—I went back." I was swaying dizzily but it couldn't be helped. He held my shoulders firmly and asked, "Steady now?" I nodded, and he knelt to take off my left shoe.

I said, "No! Please! I can do it—later—just help me to the house."

But already his sculptor's fingers moved as knowingly as a surgeon's, but no doctor's touch had ever burned through my skin!

"You can't walk on this, you little idiot." He sounded angry, even furious, and not—thank God—at all kindly. "Haven't you even a *smattering* of common sense? Born with no instinct for self-preservation? One of nature's wonders, are you, my girl?"

All this time he was lifting me and turning to the house. "It would help," he suggested, "if you would try not to stiffen every muscle. But I've carried boards before and I can again."

"I wasn't born crippled," I sniffled.

"Crippled is as crippled thinks." His voice could freeze frogs, as my father used to say. But my father had been describing winter weather—not a wintry young man who was trying to carry a stick of a girl and climb redwood stairs, then kicking at a door with his foot, yelling, "'Savannah, get out here fast!"

She came on the run, looking scared. "Oh, my God, what now? Here, Blase, let me help. Blase, she'll be easier in this chair. We can both haul her."

They put me in a canvas deck chair and gave me a minute to settle myself. Both scowled at me.

"I lost my bracelet," I told Savannah, still dizzy.

"Is *that* all?"

"Don't look at me," Blase said. "I just got here."

They tried lifting me, but he told Savannah to forget the idea, it was easier to tote the bones by himself. "She's loosened up some," he mumbled. "Decided I won't rape her with you for witness. Run on, *tesoro!*" he was still talking to Savannah, "get her bed ready. Where's Alison, damn it all—off in her ivory tower? Tell her to get on the phone and sweet-talk some doctor into making a house call. Any doctor will do at the moment."

"She's gone. So's Miles. Maybe Stella's back."

"I don't need a doctor," I said, but nobody was listening.

"Stella's here, but you and I will handle this," Blase said. They exchanged a look, unreadable to me—a look of complicity, I thought—but apparently satisfactory to both of them.

"I'm on my way," Savannah said.

"I don't need a doctor," I said again, as soon as Blase had put me down on my own bed.

He stood back, hands on hips, studying me. "I don't like the look of that foot," he said vaguely, more as if to himself than to me.

"It do look a mess," Savannah agreed, brows drawn in a straight, worried line.

"Don't worry about it," I snapped. "It didn't happen today—the bad part. Nobody asked you to look, anyway."

"Why don't you take it easy, Tyler?" His voice all sarcasm. "Let Savannah help—she's got roots and rhythm, black magic, all the good stuff. She's even got good sense—maybe some of it will rub off. Anyway let her get you undressed while I'm gone. She'll be careful."

Savannah had smacked him soundly on the seat of his jeans as he spoke. Now she said, "Just you be careful, Blase Clinton. Keep your eyes open. Hear?"

He nodded and moved backward to the door, still studying my foot doubtfully. "If a nurse would help, I can get one easy."

"Then *git*," Savannah said.

He was gone, running. "Roll over to one side, if you can, girl," she directed. "I want to turn down the spread. You want your nightgown, robe?"

"I feel rotten to cause all this fuss," I apologized as she helped me change.

"Don't fret it. Blase Clinton don't bother 'less he feels like

91

it. You sure stirred up something. What happened, girl?"

I told her most of it, leaving out the clearing and the studio. She frowned in concentration. "Who would be so low-down mean? 'Less it was Miles, drunk and feelin' ornery."

"Miles wasn't drunk. We saw him earlier."

"Don't take Miles *any* time to get a load on, honey."

"Why would Miles Burton want to hurt me?" I asked, indifferently now. Savannah had already fetched a soothing, warm washcloth and towel and was doing her best to clean me up.

"I don't exactly know—and who *says* it was Miles? And anyhow he never needs a reason for half the stuff he does. Can you turn over? I can brush some of that tangle. You got weeds even in your hair. Why do you and Colin wander all over? Them woods ain't safe to walk around in, let alone run in. I thought you wasn't too good at running anyway."

She was getting fresh towels and warm water and talking sixty to the minute I thought. I was soon feeling wonderfully well cared for. Savannah's movements were as gentle as a mother cat's. When I complimented her she looked embarrassed.

She reminded me, almost gruffly, "I got seven kids, and five of them is daughters. I wouldn't want *one* of them looking the mess you was when Blase came up them steps. Scared me half to death."

"I love you, Savannah," I said. I was almost drifting into sleep, but I meant every word and I was glad to have a friend nearer than Borneo or wherever my only relative might be. "What's your last name, Savannah? If you ever told me I forgot."

"Savannah Bertrand Hamilton," Blase's voice told me. "How could you forget that? And how could a lady who's three-quarters Cherokee get a name like that?"

"One-quarter to a half maybe," she corrected him. "Where's that nurse?"

92

"On the way." He stood by the bed and stared down at me. "What'd you do—give her a sleeping pill?"

"A face wash and a hair comb," I murmured. "Go away."

Oh, wow! I thought, with sudden glee. Catherine Linton had never told Heathcliff to go away. Jane Eyre had sort of ordered Rochester to keep his distance, but she hadn't meant a word of it. I was recovering my senses, even if my toes were gone forever. I, Tyler Ames, had told old golden boy Blase Clinton to beat it.

I opened my eyes to see how this sat with him. He was laughing. "Well, how about that for gratitude? Mutiny on the *Bounty*, too, and high time."

"I got here as fast as I could," a blithe voice spoke from my parlor. The girl who came through the doorway was a small blonde with sparkling eyes and a smile that welcomed the world. No fake nurse's smile; real.

She was quick and competent in her examination, and soon grew more somber and sympathetic, but bearably so. Her questions were brief and to the point. She'd handled prosthetic parts of patients before and would again. No big deal, her eyes and voice and hands told me, reassured me. She gave me a friendly pat on my good knee and said she'd have a doctor look in by nighttime unless I preferred to see my own physician.

"He's in Kansas City," I told her, smiling. Her lightheartedness was infectious.

"Kansas is a bit far, we'll send somebody else."

"Missouri," I said automatically. Adding quickly, "Everybody makes that mistake unless they're natives." *Unless he or she is a native,* my tutorish mind put in the correction, but at least I managed to keep quiet about it.

"Plenty of good Illinois men. Could I see what medications you have? How bad is the pain?"

"Better."

She turned to Blase and Savannah who had stood by in

silence. "I don't think there's an emergency, but a checkup is certainly advisable. Meanwhile she can use some rest, and something to ease her."

"Toothpaste," I said. "That's about it—I ran out of pills."

"I brought Empirin with codeine. One won't hurt you. You can have another later if you need it."

I smiled gratefully at her and she cocked her head, looking first at Blase and then at me. "I'd certainly like to know what brand of toothpaste you use; your teeth are beautiful."

Blase spoke unexpectedly. "The whole girl is beautiful. Witless, but lovely to look at."

"I thought you'd notice that," the little nurse said. She took his arm breezily. "Now for the Country Bumpkin—you promised!"

"I promised," he agreed, "and I'm a man of most of my words."

As soon as they had gone, I asked Savannah, "What's the Country Bumpkin?"

"It's a Chinese restaurant—ain't that what it sounds like? You want something to eat before you try to take a nap?"

"I'm not hungry."

"I guess he had to promise her a free meal to get her all the way out here. Townspeople don't like to come here—I'm lucky I got that cabman buffaloed. He more scared of me than he is of— Well, no mind. You better eat."

"It's supposed to be the white man speaks with forked tongue, Savannah baby, not the Choctaw, Cherokee, whatever Blase said. When are you going to tell me what's really going on—or what went on—in this place? Ever?"

She stared at me impassively, arms folded, waiting.

I said, "Anyway, I bet that nurse would have come even without a free meal."

"You going to sit there and pout about it, or would you like to try a little of my veal Prince Orloff?"

"Both," I decided.

11.

My bracelet was still lost a week later. Nearly everyone had helped look for it on the path to Blase's studio. Colin and I had doubly searched the secret clearing, but with no luck.

First I had been driven to the local hospital and carefully checked out. My health was fine and now the swelling in my abused ankle had receded. Colin was getting restless again after being amazingly patient with my brief convalescence. He'd brought his own TV set for my use in the bedroom. We worked lessons and played board games until I complained that I was beginning to feel like Robert Louis Stevenson and his counterpane. To my astonishment Colin had never heard of *A Child's Garden of Verses*, though he knew *Kidnapped* and *Treasure Island*. I told him about the pleasant land of counterpane where the ailing Stevenson had played with his toy soldiers.

I said, " 'I should like to rise and go—where the golden apples grow' right about now. That's another poem."

"How come he wrote about his bed?" Colin asked.

"He was sick a lot."

Colin looked thoughtful and then pleased, having been sick rather a lot himself. And now a famous author had gone that route and lived to write stirring adventure tales. I decided not to tell him how Stevenson's life had ended all too early, adventures or not.

In any case, Colin probably would look it up for himself and also, more than likely, would memorize most of the garden of verses, as I had done long before him. What mattered was that I was back on my feet and feeling nettlesome. Ready to take on new projects. Miles, as it happened, asked if I'd like to drive the Land Rover. "Nothing to it," he said, and gave me a lesson in mastering the clutch. We were returning to the house when he asked, "Did you ever find that bracelet you were looking for?"

I almost stalled the vehicle. "No, have you seen it?"

"It'll turn up," he evaded. "Most things do."

He jumped down from the car as we reached the front door, and Colin was waiting, dancing on one foot, eager to be off.

I drove slowly down the drive. Dust rose as Colin bounced on the seat beside me. We progressed in a series of jerks, and I hoped Miles had gone on about his business. Once we reached the highway, I relaxed and we rode in relative ease.

"You're doing okay," Colin complimented. "Not as good as Miles, but he's had lots of practice."

"I'll get the hang of it."

Colin sat daydreaming, or had the look of it. "Maybe Blase'll let you take his Alfa. It's neat and sometimes he doesn't use it for days when he's at the cabin. If he's working. I can tell him you're a good driver."

"Don't tell him a damn thing," I said. Then added, "Sorry."

"Why don't you like him, Tyler?"

"That's a dumb question," I countered. "Listen, I can't talk and drive, too. Not yet anyway. So just kindly shut up for a while, please?"

He was quiet for nearly three minutes. "His car is real close to the ground. This is like a bus. I mean high up."

"It rides like a bus," I said. "But promise me you won't ask Blase for his darned old car."

"Stella drives it when she wants."

"Colin, promise me."

"You always look kind of funny when we talk about Blase," he protested.

"We *don't* talk about him!"

"I mean whenever anybody talks about him, you look funny. He's kind of hard to get to know. Like my father—" He hesitated and I swallowed an "Oh, boy!" then Colin went on. "Sometimes I guess they both hurt people's feelings, but they don't always mean it."

"We all hurt other people, Colin. You misunderstood me —that day in the clearing, remember?"

He nodded. We had reached the village and I had to concentrate on maneuvering the Rover in traffic. We parked by the stationery store and took our time looking over supplies. Colin selected a yellow note pad and a green felt-tip pen. "I'm going to keep these special," he told me. "Just for letters."

"You write letters?" I must have looked my surprise, and my voice rose on the question, but he merely nodded and said, "To my dad. I write to Jonathan all the time. Savannah delivers my letters on her trays."

"Does he answer them?"

I was sorry I had asked. His face looked somber. "He used to."

"He will again," I said quickly, "as soon as he has time."

97

And I would ask Alison to demand time. The great man could surely forego one sailing day, one midnight beach walk, long enough to answer his son's notes.

As we came out of the store into the brilliant July sunlight, Colin yelled, "Hey, there's Ruby waiting for her bus."

Ruby waved to us and we joined her for a few minutes. Colin followed an ant a little distance down the sidewalk and Ruby said, "It's really been a blessing since you came, Tyler. That boy is a different child altogether. I don't mind coming to work anymore."

"*Did* you mind?" I had to ask.

She grimaced. "Some days I was scared to come," she said in a near whisper. "Listen, Tyler, I can tell you—" But Colin was back and she stopped speaking. The bus came and Ruby was gone, along with whatever she might have said if Colin hadn't returned before the bus arrived.

I tried to console myself that there'd be other days for Ruby and her confidences. The young black woman was an intelligent observer, an outsider but with some knowledge of the household and no emotional involvement to affect her judgment. By now Savannah had invested plenty of herself in the Clinton family. She couldn't be disinterested, no matter how strong the pull of her own life in Evanston. To question Ruby wouldn't be to pry or to break the good-conduct rules by asking a servant about the employer. It was what they call need-to-know in spy stories, wasn't it? Didn't I need most desperately to know more about this child's home and his true place in it? Something had to change before I could turn my back on it, job done or not done, in the fall.

Colin was clearly puzzled at my reverie and I managed a smile. "Let's go home and shop another day. I'm not even in the mood for the library."

Before we had left the village limits the sky had clouded over. It was beginning to rain as we reached the house.

By late afternoon the storm had crashed, thrashed, bumped, thumped, and whistled to a sort of crescendo, sending sheets of rainwater against the long lounge windows in shivering patterns that descended in slanting lines. Colin and I had described the various sounds as they seemed to us. I said, "It rains on the bias, have you noticed?"

"Yep, I noticed." He was making a manful effort not to wince at lightning flashes. "Hey, maybe we can bet on which one hits bottom first."

He meant the sidelong rivulets, I decided, and pulled a spinsterish face with pursed mouth. "I don't approve of gambling at age nine. Could lead to a roving life—" Homeless, I almost added, but remembered in time that he was virtually homeless now. No mother, and a father usually beyond reach. Add to that a brother who seldom phoned. I said, "I'm glad you're not bothered by storms—that *would* be a waste of time."

"I'm not scared of *anything*. You want to play poker?"

"No! And I don't want to whittle ships in a bottle." I had spoken much too sharply and I apologized. Colin asked if he could go to his own room and watch television. I nodded. *Go ahead and jump without an audience*, I told him silently, and took myself to the kitchen and Savannah's company. Stella, in full rain gear, was paying for the week's work and getting ready to leave. She was unusually pale, with dark circles under her eyes. No lipstick, and her shoulders slumped. Usually she stood erect and had a word or two of no great importance but was friendly enough when we passed. Today she merely nodded in departure.

"She really lookin' bad," Savannah commented as the housekeeper's steps died away across the deck.

I said, "The storm's going away."

"You want coffee?" She poured without waiting for an answer and I settled down to listen to her gossip. Obviously

99

Stella was on Savannah's mind. "Them two met in Paris, somewheres like that. Never seemed a good match. Kids might've helped, but she never took to Colin. They don't sleep in the same bed—Miles and her. Not even in the same room. How about that?"

The dark eyes watched curiously for my reaction. I shrugged. "They don't seem particularly 'loverly,' to borrow a word from Eliza Doolittle or whoever wrote the song."

"Eliza Whoever said a mouthful."

"Anyway, these days it's the kids who buy the double beds. Older people—my folks and their friends—were the twin-bed set. Sleeping together doesn't seem to have much to do with beds. Or sleeping. How do you like all this news from a purely involuntary bystander?"

"You talk a lot. I got eyes."

"But I got no hopes and no plans, Savannah baby. Tell me about Agatha and Jonathan—were they very much in love? Was it wonderful then?"

She looked thoughtful. "They was good friends. They liked each other and nobody got in anybody's way. You know what I mean? She was older than him and he was gone a lot and working a lot, but so was she. He was one handsome cat, I can tell you that."

"Still is, I think. At least, from the only glimpse I ever got— Was Agatha jealous at all?" Thinking I'd have been a hellcat if I'd been Agatha Clinton.

"I doubt it. She had her work, like I said. That was good. They didn't sit around waiting for the other all the time or getting mad about it and looking somewheres else." She drew herself up suddenly. "I oughtn't to be running on. What I know and what I guess about is nobody's business."

I looked around quickly to see if Colin had come in, but for once Savannah had chosen discretion for no obvious reason. Two long and one short beeps of a horn announced that

Miles was ready to drive her to the station. I went back to my room, but the lingering black clouds had ended the day all too early. I finished the only library book I hadn't read and still was restless and unaccountably aware of being alone. I was used to solitude, preferred it. So what was the matter?

Alison had said I could use the library here, but I hadn't yet visited the room which lay beyond her office. At the moment the house felt empty and abandoned, although Colin, at least, was in his room. He and I had been the only ones for supper. I hadn't asked Savannah if the Clintons had finally gone somewhere together, though no red or green light showed in the kitchen. This was a day of missed opportunities and the sooner over the better.

Sometime I intended to investigate the maze, but only after Colin was safely asleep and only when the moon was high. Tonight the grounds were probably still too wet for strolling. I was tired of stereo and I couldn't think of a soul on earth I cared to write a letter to.

All lines of thought wound back to the Clinton library—even if a visit meant crossing Alison's office. She might easily consider it an invasion of privacy at this time of night and in her absence. But I needed something to read. It was sensible, not just an impulse. I needed to improve my tutor's mind. Thus I cheer-led myself all the way upstairs.

I moved swiftly, listened at the office door, and opened it without a sound. Indirect lighting glowed here as in the other rooms, but the telephone showed no red or green blinker. I felt as if I were walking on stilts, taking awkward balancing strides, trying to hasten across the room which bore the scent of Alison's perfume. Jade, musk oil, whatever. Something that marked her territory was too exotic, too falsely promising, too heavy, like her lashes. But so fitting I hadn't been so aware of it until now—in her absence.

As Savannah had hinted, maybe Alison looked for someone

else in her husband's long withdrawals. I suddenly prayed it was Randolph Paul as it seemed to be, and not a younger man who appeared to dislike his stepmother.

The library door, too, opened easily but the room was dark. I fumbled for the switch, pressed, and found that table lamps were lighted on two levels. One side of the room, like the gallery, had the tall window-wall, with heavy linen draperies pulled back now, showing the storm-swept night, all the more lonely for a tiny moving light far out on the rough waters.

To my left a wall of bookshelves gleamed softly with polish and was packed from floor to ceiling with volumes irregular in height. I was glad to see they were not sets, but books which must have been chosen individually, taken out and read occasionally, and returned haphazardly, as our books at home had been. On a lower shelf someone, maybe Stella, more likely Colin, had arranged a row according to size like schoolchildren in old-time photographs. Then I saw the objects which decorated the front of the shelves at shoulder level, and caught my breath.

Dozens of small skulls grinned fiercely or stared empty-eyed into the shadows cast by the candle lamp on the desk which dominated the far end of the room. *Memento mori*—only that and nothing more—but coming upon them suddenly and in a guilty mood, they were almost as bad as if I had encountered Alison when I was feeling off limits. I took another moment, then stepped fully inside the room, shutting the green, suede-covered door firmly. It was bronze-bound, with a tooled bronze doorknob, and it was beautiful, but I had to turn around sometime.

I found the skulls were ivory, rock crystal, silver, and gold. Many were two-faced—Life and Death. Enormously valuable—undoubtedly—but I wished they'd been Venetian paperweights, or Toby mugs, or Hummel figures.

102

On the desk a little ivory anatomical eye sat on a silver stand. As I drew near to it I saw that it could be broken down to demonstrate the structure of the human eye, but I didn't touch it. I turned and jumped slightly, seeing a real skeleton on a jet base, standing beneath the balcony which ran along two sides of the room. Thank God, Colin wasn't here to see my edginess. An artist, even an abstract expressionist, must know his bones. I said, "Hi, there, Smokey Joe," but not out loud. Smokey was—had been anyway—the art department skeleton one of the instructors had bought with his own money to show us how the hipbone connected to the thigh bone and all the rest of it.

I ran my fingertips on the green-leather and gold-embossed desk top. Its supplies lay in perfect order as if waiting for someone. Someone who would never come again, I thought. The clock in ormolu and carved steel was French and very old, and the astrolabe on its heavy base was signed in Latin. I backed away. No wonder there was only one entrance—the windows should have been barred. A sofa, upholstered in velvet, had a long, low table in front of it, with an agate top inlaid with shells and a star. A man's room, it seemed, until I saw there was an architect's drawing table. Its lid was open. An instrument case in red morocco and gold had diamond initials—ADC. An architect's compass, a sundial of antique gold, and drawing pencils in a silver bucket. *Memento mori* of Agatha Dornblaser Clinton. Priceless items, but I shuddered and moved toward the nearer of two circular staircases which led to either end of the L-shaped balcony.

The upper level was partitioned by shelves, making individual libraries, each with its own chair, desk, and lamp. I remembered Colin had said it used to be his favorite place, and no one was allowed to borrow from another's "stuff" without asking. He'd also said that nobody ever spent much time here now.

103

"My mother used to work here at night, sometimes. She had a heap of things to do, but I could always keep quiet and pick anything I wanted her to read. Bedtimes anyway." He'd looked sad but not resentful when he added, "Blase used to read to me, after—you know, after— Not anymore."

"Now that you can read so well for yourself," I'd pointed out.

"Yeah."

Colin's section was easy to recognize. A stack of books was on the chair seat. The desk was cluttered with animal figures in hardened clay, silly putty, and a rock collection. I picked up a large child's geography of the world and found that it fell open to a map of Spain, and there were smudges on the page. In the year following his mother's death Blase had gone to Madrid, Granada, Málaga, ending up in a mountain village that Savannah said she couldn't spell much less pronounce but she thought it was near the sea. "He was running away, anyway, so what do it matter where? I ain't about to blame him, then or now. He was too young to take Colin and that's a pity."

But motherless Colin, abandoned by his brother as it must have seemed, alienated by his father's undoubtedly bewildering marriage to the peerless Alison, must have tried to follow Blase as best he could, huddled forlornly in his once favorite spot, with a map he could cry over.

I switched off the lamp, which had a Roman soldier standing endless guard as its base and a cheerful red lamp shade, but I was in no mood for cheer. I moved on to the section which must have been—or still was—Blase's.

Here the shelves were wide-spaced and deep to hold tall and heavy volumes on sculpture and art, thick books on anatomy, a few paperback thrillers, Michelin guides. There was an open portfolio on the desk with charcoal sketches of nudes and parts thereof on a drawing pad. I moved along to glance briefly into the areas once used by Agatha and Jonathan Clinton. I paused only to turn off the lamps in each and returned to Blase's quarters, then switched off this lamp, too, though it was a beauty and lit the floor on which it stood as well as the desk. I could imagine Agatha searching fine shops for the perfect lamp for an artist son who liked to sit on the floor. Or perhaps she had designed it just for him. Colin had told me that his brother always preferred the ground or the floor when he was sketching. In the dark I sat, too, and leaned against the shelves. My mind drifted back to a vanished topsy-turvy household where everyone was known and loved and mostly understood. Where life was not elegant, but not a set of puzzles, secrets, disappearances. I shut my eyes. My eyelids stung, but eventually all my worlds slid away soundlessly.

12.

Bees were buzzing in my dream ear. The storm had come back. Which was nonsense. Wrong direction. I woke fully, without moving, as I had learned to do in the hospital months. It had been a sort of game to play. Be awake and listen. Learn something. Maybe you were getting well and didn't know it. Better off than you felt. Nobody ever told you the truth in a hospital.

But I was in the Clinton library. The main part was lighted, and the balcony was still dark because I had switched off all the lamps for no particular reason. And I was hearing a meant-to-be-private argument. Voices shouting obscenities. I tried not to sort them out, but it had to be Jonathan and Alison. I had heard him speak only once but that had been enough. I lay still and cursed my blundering self once again.

And wondered how long I had slept.

He was saying, "It's a little late to be whining about desire, toots." And Alison: "For God's sake, Jonathan, nobody has said 'toots' for thirty years."

"And you haven't put out for thirty years. Not for me, at least."

His laugh sent shivers along my spine. I was wearing a sleeveless shift, bare-legged, my feet in terry-covered ortho-pedic slippers, and someone must have turned the air condi-tioning to sixty degrees or lower. I was shaking and my teeth chattered, but I heard Alison ask, "Why *did* you marry me, then, you bastard?" And his answer: "I thought the boys needed a woman's touch. *Both* boys, my dear."

"I've tried, God knows. I even offered to adopt Colin. I still could."

"I don't want to discuss it. As a matter of fact, I don't remember your offer. But I don't remember much of those days. And it no longer matters."

"Jonathan, I do wish we could get back to—to an under-standing. I wish you'd share your thoughts with me. Could you—would you let me take you to a doctor, my dear? I know a fine man."

His answer was too brief and too low for me to hear.

As if she had remembered that Colin and I were some-where in the house, she lowered her voice, too. Some of her words were audible, not all, and I wished I could hear none of it. She was trying to talk him into getting medical advice. She wanted him to understand how expensive hospital care had been for his dear friend Paul and how important that he keep on working—that there be new material for the exhibi-tion.

"Randy cares about you, too, Jonathan. You shouldn't shut him out. And will you ever, please, let me know what's gone wrong with you and Blase? If you can't stand the sight of your own son, why won't you tell us?"

"Us?" he came back at her. "Who exactly do you mean by 'us'?"

She lit a cigarette and blew smoke upward. I prayed heaven I wouldn't sneeze. Instead of answering his bitter-sounding question, she hedged, it seemed. "You've got to work harder, my dear. Randy needs the canvases. The show must be your best ever."

"Why?" Then he said, "To fill Randy's pockets? What Randy wants, Randy gets?"

"Do you care?"

"I really *wish* I cared," he said wearily.

Ages passed and I had a cramp in my shoulder. I longed to rub my back, but dared not move a finger.

Alison said, "Think of your friend, then. Think of Paul Senior. He's still far from well. Worrying could be fatal."

"You have a point," the tired voice responded.

I eased my head sideways while shifting weight as quietly as possible. Luckily for me, Alison was pressing her advantage, demanding to know when the canvases would be ready. I could see them both now. Jonthan Clinton walked to the windows to stare at the black night. An after-the-storm wind rattled the panes, it seemed, though I knew they were solidly built, double-hung, flawless in their custom-fit casements. But it was Clinton, beating his fist against the glass in a tattoo of fury or despair. He turned to Alison, and I thought I had never seen such frustration, such longing. *Run to him, Alison, run!* I bit my lip, tasting blood, to keep from shouting.

But she had crossed to the green suede door and turned its knob. Her back was rigid with anger. She left without speaking.

For moments Jonathan Clinton stood gazing at eye level—at the skulls. I lay awkwardly, helplessly staring down at him, erratically remembering a long-ago chem-lab experiment. Cobalt burns with a blue-green flame on a Bunsen burner. *It's blue,* I'd said. *It's green; any fool can see; are you color-*

blind? A lab instructor had glared at me. *Why won't you date me, Tyler? What's so wrong about me?* I could have said, *It's the pimples. No, it's the begging I can't stand.*

Jonathan Clinton had no pimples and his begging was silent. Maybe Alison was not what his whole body pleaded for. He looked young, as taut muscles pulled at his narrow face. "Everyone looks younger from above"—another bit of knowledge from the past—another boy—a photographer—faceless in memory—adding, "So does sex. That's why so many of these old lovers like mirrored ceilings. But that's not your problem, child. Say, twenty, thirty years from now, when you're a big-shot art critic, get the *People* people to shoot you from above—no chins. Remember that, baby girl."

I was no longer a child, no baby girl, and Jonathan Clinton was not a young man, but I had a childish urge to rush downstairs and gather him into my arms for comfort. My fingernails bit into my palms.

Young or not, he was still strong. He strode to the desk and lifted the heavy astrolabe as easily as if it were a plastic toy and held it aloft, studying it. For a dreadful pause I thought he meant to smash the precious antique instrument against the desk as a small boy might destroy a plaything. But he blew upon it. No dust. Stella would have seen to that. I tried to work myself farther back into the shadows. Suppose his wandering glance found me next?

But he placed the astrolabe back in place and let his hand caress the leather desk-top though he touched none of the lined-up objects: ivory, jade, alabaster, silver items. Letter openers, paperweights, elaborately carved antique boxes, a shell ashtray with a matchbox in the center of it. *A brilliant purple satiny matchbox!* Even from here I could see it! I hadn't thought of my lost bracelet for hours, but I thought of it now. Who would carry matches that must have once belonged to Agatha Clinton?

While I tried to think, the room went dark again. Clinton

had gone. I stood up too quickly and stumbled over the chair. Almost at once a pencil of light darted somewhere below me, casting giant, grotesque shadows. The stairs creaked under someone's weight. I shrank back against the shelves as the beam of light and footsteps came nearer. All my courage seeped to my feet. My steel-protected slipper weighed a ton. I couldn't move, so I cowered and shut my eyes.

"Supposing you had a reason for being here—here in the dark," a voice said, "what would it be?"

I struggled to open my eyes, wanting to vanish. Blase Clinton had tried to turn on the desk lamp with no success. The flashlight he held made a bobbing tennis ball of light across my skirt. I kept my head down. My throat ached fiercely and my mouth was dry.

"I needed something to read and I fell asleep, I guess."

"How long have you been awake, would you guess?" Sarcasm tinged his voice. The flashlight beam explored the area around me, but he refrained from shining it into my eyes.

"Too long," I murmured. If only shame could make me invisible, but I disappeared only when he turned the beam elsewhere. Always it came back to me.

"Do you have a tape recorder?" he asked.

Perversely the moon came out, strong and clear, wherever it was, so that even in this east room there was a dimness that made our shapes visible, if not our features.

He grabbed my upper arms and gave me a little shake. "I repeat, have you been taping all this?"

Astonishment kept me silent as his hands slid down my body. He was searching for a recorder, as fast, light-fingered, but as thoroughly and impersonally as an airport examiner.

"Stop that! Please!" The words came out of my dry throat in a squeak. "Taping what, for God's sake?"

"*The Taming of the Shrew,* of course."

"I didn't mean to eavesdrop."

"She 'didn't mean to eavesdrop,' " he mimicked, then his hands clasped my upper arms again. "Well, you're clean, as they say. And unless I'm mistaken you're having a chill."

"I sh-should h-have b-brought a sweater." Teeth chattering the stutter.

"Try mine," he suggested, and pulled me into his arms. I leaned against the softness of a cashmere pullover and felt the muscular body beneath it. Felt his heart beating and scarcely heard his words. "The damned air conditioning has gone haywire in the other direction. We'll have icicles by morning. Hope you've got some Viking blood." His sweatered arms warmed my back. I strained to look up at him. He released his grip slightly and the flashlight beam bounced crazily. I said, "Supermarket opening," meaning the zigzagging light, embarrassed out of my wits now, and terrified that he'd let me go.

But he kissed me. Sweetly, warmly, with infinite tenderness.

I kissed him back, hard and hungrily. Desperately it must have seemed, for he gave me a little shove away, into the blackness, against the bookshelves. I heard a wretched, "Oh, God! Oh, damn you all!" and he was leaving. But as if he'd just remembered it, he brought the flashlight back and let it shine from the desk. I heard him bounding down the steps. He hit the switch at the door as he departed on the run. All the lamps glowed again. "Damn WHO all?" I screamed at him, but he was gone.

I went back to my room, putting one heavy foot before the other, in turn, counting endlessly and to no purpose, trying to think of nothing at all.

At half-past one, two, two-thirty, I stared at the luminous dial on my bedside clock. Why had I never asked if the cabin had a phone? Why had I never looked to see if his number in town was listed among the scribblings on the kitchen message board? At ten minutes past three I went into the bathroom and looked for aspirin. Painkillers were a month behind me now. I wondered if the damned toothpaste could be a sedative.

Could I hypnotize myself by staring into the mirror at the thin face? Too bony, but my skin was clear and my hair was clean. I had a tan and my eyes weren't crossed. My mouth looked the same as always. It hadn't been burned to a blackened crisp by his kiss, though it could have been. The heat was there. Still there. Might always be. I drank two glasses of cold water and wondered how long moping over a hopeless infatuation usually lasted. *Keep afloat, old girl, bumble through. Take it one day at a time. You'll either survive and get over it or you'll bore yourself to death with tired, old get-well messages.* At least this time my wounds didn't show.

I went back to bed and punched the pillows into fluffiness. And reminded myself that everything looks worse at night. Wait until morning.

Waiting until morning took all night.

He went racing uphill to the cabin, not even panting at the climb. His mind was seething with anxiety, his emotions too torn, ripped, jagged. Miles had been right about that bastard knowing exactly what kind of girl to hire. What lure would work best.

He kicked at the cabin latch to open the door. It used to be a trick to undo a door; now it was habit. He'd been only a kid when Miles set out to make him the true successor to the Great Houdini. Promised success. Miles, who could slip in and out of the eye of a needle unobserved even by the stitcher. Nothing to it, if you paid attention. Pay attention, boy, and you can learn the rope trick, the box trick, saw-the-illusion-in-half, if that's your pleasure. The conjurer's conjurer. Nothing at all if you practice.

The girl's hair had smelled fresh, sunlit even in the dark, like a lemon grove in the morning, or honeysuckle, sweet and tangy, and he'd almost dropped the flashlight. What if it had bounced off her bad foot?

She'd wanted him. He'd believed it for a mindless moment. If she hadn't clung, kissed back so sweetly, overplayed it. Like the blond thief in Casares. He winced even now. The memory stung. He'd been a green American overgrown kid and the Spanish beauty, blond like this Tyler Ames—in the ruins of an Iberian castle. Once a Roman enclave, once an Arab fortress. In moonlight. Well, it had been a long walk back to Málaga, with no wallet, with nothing but pain and a lesson learned.

The Ames girl was smarter than the Spanish beauty. She hadn't held him back, hadn't called him back. Hadn't laid a finger on him actually. He groaned, making his way easily across the cabin in the dark, not stumbling, sidestepping the furniture, the easel, the worktable, the granite, throwing himself on the couch.

He lay wide-eyed until dawn light showed the flaking ceiling.

13.

The day grew hot and humid. Colin and I were doing the lessons on the back deck until the serviceman had once again come and gone. He'd arrived half an hour ago and was now leaving, shaking his head as he passed us, saying loudly he didn't understand how one house could be so much trouble. "Somebody must fool around with the thermostat or the main switch." He looked darkly at Colin, who stared back calmly and wide-eyed, saying nothing. "Well, it's your money," he was directing this preposterous statement to me. I shook my head.

"You people sitting out here on the lake—you got it easy. You can't stand one minute of real weather, right?"

I said, "Wrong, and don't take it out on us, okay?"

"I hate basements," he confessed with a heavy sigh. He took off his serviceman's cap. It could have been a golfer's or a baseball player's, but it was a workman's cap, emblazoned with his company's logo and slightly stained. He wiped his forehead with the back of his hand. He grinned an apology at me. "I'm sorry, little lady. You want to know something? I hate basements, cellars. I hate rats. I don't even like mice, spiders."

"I'm not too crazy about them either. I didn't know this house had a basement," I said. The heat was getting to both of us.

"Why should you? You ain't never going to need it." Savannah brought out more iced tea, with an extra glass for the serviceman. "They had to tear down an old house to build this place, Mizz Agatha told me—sealed off all but a quarter of the old cellar, kept enough to put in the heating, that's it. They kept a fruit cellar, too, but I don't use it. You couldn't hire me to use it."

The serviceman accepted the tea gratefully and nodded genially now at her comment. "It might come in handy in a tornado. Them rock walls must be a hundred years old; two hundred maybe."

"I'd take a tornado any day," Savannah said.

The intercom bell in the kitchen shrilled insistently and Savannah ambled back indoors, taking her time. She returned to the doorway and called, "Tyler, it's herself, wanting you at headquarters. On the double."

I said, "You can stay here, Colin, and enjoy the heat or go down to the lounge; I'll find you. Good-bye, sir, and excuse me."

The serviceman tipped his cap to me, and for a fleeting moment I wanted to say, *I don't belong here! I'm from the real world—like you. I wish I could leave right now. Hitch a ride in your truck and go somewhere, anywhere, away from here.* And then I looked at Colin's bright head bent over his tablet, the eraser of a yellow Ticonderoga No. 2 caught between his teeth, saw his confidence that I was here and would be back, and I knew I couldn't leave him. I headed for Alison's office, thinking crossly, *What the dickens now?*

Alison was her impeccable self in a white sharkskin suit, seated at the desk-without-clutter. A green light showed on the telephone. The temperature was perfect. I gaped as I looked at my employer. She was glowing with confidence, smiling, welcoming me to be comfortable in the chair nearest her throne. "Isn't this a delightful change, after the breakdown?" she asked lightly, and I realized she meant only the atmosphere. But I blushed momentarily, remembering my own mental breakdown of the hideous night past.

Something wonderful had happened to Alison, but what? Even *where* was a legitimate question, I decided. But she could have changed her mind and gone to her husband in his studio. *She looks like a woman in love*, I marveled. *Thank God, something is working out for someone around here.* Maybe now the young-old King Lear would move back into the house.

"I truly want to thank you, Tyler, for the help you've been to us all. Colin has never been so happy—not in recent years anyway." Her voice rushed along—a brook bubbling over pebbles, sparkling, pleasure-filled—as she continued to thank me for giving the boy friendship as well as "excellent" tutoring. "He seems to have caught up with most of his lessons, but we want you to stay on and prepare him for the year. You will stay, of course? Randy said he made that clear—"

I said, "Yes, he made that clear." But wondered about the "we." Randy Paul and Alison, or did Jonathan Clinton know I was here at last?

"Is there anything you need, Tyler? Would you like a *little* more time off? A day or two could be arranged, but not much more, I'm afraid. We still haven't anyone to stay over with Colin, unless we put the burden on Savannah again. From now on, Randy and I will be doubling our efforts to help Jonathan in every way we can—"

116

"I don't need days off," I said. My mind was tumbling with questions. When—since the fight in the library—had all this been decided? It was only a little past eleven, but Alison had made peace, and probably made love—from the look of her —and made plans to increase the chores, hers and Randy Paul's. *And* was taking time to thank me for a job well done. So she must, also, have checked on the lessons.

In a careful tone, she asked, "What's the matter, Tyler? You can tell me—is something wrong?" She took my silence of indecision, of not knowing how to answer, for shyness— and put out her hand in a soothing gesture. "I wonder— Tyler, did you—were you disturbed by noises in the night?" She hesitated again.

I struck out wildly, thinking that honesty might indeed be the best policy, but not knowing how much to reveal, nor even how to begin. And I found myself floundering. "Looking at a Jasper Johns painting is like overhearing a quarrel— I read that somewhere—an art critic in a magazine pointed that out."

She looked bewildered, but also wary. Little wonder, I thought; I sounded like a madwoman. What the critic had written was that John's *Arrive/Depart* was like hearing stray words through the wall. "Chromatic sputters," the phrase.

But I looked at Alison's narrowed, thoughtful, and concerned green eyes and chose not to admit I had actually overheard their quarrel—not through any wall, heard some of it, understood little, and intended to forget every word as soon as possible.

"It's the heat this morning," I said. "Colin and I must have got too hot—we were on the deck for more than an hour. I did anyway. I guess he can take it. I didn't sleep well. Wrong time of month." A lie, that last, but it erased the doubt from her eyes. She smiled again understandingly.

"I hope you're feeling better, Tyler, because I have marvelous news for you—he wants to see you. Jonathan. In the studio." Her glance went to the green light and back to me. "I'll let him know you're coming. Isn't this what you've been hoping for?"

"I guess it is." But I didn't know whether it was or not by now. Not after last night. Was he still deeply disturbed—or smooth and glowing like Alison?

"Does he want Colin, too?" I asked hopefully, but she shook her glossy head. She was so carefree today the expensively cut hair fell across her forehead, but it fell in an expensively attractive way, giving her a gamin look. Lady in the wind and rain, durable, even in this perfectly controlled room—for the moment, at least, the right temperature—no breezes stirring.

Something else was stirring though, and it bothered me.

"Jonathan wants to get to know you. We've all told him how improved Colin is, and he can spare you a few minutes this morning. Shall I call him now?" The perfectly manicured hand poised above the phone.

"Well, of course."

"You know the way, Tyler?"

"I know the way." I stood up. "Am I supposed to—" *Report back?* would have been the rest of it, but I let the question dangle. She was already speaking softly into the phone. Something was wrong about that. Something was off center, too subtle for me to grasp, with my nerves jumping at the prospect of meeting Clinton. I couldn't put the scene in order. It was as if a stage manager had forgotten an important prop, but I couldn't handle it now. I'd think about it later.

I was wearing khaki shorts and a sleeveless, tie-dyed tank top and I had perspired the same as everyone else had who'd stepped outdoors this morning. I did not intend to meet Jonathan Clinton formally, as it were, in this condition. He'd waited most of the summer; he could wait a few minutes more. Defiance perked me up. I almost sang in the shower. At least, this wholly unexpected development had taken my mind off Dornblaser Clinton, the great kisser. I could almost laugh. Kiss and run. Maybe he likes boys, I decided, feeling nasty and fine at the same time. Dornblaser Clinton could go to hell. I was going to meet the big chief around here. And high time, too.

I chose my only good dress, a paisley-printed crepe de chine, "light and pretty as a butterfly," the clerk had said, trying to justify the price.

Excitement had put a new shine in my eyes, sleepless though they were. My tan was a rosy bronze now and the pale green paisley set it off. I looked—very nice, very lady-like, I decided. And all wrong. I was a tutor, a hired hand, not a guest arriving for tea. I changed into a yellow cotton shirt and a khaki skirt. I had a pair of beige orthopedic shoes, in addition to the green ones, and my slippers. Extra shoes and my good dress had been my only real indulgence, but today I was glad of it. I tied the laces of the beige pair and could delay no longer.

My route lay through the kitchen. "Savannah, try to guess where I'm headed?" I demanded in passing.

"Going to meet the man, right?"

"Right. Pray for me."

"Already am."

I broke stride. She sounded so earnest I shot a wild-eyed glance at her. "He won't bite me, now really. Come on, Savannah, say it won't be so bad."

"Maybe it won't." She shrugged and kept on cutting radish roses for a salad tray.

"How anybody can think of food at a time like this!" I stormed irrationally, but suddenly so weak-kneed I couldn't make it to the door. I leaned against the bar peninsula, gath-

119

ering courage, and Savannah said gently, "Oh, I was just teasing you, girl. He be fine. And it's a good thing you two going to get together. Make him promise to do something about— you know." Her head inclined in the general direction of the lounge and I knew she meant Colin. "Just remember to sass him back. He don't bite, but his bark is near to killin' some days." She pointed with the radish cutter to the back door. "Get on with it, child. Go along now. Tell me all about it when you get back."

I sniffed the scent of pine from the woods along the winding, white-graveled approach to his studio. The walk was well planned with gentle rises leading to a set of three steps, with a rustic fence, and a cleared space surrounded by trees and shrubbery gone wild, tangled and woody honeysuckle and other vines, some with foliage like barbed wire.

There was a level area like an outdoor living room, furnished with bamboo and wicker chairs, waterproofed cushions, umbrella tables, a chaise longue with its pad missing. A long, low redwood table had pottery pieces strewn hit and miss. They looked priceless but were scattered as if in the wake of a garage sale. Larger sculptured figures stood at the edge of the clearing. A giant red clay sun-god adorned a stretch of wall which matched the building. Both were of wide, rough-sawn lumber that looked ancient and had been weathered to an ageless beauty. As I already knew from Colin's lookout, the studio was designed to fit the hillside. No windows overlooked this entrance. Probably there were skylights indoors, in addition to Colin's showcase, but at this moment I faced a blank wall as I had on the day I arrived at the main house.

And I felt chilled although the sun was strong. I felt *watched*. But Colin hadn't known where I was going. Savannah had promised to keep an eye on him. He couldn't be on the bluff, so why did the back of my neck feel cold? I had rotten nerves, an emotional hangover, and if I stood here any longer I'd never knock on that door.

But I gave it a rat-a-tat-tat fit to wake the dead. At least this time I was expected. Alison had phoned. I had seen her, I reminded myself, and felt queerly disturbed again. I hadn't delayed very long, showering, changing my clothes twice, not more than twenty minutes. Not bad for a limper. I banged hard on the door again and eventually a voice yelled back, "All right, I'm coming. Keep your shirt on."

I wasn't ready, after all this time. When the door opened with a jerk, the movement nearly threw me off balance, but I stepped inside, blinking in the dimness of an entry hall.

"Booze or what?" he asked.

"I'm not drunk, I'm lame!" I snapped at him.

"I was asking what you'd like to drink," he said, "as long as you're here."

As long as I was there— "But you were expecting me," I nearly shouted. I stood shivering instead.

He was standing on the tiled floor, hands on his hips, feet apart, his vivid blue eyes studying me. He wore a white shirt and jeans. Sandals on his bare feet. "They forgot to tell me you were Botticelli's Venus. How could Miles miss that?"

I grinned, feeling an immense relief—and total calm. "She has a few pounds on me and my hair is shorter, but you're right about one thing—her feet were ugly, too."

"How about a Scotch?" he said, smiling back at me.

The shutter clicked and she tried to cock the camera for the next frame, but she had reached the end of the film, of all stinking, rotten times to run out. Her upper lip was beaded with moisture. She wiped it with the heel of her hand and sat back on the log too hard, but scarcely feeling the pain. Tasting her own salty perspiration and not thinking about that either, but she looked at her watch and paid attention.

One-ten exactly. No need to mark it down. She'd remem-

ber. *Where the hell were her cigarettes? She had matches. Oh, she had plenty of matches. Satiny purple-lavender matches. God! it was hot enough for snakes and there were gnats here, too. But at least Colin wouldn't surprise her here. He was hooked on that TV soap junk—the one that had gone to a full hour, and much obliged to whoever expanded the damn thing.*

Her fingers searched her pockets and found a crumpled pack. One lousy cigarette and no film. But there hadn't been time to prepare for this. Who could have guessed he'd take it into his head to see the girl today, after all this time? Let him get a look at her and get her out fast. There wasn't too much time to waste—even if Colin didn't start wandering around once his show was over. She had to get to town and back before four. See if those goddamn films were finished yet. She could have sent them to the North Pole and got them back faster. This uppity, one-horse town, rich or not, it was the boonies. Nobody ever in a hurry. Why should they be? That customer last week, that old fag, shriveled like a peach pit, saying, "There's no need to rush, dah-ling. I'm off again. Taking a cruise to Australia—isn't that the maddest? This time of year?" And old Trynne and his wax mustache wheezing over him, letting the real customers wait.

One of these days, one of these days, soon now, soon, she'd be rich enough to buy Australia, if she took a notion. But today she had to get to town and back before four o'clock or all hell would break loose.

What if Blase decided to show up at the house, or the cabin? Miles was lying in his teeth when he said Blase was already back. He'd have let her know, first thing. Foxy Miles didn't know half what he thought he knew. Not anymore. His brains were fried.

One of these days, though, they'd all find out. Find out who was smart. Who had figured it all out. And could settle it even, come to that.

122

14.

There was a compact kitchen in the rear of the studio. When
I said I preferred a soft drink, Clinton shrugged but brought
me a tall, tinkling glass topped with a sprig of parsley.

"Try to pretend that's mint," he said. "It's cranberry juice
and Seven-Up. You'll like it."

He was right. It was delicious, but maybe at that moment
anything would have been. I was here at last, seeing where
the great man lived, most of the time, and worked . . . and we
were chatting as if we were very old friends. I saw that Colin's
window was clear again, the pane sparkling with midday sun.
I nearly blurted out, "I loved the watercolor you made so
spontaneously with the music," but just in time I remembered the circumstances were secret. The near slip startled
me into silence which he noticed at once.

"Tired? Feel like sitting a bit? Here or outdoors?"

"Here, please."

He held an Eames chair steady for me, and lifted my legs,

placing them gently on the footstool which matched the chair. Then he sprawled in another Eames creation and his head went nearly lower than his backside. "Damn spring's busted," he said cheerfully. "I never remember to get Miles on the job till he's past fixing it."

"What about your son? Blase—is he a handyman?"

"I wouldn't know."

The ice in my cranberry drink couldn't have been as hard and cold as Clinton's eyes then. Blue agates, for all the feeling in them.

I stood up and wandered around the room, staring at its contents. But not really seeing them at first. Then I paid attention. There was a lovely lacquered Chinese screen which somehow fitted the almost rustic interior. The ceiling was also rough-sawn wood, with tempered glass skylights.

A metal circular staircase led to a sleeping area overlooking the main studio. Clear glass on two sides of the building left it less exposed than I would have guessed because treetops rose from the cliffside and almost hid the view of the lake. Sliding glass doors here led to another small outdoor living space, but this was screened and roofed.

I passed a bamboo clothes-tree, holding smocks and a collection of straw hats, near his worktable. The table itself was a clutter of equipment. A small, unfinished painting stood on a light but floor-length metal easel. At the back of the main area, canvases were hung from steel racks in the ceiling, as they might be in a gallery. The painting that had been splashed with green that dreadful first day stood in one corner, cleaned but not finished.

"Do you know who did that—the vandalism?" I dared to ask.

"Didn't they tell you I did?" he asked levelly.

"You're joking!"

"Who knows?" he returned.

"No one has actually accused anyone," I said, because he seemed to be serious. "Except perhaps Colin—some think—he might have."

"That's a— Well, let's say Colin's all grown up now."

"No, he isn't. Not by a long shot. And he needs you. He needs to see you, maybe go sailing, have a picnic—"

My own audacity made my voice shaky and my hand trembled. I put the glass down and sat on the edge of my chair, waiting for Clinton to speak, if even to put me in my place or throw me out.

"Sailing can be arranged," he said at last. "Tell me about yourself, Tyler Ames. First a refill, though." He held out his empty glass. I trotted out to the kitchen and made him a drink strong enough to match the color of the first one. He held it up to the light after I handed it to him. "Not bad," he commented. "So begin."

He propped his feet on the other side of the wide footstool. It was black leather, like the chairs, beautifully padded.

"I've got all day," he added. Then he made a queer grimace. "Or let us say I've got till deadtime."

I was looking at his skinny crossed ankles, his shabby jeans, his lean face, and brilliantly blue, intelligent eyes. The intense set of his mouth. His thick shaggy hair, springy as a young man's, not balding at all. There were sun wrinkles in his face and he hadn't shaved today, but he was beardless, thank God. The great, gray-bearded painter would have been too Walt Whitmanesque to bear. I took a long, uneven breath and wondered if it was possible to fall in love with two men in one day. A night and a day. Half a day. *Is that how you get over a hopeless fascination, you develop an equally impossible passion for his father?*

"Well, then," he said, smiling at my silence, but not rushing me.

"In a minute," I said. To my own astonishment I found

125

myself bending over, unlacing my shoes, and putting my feet on the other side of the footstool which separated us. He studied my prosthesis somberly. "Not bad, not bad, but I could have sculpted a better one. Indeed I will, if you like."

"You wanted to hear about me—and my family," I said, feeling oddly driven to talk. Pressured by a queer sense that —no matter what he'd said—there was not much time to spare.

"Sing out," he said. "And if all this is leading to a proposition—" I must have jumped. He grinned wickedly. "I mean if you intend to ask for my son Colin's hand in marriage, I shall give it every consideration. You've charmed the kid out of his wits."

"I didn't know you'd seen him!"

"Sometimes at night, late at night, I take a lingering look. Someday soon I'll take him sailing; you, too, perhaps. But get on with your sordid story. How did a nice girl like you lose a few of her toes and land in a nest of Clintons?" He closed his eyes and waited.

"It was my graduation day," I said. "We were headed home—"

I don't know if he dozed or listened. I only know I felt immensely comforted.

He reached to take my hand in his and give it a little friendly shake. "Do you realize how far we've come in one short afternoon?"

I nodded. "I've always found it easier to talk to strangers; no—not always. Only lately."

"Now that we aren't strangers, Tyler, don't clam up, promise me?"

I nodded. He stood, taking up his empty glass, staring at it as if it were a foreign object.

"I wish you knew my Aunt Lynne," I said unexpectedly. "You'd hit it off instantly. She comes and goes and never bothers with the in-between."

126

He smiled at me but he said, "I need to ask you something, Tyler. I want you to promise me, if you can, to keep clear of—well—entanglements here. Don't invest your emotions—any more than you may have already. *Can* you promise?"

"Not entirely."

He sighed, not looking surprised, and went to fix his drink. "I want you to leave us on the vertical in September."

"Well, of course. As soon as Colin's back in school."

"He'll be ten in September—did you know that?"

I shook my head, wondering what digression now. "I hope you have time to celebrate with him."

"Celebrate," he repeated and fell into a long silence. When he spoke at last, he addressed himself to another topic entirely. He spoke of painting and painters. "Did you ever study the Germans? Friedrich? Kaspar David Friedrich?"

"About two hundred years ago, as I recall."

He smiled. "You must have been a pleasure to your instructors."

"I remember only dimly. Landscapes, I think."

"He took long walks along the Elbe, all around the countryside, and drew what he saw. The thing to remember—you could tell what hour of the day it was by the light and shadow in his paintings. And he made you dream of far-off things, long agoness, seasons changing, time unending—"

"And you like that, too? He was literal—" I hesitated, not wanting to break his line of thought, but thinking about Clinton, the abstractionist, admiring a landscape artist.

"He could paint *time*. Carpaccio, an Italian, painted a pair of Venetian courtesans 'taking the air'—you might say—on a balcony with their dogs, a few turtledoves, a peacock. Ruskin called it the best picture in the world—"

"I wish—" I began to say how I would have liked to have Clinton for a teacher, but he held up his hand to silence me. It was not peremptory. His forehead was suddenly damp with tiny beads of perspiration. The blue eyes seemed glazed,

127

almost like enamel in sunlight. *He's ill,* I thought, with an alarm that nearly doubled me over. *Perhaps he's dying, and he knows it!*

"Well, sorry, my dear—I get these little breathless attacks, nothing to it—what I wanted to mention—they were called *minor* painters by some know-it-alls. I have never understood the term. Nor minor poets. Have you?" He was wan despite his deep suntan. His lids came wearily over his eyes.

I hastened to put on my shoes. I murmured that I had to get back to Colin and lessons, and dared to suggest that Jonathan Clinton should take a nap. "A man who works all night needs his rest."

Not even stopping to think how presumptuous for me to tell my host what to do. But he seemed to accept my excuses for running away.

"We'll sail," he promised. "You and I and Colin. Minor sailors all, right?"

"Right!" To my horror tears filled my eyes. He observed me sadly. Presently he shook his head. Then he patted my knee gently.

"Whatever you think you know," he said softly and very slowly, "it's between us, Tyler. Our secret, my dear. You and I have spent a peculiar day, shared a strange and immediate confidence. I never looked or—dared hope to find a friend so late—" He cut himself off. He was tiring fast. "We'll talk again."

I let myself out and ran down the walkway. Beyond earshot and out of sight of the studio, I dropped to my knees beside a tree trunk and sobbed against its mossy bark. The weeping was therapeutic. When my private storm had wept itself out, I was able to begin thinking again. How many people in this household knew or suspected that Jonathan was maybe dangerously, even terminally, ill? And were pushing him beyond his capacity to work? How would it affect them if—if the worst happened. They'd been so much a part of this queer establishment. Even Savannah had been here for years, but she was a survivor.

I thought of the vast house and its treasures and the pack of hunters who could descend upon it. And grew even colder thinking of the greed that even now might be fermenting within its walls.

My father had been fond of Chinese philosophy. A fragment he'd often quoted slipped into my mind: "There is no calamity greater than lavish desires . . . no greater disaster than greed." Lao-tzu, six centuries before Christ.

A modern thought took over. The green light on the telephone was still burning when Alison called Jonathan to say I was on my way! She had been talking to someone else, or the light would have gone out.

He had not been expecting me. And when we parted he had said, "I'm delighted you finally decided to beard the mangy old lion in his den, my dear."

I decided! Someone had decided, and it hadn't been Jonathan! It was chilly in the shadows. I shivered as I stood up and went back to the house. I would watch and beware.

She looked at her watch again. The girl was never going to be out in time. What in hell was Clinton doing all this time? A touch of rape in the afternoon? Not likely, not after all these years. And he'd never had to force himself on anyone.

Too bad I can't wait around to see if she comes out smiling or bawling her head off. Got to get to town now or that damn Snap and Shutter will be closed.

It was closed anyway. A handwritten notice said Mr. Kermit Trynne expressed his regrets, but the shop would be closed until Monday next. Until Monday! *Jesus Christ!*

15.

Colin had finished his lessons and was waiting impatiently on the back deck. Our luncheon trays were waiting, too, in a cooler. Savannah had told him there was no telling when I might decide to come back and he had better eat, but he had waited.

He was the Cheshire cat when I climbed the steps at last, but my eyes were still red and his grin faded fast.

"It's an allergy," I lied. "I think I'm allergic to pine trees. Sam was." For a stricken moment I couldn't remember Sam's face and I nearly burst into tears again. "What's for lunch?" I asked, trying to look interested. "And what are you hiding behind your back?"

He brought it forth triumphantly—a folded yellow note. I recognized the paper he had bought in town for writing to his father. "It's an invitation—for both of us. We're going sailing with Jonathan. Didn't he tell you? He phoned and Savannah wrote it out for me. Maybe tomorrow. This week anyway. How about that?"

I needed to slow him down. What if something happened to Jonathan? Colin needed to be alone with his father. "I'm no good in boats. What if I get sick?"

"You're kidding."

"No, lots of people are bad on water."

"Well, he's got buckets—or something!"

"We'll see how the weather is."

"You can call the weather bureau," he pointed out.

At dinner he announced as calmly as he could manage that he and his father were going sailing and I'd been invited to come, too. Alison looked startled then thoughtful.

"You'll be interrupting his work, Colin. Was this *your* idea?" She turned to me.

"I'm surprised, too. I'm not going anyway. I don't want to tag along and spoil their day. I am a rotten sailor."

She thought about it. "I'm not at all sure Colin should—" she began, but stopped. Savannah had been pouring milk for Colin but she tilted the pitcher up and stood perfectly still.

The sudden quiet in the room seemed thundering. Probably all our expressions had halted Alison's objections. I glanced at Savannah and almost laughed despite my nervousness. Savannah's glare would have turned back Hannibal and his elephants.

Alison said presently that perhaps the outing would be good for both of them and I could do as I liked.

We ate in silence. She was unusually reflective this evening. Maybe we all were. She had asked politely how my meeting with Jonathan had gone. Did I like him? Had he served anything? Was he getting a lot of work done?

Savannah had also asked questions. I had dissembled like an old hand at evading direct answers. Even though Savan-

131

nah and Colin were my friends, I was not ready to confide my fears to anyone.

The only positive thing I knew was that Colin deserved the day of sailing alone with his father. It might be his one and only chance.

Savannah, bringing in dessert and after-dinner coffee, remarked, "My ain't we a bunch of chatterboxes this evening."

Alison looked at me and said seriously, "It might be best if you joined the sailors tomorrow. But do you see what I mean about Jonathan? He springs his plans without warning. All the time. Never asks first about anyone's schedule."

"Most artists must live that way."

"*This* one certainly lives as if he were alone in the world."

Colin asked if he could be excused. He was too excited to linger while we drank espresso.

Alison waited until he had gone. "I wanted to adopt him, you know. When we were first married. I wish I had. I may talk to Jonathan about it again. It might be best for all."

My mind went blank for a comment. I thought it was a dreadful idea. Or maybe Alison was right. But wasn't it almost too late to win Colin over? If anything happened to Jonathan, Alison would be in charge of Colin, for sure. Not Blase, or a guardian, but the woman who had adopted him.

She was watching me. She said, "Of course, that's something for the future. Tyler, you look worn out. You've earned some time on your own. I'm sure you can go sailing another day—" Her eyes lingered on mine. It seemed to be important that I answer her hesitant question. "Tyler, you will—let's say, *promise* me, you'll go with them one of these days? I'm afraid Jonathan's feelings would be hurt if you refused his invitation twice—"

Curious, I thought, that she was so intense about it. But what wasn't curious around here? I reassured her: "Of course I'll go. I might even enjoy it—a new experience. We didn't live near water. Certainly nothing as big as Lake Michigan. I never got used to the water. I never even liked Tippy-canoe, my dad's boat."

She said, "Well, that's settled, then. These are sale days. You can shop without Colin at your heels." And she smiled.

Colin was in the kitchen early, waiting, when Savannah arrived. He tied and retied his oldest pair of tennis shoes and announced what he thought would be a suitable lunch.

"If it ain't a tray, it's a picnic lunch," Savannah grumbled, but she sang as she made sandwiches, three-bean salad, and filled a Thermos.

"Don't forget the chocolate cake," Jonathan Clinton said, opening the back door. He was in jeans again and a denim shirt, but he carried a bright red windbreaker over his shoulder. He saw that I wore my terry beach-or-bath robe and hesitated. "I can't tell if that's a sailing outfit or not. Sure you'll be warm enough if the weather changes?"

"I'm not coming. Not today. Later, okay?"

I felt a stab of pain even as I spoke. He had looked so eager, lithe, and confident, his eyes bluer than the lake and the morning sky. Now the corners of his mouth twisted downward, but when he looked at Colin, who had bounced up to take the lunch basket from Savannah, the boy's delight with the world was infectious, and his father beamed at him. Savannah gave Colin a hearty slap on the seat. "Don't you jump yourself right out of that boat, hear? You be calm now, boy."

"Oh, Savannah! I've been sailing for *years*."

Just beyond the door, Clinton stopped and turned to look back at me. "I hope you're taking the day off, too. Enjoy yourself."

"I'll probably read." I made a face. "I'm not very athletic, not anymore, and I can't think of anything to buy." I was glad Alison wasn't here to learn that I had no intention of wasting a beautiful midsummer day shopping.

Clinton asked, "Do you know *The Jade Mountain*? It's a

133

Chinese anthology. I mean it's a collection of Chinese poetry translated by Witter Bynner."

"I'll try the library." I looked to Savannah for paper and pen to make a note of the title, and he guessed my intention.

"Don't bother—I'll lend you my copy one day. Meanwhile —'I shall think of you in a floating cloud; So in the sunset think of me.' "

"You ain't comin' back till night!" Savannah cried. "You be inside for dinner?"

He shook his head as he left the room, while inwardly I mourned. If she hadn't interrupted, he might have gone ahead with the quotation. And he wasn't coming back to the house. I felt let down that his place at the table tonight would be as empty as ever.

Savannah looked at me shrewdly. "Guess you lucky you be a little too young, right?" When I said nothing, she changed her tone. All business now. "I'm wondering if you could do me a favor this afternoon—long as you ain't going into town? Could you run up to the cabin and see if Blase is coming for supper? I'd like to have *some* idea of what to fix."

"I can go as soon as I finish breakfast, and get dressed."

"Nope, you can go as soon as you finish lunch. Blase likes to stay up all night; he don't get up early, lessen he's changed his ways and I doubt it."

I hated to think that I had a whole morning to worry about how Dornblaser Clinton would take my invasion of his private property, but there was nothing else to be done. No use arguing with Savannah when she had her chin set as it was now. I went back to bed and took a stack of poetry books with me.

The afternoon was warm and dry. I wore my shorts and tank top, tennis socks, and my beige shoes. The path seemed to climb forever, and I worried that I might have taken a wrong turn in its twisting route. But only a bit farther on I reached a grassy plateau. From there the trail turned sharply to the left and rose to another level, where a rough log cabin was set in a stand of pines.

There was a little clearing at the house itself. Like the studio, the approach was forbidding. There had been windows, small and high, the sort early settlers might have put in, but they were boarded over. If you were to come across the place by accident, you would think no one lived here.

The other side would overlook the lake. I presumed that windows had been installed there, and possibly skylights. Jonathan and Blase might not be friends these days but they were alike in presenting their backs to the world.

I would have bet the other side was open to the distant horizon only because there would be an impassable drop-off and only birds or passing freighters, too far away to be sightseers, even if they cared to be. But natural light was needed. Colin had said his mother had planned a new studio for Blase, but it had never been completed. And how long did I intend to stand here musing on the past and gaping and delaying? I moved forward reluctantly.

Split wood was piled the height of one wall beside a chimney. An ax was imbedded in the top log. Whoever had swung it last had sunk it deep.

The door was made of rough-sawn lumber, the boards of varying size, with a latch, unhooked at the moment. I put my fingertips to the sun-warmed wood and the door swung inward briefly, then settled back, nearly closed. I knocked but no one came, and the knock itself on the weathered wood made very little noise. I thought of calling, "Is anybody home?" But I stepped inside. Into a sort of catchall entrance room. Two large logs standing on end looked as if they had been used for wiping paintbrushes. Blocks of wood and stone and one great chunk of marble filled nearly half the small space. The floor was littered with wood chips, sawdust, and pebbles.

There was a second door. I knocked on it and heard a voice, or thought I heard it. Blood rushed in my ears. A pain I had nearly forgotten stabbed my left leg.

"Well, for God's sake, come *on* in," the voice said. Louder this time and no mistaking it. I wanted to run anywhere, off the edge of the world, if possible, but I went inside.

"I thought you'd get here, sooner or later," she said.

Stella Burton lay on a couch. She was smoking a cigarette in an ebony holder. Two apple cores were turning brown on a plate on the low table beside her. She wore my Mexican silver bracelet and nothing else.

Nothing at all.

16.

Blase Clinton sat behind a slab of gray stone, holding a chisel. He must have wondered why I gave him only the briefest of glances and returned my stare to Stella and her golden wrist. To the bracelet with the serpent of Teotihuacán on its linked rectangles.

"What's the matter?" Blase asked. "Never seen a live model before?"

I said, "I believe I've seen the bracelet before. It's mine."

Stella said, "Prove it." She lay, blowing smoke rings toward the raftered ceiling. No skylight. But the east wall was almost all glass. There was no traditional north light. The fireplace, big enough to roast a Texas longhorn in, was black and cavernous now, but it occupied the north. I didn't care what occupied the rest of the room. Not now anyway. I stared once more at Stella. Her skin gleamed, apricot-colored in the half-light. The body shone as if it had been oiled. By

whose hand? I felt myself blushing and clenched my hands
into fists.

"Sit down, Tyler," Blase said. "What's this about the
bracelet?" His voice was unexpectedly serious and I flashed a
grateful look in his direction. He waited a proper pause for
my answer, then prodded gently, "Are you sure it isn't a *simi-
lar* one? Bracelets don't come one by one, not these days.
Cellini's time, maybe, but—"

"In Victor's time!" I exploded. "He was a Taxco silver-
smith and he's dead and he didn't turn out bracelets by the
dozens. My—my father picked it out for me. I lost it weeks
ago. I told you!"

"Where?" His eyes were cool. "You didn't tell me where."

Stella seemed to be no part of this. A piece of furniture,
except for the bracelet. She had put out her cigarette—in an
apple core! The meticulous Stella Burton!—and had covered
her wrist and my jewelry with her left hand. Then she lay
without moving.

"I'll tell you! I'll prove it!" I yelled at Blase. And then
remembered that I could *not* tell him. I could not betray
Colin. My eyes rolled back to Stella. She was smiling slyly,
quite content with my dilemma. Enjoying every minute.

Blase threw the chisel on the floor and stood up. His white
shirt was unbuttoned, the sleeves rolled high on his arms. He
was deeply tanned now, leather brown. His jeans were paint-
stained, more so than before, and his feet were dirty. Clean
dirt. I was able to judge because I had tried to move toward
him, to take hold of him, to plead for understanding without
details, and I had stumbled and fallen again. I lay on the
rough flooring. My leg burning.

He was laughing as he gazed down at me, one brow lifted
quizzically. "Really, Tyler, if you keep throwing yourself at
my feet, people are going to talk."

Stella had moved at last. She had put on a man's blue work

shirt—at least she had thrown it loosely over her shoulders—
and was actually coming to my rescue. "Take hold," she said,
extending a hand. Her grip was firm. She helped me to a
chair. I caught an odd expression on Blase's face. It was only
momentary, but he looked as if he were sorry that he hadn't
helped. Looked concerned for just an instant. Then angry.
And from that to stony. Blank. *What is this—a screen test?* I
wanted to snap at him. *Showing your great range of expression, from rue to fury to indifference?*

I closed my eyes and let my head whirl for the present. I
was exhausted. What on earth was I doing here? Savannah
wanted something—said Blase had no phone up here—I
should ask him something— It would come back. The climb
had been far worse than I had expected. The cabin was hot
and dusty. I wanted Stella to return my bracelet. No. In
truth, I wanted to snatch it from her and hurt her wrist in the
snatching. Let somebody else feel a little pain around here.
Pain and panic, I had a monopoly. I was sick of the whole
household, the whole secretive summer. God get me back to a
sane place. Let it be the dullest spot on earth, but with normal people doing everyday things.

I fought against opening my eyes, raised heavy lids, and
stared at the brown apple cores. *Comfort me with apples—*
Song of Solomon, wasn't it? But there was no comfort in this
room. Not for me, at least.

Stella was making rattling noises in a kitchen corner. She
had filled a teakettle and put it to boil in the compact little
utility area. Blase Clinton could be holed up here for days—
and nights—all summer if he chose to be. The cupboard
Stella opened was packed with canned goods, bottles, packages of supplies. She reached for a green bottle of reconsti-
tuted lemon juice and packets of sugar and put them on a
tray. She had already laid out two plastic cups and one large
crockery mug.

Blase had tossed his white shirt into a corner and put on a fresh blue work shirt, matching Stella's. Waiting for the kettle to boil, the model went to stand beside the sculptor. The silence between them screamed with intimacy. Her apricot thigh pressed against his shoulder. He had sat down again. His elbows leaned on his worktable. He looked as hard as the gray slab in front of him.

I sat still while anger out of all proportion swelled inside me. *Nothing* was *going* on. *Nothing would* go on while I sat here intruding, uninvited, unwanted. I had been a yeller in my day, but not a thrower. Not a hurler of hard objects. Now I longed to throw the plate of apple cores at Stella's beautiful, closed face. To make an opening, wide enough to get inside her head and stomp around and holler, "What's going on anyway? Why did you steal my bracelet? Where is it now? Never mind that, just please tell me what's going on? I don't want to be the outsider anymore! I want to know the truth, just for once, about any one of you!"

Then amazingly I felt as if I were sitting underwater. The light seemed faintly green, objects floated, glistened, shimmered. Not so amazing. I'd had this frightening experience once before and it was sheer spookiness. It had been diagnosed—pre-migraine. But everyone moved, or stayed still, spoke or did not speak, in slow and waving motion. I hoped it was a nightmare and I would wake in my own bed, with a headache, nothing more. Knowing it was real enough.

For one thing the teakettle was whistling and Stella was making tea.

Over her shoulder, she asked matter-of-factly, "You've got the proportion now, right? I can get away this week? I told you—it's my vacation time, lest anyone's forgot."

Blase nodded, tipping back his chair to gain perspective on his work. Without even looking in my direction, he threw a question. "Where's my brother?"

"Sailing. With his—with your father."

His brows flew upward. "Miles go, too?"

"I don't know. I hope not. Shouldn't you—" Looking at Miles's wife, *ask her*, implied. But maybe Stella had been here overnight. I blushed deeply again. Damn it all, this getting senselessly red in the face had to stop. I had to control myself. Better off dead than a blushing damsel in distress for the rest of my life. Lucky to be alive, remember? Hang on to clichés and hang in there.

"Hey—" Blase's dark-as-navy eyes now were concerned. His voice was urgent though it came from miles away. "Hey, Tyler, wake up! Hey, baby, breathe deeply! Can you hear me?"

Shaking me hard. Looking frightened. About what? About me?

"A fainter," Stella's voice, acid edged but a long way off, too. "That's all we need around here, a sleeping beauty who gets her feelings pricked on a thorn and swoons every time it seems to come in handy."

"Stella, for God's sake shut up!" Blase said.

I said dreamily, "Who would ever think you'd read all those fairy tales."

His arms were around me. His hands warmed me again, holding my shoulders. He leaned forward suddenly and kissed me lightly on the forehead. "Testing," he said. His voice as light as his lips had been. "Just testing. She doesn't have a temperature." This last to Stella, who said, "Well, hallelujah and all that."

But Blase was sending me that dazzling smile. The one I had seen only once. That brief, splendid, welcoming time when we met. Until something went terribly wrong. Until Alison said something so perfectly natural I had missed it. I couldn't think now. With Blase warming my hands, rubbing them between his, I couldn't have heard Gabriel and his heavenly horn summoning us all to that Great Getting Up Morning. But there was a recorder in my head and I could play it back if I worked hard at it. And I would concentrate. Later.

I murmured, "I've never fainted, all the way, in my life."

"Nor anything else all the way, if you ask me," from Stella.

"Will you shut up!" from Blase.

"Can I leave now, master? Or must I stand here and chaperone this love scene?"

"What about her bracelet?" he demanded. "Want to give it to the lady?"

"I dropped it somewhere," she answered. "Let her find it if she wants it."

"Get it, and get it now," he ordered.

"Find it, kiddo. How can she prove it's hers?"

Another voice spoke from the doorway: "Have all the cards been dealt—or can anyone get in this game?"

Miles came in holding an open beer can. He looked at Stella and said, "Why don't you just slip into something comfortable? I forgot you had your appendix out."

My eyes seemed to roll without my control. Stella had no scar on her lower right abdomen. A pucker, like a little row of dimples, in the middle of her body, below the navel. Stella said, "Seen enough, kid?" And I swept my glance on around to the safety of Miles's beer can. He held it up and asked, "How's *your* belly, honey? Clean as a whistle? Hound's tooth? Want a beer?"

Blase said, "Tyler, try to relax in spite of these comics. You should see yourself—you'd make a great lay figure right about now."

Miles headed for the kitchen and another beer.

I smiled dazedly at Blase. I knew what a lay figure was—a jointed wooden doll artists had to use for proportioning when a living model was not available. "I wouldn't even be any good at that, I'm missing a few parts," I said, but without apology. I wanted to get out of here and go somewhere and die quietly. I wanted to leave at once but Stella went to dress behind a screen that served as a room divider. She and Miles probably would be heading down the path, and I didn't want to go with them, or go ahead and be overtaken by them. The only thing to do was wait.

Miles had opened his beer and gone to study Blase's sculpture. He said nothing for several minutes, even though Blase seemed to be waiting. "It's coming. It's even good," Miles said finally. Then he headed for the door. "We're probably going up to Charley Chan's tonight; want to see us there about eleven?"

Blase was picking up tools from the floor, dusting them against his pants leg. "I don't know yet," he said. "I'll be in touch."

Stella emerged from behind the screen. Once again she was the immaculate housekeeper in the spotless uniform. She was carrying a shabby leather purse. I wondered if it held my bracelet, but I was past asking. Asking would only get another jeering remark.

As if Blase had read my thoughts, he said, "Aren't you forgetting something, Stella?"

"No. I threw it in the sink. You'll get around to it. You'll have to wash up afterward."

There was no mistaking her meaning. But she had a parting shot. "Anything you can tell Alison, I can tell Alison, right?" This was for me. I didn't redden. I didn't even blink. For that I thanked God.

I stood up clumsily as soon as they had gone, and said, "I remember now—Savannah wanted to know if you are coming to the house for dinner. That's what I came to ask."

He shook his head. "No dinner, but sit down a minute. Please. Take it easy. We've never talked, do you know that?"

143

And then his look went past me to the doorway, and he sighed heavily. He asked, "When did my little gray home in the West get to be O'Hare Airport?"

Randy Paul stepped breezily into the room. "Heard you were at work again—wonderful!" Then he saw me and his surprise was as synthetic as his heartiness. Savannah must have told him I was here and had been gone longer than she expected. I was convinced she'd sent Randy to the rescue, just in case I wanted help, or lay on the path again tripped by an unseen enemy. Unseen and unknown, but not unsuspected. Not anymore. Stella had found the bracelet and therefore had found the hiding place. At least had dropped the matches there. Who steals bracelets, steals matches, probably without even thinking about it. *Why* was something to sort out later. I would have a busy night, adding up scores, putting twos and twos together and trying to find one solid four—new or old math.

Randy had walked over to study Blase's work, as Miles had done only minutes earlier, but unlike Miles he said at once, "Magnifico! Really great you're working again."

"Hacking away," Blase said noncommittally, as Randy bent closer to the sculpture.

"Looks exciting. Good lines."

"Thanks. That's the main aim."

"God! What I'd give for your talent—" Randy's voice was wholly sincere now and for once his face was revealing. He yearned toward the sculpture, reached out and touched it with appreciation. Genuine envy, honest envy. I glanced at Blase to see if he understood, but Blase was paying no attention. Downplaying Randy's appraisal. "Like the man said, you want to sculpt an elephant, you just cut away everything that isn't elephant."

"Stella is no elephant," Randy said. His eyes were still shining in appreciation, but as if he realized I was watching,

144

he turned and winked at me. "And neither are you, Tyler, but don't let this fellow talk you into modeling for him. No matter how good he is. Colin needs all of your attention. As a matter of fact, he—"

"I was just going," I interrupted. Spare me the reminders. And I would spare him any explanation of why I had been here so long. I supposed I was glad he'd come running, at least climbing, to save me, if needed. But why did White Knights have to be such god-awful bores? And with such deadly timing! What if he'd been late? Too late. I slid a look at Blase Clinton, standing with arms folded on his half-bare chest. A Mohawk Indian. Impassive. Certainly not a man planning a fate worse than death for the Fainter. But we could have talked and I might have learned some of the answers the easy way. By asking him the right questions.

He became aware of my scrutiny and stared back at me.

Randy had stepped to the kitchen and turned on the tap to let the water run cold for a drink.

I said, barely above a whisper, "I met your father and I'm just *foolish* about him. I'm smitten. And I'm terribly worried about his health. It's not my business to interfere—if you and he don't seem to be getting along—I *know* that but—" Oh, damn, damn, Randy was coming back. Blase said in a low voice, "Don't mention it to anyone. Promise me?"

I nodded.

"Not to anyone."

Randy was back. "What not to anyone? Secrets?"

"Yes," Blase said easily. "I don't want the great big art world to know I'm hacking at a piece of rock. I don't want reporters getting their pads and pencils up here again."

"Oh." Randy's face fell, but soon he looked more cheerful. "I hope you'll let us know in plenty of time to represent you properly, old boy."

Blase said nothing. I said I had to get back to Colin, and

145

Randy and I walked Indian file down the bluff. "Tyler, what do you think of Jonathan—or Blase, for that matter?" Randy asked. "I feel sort of responsible for your being here, after all. I hope the summer is going well?"

"I like them both and respect their talent. And I adore Colin."

Safe, safe, safe.

"Did Jonathan mention the painting—that crazy business with the green paint?"

I shook my head. "Are you counting on it for the fall?"

"Hoping for, let's say. No one who knows Jonathan ever dares *count* on anything. Well, at any rate, if he's opening the door again, maybe he'll let some of the rest of us in. I really need to talk to him—and my father is expecting to visit again soon."

"I'm glad. Colin tells me he adores your father." Adore was not in Colin's vocabulary but the meaning was right.

"It's a mutual admiration society. You will like my dad, too, Tyler, and he will be absolutely delighted that you and Colin are such friends. He was worried about the boy, thought he was growing dangerously introverted."

"Colin couldn't help it. He has his private fears." I quickly added, "All of us do, including little boys." *Get on another subject, fast. Stop playing with semantics. Back off.*

"Jonathan's style is out of style, many critics would have you believe, but we expect a splendid crowd—and not just old-timers, old friends. Who knows? They may be surprised at his new work. Something is changing."

We had reached the driveway at last and I was grateful that I didn't need to comment, only to wipe my face with my handkerchief and thank him for escorting me. Only now did I remember I had gone off without my bracelet. And Blase Clinton might think I had forgotten it on purpose. I would send Colin for it tomorrow.

Miles seemed to appear out of nowhere. And Randy shrank back from the smell of beer and sweat.

"You've done it now, girl," Miles told me. "I just saw the old boy and you've got him quoting Eliot. We *endured* before you came—I think that's Faulkner. Anything better might kill us." Then he laughed, with his head thrown back in a carefree manner, but the muscles in his neck were strained above the bandanna he wore so constantly. I got a strong impression that he was listening, not laughing, waiting for a reaction.

Randy said, "So everyone is getting in to see Jonathan, is that it?"

Miles's head was lowered again. "I think I'm the last. I wouldn't bother him today if I were you."

"I have no intention of bothering anyone," Randy said stiffly and headed for his Lincoln Continental. "Good-bye, Tyler. Be seeing you."

I said, "I hope Colin's back in a happy mood."

"Is that what you hope?" Miles asked. Then he went reeling toward his apartment stairs.

Savannah was snapping the ends of string beans when I entered the kitchen. "Seems like somebody got herself all hot and bothered today," she remarked after one look at me.

"Thanks for sending the escort."

"I ain't sent nobody nowhere." She snapped faster and threw beans into a stainless-steel bowl. Ends went into a paper bag. "Looks to be your lucky day, anyway, girl."

"Not from where I'm seeing it," I said sourly.

"Get yourself downstairs, maybe you see better." She fished in her apron pocket and tossed something at me. "Here's your key."

I looked at her. "My key? I never lock my door anymore."

"Bet you do now."

147

17.

I opened my door as slowly as ever a television actor turned a knob with a camera panning in on his hand. There was no dead body beyond, but I gasped nearly as loudly as if there had been.

A painting stood on a mahogany easel. Furniture had been moved so that my favorite armchair faced it and not the lake, where the fading day now blended into the water.

Windless Afternoon—with Clinton's bold, unmistakable signature in black. Parallel cantilevers and perpendiculars, triangles and waves of pure color. A Clinton original. Proto-abstractionist—would they call him that now? A Jonathan Clinton not dying but joyously on canvas and magnificently alive.

I sat for minutes thinking, *Why here? What is it doing in my room?* Then Savannah's dark face, beaming from ear to ear it seemed, looked in at me.

"Why the watermelon grin?" I asked, beaming back.

"You pretty sure of yourself now, right?" Then she came in and stood with arms folded and admired the painting in narrow-eyed silence, with only a husky, "That's more like it," to let me know how she felt.

"He wants you to get Miles to hang it," she said later, after she finally turned away from the canvas. "You can figure out where you want it."

"Where *I* want it?"

"It's yours—that's what he said."

I said, "Oh, my God!"

She nodded. "Yep. I told him it would cause hell on wheels around here. He don't care about that. He says you can handle it."

"I'm scared," I said. "Frankly, I'm terrified. I am certain Alison will be furious—and she's got every right to be. She'll think—" I couldn't finish the appalling but obvious conclusion Alison might draw when her husband had given me such a priceless, timeless piece of art. "I'm sure he only meant to lend it to me."

"That's a good line to take," Savannah said somberly. "Anyway, you want me, you know where to find me." She fished in her apron pocket and brought out a torn piece of Colin's yellow paper. She had scribbled her Evanston address and telephone number on it.

"There's a book, too," she pointed out, just before she left.

The book lay on the desk. Its cover was bright with a detail from Manet's painting of his friend Monet at work in his floating studio. The Seine on a sunny afternoon, long ago. I couldn't for the life of me think of the name of the painting.

I was dazzled, blank, and drained of memory, even of reaction, at this moment.

The book was titled *Through an Artist's Eyes*. No, that was a subhead. I saw an envelope lying beside the book and I raced to open it. Colin's yellow paper again, giving me a page

149

number, and a brief note asking me to see that Colin read the book, too. "This stuff was written for kids. Colin probably knows most of it, but he'll enjoy meeting all these fellows again —Apuki in Thebes, Henry Moore, Juan O'Gorman. Picasso. You keep the painting. Colin gets the book. J.C." And then, maybe after Savannah had warned him about hell on wheels, he had carefully added "Jonathan Clinton, his signature," and drawn a smashed-looking heart.

My own heart felt as if a giant hand had squeezed it hard. I breathed like an asthmatic. And turned to the page in the book he'd made a note of.

There was a charcoal drawing of Kaspar David Friedrich in an all but empty studio, in Dresden. I skimmed the words opposite: ". . . paint-boxes, bottles of oil and painting rags had been banished to the next room, because Friedrich believed that all extraneous objects deeply disturbed the world inside the picture."

I walked outside and looked at the lake and sky, all one now. No extraneous objects.

Jonathan had said I could handle it.

I could try.

First I locked my doors. All of them. Then I showered again and put on my nightgown, and went to bed, taking Colin's book and an unfinished biography I'd begun weeks ago and never opened again because it was about a poet who'd killed himself and I had found it much too gloomy. Tonight I could handle it.

I didn't need any supper and Colin could look out for himself. Just to make sure I phoned Savannah and passed the word along. Splitting headache. Sorry.

"You doing real good," she said.

He used plenty of chloroform to knock the bastard out so he could slip him into the heavy-duty trash bag. Not that the

150

body weighed a lot, but it was hard to handle. Just let the heavy-duty be as tough as advertised. It would have to stand dragging, not too far, but don't let it rip, for God's sake.

Thank heaven he'd been able to talk the old boy into meeting him on the beach. There wasn't too far to go. Just get him up those rocks and let him fall free. He'd sink all right.

The man stopped to get his breath, having dragged the trash bag twenty feet at least. He'd thought about putting something in the pockets to make sure the body never surfaced again, but that was risky. Better not. Better, in case it ever was found, to be a simple case of drowning. Drowning while under the influence. Or suicide. Who the hell cared?

He would have to get rid of the trash bag, but that wouldn't be hard. Take it into town and throw it in one of the city's litter barrels.

18.

"*She quit* this morning."

"She quit? She can't do that!"

I sat on the back deck but I couldn't help hearing Savannah and Stella indoors. Both were speaking louder than normal.

"Well, she did," Savannah said.

Stella sounded totally exasperated. "Did she give any reason at *all?* Ruby's young, but she's very good. I won't find it easy to replace her. I thought she liked it here."

"She liked it here, but she stayed over last night. I *ast* her to—" In her upset state, Savannah slurred her words.

"*Why?*" Stella waited and then burst out, "There was no entertaining here last night. Why in God's name would you ask Ruby to stay over?"

"Miss Ames—she wasn't feeling too well. I thought Ruby could keep an ear out for Colin, if he took sick."

"I see." Flat, noncommittal. "And I *don't* see," Stella added after another pause, "what that has to do with anything, with Ruby's walking out on us." But now her voice was wary. As if maybe, suddenly, she did see—or suspect— that staying over had everything to do with Ruby's absence this morning.

"I suppose she got scared. Night noises. Country sounds. She's a city girl, after all. Poor child. I thought she needed the job."

Savannah said, "She did, but she'll find another."

"What are we supposed to do meantime? I should think she'd give notice."

"When you runnin'," Savannah said slowly, "you ain't thinkin' about no notice nor nothin' else. She ain't coming back. I got to get her check and take it to her. Anyway, I think I know a girl can come for the time being. Leastways till she starts hearing the talk."

"Would you mind explaining that?" Stella was being very patient.

"You knows they's talk. Whut you *don't* know is that Miss Ames is sittin' out there havin' her breakfast."

This announcement must have startled Stella into silence. After a pause, she came to the screen door and looked out at me. "Hi," she said, "you want more coffee or anything?"

"I'll get it," I said, coming inside. "I couldn't help hearing about Ruby. That's a pity." In more ways than one, for me, too. I liked Ruby and I had never remembered to ask her what she had intended to tell me that day at the bus stop. Now, apparently, I'd never know. Stella was studying me with eyes narrowed, probably trying to figure out how much I'd heard or interpreted. Then she sighed. "This talk about *talk*, y'know?" Lifting her brows. "Everyone gossips about celebrities—and the Clintons are that. It doesn't mean anything."

"I know. I felt it at the library—and in the cab. And I'm sorry about it—for Colin's sake."

"It's nuisance talk, nothing more," Stella said. Savannah

snorted and went back to loading the dishwasher. Stella stared at the intercom as if trying to decide whether or not to let Alison know she was minus one cleaning girl. "Savannah, who've you got in mind? Can I reach her by phone?"

Savannah nodded. "Alice—there's the number on the board."

Stella made a note of the name and the number. Then she squared her shoulders and headed toward the hall door. Over her shoulder, she called, "Will you give Alison a ring—tell her I must see her—just for a minute?"

Savannah took her time about it, but attended to the matter. Then she poured fresh coffee for both of us.

I said, "I don't like to talk about it, but Colin has a crazy idea that his mother didn't just"—how to say it?—"die in an accident. He thinks—" Again I hesitated, but Savannah said, "I know what he thinks."

"But surely there must have been a medical examination? It must have proved she either died from the fall or drowned. Maybe it's time someone discussed it with him—I really don't know. Maybe he's just outgrowing it—his fears, I mean. He's so much happier now than when I came." I stopped abruptly. I sounded as if I were trying to pat my own back.

"There wasn't no medical examination."

"But there always is! I'm sure of it!" What did I know about it except on television? Except in highway accidents. I bent over, holding in a sudden, sharp stomach spasm.

"There wasn't no body," Savannah said. I thought she was slurring her words again.

"They didn't *call* anybody?"

"Look, girl. What I'm telling you, there wasn't any body. It never came back. It's deep there by them rocks. Everybody's been warned about that. Nobody goes swimming around here. Anyway the body never came back up. So what

154

was there to examine?" Her face was closed against further discussion. She said, "Why don't you eat a piece of toast or something? You don't eat enough to keep an ant alive, let alone a bird."

"Poor Colin, poor baby," I was talking mostly to myself.

"You got *that* right," Savannah said.

"Maybe last night Ruby was afraid of—well, of a ghost? Some people are—lots of people." I didn't want Savannah to get on the defensive. "Lots of Southerners, English people— the government even has a list of haunted houses. My aunt wrote a piece about them."

"Ruby didn't hear no haunt. She heard something funny. People up late. I don't know. She didn't want to talk about it."

I looked at the red light over the back door. "Maybe it was just Mr. Clinton taking one of his midnight strolls."

Savannah shrugged. "Leastways it wasn't Miles or Blase— they both gone."

"Who's gone now?" Randy Paul asked, putting his head around the door frame, and then quickly coming in from the deck. He tossed me a smile. "Savannah and I don't like flies. I didn't let any in; does that entitle me to a cup of coffee, Mrs. Hamilton?"

She reached for a mug and poured coffee, saying nothing.

Randy looked at me. "Who's gone?"

"Ruby has quit without notice, but I gather it's all right. Someone else is willing to come."

"Just so *you* don't quit with or without notice, Tyler." He said it easily, making it a joke, but his eyes were watchful. I shook my head and said, "You couldn't pry me away—not as long as Savannah is the cook."

The hottest part of the summer had arrived. The house was cool and quiet. Clinton, apparently, had submerged himself in his work again. I bought color film for the Minolta Blase had left behind that first day and took pictures of *Windless Afternoon*, the painting I would have to give back someday.

When Alison had first learned of my gift she had been understandably surprised and a little cool in manner but had melted as soon as I said I knew it was only a loan, a mark of kindness, an impulse. She had told Randy Paul all about it and added, "I'm truly pleased with this girl for possessing wisdom and tact not common in one so young." I could understand her relief that I understood a painting worth a small fortune couldn't be given to a hired hand, virtually a stranger. "But I hope no one minds if it stays in my room until I leave?" I asked.

Nobody minded. They wouldn't have it any other way. Jonathan would be very upset if he dreamed that I wasn't accepting his gift. When he was going in and out of busy spells, like this, with an important exhibition ahead, he was not altogether responsible for his changeable emotions. Did I understand that? I understood.

"I feel vindicated in selecting you as Colin's tutor," Randy said, maybe a little too heartily to please Alison whose smile was strained at least momentarily.

Colin was pleased about the gift. The idea of the gift was what he liked the most. One painting was very like another to him, but the fact that his father wanted to give me something of his own, something of value, was wonderful. Blase had not been around to comment. Stella had said I should consider myself lucky, even if I didn't intend to keep the painting. "He takes dislikes to people for no reason," she said. "I can tell he and you hit it off."

One morning my cherished bracelet lay on my bureau and I decided Stella had brought it back. I wouldn't ask. I wouldn't wear it either. I put it in an old candy box along with other pieces of semijunk, semiprecious jewelry my mother had saved. The satin-covered candy heart box had been my grandmother's. I had come from a long line of Valentine types, I thought, but the sweetheart Ames girls were all gone now.

Alice was working out fine. She was another slim, young black as Ruby had been, who did her job easily and kept her own counsel. She carried a pocket transistor with an earplug and stayed tuned to rollicking rock sounds or woeful country ballads while she dusted or swept or mopped. She was cheerful and pleasant to pass in the halls, but she never even took a coffee break, much less sat and gossiped with Savannah as her predecessor occasionally had done.

The Clintons could have been the Rockefellers, the Jimmy Carters, or the Paul Newmans, it would have made no difference to Alice. Her mind was strictly on her schedule, her paycheck, and five o'clock, quitting time.

Once I overheard Stella asking Alice if she could plan to stay all night, if needed. "No way, ma'am," Alice said. "Ruby told me about this place. Five o'clock, I'm gone."

"Exactly what did Ruby tell you?" Stella had tried, but Alice had plugged in her transistor again and danced away, disco-style, waving one hand good-bye in tune to the music only she could hear.

Again I regretted my lost chance to question Ruby. What unexpected noises could reach a person sleeping in the back room beyond the kitchen and Stella's office that I would not hear? Now that I locked my doors day and night, I slept soundly. The air conditioning worked flawlessly. There was no need to keep windows open at night. Quite the opposite, in the really oppressive heat that lingered long after sundown.

Beebee had been here twice and Colin and I had met him once in town for a movie. We were fairly evenly matched now at board games. One lovely evening we'd had a small

157

driftwood fire and toasted hot dogs and combined talents to sing old and new songs. I had taught some, learned some. Beebee had decided he didn't want to go home ever. He'd rather move in. I had hugged him for the implied compliment and his mother had swatted him good-naturedly. We parted on Sunday morning, buddies forever, promising to get together again soon.

Sunday noon, Alison said Randy's father was coming for a late afternoon tea, would I like to meet him? It was a silly question, but she had a lot on her mind. "What time?" I asked. "And what should I wear?"

Four o'clock and my best dress would do nicely.

"Randy is bringing him. He doesn't even need a nurse these days," she added.

"Is Savannah staying?" I asked and got a blank stare. "To make the tea for Mr. Paul—" Savannah usually went home after brunch or Sunday dinner. Today it had been brunch.

Alison laughed, "Oh, no, I can handle it. Tea is usually cocktails; I thought you knew. I believe even hospitals favor sherry or a glass of wine for the elderly. We'll be very British today, m'dear."

"Okay, I'll be here." I gave her a little wave in leaving.

There was something about Alison in a joking mood that put my teeth on edge. I liked her better when she was herself, intent only on business. She had no social ease, I decided, and wondered again as I had all summer, in off moments, *Where did Alison begin?* Not in Lakeview, I would bet. Not on this side of the tracks, manner of speaking. In Lakeview if you got far enough away from the tracks in either direction, you were in pretty rich territory, though the older, grander homes were still mostly on the side toward the lake.

Colin and I had spent one lazy day driving around while he pointed out at least the gateways of estates his mother had been the architect for. "She knew landscape architecture, too,

Blase told me. Not very many had a degree in both, specially a woman."

"I can believe it," I'd said. Maybe it had helped being a woman, with a wealthy husband, to get any degree you had your heart set on. I'd asked Savannah in one of our gossips if Agatha had been a perpetual scholar, thinking out loud that a lot of us would be, given the time and the money by a rich and busy husband.

"She had more'n him," Savannah had scoffed. "It was the other way around, you ask me. He wouldn't of got so big so fast, hadn't been her backin' him, maybe. Who knows?" Savannah had looked very thoughtful. "They both got plenty —had plenty—before she died."

Now I headed for the kitchen where Savannah was making tiny watercress and cucumber sandwiches and wrapping them for storage until teatime.

"Can I help?" I offered. "I know you've got a picnic planned; Beebee told me."

She shook her head. "Just about through. Anyway, you want to ask something; I can always tell. So sit yourself down and ask."

"Well, it's none of my business—" I began.

"Granted," she said, "so get on with it."

"Well, if Agatha Clinton was wealthy—"

"Rich as Croesus," the dark head affirmed, with a positive nod.

"Well, did she leave all her money to Jonathan?"

Savannah stopped for a moment. The bread knife glittered in a shaft of sunlight. "Some, I hear, and Blase got some—we was all taken care of—or will be—but Colin gets the bulk. When it's settled."

I said, "I don't understand." But I was chilled as if an icy blast had struck. "Colin *gets* the bulk? You mean in a trust, something like that?"

159

"Don't know. He inherits—ten, twelve million, way up there anyhow."

I felt a pulse beating in my cheek. I asked, "Why wasn't it settled a long time ago?" What I knew about wills was minuscule. She mumbled something about matters taking seven years in some cases. Even Savannah's usually expectant Sunday face was bleak for the moment as we contemplated a lonely little boy inheriting ten or twelve million dollars in a largely hostile world. There would be flunkies galore, but friends?

And I thought about Jonathan and his chances of being here to soften the blow. And how would Blase look on a millionaire kid brother?

"I don't understand," I said again. "I mean—why Colin? Why not spread it around evenly?"

She shrugged in an I-don't-know-either gesture. "Could be Mizz Agatha figure her husband already got his, and Blase's got talent, what they call it, and plenty of gumption—you don't know Blase, honey. You don't see past that good-lookin' face, them muscles. Don't nobody in this world have to look out for Blase, and I reckon Mizz Agatha knew that—but Colin was just a baby. And who knew what he might need?"

I had an awesome thought. "It almost sounds—I mean, well, was there ever any question of suicide?"

"No way." The black head shook from side to side like a metronome. "She never would've left till she had to. She was sick, but not *that*— Nothing wrong with her mind, Tyler."

She looked at me and said, "Don't frown so much. You going to get wrinkles. If it wasn't for Mr. Paul comin' today, I'd of asked you and Colin to our barbecue. Now look, child, I got the lemon slices fixed and they're in this bag. And this here is fresh cookies. And I made a lemon cake." She pointed to a lovely pale-yellow, three-layered concoction in a plastic-covered container. "The silver's laid out, cups 'n' stuff, too—"

I interrupted, laughing. "No wonder Alison says she can handle it."

Savannah said, "She'll do all right with the serving. She used to be a waitress. Ruby found that out."

"Well, good for her." I was beginning to feel far too conspiratorial against an employer who had been nothing but kind to me. "I admire self-made women; men, too. I hope I can be one."

"Don't make yourself no promises you may not need." Savannah was knotting a scarf around her hair. Her eyes turned in the direction of the woods and the cabin beyond. "Wonder when he plans on gettin' back wherever he went. This family—I swear, if I didn't have it so easy and such good pay—" She went on talking but I studied my red face in the tile floor.

Randy's father was a charming man, frail as I'd expected, and older than his friend Jonathan by several years, I suspected. His eyes twinkled with interest and good humor. "You've no idea, Tyler, what a smashing debut you've made here." He took both my hands in a gentle clasp. "When they give you up, I hope you'll consider coming to work for me. I can use someone who knows her way around a gallery—"

"Oh, but I don't—but I'd love to try!"

His warm brown eyes rolled meaningfully toward the walls and he said, "I think you've had a crash course in galleries and the eccentrics who go with them."

Randy said, "Dad, try not to get too excited, about anything. We'll talk about work and hiring and firing later. Remember you promised the doctor to keep your mind easy—"

"How could I meet a girl Jonathan has already fallen madly for—and not get a little excited?" Oh, he was foxy, too. Charm, but plenty shrewd, as his bright glance darted to see

161

how this thrust affected Alison and his son. Colin and I made up the rest of the tea party. Jonathan Clinton remained in his studio, with the red light glowing probably. At least it had still been on when I was in the kitchen. Was it possible he would not come into the house even to see his good friend after all this time? Not just to change the embarrassing subject, I asked quickly, "Isn't Mr. Clinton coming to join us?"

Alison blew smoke rings. "Who can ever tell?" she continued. " '*Mr. Clinton?*' Surely, after he presented you with a painting, you can use his first name?"

"I want to see that painting," Mr. Paul said, but Randy said firmly, "Not today. We've overstayed already. I've got to get you home or you can't come out again till who knows when."

Randy's concern was genuine and his father responded to it, only pretending to protest, but probably exhausted by his first real outing. We shook hands in parting, promised to meet again soon, and I escaped before Alison could drop her hostess politeness and ask me anything at all.

I was sitting in the twilight studying my painting—the soft light changing as the day grew dim had altered the colors, creamy tones went pearly, blues deepened. The strokes seemed almost to move as the light itself faded. I was held dreaming, half awake, when the knock sounded briskly on my hall door. I heard Alison calling, "Tyler—it's long distance—for you!"

I nearly leaped from my chair to cross the room and open the lock. "For *me*? Long distance? From where?"

"Srinagar," she said, watching me. "We thought it must be a mistake, too, but the operator spelled out your name. And spelled Srinagar, too, I asked her. That's in India. I—we thought you had no one—I mean, well, it was the impression Randy got—that you were all on your own now."

"I've got an Aunt Lynne," I said. "And that's who it would

162

be. I guess the news of the—accident finally caught up with her." I straightened my shoulders, having almost fallen into what my doctor used to call my hospital slump. Just remembering the disaster and the times of trying to reach my itinerant only relative brought it all back. "She's a travel writer," I told Alison. "I left your number with the travel writers' office in Washington, just in case. Even they didn't know where she was."

"You want to take the call in my office, dear?" Alison looked solicitous. "There's an operator's number we're to call back—"

I followed her numbly. I could have taken it in my own room, but I didn't think of that. Not that it mattered. I was remembering Aunt Lynne, who was tall and wiry like Savannah, and intrepid. Who'd walked on glaciers in her tennis shoes and flown in a rebuilt Messerschmitt, or repaired anyway, somewhere in Texas, the Confederate Air Force base, pretending she was the Red Baron with her camera and later her typewriter. Who'd climbed the Matterhorn and sailed around Tierra del Fuego with the last of the great sailing captains. Who'd tried to follow Magellan's footsteps—or maybe sea legs—and we'd read all about it in *National Geographic* before we heard from Lynne again.

She didn't mind caves, hang gliding, snakes, shooting the rapids, or diving fathoms deep for a story, but she hated civilization if it happened to be crowded, and she loathed telephones. I had expected a beautifully written letter when the bad news caught up with her, but I hadn't expected a telephone call.

"I had to ring, Tyler, and now dammit I'm only able to bawl." We both wept expensively across the world, but it didn't matter, and I didn't think about it until long later, and it still didn't matter. "What I want to tell you, darling, is that I've finally been to the caves of Marabar and I wanted

163

you to know. I wanted Tom to know and maybe he does. Maybe he and E. M. Forster are having a good talk about it." Tom was my father and E. M. Forster, who wrote my father's favorite novel, was in heaven, too. "I yelled hello to Dr. Aziz and Miss Quested, in case they're still hanging around there." She went on talking and crying a little, and I leaned against Alison's desk. "I'm coming home soon, Tyler. Hang in there." I could see her face all streaked with tears like mine. I couldn't see Srinigar, but I could see Lynne's sad but brave face, and it helped. I had some of the same kind of bones in my spine, after all. Maybe some of the Ames spunk. And I might need it. "I—I'm all right—g-got a job here."

"I got your letter a little late, dream face," her voice was saying matter-of-factly, but as clearly as if she were as close as Alison, who was very nearby indeed, actually hovering, as if she were afraid I would keel over. I shook my head at Alison with thanks for her concern and smiled, with tears running down to my chin. At least it had quit wobbling, and my voice sounded almost normal.

"I'm all right, Aunt Lynne. I'm fine. Glad you found me."

"I'll be there, baby, one of these days when you least expect me." Then a chuckle. "That won't be any change, will it?" I thought her voice faltered, too, all those thousands of miles across the world, but she signed off with her usual, "Pip pip, adieu!"

I said, "And toodle-oo," as Tom, my father, would have done, had done, for years and years. It was a family joke, stemming from their adolescent years, when Lynne had hoped to be a great writer, the female Thackeray of the twentieth century, she'd said, but she'd actually sold a greeting card verse out of tons of stuff she'd mailed off to editors, and after that she thought she was on her way to the Pulitzer Prize for poetry.

"My goodness," Alison said, breaking a silence that had

followed my hanging up the phone, "a call from India—I'm impressed. Jonathan used to get calls from all over the world, but—well, I'm impressed." She reached out to pat my hand still resting on the phone. "Tell me about your aunt. Does she *live* in India? Do you have an uncle, too, and cousins? Dozens of cousins you forgot to tell us about?" She was laughing, making a little joke of it.

"Not married now. A widow."

"And lives in *India?*"

"She doesn't really live anywhere," I responded. "She's got a room she keeps in a little town in Tuscany—at a hotel, the Conca Verde, means the Green Shell, I think, and sometimes she keeps an apartment in Paris—just a walk-up, I guess. I've never seen it. She's a travel writer. Or did I say that?"

"What did she say about a cave?" Alison asked, giving me her full attention. "I could hear some of her words; that is, I couldn't help hearing. I was afraid to leave—you looked so pale."

"It's all right, thanks. She was talking about *A Passage to India*—it was one of my father's favorite books—by E. M. Forster. I like it, too. There were caves in the novel, you see."

Alison politely tried to look as if she understood why a person's only living relative would call half around the world and talk about a book, or a hole in the ground.

"She's crazy. We all were," I said, and let it go at that.

Dearly beloved Aunt Lynne. If only she could show up tomorrow, or the day after! I suddenly yearned intensely for the comfort of a familiar presence, if only fleetingly. But she was too impossibly far away, too busy, and I was a grown-up now. Expected to fend for myself. Like it or not.

"Just a minute." Alison had caught me at the door and put a detaining hand on my arm. "Did I overhear right? Is your aunt planning to see you *here?*"

165

"Oh, no. She always says that. She never knows where she'll be from one week to the next. She always thinks she'll be here—" I stopped. "I mean, Independence, Missouri, of course, not *here*. Where—we all used to be. It's just the way she talks."

"Oh," said Alison. And then as if I might have read her expression of relief correctly, added, "Not that you wouldn't be welcome to have a guest drop in—"

"The only possible guest I can think of is my Aunt Lynne. And she's in—where was it?—Srinagar? Not exactly next door. One of these years she'll show up, and find me, wherever I am—and I'll be glad to see her. It'll be as if she'd never left at all. She's like that. I'm sure you'd like her."

"Yes, I'm sure I would," Alison agreed vaguely. She was already thinking of something else.

19.

I couldn't sleep. I saw the caves of Marabar. And elephants. White elephants. And stray lines from Forster. I couldn't by midnight begin to remember which came from what, or care at all. Some of the words came clearly, as if summoned:

"But at the supreme moment, when night should have died and day lived, nothing occurred. . . . The hues in the east decayed, the hills seemed dimmer though in fact better lit, and the profound disappointment entered with the morning breeze." And then the line, the question that had followed; all these years I could hear it in my father's absorbed voice, reading aloud, though I hadn't understood it then, and didn't now, perhaps: "Why, when the chamber was prepared, did the bridegroom not enter with trumpets and shawms, as humanity expects?" Shawms?

Why had I never, ever, looked up the word? I snapped on

my night lamp, got out of bed, and sought a dictionary in the lounge. "*Shawm* (shôm), n. an early wood-wind instrument with a double reed, forerunner of the modern oboe." There was more but I didn't need it. I had stopped thinking about bridegrooms coming. Or had nearly stopped.

I went upstairs, and got a cold drink and an aspirin from a bottle Savannah kept in a cupboard near the sink. It was two o'clock. The empty walls of the dining room were luminous. The electric bill must be enormous, but a Clinton could afford to be afraid of the dark. Some of them anyway.

I went down the corridor and into the gallery. Its heavy draperies were open to the black water beyond. I walked over to the window and gazed out blankly, hoping to feel even a little sleepy. A cloud drifted over the moon, perhaps. The water seemed blacker than before. I turned to leave and saw a flicker of movement in the L end of the room.

But I had imagined it, along with my white elephants. When I walked across the carpeted area to the L, where the floor gleamed perfectly, as always there was no other living thing. Only a new painting!

I raced to switch on the spotlights and hastened back to see the canvas. Lots of drips and sloshes, as someone had said of Willem de Kooning, but spontaneous, dazzling with vibrant color and unique. I drew in my breath. My knees were wobbly. I sat on the floor and gazed for a long time. I wanted to applaud. Tomorrow if the green light were showing, I would take my congratulations in person. I stood up painfully after a long, long time, moved forward limping, and pressed my fingertips against his familiar black signature. The same signature as on my own, well my own for the summer, painting below. As dawn light broke I went at last to bed.

Day lived, as Forster had said, but nothing happened. The red light was on. All the talk in the household was of the magnificent new work. When I had a chance to be alone with it again, shortly before noon, I took a color picture. The roll was finished. I would get it developed. After lunch and an hour of math, Colin and I could take our books back to the library.

The day was fair and cool. Colin would enjoy the trip. I was leaving the gallery when an argument broke out in Alison's office. The voices were so loud I couldn't escape all of the dispute. Stella Burton was virtually shouting, "I can't take much more and I don't intend to take much more! You'll see! You'll all see! And you'll be goddamned sorry you didn't wake up a whole lot sooner."

And Alison demanding urgently, "How much, for God's sake, Stella? How much more do you want? I'll manage it. You've got it coming—I know that. But it will take a little time. Can't you hang on for just—"

"Hang on, hell!" Stella yelled. "I've warned you for the last time."

I had reached the hall door. I closed it behind me. Then tried to remember: had it been open or shut when I arrived? But what did it matter? They were both too upset to think about someone's overhearing the ugly exchange. I fled for the stairs. It wasn't until I was safely back in the lounge that I realized I had moved as fast as I did before the accident. Without even thinking of caution. And with no twinges of even the slightest pain.

Colin was reading his art book. I leaned over and hugged him hard. "It's a superdelicious day," I told him. "Just look outdoors. This afternoon, I promise you, we'll go adventuring! We may never come back!"

His eyes widened. His grin spread. "Never?"

"Never. Not till supper."

"Oh, Tyler!" Male contempt for female exaggeration, but the grin stayed wide.

"And for later, we may even make fudge. And popcorn. I

169

might even let you see whatsisname—that rowdy cop who says 'I'm da heat.' I'll bet you my steel-toe sneakers no real cop ever said 'I'm da heat, man.' "

"If Baretta says it, they do." He was loyal, but he looked doubtful.

"We can stop in at the police station and ask—offer a dollar to any *one* of them that has ever said, 'I'm da heat.' "

"They aren't real cops!" he complained. "They give traffic tickets. Nothing ever happens out here—" His voice dribbled into silence. Something had happened here six years ago, almost seven years now. I could have kicked myself for letting exuberance make me so careless.

"What's got into you, Tyler? You're so bouncy today?" he asked, getting past the tricky remembrance on his own.

"I've got a relative in this world," I told him. "Do you know, for a fact, I'd nearly forgot. I have an Aunt Lynne Babcock, and someday she's coming to see me."

"And me?"

"Well, of course, you!"

"Let's go tell Savannah—" He was already on his feet, book forgot.

"Now just a minute, hold on—she's not coming today—or even soon. Just one of these days."

"Has she got any kids?"

"No, her husband died a long time ago. He was a photographer, same as she is, and he was killed in the war. Korea. She never married again and she never had any kids—except me. Sometimes she borrows me for a weekend when she's around." I looked at him. "The same as I might borrow you, this winter. If your folks let me. Especially if I go to work for Mr. Paul. I'm sure he wouldn't care."

This was a new idea, full grown at birth, but it seemed a dandy. "Hey, Tyler," Colin said. "Hey, that would be great. And Beebee, too?"

"Beebee, too. I wouldn't be surprised if I could ice-skate again."

His excitement dimmed. "I never did."

"So we'll give it a try."

The back of my neck prickled. I turned and Miles was looking at us from the doorway. "As long as you've got the winter schedule set, mind giving me a hand for a minute?" he drawled. He was totally sober. His flannel shirt was still buttoned at the cuffs and he wore a blue bandanna tied at his neck, but both were clean and so, relatively, were his white jeans.

"Me, or Colin?" I asked.

"Why not both of you? Follow me."

Mystified we trailed after him. He led us outdoors and across the back driveway to the vegetable garden he'd put in. Then beyond it to an overturned wheelbarrow where he stopped and pointed dramatically with a bony forefinger. "There's the problem," he said. "What am I going to do about this?"

Colin kneeled first to look. At his squeal of delight, I leaned on his shoulder. Stella's cat had four, no five, newborn kittens.

"Can I touch 'em?" Colin asked, awed now at their tininess.

"Better not yet," I said, and glanced at Miles. He tugged at his beard. "Stella's going to believe in immaculate conception, after all. She thinks Plaid has never been out in this great, big, wonderful world. Not only that but we may have the first bisexual cat in creation."

Colin was too mesmerized by the squirming new life to listen to us. "I know," I said. "She called this cat 'him'—the only time I ever saw the animal. How about that, Plaid?" I caressed the calico ears, the nape of the neck, and heard the little motor running. Mama Plaid was very pleased with herself.

"*Stella* is not going to purr over this," Miles commented. "She's not exactly the motherly type. Built for it, I grant you, but nature goofed."

Stella was having a bad day, I reflected. First her argument with her employer and now a litter of unwanted kittens.

"Can I keep 'em?" Colin was demanding eagerly.

"I doubt it very much," I said reluctantly. "Maybe Savannah can find homes for them when they're ready to travel." I'd already asked weeks ago if Colin might have a puppy or a cat of his own and the answer had been a definite no. Alison was sorry, but no. Jonathan couldn't stand the noise there'd be, was her excuse. And at the time I'd thought it a lame one. But Colin *would* make noise, playing with a dog, and dogs do bark, and we'd once had a cat that was almost as noisy as a baboon. Trouble, his name, and he'd complained day and night, even with a full stomach. Then I remembered Picasso, Blase's dog. I hadn't thought of him for weeks, but he must be here sometimes.

I backed off and sat in the hammock. As I'd hoped, Miles strolled near enough to converse, and I asked about Blase's lordly little mutt. "Dead," Miles said. "Poisoned."

I gasped. "Somebody in town?"

"Somebody here, I'm afraid." His eyes, looking beyond me, at the white house shimmering in early August sun, were hostile.

"This is not exactly a health spot for the uninvited," Miles said. "Or the unwary." I wondered if this was intended to be a warning, but I hadn't time to think about it. Savannah had walked out on the deck and was peering in our direction, her hand covering her eyes from the sun.

"What's all the commotion?" she called.

"You've got a problem, baby," Miles shouted back to her.

"Is that a fact?" She slip-slopped toward us, her feet flopping in shoes that had been cut for comfort indoors but not

172

for walking on gravel. "Oh, ain't they sweet!" when she saw the litter. But a moment later, she looked to Miles and grinned. "Now you got a family. You be tied down like the rest of us, right, man?"

"Wrong, lady." He headed for the garages.

"Where you off to now?" she demanded.

"Anywhere away from here, baby. I intend to be long gone when Stella gets the news she's a mother-in-law. Grandma, maybe, whatever. I'll be back when the sun shines, Nellie, or maybe not."

"Ain't that the limit?" Savannah remarked, then she, too, succumbed to the tumbling newborns and their instinct for survival. She was cooing, almost crooning, when Blase spoke so suddenly we all fell silent.

"I thought I'd have lunch," he said. "What's the excitement here—killer bees?" Then he saw the kittens and his grin matched Colin's.

"Fancy that," he remarked. "Plaid's been to Sweden? Or wasn't he all that he seemed to be?" Then he bent over to touch the newcomers gently, and gave Plaid a congratulatory scratching, under her ears. She licked his hand.

"We better get back to the house and let this mama alone," Savannah said. "What do you want to eat, pretty boy? It's been so long I done forgot."

"How could anybody forget peanut butter and jelly—even you?" He clasped her shoulders as they walked side by side. The golden hairs glistened on the bronzed arm. His head was darker gold. Colin, his red-gold curls bouncing as he hopped along, was begging, "Can I keep 'em, Blase? Please can I keep 'em?" But Blase was not answering. He put his other arm around Colin's shoulders, but he said nothing.

20.

I was stumbling through a tunnel in a dream and there was a man's waiting figure at the end with arms outstretched. I awoke crying. It was morning. My pictures should be ready today. Colin and I had taken them in last week. The day the kittens were born.

I pulled back the draperies to find that the morning was already brilliant and I went into my sitting room to see how this light changed my painting.

No change except to make it even more beautiful, I thought, and then a chill shook me. Something was wrong. Before long I found the black line. It was narrow, extending no more than an inch, say. I touched it and found it sticky but not wet. Sometime during the night someone had got through my locked doors or windows and added about an inch of black line to a most valuable painting. Why? That was even more important than how. Who—was also impor-

174

tant. Not only who got in but who—whom—could I ask about it?

I phoned Trynne's Snap and Shutter Shop as soon as I reckoned it was open. Mr. K. Trynne was terribly, terribly polite, but my films were not ready and he wished really, truly, I would try to show a little more patience. He said something else but I wasn't listening. I was waiting to ask if he had the least notion when they might be ready. He thought Thursday. Thursday afternoon.

I went to my armchair and sat down again to study the painting. Then Trynne's annoyed words played back in my head. "Would I please stop asking about them!" But I hadn't asked!

I stared at the work of art and wondered if all the real world had gone mad and only art was true. And soon saw other subtle changes. A slight wisp of scarlet, a yellow tail on a period of sorts, making it a comma. They were sticky, too! Almost imperceptible to the eye but as readable as Braille to my exploring fingertips.

The day passed. Early evening came for me. I begged off from supper. Savannah gave a short speech on what birds eat but I said I really had a headache and no joke about it. I wanted only peace and quiet.

I sat and gazed at my altered painting, trying to keep fright away. All my doors were locked again, but would that help? Someone could get in. Had proved it. A knock sounded, a sharp tap, on my balcony door, and I nearly screamed. Thank God I'd put a hand over my mouth and kept quiet. It was Mr. Paul, Randy's father, who stood on the narrow redwood balcony. He had turned away politely after his brisk knock and was looking out across the lake. I almost ran to welcome him.

"Mr. Paul! I'm so pleased to see you! Come in, come in!"
He looked happy at the genuine warmth in my voice.

175

"Miss Ames, I was afraid I might be disturbing you. Alison thought you might be napping. I've just had a sherry with her—"

"I'm fine—I was tired—but having you here has helped. I feel much better. I'm sure you'd like to see the painting, have a little time to study it?"

He nodded. I wondered if he noticed the changes. But of course not—he'd never seen the original. I yearned to tell him about the strange thing that was happening, but a man recovering from a heart attack was not to be leaned on, no matter how kindly, how wise he was, and how interested he would be.

He stood in rapt attention before the easel, with his hands clasped behind his back. Presently he nodded in great satisfaction. "This is truly magnificent. Frankly, my dear, Jonathan had me almost convinced he was nearing a stopping point—he as much as hinted that he was through—but this is superb."

I urged him to rest for a few minutes. "Can I get some tea—or more sherry?"

"No, my dear, I'm on my way to talk with Jonathan." He looked at the room and said, "I'm so glad you're here, and we'll get better acquainted this winter when all the excitement has simmered down. Things are always disturbing when there's a deadline to be met—invitations and all that. Though I am not allowed to do much of the work—or the worrying. Easier said than obeyed." He hesitated. "I hate to interrupt Jonathan for even a moment but something important has come to my attention."

He straightened his shoulders and added, "One of these days we can try backgammon tournaments—you and Colin and I."

"I'll look forward to it." I smiled. "And Colin will be delighted."

176

He was such a kindly man. He said, "You've been a life-saver for him. And I haven't forgotten about that job we mentioned."

"I know. I'll enjoy being close to Colin, too."

He suddenly quit smiling and peered at me solemnly. "Tyler—may I call you that? Do you think Jonathan is well?"

Once again I had to remember that Mr. Paul was a convalescent. But I wanted to be as honest as possible in the circumstances. "I spent an unforgettable afternoon with him," I said. "I was a little worried that he might be—a bit ill, but since then, well—you see for yourself—" I pointed to the easel. "It's dancing with life and good humor—it's nobody's *Black Painting*—don't you agree?"

His look lightened. His pale eyes were tired but the gaze was steady. "You're good medicine, Tyler Ames. Probably at my time of life—and with my recent scare—we—I tend to expect the worst, rather than the best. I find it hard to lose even one friend, but we all must. Oh, my dear, I'm sorry, I forgot all that you have suffered so recently." He looked so contrite, I longed to throw my arms around him for comfort. I hastened to say it was all right. Then I sat on the floor and put my head on his knees for a moment. He smoothed my hair with a shaky hand, and I sat back, smiling now, feeling worlds better.

"Jonathan and I like so many of the same things," he remarked. "The same poets, dramatists, and—some of the same music—not all of it. Bartók." He made a face and I laughed.

Poets! "Mr. Paul, are you familiar with *The Jade Mountain*?"

He nodded. "Ah, so Jonathan got to that. I'm sorry I didn't share your golden afternoon."

"So am I—but the library here doesn't have a copy of the book and I haven't wanted to bother Mr. Clinton—Jonathan —the red light has been on most of the time—"

177

"I know—it's on now but I'm going to break in anyway."
His eyes twinkled. "I believe I have a copy of the book I can
lend you."

"What I wanted to know, in particular," I rushed on, "is
the poem with the lines . . . 'I shall think of you in a floating
cloud; So in the sunset think of me.' Do you remember that
one?"

He concentrated for a moment and then said, "Yes, Li
Po—T'ang dynasty. Died too young. Jonathan would know
his dates—704, no, maybe 760. How splendid that you like Li
Po." He beamed at me. He clasped his pale shaky hands on
his little potbelly and sat like a small, benign Buddha.

"Oh, please." I leaned forward eagerly. "Please tell me the
rest of it—anything you remember."

Once more he looked far away and his pinkish-blue lips
moved silently. Then he smiled again. " 'We wave our hands
to say good-bye, And my horse is neighing again and again.' "

We stared at each other. Then I closed my eyes to hide my
fright. Something shadowy seemed to flit from behind my
lids. As if a bat had suddenly risen from the floor of my mind.
I looked at my guest again. He was rubbing his own eyes
wearily. "Did Jonathan say those lines to someone, Miss
Ames? Tyler?"

"To me."

"I see." He went away again, in his thoughts, and then he
said, "The title of that poem, Tyler, is 'A Farewell to a
Friend.' "

"He was only going sailing!" I cried. "With Colin. And
they came back, of course. Days ago."

"He wouldn't tell me what his doctor said in his last examination. Nobody, lately, has cared to tell me much of anything. But I intend to find out." He was smiling faintly again.
"If he won't answer the door, I'll go in anyway." He pro-
duced a key on a gold chain from his vest pocket. The key
and the fine linked chain both had been tucked completely

out of sight. "He's undoubtedly forgotten that I have this. And I'm not above using it, if I have to."

"Do you want—should I go with you?"

"No, my dear, I'll be all right." He rose just a little unsteadily after sitting so long and as if his joints pained him. He took a last look at the painting. "I'll just slip out this way and not bother anyone. Good-bye, my dear. Good-bye for now."

I huddled in the chair, still warm from his sitting there. What a charmer he was! A thousand, no, ten thousand times more fascinating than his son. *I've got a new friend*, I exulted. *Next time, if he's well enough, I'll ask him what he thinks about the changes.*

A scream and the sound of breaking glass shattered the twilight. I thought I was dreaming again and I sat up with a start. But the scream came again, and the sound of feet running. I glanced at my watch. Mr. Paul had been gone for half an hour or more.

I ran toward the kitchen and found Colin, anxious-eyed, peering out the screen door. "It's Savannah. She took the tray. Tyler, I'm scared!"

"Stay here, Colin," I said urgently. "No, find Alison, Miles, anybody, and tell them to come running but you stay here."

I flew over the deck and down the steps. The piercing note in Savannah's voice still rang in my ears. My feet in the slippers—looser than my shoes—skimmed the walk. At the second curve I saw her, standing. Thank God! She was wringing her hands and moaning in a singsong daft way. I couldn't see just beyond her for a moment. Whatever she leaned over. The glass crunched under my feet and I saw Mr. Paul lying in a pathetic heap on the top step of the little flight of stairs that led to the clearing.

He seemed as if he might have sat down to rest and crum-

179

pled over. But rice dotted his dark suit, a lamb chop lay on his shoe, broken shards of glass and bright green peas covered his trousers and the steps.

"I almost stepped on him!" Savannah keened.

"Did you take his pulse?"

"I—I—no—I, Ty-lerrr!" She was keening again and had hidden her face with her hands.

I knelt, but even as I reached for his wrist, I was somehow certain he was dead. I put both my hands around his, warming the veined old fist, trying to loosen its clasped fingers. Vaguely I remembered someone's telling me to warm a half-frozen hand under an armpit—centuries ago it had been, in a skiing time—but as if I could bring his hand back to life, I pressed it under my arm and the dead fingers let go their prize. A key on a tiny gold chain, a small, oval pill case, silver and jade. Its lid was loose. One pill rolled into my sweating palm. I glanced wildly at Savannah. Her own eyes were closed. She seemed to be praying.

"I've found a pill. Should I try to force it under his tongue? Should I, Savannah? Please, what can we do?"

She'd got control of herself now that I was here. She shook her head. "No, child. He be gone."

"What shall we do? What about—" I was thinking of mouth-to-mouth first aid. Should I try to turn him over? I lifted and turned his head as gently as possible, and knew by his shocked and staring eyes that Savannah was right. I closed his lids. I'd always heard—I'd always hoped—that the dying are at peace. Poor Mr. Paul looked as if in the instant of departure he had seen the Gorgon.

I stood up and Savannah and I clung together in the deepening shadows. Then I said, "I'll try to get Mr. Clinton—will you see if Colin has roused anyone? Don't let him come—oh, I'm sorry, Savannah—you know that."

The sun had dropped below the trees and the clearing

180

around the studio hummed with night sounds. I banged on the door and called Clinton's name repeatedly. Nothing happened. With tears half blinding me, I kicked my good foot at the door. And then I rested my head against the wood and sobbed.

"Tyler, that won't do a bit of good." Alison was here at last, speaking slowly and sensibly. I turned and looked dully at her. "Tyler—Jonathan isn't there, you know. Well, you don't know, but *I* do. He's away. Where—I couldn't begin to tell you." Then her voice changed to a command. "Tyler, come away from that door!"

"He didn't cancel his food tray!" I said overloudly, on the edge of hysteria. We faced each other. Her green eyes were glacier cold, and deep. She took my arm and led me to the other side of the clearing. She cleared her throat and seemed to make an effort to speak more gently. She said at last: "Well, that's Jonathan. I've tried to warn you, dear, he's not very thoughtful—about others. He's off somewhere. The light is out. He at least remembered that."

She urged me to sit down, to remember I needed to rest my foot. I was peering at her in a glazed, out-of-focus way. She had never before referred to my handicap. But the death had shifted everything out of focus.

I said, "What about poor Mr. Paul—is anybody coming?"

"Of course, Tyler. Why don't you sit down till you quit shaking? You've had a nasty shock, dear. It's even worse for us—we knew and loved him."

"But—"

She put up her hand gently to ward off my protests. "I know, Tyler, any—sudden death must bring it all back. Please, my dear, sit down. You look ready to pass out."

I let myself be led to the chaise longue. I observed the pad was back in place. I sat gingerly on the edge of it. I would not lie down, though Alison indicated that it might be best. "If I

181

feel in the least faint," I said stubbornly, "I can put my head between my knees. Did anyone cover Mr. Paul, at least?"

I was almost insolent in my whirling state of mind, but Alison seemed to understand. "Everyone is functioning—" Except you, implied but not stated, and I squared my shoulders. I stood up and said I was fine now. I wasn't even having a chill. I had been wearing a summer sweater when Savannah first screamed. I wore it now and I put my hands in my pockets. My fingers closed around hard objects. The key and pill case. I must have put them there when I was still thinking about trying to breathe life into Mr. Paul. I thought I'd better give them to Alison, but she had turned abruptly and headed back for the steps. She stopped once, to look back at me, to say, "You must help me make them understand. We must get him away from here. Jonathan must not see this tragedy." I nodded, fully in agreement.

Stella Burton was standing vigil in the path. The tray lying on the path near her was filled with silver, food, pieces of glass now. The evening shadows covered Mr. Paul, nothing else. Then Savannah trudged heavily up the path and tenderly placed an afghan over the body. Stella's face was taut and white, as if its features had hardened into clay. She stooped to pick up the tray. "I'll take this back." She looked to Alison. "Should I open the downstairs guest room?"

"Yes, that's probably best—it's good of you—" Alison's voice trailed off as if her mind were elsewhere. As well it might be. How would Jonathan Clinton take it if he came back while his best friend still lay on these steps?

Savannah said, "Blase and Miles gettin' somethin' to carry him on. They be here directly." She stared at the ground, not at the afghan and what lay under it. "All them peas gone to waste." I was sure she hadn't the faintest idea of what she was saying. A tear had slipped down her dark face. I moved beside her and tucked my arm in hers while we waited.

Stella was stepping carefully down the path, holding the tray to one side so she could see her way in the gloom. Before she was wholly out of sight, Miles and Blase came around the last curve of the walkway. They were carrying a folding camp cot to use as a stretcher. Blase called out, "We've called an ambulance, and his doctor. He said it's all right to move him into the house."

"Well, of course, it's all right!" Alison snapped. Everyone's nerves were frayed at a time like this, I realized. Miles looked shocked sober, it seemed. "If his own doctor gave you the go-ahead, we'll move him," Miles said. "I guess it had to be his heart."

I slipped my fingers into my pocket for Mr. Paul's possessions as Alison said, "Yes, it was his heart. Poor man—he never even had a chance to take his pills. I found this—you can see it's full. He couldn't have had any time at all." She held out a silver and jade pillbox while I stood aghast. I must have made a small cry. Everyone looked at me, but only briefly. Nausea was rising in my throat. I bent over fast, gazing blankly at my slippers, while my mind seem to whirl in my suddenly empty skull.

Savannah caught my arm. Then stronger hands took my shoulders. Blase was holding me up. He took his right hand away to reach for his handkerchief and gently wiped my forehead. "Easy, easy, Tyler," he said, "we can't help him now." It was queer, I thought, how his voice sounded like his father's. I'd never noticed until now. But seldom had he spoken to me so considerately. As on that forever-ago first day, when he'd offered a chair—

"I'm sorry," I whispered. "I'm okay now." I slid my fingers back into my pocket and closed them over the matching jade box, as if it were Mr. Paul's secret, and I was protecting it.

"Nitroglycerin, I suppose," Alison was saying. "I believe most heart patients carry them."

"They might have eased his pain," Blase said in an odd flat way. "I don't think they would have changed the outcome."

Miles said, "Where were they anyway? How come you've got them?"

Alison looked annoyed at his brusque questions, but—surprisingly—she answered, "In his hand, of course. I told you—he must have been trying to open the damn case. I wish I'd never given it to him—maybe it stuck."

"No sense worrying about that now," Savannah said.

The two men had already carefully lifted Mr. Paul's body and placed it on the cot. They had also brought a blanket to cover him. Miles handed the afghan back to Savannah.

"He treasured it," Alison said absently while my thoughts continued to race. Could there have been another box in his other hand? I couldn't remember the position of his left hand. He'd been slumped on it. His right hand had held, and released, the key and the pillbox, now in my pocket.

Alison moved impatiently as Miles tucked the blanket around the dead man. "Can't you please hurry? It's getting dark—we can't stand out here all night."

Miles said, "He probably shouldn't have climbed those steps. They aren't steep, but what was he doing out alone anyway?"

I waited for Alison to tell him, but she stayed silent and at last lifted her shoulders in a helpless shrug. "Who knows? I suppose he wanted to see Jonathan—"

You suppose! We were all heading back for the house, in a straggling procession, but I felt like shouting at her back. *You know he came to see Jonathan. You had sherry with him! He surely told you, as he told me!*

"Take him to the back room," she was directing the men. "I'll see if the doctor is on his way. Let me get past you, please."

Blase, who was in the lead, halted at her words and spoke

across the poor blanketed heap on the cot, "Miles, hold up a minute, just a goddamn minute— Alison, don't you think someone had better call *Randy?* The doctor *is* on his way. I told you that."

Alison drew herself up, but said nothing at all. She stepped past Miles, the cot, and Blase, walking head high, her spine like a ramrod. The odd image that leaped into my mind was that Alison could be an Indian princess alone in a Mayan jungle. Her shining black hair, her olive-toned skin tanned almost as dark as Savannah's, tight on her high cheekbones; her dark red lips were pulled tight, too, as if she were biting the insides of her cheeks, her jaws clamped. Slowly, slowly, she stepped down the path. Regally, the mistress here. And don't you slaves forget it.

But I had forgotten Colin and I hurried to slip by the others and reach him before he saw the pitiful burden Miles and Blase were carrying. They were very solemn in the deepening night, as if they remembered that Mr. Paul was leaving his old friend's studio for the last time.

Colin hovered by the kitchen door, peering out. His eyes were wide and excited. "Stella won't tell me. What's happened? Please, Tyler!"

"Savannah!" Alison broke her silence. "Will you get him out of here!"

I held out my hand. "Let's go to my room. I'll tell you about it."

But for the first time Colin did not respond. He remained by the door as if rooted, waiting to see what was coming. I groped for his hand, trying to pull him toward the hall, but he jerked free. Any minute now Blase and Miles would be coming through the door. They had to pass this way to reach the downstairs guest room, past Stella's office.

"Colin, get a move on!" For the first time I was yelling at

185

him. It startled him but he did not move. I grabbed his wrist and tugged, but it didn't work. He looked rigid, as if he might never move again. Then Stella came out of the back room where she had been checking to see that the bed was made properly to receive a dead body and walked across the kitchen, not to open the door for Blase and Miles, who had reached the deck, but to Colin and me. Without speaking, she twisted my hand still on the boy's wrist.

"Let him go. You'll wrench his arm from the socket." Both my hand and my jaw dropped open.

"She didn't hurt me!" Colin said instantly, but his interest was finally caught by something besides the burden on the deck.

"Come with me, Colin, I've got something to show you," Stella ordered, and he obediently trotted along with her. She closed the hall door as they departed.

"Well, I never—" Savannah said.

"Make coffee, lots of it," Alison ordered. "See what's needed at the bar."

"For who?" Savannah asked, still looking like a sleep-walker.

"For Mr. Paul's chauffeur, for one. He's been waiting out front all evening. Somebody get him in here. Miles, as soon as—" They were passing through the kitchen.

"I'll get the chauffeur," I volunteered, glad to escape.

An ambulance was turning into the drive as I reached it. There were no sirens. A doctor's black limousine followed. I stared at the license plate holder and its metal caduceus. Memories of the hospital and the doctors' parking lot flooded back, but I brushed them aside easily. I hadn't spent much time outdoors, even in practice walking.

Dr. Gibson was a brisk little man, who introduced himself and hurried indoors. Underneath his professional calm he looked sad, I thought. Everyone had liked Mr. Paul.

I wandered back indoors, feeling sorry for Randy, wonder-

186

ing where he could be this evening that a phone call couldn't reach him. I saw Alison coming out of the gallery. She said, "I've found Randy—he's on his way. This will be very hard for him."

I said, "I'll get Colin to bed, read to him."

"Yes, that's a good idea."

After Colin was asleep, I went to the kitchen. Savannah was still on duty. She looked at me guardedly. "He finally give up, huh?" It was half-past eleven.

"You're staying over?"

"I got orders," Savannah said. "I'm staying but I'm not sleeping."

Miles, of all people, came to the rescue. He was seated at the kitchen bar drinking coffee. "Yes, you are, woman. In *my* bed." He tried to leer at her, but it was a poor effort. Nobody felt like smiling, but I felt like backing him up. Felt that for the moment, at least, I understood Miles. "You do what he says, Savannah. Stella will be in her room and Miles will stay here, am I right?"

"Right," he said, peering at me over the top of his coffee mug.

Savannah's eyes rolled back in her head. "I be so tired," she said. "Maybe you *are* right for once."

So it was settled. Miles even escorted her to his quarters, and I made hot milk for myself. The house was ghostly quiet. Mr. Paul had been taken away. But where was everybody else? I looked out the back door. Stella's light was on, so that was all right.

Randy Paul must have come and gone while I was still trying to get Colin to settle down. There had been a lot of cars in and out of the driveway; I hadn't looked to see who might have arrived or departed. I was burying my own head in Colin's book while trying to lull him into dozing off.

Had Jonathan come back? Did he *know?* Where had Blase

gone? I could hear footsteps crunching on the back gravel and I fled the kitchen. Having a middle-of-the-night, one-on-one conversation, or confrontation, with Miles Burton was more than I could take at the end of this chaotic day.

I slipped into my sitting room, not wanting to make any noise in a house which already seemed to be in mourning.

Blase Clinton was sitting in the brown armchair. He was asleep.

21.

He came awake almost instantly. His tired, red-rimmed, navy
blue eyes considered me solemnly. His hair was rumpled, sun-
streaked, as if he'd combed it with his fingers. He hadn't
shaved since morning probably. I was mildly, and distantly,
surprised that his beard was so dark. His lips parted. I
thought, *Oh, my God, he's going to cry*.

I said, "Would you like some hot milk?" I offered the
steaming mug.

He said, "No, Tyler, I want you."

For a blank moment I gazed wide-eyed at him, and then he
reddened. "I was dreaming, sorry. I want you to lock your
doors, that's what I want."

"Okay," I said. "Of course. I usually do, lately." I went
to my balcony door and tested it. "Poor Mr. Paul." Thinking
how short a time ago he had left this way, looking forward to
his talk with Jonathan. "I guess when I heard Savannah and

dashed out of here I didn't stop to lock up. But I usually do."

"That's sensible," he said wearily. "Good night, Tyler."

The man stepped carefully through the studio, not turning on the flashlight which was shaped like a pocket cigarette lighter. He had another lighter that was a camera. He didn't need either one of them now.

The bastard had been here all right. The smell of paint was fresh. He found his way to the worktable and felt the brushes soaking in thinner. The palette was sticky. He moved across the room to the clothes tree. One of the smocks was damp in spots.

So it had begun. He didn't need to touch the easel or the canvas. He couldn't see how much had been accomplished— not without turning on the flashlight. He didn't need to see it now. The windows would be smeared, too. He checked and found he was right about that. Following Jonathan's lead but for a reason. So that no one could see in. Jonathan had only felt like painting to music. It was a whim.

The man rubbed his ear. He needed to do some heavy thinking about what was scheduled to happen next. Old Paul apparently was an accident. Nobody had counted on that. It ought to delay their schedule, too. Nobody, he was damned sure, wanted the old man involved. Everybody liked the old man. But maybe he'd caught on to something, even if he'd been laid up all these months.

In that case, had his death been an accident?

The man stood very still in the middle of the dark studio and pressed his fingers to his lips while he thought about it.

The main, immediate, problem was if Stella had gone sour and struck out on her own, maybe aiming in some crazy way to get it all for herself. She'd been acting peculiar, damned peculiar these last weeks. Secretive as hell and wacky. And

*she was drinking too much. Drinking and popping pills both,
a dangerous combo, which she ought to know.*

*Well, he'd tried to warn the others and they'd never be-
lieved him. Said she'd never in a million years turn against
the kid, or any of them.*

*"Don't worry about a million years," he'd said. "Give
a little thought to a million dollars. Twelve million dollars.
That could influence a weak mind. A head jazzed up with
booze and pills, am I right?"*

*But the argument had gone on all night and nobody had
thought he was right. Trust Stella. She could handle herself
—she always had. He was worried about Blase, too. Blase
could fall into the old romance pit. The old Adam and the
apple bit. That was the oldest trick of all, and Blase was
young enough to be tempted. Even if he was old enough to
know what was at stake.*

*In the dark the man cracked his knuckles, one by one. It
helped him to think. There was still time to check all pos-
sibilities, if he was clever enough. And lucky. That was the
hitch. Plain fool luck had to be a part of it, a bitter pill to
swallow.*

*He hesitated, halfway across the studio toward the dumb-
waiter. Old Paul hadn't taken his pills. Was that important or
just chance? It would bear thinking on. That, and if he'd
been able to see in here. He couldn't get in, but maybe he
had walked around to where he could see in, see something
that might give him a heart attack when he thought about
it.*

*The man snapped on the tiny beam just long enough to
check the time. Four thirty-two. He let himself out, the same
way he'd come in, the dumbwaiter, the food trolley. He
maneuvered the pulleys. He didn't even wake up the flies.*

22.

I woke with an odd feeling of expectancy. But day lived and nothing occurred, as Forster had written. I stretched, wiggling my toes, all ten of them, still half in my delicious dream of a world in which I was whole and loving and loved.

And then I remembered. Mr. Paul was dead. Blase Clinton had sat in my parlor and fallen asleep for a time. Savannah had stayed for the night and there'd be funeral details, maybe a wake. And probably Alison would have to help with them. I wondered if the Pauls had other close friends and family to take over, but no one had ever mentioned anyone else. Mr. Paul, in his illness, had been taken care of by a hired nurse.

There was a polite knock on my door. I unlocked it at once, and Savannah came in, carrying a breakfast tray. "I thought you might need some extra sleep today. We all could use it," she said.

I stared at my clock. It was past ten! "Why didn't anyone wake me?" I cried.

Savannah said, "Blase took Colin into town with him. I guess you got the day off—too bad it ain't a better one."

At the windows, rain was drumming steadily and I hadn't even heard it. "Where—I mean, did Mr. Clinton come back?"

She shook her head. "They's all gone. I don't think he's been back. The light's off. But that ain't too unusual. He goes off on his own from time to time. They got a place up north, way up in Michigan—"

"Upper Peninsula?"

"Something like that. Is that where Lake Superior is? Farther then. No phone and no tracking him, less he wants trackin'."

"Isle Royale?" I murmured, but she was intent on her own thoughts. I spoke louder, "But he'll want to come to the funeral!"

"No, he won't." Her tone was firm. "He didn't go to hers either."

Hers. I thought about it and remembered bleakly another death here. "But—if the body didn't come back—I mean—"

"They had a memorial service, what you call it. We all went, except the mister. He stayed to himself and played that god-awful music. All day and all night. Him and Miles got drunk for two days—and that was that. Leastways we don't need to figure him showing up for no funeral."

"Is it scheduled?" I asked. "I want to be there."

"Tomorrow afternoon. You 'n' I and Colin can go together if that suits you."

I nodded. "Is Randy all right?"

"He wants to talk to you, Tyler. He's pretty shook up."

I was shook up, by her words. "Wants to talk to *me?*"

"He been talking to us all. He just reckon *somebody* must've seen his pa—and nobody seems to recollect—"

193

"But Alison—" I began and then stopped. Savannah eyed me shrewdly.

"You was saying—" she prodded.

"I thought Alison saw him," I said. "I know I did. He stopped to see the painting."

"Well, you better get dressed and when Mr. Paul, Junior, gets back, you tell him, honey. Maybe it'll comfort him. I got a feelin' he's scared that not findin' the mister in was what done it—shocked him into overdoing. Who's ever going to know for sure?"

"I'll tell him what I can," I reassured her, and headed for the shower.

Alison called me to her office at three. Randy was there with a light drink in his hand. He looked white and shaken, but his summer suit was immaculate, his hair perfectly combed. There was no mistaking his sorrow, however. I murmured words of condolence, knowing how little help they were.

"Tyler, thank you for coming. Could you tell me about your visit with him?" His eyes were red and curiously anxious as if the worst blow had not already fallen. He seemed braced for something more. He searched my face and then turned to Alison, handing her his empty glass. "Could I have a refill? Would you like something, Tyler?"

What I'd like, I thought with sudden anger, *is to know why Alison hasn't spoken up.* I looked at the rolling cart which held a supply of bottles, bar materials, glasses, the works. The sherry bottle was unopened.

Alison said, "If you don't see anything you want, I can ring for Savannah."

"Sherry," I said, surprising myself. "That is, if you have some opened."

Her head snapped up. The green eyes leveled at me, but

194

all she said was, "I thought you didn't like wine in any form."

Randy said, "For heaven's sake, Alison! Let the girl have whatever she wants!"

Silently Alison opened the Dry Sack that sat prominently in the front row of bottles and poured a glass for me. It was much too much but I accepted it, sipped, and then added a cube of ice from the silver bucket.

"Do you think you could talk about it now, Tyler?" Randy asked tiredly. Alison had moved to her desk, but she sat on the edge of it instead of in her chair. The telephone had no lights glowing. She looked at me as she spoke. "I've already told Randy that his father waved to me as he came in. I wanted him to stop but he insisted that I ignore him. He knew I was busy. He was looking for Jonathan, of course." Her voice went on carefully, in a monotone; when at last she stopped, I said, "But I thought he mentioned—"

"Mentioned what, Tyler?" Randy was alert at once.

I flicked a glance at Alison, who stared steadily back at me. Waiting politely, with Randy who was so impatient he was standing.

Well, I could forget things the same as anyone else. Get things wrong. I'd had a headache yesterday, had been planning to go to bed early. And I'd been puzzled and worried about my painting. Maybe I was imagining things. Had Mr. Paul actually told me he'd had sherry with Alison or had I dreamed it?

She smiled at me encouragingly. "He probably wanted to see the painting, am I right?"

I nodded. I took another swallow of sherry. "He was so charming, Randy. I enjoyed his visit. We talked about—oh, lots of little things—poetry—"

"Did you talk about Jonathan?"

I nodded. "Some. He told me what friends they are— were—"

"Did he know Jonathan was away?"

"I don't think so. I believe he thought Jonathan was just—just keeping to himself—as usual." For the first time I wondered if Mr. Paul had died before he got to the studio or after. The way I remembered his poor body on the steps it could have been either arriving or departing when he fell. He—it—a beloved living man, and a puzzling corpse. I thought again of the pillbox and the key. Everything else had driven them out of my mind. They were still in my sweater pocket downstairs in the closet. Blase's closet. My face reddened against my will, and the blush must have confounded both of them. Two sets of eyes pinpointed me. I stared at the floor—recalled my rule about silence, about never volunteering any information around here. But I was stirred to pity by Randy's slumping shoulders. He'd sat down again and put his face in his hands.

"If he went to the house," I said, "he knew Jonathan was gone, for sure."

"What makes you think that?" Alison demanded.

I meant to say, "Well, Mr. Paul had his own key, didn't you know?" But I stayed quiet. "I just thought—he might have walked in—if the door was open."

Both gazed at me and Randy finally asked, "Why on earth do you think he went into the studio? He wouldn't bother Jonathan if he knew the red light was on. We—none of us—ever have."

I said, "I'm sorry—I'm upset and confused." I looked at Alison and thought I had better forgive her for forgetting about the sherry. At least give her the benefit of the doubt. Anybody could forget anything at a time like this.

"Tyler, you can go back to your room and rest if you like. I understand that Blase took Colin off our hands for the day. Randy, I'm sure you need some sleep. Dr. Gibson will give you a tranquilizer if you need one, I am certain. You should rest—there'll be so many people coming later. We can have—"

"You're right," he said dully. "I'll go home now."

Wednesday. It was still raining, a steady downpour. Miles drove the station wagon. Stella sat beside him and was silent. Colin, between Savannah and me in the back, was quiet, too. We all listened to the whirring of the windshield wipers, and talked about the fact that time seemed to drag. Trivia talk for a solemn ride.

At the funeral home, too many people and flowers seemed to fill the room. "Flowers are real pretty," Savannah said.

"God-awful," I said. "Artificial."

"They're real, child."

"They never grew outdoors. Mr. Paul wouldn't have liked them. I don't blame Mr. Clinton for staying away." Flowers grown indoors, preserved in refrigerators, and now meant to dazzle the eye on their green tape wire spines, long enough, at least, for the names on the cards to be read and noted and commented upon. The conversations were hushed, but the crowd milled and whispered and observed who was here, who was not.

A handsome shrub with no adornment stood in a plain white tub in a hallway. Savannah nudged me. "That's his." She meant Jonathan's, and she was right, but the engraved card was filled in by the florist. The bold black signature was missing. I thought abruptly of my painting. I had locked my doors, but what good did it do?

Soft organ music grew louder, changing to signify that the service would begin. I saw Alison raise her black-gloved hand to beckon for me to bring Colin forward to sit beside her. I slipped my hand under Savannah's arm to urge her forward, but she stepped back. "No, no, I'll wait here."

Then I saw Blase, across the aisle from Randy. His blond

197

head was bowed. He wore a white shirt and a dark suit, a plain blue tie. He looked at no one. Randy shared a pew with two frail women who—Alison whispered—were cousins from California.

I kept my eyes open but shut my ears and tried to turn off my thoughts. I concentrated on the painting in my room. Fitting it together, putting piece after piece in place, as if it were one of Colin's jigsaws. Curve within curve. And saw that a piece did not fit. Another line had been added. I had seen it, registered it, sometime last night or this morning, but only in the back of my mind. Lord God, why?

The music came up. Alison touched my arm. People were leaving, row by row, filing out as waved on by the ushers. I glanced at Colin, who was solemn but perfectly composed. His dark suit seemed to match his brother's. When we reached the sidewalk, he went to stand with Blase and slipped his hand into his brother's. Donatello might have sculptured Blase's hand, I thought.

Alison said we could go home with the Burtons. She would go to the cemetery with the family. I gave her a grateful glance and we escaped, dashing across the wet pavement when Miles brought the car around. Stella was already seated and seemed mesmerized by the slashing rhythm of the windshield wipers. Savannah, breathless, fitted herself beside us and shut the door with a solid, reassuring thump. "Get movin', man," she told Miles. "I got to get tea stuff ready. They'll all be comin' back to the house."

"I'll help you," I said. "I want something to do."

Stella said nothing, but as soon as Miles let us out at the back deck, she turned to him. The belt of my lightweight raincoat had caught in the door. I was trying to release it. Therefore I heard Stella say savagely. "One more day and that's it. One more stinking, rotten day! And I'm making

198

tracks—or I'm blowing the lid off. Take your pick, mister!"

Colin had already gone to his room. Savannah was shaking out a starched and frilly apron and a ruffled headpiece, like a maid in a late-night movie. I watched her in silence. I thought of telling her what Stella had said, but while I hesitated, she swept a hand toward the counter which was heaped with gleaming pitchers, trays, monogrammed tea- and coffee-pots, glistening holloware and rows and rows of spotless crystal.

"The Lord giveth and the Lord taketh away," Savannah said to herself. "You going to give me a hand, like you said?"

"Yes, sure. Is Stella coming to help?"

"Stella quit," Savannah said. "Sometime yesterday, day before. Anyway I'm glad she stayed for the funeral."

"You're kidding!" My mind raced. "Miles, too? Why didn't you tell me?"

She tied her apron and double-knotted it. Her lips were grim. "I can't tell what I don't know, now can I? Besides what business of yours? Or mine either? Now let's get crackin'— how many you s'pose going to show up here?"

"Here?"

She flicked me a glance and I flew to take the tray she was stacking sandwiches on. "I'll finish that," I said and then clamped my jaw as firmly shut as hers looked to be.

We worked silently and swiftly, and by the time the first of the sleek black funeral cars swept into the driveway, the dining room was beautifully laden with food and drink. "Didn't they talk about 'baked meats' in the Bible? Savannah, I never saw such a spread. Mr. Paul would have been proud." It was the first time I had spoken in an hour, at least, though I was bursting with questions. I thought I might die if I didn't get a few answers, a whole lot of answers, but nothing in Savannah's stormy face indicated that I could get even the right time of day if I asked.

She shot one more blank and hostile look at me and then abruptly relented. As if she had just recognized me again. She beckoned me back to the kitchen and poured two cups of fragrant coffee, using the breakfast mugs and filling them to the brim.

I said, "I know there's no time now, but just one thing, please Savannah—did Stella's leaving have anything to do with Mr. Paul's dying?"

"I doubt it. Nor her staying on either. She's got something big coming up for Thursday. I heard her talking on the phone. That's why she still here—*why* she *going* I do *not* know!"

For the next two hours the house was filled with gabbling strangers, and we ran to and from the dining room and the bar that had been set up in the gallery and was manned— superbly—by Miles. I was beginning to think if he'd ever had a drinking problem it had vanished. But Savannah disillusioned me when I mentioned it. "That ain't a pitcher of water he's got there by his elbow. That's pure Roosian vodka. You ought to try it."

An assistant from the undertaking establishment came in the back door, staggering under the weight of Jonathan's tree in the white barrel. "Take it right back out," Savannah ordered. "It's just the thing for the deck."

He muttered to himself and I giggled. "Whut he say?" she demanded. Her glower was back. "He's praising the Lord you don't think it's just the thing for the upstairs maid," I told her.

"We ain't got a upstairs maid!" But she grinned. She called the perspiring and rain-soaked young man back inside, reached under the sink, brought out a bottle of twelve-year-old Scotch and asked him how old he was. "Old enough," he said gratefully.

"Here's to black power!" he said, raising a glass.

"I'll take a swig of that myself," Savannah responded. Her eyes went beyond me. She said, "You, too?"

I turned to see Blase had come in from the outdoors. He was wearing his jeans again and a torn red windbreaker. His damp hair clung to his forehead in upside-down question marks. "I came for refreshments," he told Savannah, grinning at her.

"Well, help yourself. You always have."

But he didn't turn toward the dining room or the reloaded serving tray on the counter. He turned to me, swept me into his arms, and kissed me with tender skill. He didn't even seem to mind that the coffee in the mug I held sloshed on his jacket and was still near to scalding. "That's what I needed," he said to no one in particular, least of all me, it seemed. "See you around," speaking to Savannah. "I'll be back, though God knows when."

"Well, I'll be damned," Savannah said.

"Oh, my, oh, my," I said, scarcely breathing.

The undertaker's assistant reached for the bottle and filled his glass. Then he asked vaguely, because no one was paying much attention anyway, "Does anybody care if I take this with me? I feel a cold coming on."

23.

The night remained as monotonous as the rainfall, which slowed and stopped entirely by morning. We all moved rather like sleepwalkers in the aftermath of the unexpected entertaining. Alice came to help with the cleaning up.

In the early afternoon when lessons were over, I borrowed the Land Rover and took Colin to the village. Though there were puddles in the roadway and on some of the sidewalks, children on bright tricycles raced one another, joyous to be outdoors again.

The village, too, seemed to be in a stage of cleanup under the newly blue sky. Windows were being washed, awnings rolled up and down, gutters swept. Colin bounced beside me. But I had to think about the film to pick up and the new lines which had been added to the painting the night Mr. Paul died. Nothing had changed since then.

I parked near the Snap and Shutter with no trouble. Coming in from the brilliant daylight, I saw only that someone else was ahead of me at the counter, but Colin dashed forward, skipping lightly, and yelled, "Hey, Stella!"

"I simply cannot believe such incompetence!" Stella was announcing in a heated tone, which made everyone in the store turn to look at her. "You promised me today at the latest!" She scarcely glanced at Colin, and threw one disinterested look over her shoulder to see that I had come in with him, then returned to her argument. Mr. Kermit Trynne had thrown up his hands and rolled his eyes for sympathy to other customers. "It happens, ma'am. I had to be away. I could only get student help. Everything got mixed up, orders were delayed. I shall *never* take a vacation again!"

Stella said flatly, "Look again. Look through the whole mess again. I am not budging from this spot if it takes all night."

"But, my dear—"

"*But, hell!* Here—" She reached for the box of yellow envelopes. "I'll look."

Mr. Trynne set his thin lips and took his box back. His mustache tips actually quivered. An outraged white rabbit, I thought, but Stella looked to be in a towering rage. "Please," Trynne said, "I have all these other customers—come back in half an hour—please."

Stella turned on her heel and walked out of the store without speaking. I chased after her, suddenly feeling sorry I'd almost laughed at the outraged little man and at the housekeeper's disappointment, excessive though it seemed. "Stella, if you'd like, we can give you a ride home—we can wait."

Then she slowed her stride for just a moment and managed to say, "Thanks, Tyler, but no thanks. I have too much to do." She went on down the street.

For a moment I stood watching her walk away, then an urgency rose in my chest almost like pain. I turned to Colin, who was lingering in the doorway of the Snap and Shutter looking uncertain, and called to him to stay there, I'd be right back. I ran after Stella and caught up with her at the next intersection.

She looked at me in amazement. "Tyler, what on earth?"

"I don't know," I confessed. How could I blurt out that I had let Ruby get away and had never forgiven myself? "Are you coming back to the house? You aren't leaving today, are you? Savannah said you had quit."

"Well, what of it?" She stepped back onto the curb and waited for my answer. We were the same height, I noticed absently. I looked into her hazel eyes as she searched my brown ones. I felt a perfect fool, but the viselike feeling was still in my chest. "I guess I'm a little lost—with Mr. Paul dying—and Mr. Clinton gone away—I—we—never got to know each other—"

"Well, maybe I can remedy that," Stella said, shocking me to my heels, with her swift change of attitude. "Tell you what —if things work out for me this afternoon, I'll drop by your rooms sometime tonight. Or the lounge. We'll have a little talk." She seemed to be thinking hard and fast. A sly smile played at the corners of her pink mouth, but it didn't seem to be directed at me. The slyness of it.

"That would be fine," I said. I could hear Colin calling me impatiently. I didn't want him to get anxious, or to join us, and maybe cause Stella to change her mind. "I get lonely in the evening," I said. *And I've got about half a hundred questions I'd like to ask,* but I didn't say that. "I'll be looking for you, anytime." And then I turned and went back to the shop.

Several other customers were ahead of me now. I waited patiently. Mr. Trynne was taking care of business as fast as he could. Taking names and addresses, sorting packages, handing them out, making change, taking in new rolls of film, and filling out blanks for the sizes wanted. By the time it was my turn he was saying that everyone was the same. Take a few pictures, let them lay around the house for months, and then want them developed in five minutes.

"Lie," I said absentmindedly, thinking of Stella and thinking it was Colin who had spoken.

"I *beg* your pardon," said Mr. Trynne.

He was startled to have been overheard and I was startled when he protested. "I can assure you, miss, it's the truth."

"Oh, I'm sure of it, too! I was thinking of something else." I gave Colin a solid pinch, meaning, *Don't you dare laugh.* Outdoors again the boy was quick to giggle and then to mimic Mr. Trynne's querulous voice: " 'Lay around, I can assure you, miss, it's the truth.' You were correcting his grammar, same as you do me, huh?"

"Are you really only nine years old?" I asked.

"Going on ten— Hey, will you be here for my birthday?"

I came to a halt and looked at him. "It's in September, isn't it?" And he would be seven years older than he was when Agatha Dornblaser died. Seven years. Time for the will to go to probate or whatever happened. Time for his inheritance.

"It won't be any fun if you aren't here," he said. "September thirteenth. Promise you'll come, Tyler?"

I hugged him. I felt cold, though it was almost ninety degrees and no wind from the lake.

"The summer is going so fast," I said. "Let's not rush it. Let's enjoy every minute of it."

He said, "Well, of course."

Stella did not come to my room though I waited past midnight, with the lamps burning and the radio playing just loud enough so that she could hear if she had been delayed and was afraid of waking me.

I must have dozed. I woke with a start, hearing muffled footsteps, but not in the hall, above my head. Something was being moved on wheels. In the gallery. I hoped they were bringing something in, not taking out Clinton's glorious latest work from the L. My watch said two-twelve. I was certain it was the dolly I heard along with the shuffling feet. Was Jonathan back and working off his grief? He could work or sleep whenever he wanted to. He set his own hours. He'd earned them.

I was sure Stella would not come to call at this hour, no matter who was shifting paintings in the gallery, but I was still dressed for company, in skirt and shirt, tennis socks and slippers.

At three the house was silent. Had been quiet for half an hour at least. The dolly wheels and the footsteps were gone. I should go to bed. Clinton or Miles was undoubtedly back in the studio, drinking the night away. I would go see the newest work for myself.

As always the halls and stairway were aglow with soft, invisible light. I tiptoed through the carpeted part of the gallery. It seemed darker than usual. The draperies were drawn. I stood still for a moment, wanting to get my night sight. Soon a chair took form, a table, and I had some visibility.

There was a painting on the west wall, opposite the window. The end of the L was empty again. So something new had arrived. The other work had been taken away.

I thought of switching on the floor lights to study the new creation, but perhaps drawing back the draperies would be better and disturb no one. Anyone might be restless in this house tonight. Most of us were too tired to sleep or too carried along by the recent excitement. I moved to pull the draperies but stopped.

There was a cough, a slight movement in the darkest part of the room. A form stood there, not a piece of sculpture, a human, man or woman? And would he or she speak to me? Had Blase come back? Would I feel this rising fright if it were Blase? Or Jonathan?

I murmured a very shaky, "Who's there, please?" And almost wanted to follow it with a, "Don't answer. I don't want to know! Just go away!" Was this what scared Ruby out of the house forever?

The shadows moved. I thought I saw a bulk with color, a smock, the folds of a yellow smock, but could such a chilling presence emanate from Jonathan? I stepped forward and a hand rose to halt me.

I was terrified but I was angry, too. I said, "All right, Mr. Clinton. All right. It was bad enough to hide from your best friend's funeral. You're not going to frighten me. I'm not a silly little girl. I'm not Ruby. But you don't have to talk to me. I don't care about that."

I cared terribly, but I would retreat in dignity. I turned with deliberate movements and walked to the door and left the gallery. Once back in my own rooms I locked all the doors again. For all the good it did. Who knew how many keys were buried in how many pockets? Or held ready in sweating palms?

Thank God for the smock! What a close one! Who could guess that idiot girl would be spooking around the house at half-past three in the morning? The smock had been pure chance, a last-minute coverall, but it had fooled her.

The man in the shadows trembled with anger, with the injustice of having a damned cripple wandering around in the dark soul of the night. He trembled, also, with desire. She had been so close. He could have reached out and taken her. Who would have known?

207

24.

I woke so late that it shamed me, but I hadn't slept until dawn. I'd watched and listened, but no doorknobs turned. No one stole along the balcony. There had been no noises at all.

It was well past ten and the lounge was empty. I went to the kitchen, not for a late breakfast, but to ask if Savannah had seen Colin, knew where he might be now.

She was filling the dishwasher. "He ain't in the house. I guess he took a walk. Stella didn't see him either. I asked."

"Stella's still here?" I remarked, past caring at the moment.

Savannah nodded. "Here but not working. Just waiting for something. What I don't know."

"For her photographs," I said, on a guess. "Mine weren't ready either. Mr. Trynne is not very reliable. Or maybe he is, but he took a vacation and everything got loused up in his shop. He had student help."

"Speaking of help, ain't you supposed to be keeping tabs on Colin?" Then she relented and offered me a cup of coffee. "He getting more independent all the time, but maybe that's all for the good."

She poured powder into the dishwasher and shut the door. "Help him more when you be on your merry way next week. Week after."

"Next week!" My eyes shot to the calendar. It was already the middle of August. My merry way—how merry would a world be away from the Clintons—the male Clintons—Blase, Colin, even the silent, frightening Jonathan of last night. I stood with my heart beating fast, looking at the untouched coffee in my hand. As if I were suddenly gifted with the ability to read coffee as a gypsy could read tea leaves. Conviction gripped me. It *wasn't* Jonathan last night. It wasn't a Clinton at all. It had been a stranger. Or, if not a stranger, someone corrupt and menacing and familiar—I couldn't shake that last feeling. It was someone I knew—that's why I had thought it was Jonathan at first. I said, "Oh, my God!"

And Savannah said, "How do you know it's that bad—you ain't even tasted it?"

I put the cup down and said, "I might know where Colin is. I'll go look."

I was terrified now all the way through. The evil person in the shadows hadn't hurt me, hadn't even tried—the person to fear for was someone else. Why not a little boy, a little boy who would be a millionaire in mere weeks? I stumbled up the path, dodging twigs and ruts, but I would never again be nimble, never again a basketball player, part of the team, a cup winner. But who wanted to go through life winning trophies to catch the dust? Catch a grown-up golden boy, for keeps, that was another unattainable. That was where the deep wound lay.

That shadow last night, early this morning—"A shadow like an angel, with bright hair dabbled in blood." No not like

209

an angel, like the Devil himself. *King Richard III*. Lines from my literary upbringing. But an angel could be a fallen angel. . . .

I did not intend to fall today, angel or no angel. My thoughts were tumbling, falling every which way, but that was all right. I reached the clearing. I called softly, "Colin, Colin, honey, are you here?"

I was blocking the entrance in case this was one of his days for darting away. There was no way to go but down the cliff and he couldn't take that chance. In the first place he might break his neck, and in the second place it would give him away, for once and all. If his father was back in the studio as—judging from the swelling sounds of Bartók he was— Colin would not plunge down the cliff toward the A-window. I pulled back a few more low branches to get a better look, lest he be hiding at the edge of the bushes. But the clearing was unoccupied. I was alone and suddenly weary, out of breath, and deeply depressed.

I sat on Colin's favorite rock and pulled my knees up to my chin and waited until my heart stopped beating in jigtime, then peered across the ravine, parting the bushes to see better. There was no painting filling the window. But there was nothing to see, either. Two enormous canvases, the backs of them at least, took up the space nearest the window, obscuring any glimpse of the interior. A blue smock was draped carelessly across the top corner of one framed canvas, its empty sleeves dangling. The window itself was gray with dust, the grime of weeks. I remembered Savannah's complaint that this time it was worse than ever. The master wasn't even letting Stella in to clean. "Lord only knows what state he's got the place into. She kept it clean as a whistle."

I wondered if Clinton had finally learned about this balcony seat for his performances? Maybe Colin had even told him on their outings together. Certainly Clinton had decided to block the opening, the view. Curtain down, at least for now. The bottom of the dusty pane was smeared with paint, more like Halloween kids would commit than a genius swinging his brush to classical music. But the curtain was down. No performance today.

The sound of twigs snapping, branches swishing back, reached me. Colin, probably, had come looking for me. I turned but not fast enough. A cloth came over my head. I drew in a deep breath, gasping to get air, and my lungs felt seared. My eyes streamed with tears. Even my nostrils burned. It was turpentine. And someone was drawing the cloth tight around my neck.

I couldn't get my breath to cry out, couldn't even yell, to gasp was to make it worse. I tried to breathe shallowly, but panic made me try to gulp the foul air. My hands clawed and caught at arms, hands, that held the bag ever tighter, then I was thrown backward to the ground. My head hit a rock. A great weight came across me. The cloth around my head was twisted. My mouth was suddenly free. For precious seconds I dragged in air. Then my mouth was smothered again by hard, crushing lips. A thrusting tongue twisted and coiled snakelike in my mouth. Hands gripped my breasts.

My head felt as if the rock had split it, but the body on mine was writhing and I tried to wriggle free. Incredibly, in delirium it seemed, I heard a soft and cheerful whistle not far away. The hands fell. The tongue withdrew as my attacker lifted his head to listen, too. Then the smelly cloth was shoved, wadded, jammed into my mouth. Then a cracking sound and my jaw must be breaking.

"Tyler, Tyler! Open your eyes!"

Blase Clinton's voice, near or far away. And Miles, too, saying, "Better take it easy. She might move, try to sit up. See if she can just wiggle a finger. Don't let her move her head."

211

"Tyler, can you hear us?"

I lifted one finger and let it drop miles again.

"Did you hit your head on the rock? You fell again, Tyler." Blase trying to sound comforting.

"Not exactly," Miles again. "Look at this." Obediently I looked though he was speaking to Blase. Miles was holding a piece of jersey cloth and sniffing it. "Paint thinner, turpentine, and something else." Blase grabbed the rag from him and sniffed, in turn. A small, scared voice asked, "Is she all right?" A small, warm hand patted mine.

I said, "Colin, I've got a fearsome headache." Then I remembered the twisting tongue, the body on mine, and I whimpered, "Is my dress pulled down?" Forgetting I was wearing my khaki shorts.

"You're covered, Tyler," Blase said, sounding terribly angry. His windbreaker covered my legs. "Colin, get Savannah and bring a blanket, fast." He was sounding like his father again.

"What is everybody *doing* here?" I asked. Miles seemed to be testing my bones gently. My wrists worked. His fingers felt the base of my neck for tender spots. "It's not as bad as it looks," he told Blase. I said, "It all happened so fast." Blase counseled, "Just lie easy for a few minutes." Miles said, "It looks as if you got a Sunday punch in the jaw—nothing broken, though." To Blase he added, "I think we can let her sit up. Easy does it, Tyler; let me help."

"Dr. Burton, glad you're on the case," I murmured when I was sitting again.

His twisted grin flicked at me. "I'm only qualified to hang out my shingle for first aid and emergencies. Learned a little in the war."

"Learned a lot," Blase qualified. "Simple life-saving, that kind of easy stuff." He was still gruff but he was able to joke now.

I shuddered, wondering what would have happened if

someone hadn't whistled. "How did you find me? This was supposed to be a secret place." Both of them grinned at me. "Don't tell Colin, but there isn't any secret place on this land we haven't explored. Before he was born. There's even a secret stairway, been closed off for years, but one of these days we'll introduce him. He'll love it."

Blase said, more seriously, "My little brother was too secretive all on his own until you came. That's why we didn't encourage him. All kids like hiding places. There seemed no harm in this one. Nobody expected you'd be attacked."

Nobody was making any guesses about who my attacker was, I noticed, even though my head was throbbing. Savannah and Colin had arrived. "Land sakes, child, what next?" she grumbled, but smoothed my hair with a gentle hand. "Honey attracts flies," she told Blase. "We wasn't counting on hornets, too."

I apologized to Colin, hoping the frightened look would leave his eyes. "Sorry I had to blow your cover, man. This is the time you should've brought 'da heat.' "

"What is she babbling about?" Miles asked. "I'm losing my touch. I'd have sworn she hasn't got a temperature."

"No, but I'm getting one." I sat up. "Fainting is not a spectator sport. Everyone get along, please, just not too far along, while I stand up and sort myself out."

Somebody else was running up the path and inquiring, somewhat out of breath, if he could be of any help. It was Randy, demanding to know what happened.

"We *really* blew your cover," I said ruefully to Colin. He was looking happier, sure now that I was far more embarrassed than harmed.

"Somebody attacked her," Blase said. "Where have you been? Did you pass anyone?"

Randy seemed not to comprehend. "You mean in broad daylight—*attacked*?"

"I mean a very short time ago—maybe an hour, maybe

less." Blase was still keeping a protective arm around me, but he seemed to realize that no one really knew how long I'd been lying there when Colin found me, which had been less than ten minutes ago. Colin had started yelling and brought Miles and Blase from the cabin. The attacker must have heard Miles whistling and run away.

Randy said, "I was headed your way—I wanted to ask about—your new sculpture, Blase. Well, it doesn't matter. Let's get poor Tyler back to the house. She looks exhausted. We can talk about art later."

I was moving my chin gingerly. Miles held out the jersey cloth and said to Randy, "Is this yours?"

Randy's nose wrinkled. He looked almost comical, recoiling from the smelly rag in his blue and white seersucker suit, his immaculate white shirt, and blue-striped tie. I had to hold back a hysterical giggle.

"Colin, you get on back down to the house and tell Alison we're on our way. She won't like it one bit if we don't tell her what's going on," said Savannah.

As soon as he had gone, she said, "Now somebody tell *me* what's going on?"

Blase and Miles filled in what little they knew. They argued about one matter—what was in the cloth besides turpentine.

"Chloroform, old-fashioned chloroform," Miles was positive. "One small, swift dose will knock you out but not permanently. And you won't even remember too much of what went on."

Savannah was scattering questions like grapeshot as we straggled down the path.

"Could I see that rag for a minute?" Randy asked, just before we reached the fork in the trail. Blase hesitated, then handed it to him. No one was saying—nor had said—that it looked like a piece of a turtleneck jersey Jonathan Clinton often wore under his smock. But Randy remarked absent-mindedly, "You know something—this looks like Jonathan's shirt—I mean—"

"One he works in," Blase finished for him. "Isn't that interesting?"

"But he wouldn't—" Randy sniffed the cloth again. "This would knock out a regiment." He quickly tossed it high and wide in an arc that landed it somewhere in the ravine.

"That's a silly damn thing to do!" Blase yelled at him. "It's evidence—such as it is!"

Randy stared at him. "Oh, come off it, Blase. You don't think fingerprints stay on a soft material like that? We can all testify whose shirt it was. And *that* doesn't mean much. Almost anyone could have taken it. Stella could have used it for a dusting cloth—"

"Are you accusing Stella of this assault?" Blase asked, in a curiously quiet tone.

"It wasn't a woman," I said, shuddering again.

"I'm not accusing anyone," Randy said stiffly. "My God, I can't even—I don't begin to understand what happened, but I think Tyler should rest before anyone—before we question her. Right, Tyler, honey?"

"I don't need to rest. Tell Colin, as soon as I get cleaned up, I'll meet him in class."

Blase said, "Miles and I will escort you to your room, Tyler."

"I kin take care a' Tyler," Savannah said.

"Sure you can," Blase agreed smoothly, "but you can also break the bad-good news to Alison better than we can. Randy was on his way somewhere, wasn't he? So get along, Randy."

"I was coming to ask you something," Randy said, sounding almost sullen. "But I think I'll go home and try to start this day all over again." He headed for his car.

Blase waited in the lounge while I showered and changed.

215

I put on a long-sleeved cotton shirt and skirt and even put on a new pair of panty hose. I wanted to be clean and covered. If I'd had a winter coat I might have donned that, as well. When I came back to the lounge, Blase was playing records.

He looked up and whistled. "I love clean hair," he remarked. "Especially real hair, blown dry." Then he quickly held up both hands and nodded toward the stereo. "Miles had a job to attend to, but I put on 'Do Nothing Till You Hear from Me'—I hope that's all right with you?"

"So you're the Ellington fan," I said. It seemed vaguely that there had been a time when it mattered. When Ellington was playing and Blase was not here.

"Takes one to know one," he smiled back. Then, at the frown I must be wearing, he added, "I'm not the only one in the household. My father, Miles, even Colin are addicts."

"Langston Hughes, too."

"Hughes, sure, but he wasn't a composer."

"I know, but a man my father knew—another friend of both my father and Duke Ellington—said Hughes left a request in his will for three pieces of music at his funeral. I forget the first two, but that was the last one—'Do Nothing Till You Hear from Me.' "

He beamed at me. "Now I know you're all right. Shall we sit down for just a minute. I also know that Colin is waiting and he comes first around here."

"Do you mind?" I asked out of real curiosity.

"I think that's the way it should be," he answered somberly.

We took the wing chairs by the fireplace. "Do you remember anything that might give a clue?" he asked. "Who attacked you, I mean? I don't like to remind you of a bad scene but it could be important."

I shook my head. "I thought it was Colin. I didn't turn my head to see when—there was still time."

"You were there before." Not a question, but a statement, as if he were sorting it out. "Is that where you lost your bracelet?"

"I think so."

"Then Stella, for one, knows about it."

"But it wasn't a woman today," I reminded him.

"Stella wouldn't attack a kitten," he said, and then looked sorry he'd spoken. After a moment of reflection he said gently, "They were drowned, did you know?"

My gasp was answer enough.

"What happened this morning—I don't mean up on the hill—you were late and that is unusual, isn't it?"

"I went to the gallery last night, about two, maybe a little later, and I saw your father."

"You saw what!" He had moved to the edge of his seat.

"Well, I thought I saw him. There was someone—in a yellow smock—but he didn't actually speak to me, and—" I put my hands to my temples. My head was aching fiercely. I remembered now my later decision. The shadow of a man had not been a Clinton. But that part was guesswork, and there'd already been too many half-truths, half-suspected matters, all summer long.

"Let me begin again," I said, and he nodded silently. "I couldn't sleep. Someone is altering my painting—"

"Sorry, but what exactly do you mean *altering?*"

"Adding lines, bits of lines, slashes of color, not much, ever so little in fact, but changes. I have wondered if it could be Jonathan—Mr. Clinton."

"I suspect that's what you're meant to think," he said very carefully. "It must be the main aim for you to be here at all. I could be wrong. It's my best guess. It wasn't my first guess."

"Well, I'm glad somebody besides me doesn't know all the answers!" I may have sounded more annoyed than I intended. He grinned at me. He reached to stroke my knee but withdrew his hand and shoved it into his pocket.

217

"To take it from the top," he said, "I can almost assure you my father is not here, nor was he here last night. That's all I can say."

I hesitated. With the bushes back in place, perhaps none of them had realized what a viewpoint Colin had, even though they'd all been in the clearing. Their attention, after all, had been on me. And one had to part the shrubbery to see the studio window.

I wondered if I should confide in him, but the decision was taken out of my hands. Alison came in, running and breathless. "Tyler, are you all right? I want to hear every word. Right now."

"Well, I was looking for my bracelet again," I said, keeping my eyes on my hands.

"But—" she began to interrupt. Then pressed two flawlessly manicured fingertips to her matching lips, a rose shade this morning, ashes of roses.

"But what?" Blase asked.

"Nothing." She threw him a glance of irritation. "Don't you have something to do?" she asked him. "I can look after Tyler. I've got—" A glance at her tiny watch. "Well, I can take the time."

"Hear, hear," he said.

I said, "Colin's already been waiting for me too long." I stood up. "I'm a survivor. Lucky to be, remember? I'd better get back to the job."

"Tell me tonight," Alison said. "Or in the morning. It's just possible I have to go into town later today."

Tomorrow would be better, in any case. Tomorrow my films would be ready. I could show her the changes in the painting.

25.

Beebee had come to spend the day with Colin even though the sun was shining. His mother had decided he'd earned a holiday. They were setting croquet wickets in a part of the grounds Miles decided could be trampled with no great harm done. I promised to hurry back from town and join them.

"I have to see a doctor—I promised Alison, and there's no telling how long that will take."

If I offered to pick up Stella's films, too, I might find out what Stella had to say, or would have said, if she'd called on me as promised last evening. I swung my shoulder bag over my arm, took a grocery list from Savannah, agreed to have it delivered if it turned out to be too heavy, and headed for Stella's office.

"She went back to the apartment about ten minutes back," Savannah said. "Something's bugging that lady. Wish we knew what."

"Maybe I can save her a trip—or she can go with me," I said.

Halfway up the stairs to the apartment I heard the angry voices. They were shouting in argument and no mistake. Stella was threatening to call the police and Miles was advising her not to be a damn fool.

"You're going to fool around until it's too damn late! Mark my words, smartass!"

"Too late for what? What do you plan to tell them? Your suspicions? They'll haul you off to the loony bin! If Alison can make Jonathan think you might just possibly be a murderer even for a minute—even when he was half out of his mind—if she can make Blase and God knows who all—certainly that girl—think you've got an active case of kleptomania—what do you think you can tell the local gendarmes?"

I turned to flee at last, but Miles had walked over to a window near the door and was staring down across his small garden. To move might bring his attention in my direction. I stayed rooted and hoped the disagreement was over. My leg was numb. The sun seemed to pour in extra strength as if in malice for an eavesdropper.

Stella said, "Tomorrow they won't laugh. I'll have proof. You'll see."

He swung around. I could leave but I felt welded to the spot. "I'm warning you, don't meddle!"

"Meddle, hell! It's too late for justice. But it's not too late for a piece of the pie."

"You don't mean that. You're not a thief, nor a blackmailer!" For a moment I thought his voice was worried, and then it was sarcastic as usual. "Takes brains, old girl."

I could move at last. I went noisily up the steps and called out. "Mrs. Burton! Stella! I'm on my way to town. Can I pick up—"

The door came open so fast its breeze nearly sucked me inside. "What the devil do *you* want?" Miles demanded.

Stella pushed past him. "No!" she said sharply, to my unfinished question. I was staring at his hot flannel shirt. It almost made me ill from the heat. Had it been Miles who pushed himself upon me? Beard! Would I have felt a beard in that moment of agony and confusion? Could I have smelled vodka with the other fumes?

"Tyler, I don't need *anything*," Stella said, with a queer emphasis on the last word.

"But I'm going to the—"

"No!" She cut off my mention of the Snap and Shutter. Perspiration outlined her upper lip. She licked at it. "No, thank you," she said.

"Well, I just thought—"

"Thought what?" Miles snapped at me.

"I thought I could pick it up for her."

"Pick *what* up?"

"A prescription," Stella said. "I have to get another one refilled." Her hazel eyes pleaded with me to go away. "Thank you anyway. I have to get another one, too, and I have to find the number first." Her freckled hand was on the doorknob in a desperate gesture of dismissal.

"Would you like for me to drive you in?" One last try, but a futile one.

"No, no, thanks very much." The door was closing. "Thank you."

I said good-bye to a closed door. "Toodle-oo, pip pip, adieu," I said, not knowing that it was for the last time.

Feeling a little like Colin who always saved the icing on the cupcake until the last, I was determined not to examine my snapshots until I got back to my sitting room. Their value lay in direct comparison with the painting anyway. Not that there was any doubt. But proof would get Alison's attention.

Blase's Alfa was parked in the shade where Randy's car often stood, near the gatehouse. If I felt like it, later on, I might show him the photos, too. I parked the jeep in the right slot in the garage and ran into the house. I could see Beebee and Colin were playing checkers now on the deck. Miles was lying sprawled in his hammock with a book. His glasses were pushed to the top of his head. The book lay over his face. He dozed.

The kitchen was empty, and for once I was glad not to be stopped by Savannah with a glass of iced tea or anything else.

As soon as I locked the door of my parlor, I pulled the draperies shut and turned on the lights. Then I pushed a low table in front of the chair which still faced the painting, adjusted the lamp on it, and put a second lamp to shine directly on Clinton's gift. At last I was ready to tear open the envelopes and spread the photographs.

Trees, trees, trees, and the back fender of an automobile. A license plate and a lump of something lying on the road. They'd given me the wrong package! Oh, damn Mr. Kermit Trynne and his student helpers! Damn them all!

There were what looked to be three shots of an indoor storeroom. Must have been taken with a flash. There were shelves. Objects, small pieces of sculpture, a couch with several pillows, and a throw blanket, and in a corner a low, slatted table holding three or four picture frames perhaps, but the backs were to the camera. Probably a storeroom. Not a particularly interesting picture, nor were the others.

I ran for the phone but it was past four and Trynne closed early. Closed early, opened late, and messed up in between. I felt like crying and kicking, but a tantrum was no help, so I stuffed the pictures back into the envelope and threw it into my top bureau drawer. I reached for a handkerchief, something solid to bawl into—not tissue paper—and there was my bracelet. Not in the Valentine box. Lying loose in the drawer where somebody had been meddling, rearranging! Nested in my little pile of Swiss linen handkerchiefs, a gift from Aunt Lynne.

I yelled out loud this time, in sheer rage that my possessions were being pawed in my absence. I took a chair and shoved it against the hall door. In minutes I had shoved furniture against all doors, and then I sat down and wept until I felt better.

Tomorrow I would get the right set of pictures if I had to stage a sit-in at the Snap and Shutter. Mr. Kermit Trynne would wish he'd gone into some other line of business, any other line of business, if I didn't get my own films back. And Alison Clinton had better plan right now, as of tomorrow, I corrected that, though I looked longingly at the phone, thinking to call her at the moment, anyway she had better plan to get all the locks changed on my quarters at once. She could take the cost of it out of my salary.

Somebody tapped on the door and I yelled, "Go away! I am NOT here!"

Whoever it was went away without a word.

Granted that most tantrums are no more than self-indulgence and plain damn silly, serving at best to work off steam, mine may have cost a life. If I had opened the door, invited the caller in, exchanged confidences, discussed the snapshots, all might have worked out differently. But it was the road not taken.

Dutiful daughter of an English prof I had memorized Robert Frost along with most of my generation . . . "Two roads diverged in a wood and I—took the one less traveled by" . . . whatever. I was safe in my own quarters. I kept the door locked. And had no idea I was making a dangerous choice.

26.

"*Where you* off to now?" Savannah demanded as I ran across the kitchen without stopping for coffee or breakfast.

"Back soon," I called, and waved to show no offense intended. "I'll be back before Colin's up."

"I'm up now!" he yelled from the doorway.

"Then wait," I said. He was still in his pajamas and I was in no mood to hang around until he could get dressed. I intended to be the first customer in line when Mr. K. Trynne opened his door.

A student clerk opened up this morning. "Oh, hi," she said, with no great interest in the beautiful morning or my look of urgency. "You again already?"

"You gave me the wrong pictures!" I pushed the envelope across the counter. She yawned and read the address out loud. "Ninety-four Ravine Drive, that's yours, isn't it?"

"Right address, wrong pictures. I'm Ames. Tyler Ames. Begins with an A. A for Awful hurry, right?"

"So hold your— Excuse me, I'll take another look."

Mr. Kermit Trynne had arrived in person. "I shall look," he announced, and I groaned. "Is all this hurry really necessary?" he asked. "What have you taken—the neutron bomb?"

"My dear man, you will think I invented the neutron bomb, if you do not produce my pictures very quickly. Sir." I added the last totally unnecessarily. His pink-rimmed eyes, rabbity Trynne, were popping. He swiftly shuffled through the A's and announced, "They're not here, but—just hold on *one* little minute, please." He kept on talking gently as if that would keep me at bay.

"Ah, ah, your envelope got mixed up with the B's. You are not Stella Burton, by any wild chance?"

So I had been given Stella's photographs instead of my own. "By no chance at all. I am Tyler Ames. A."

"Well, shall we see?"

"By all means."

He slit the envelope dexterously and daintily lifted one photograph. It showed my painting in lovely, glowing, chromatic nonglare, borderless prints. Five of them. I said, "How much?"

He said, "Well, let me see. You already paid for the Burton lot."

"Yes, I'll take them to her. Same address, you know."

"She had three more rolls due back. Tell her to be patient."

"Yes, yes. How much?"

He did some pencil work and decided I owed him $4.62. I thanked him and fled. I dropped the change in my sweater pocket and my fingers touched a metal object. Mr. Paul's pillbox! Which I had totally forgotten.

I ought to be locked up, I thought, for examination and

study. My brain is shot to hell. But this summer is going to end. And I am going out of here on the vertical. Who had said that? Ah, Jonathan, in what now seemed years and years ago. I drove home very slowly, thinking that if I drove as haphazardly as I used my poor head these days I'd be arrested in short order.

My films were safely in my purse. I could look at them in leisure and sometime today I would show Alison that some-one had been moving in and out of my sitting room with the greatest of ease and I would like new locks, thank you, on all the entrances. Even if I had to pay for them myself.

When I reached the rough part of the road, I saw a dead bird lying in the dusty bushes and thought of the lump in the photographed road. I hoped it hadn't been an animal. Now that I thought about it—could it have been a dog? I hoped Stella got the license of the bastard who had run over it, if so. Was that why she had been so intent on getting the pictures as soon as possible? I hoped she would be able to retrieve the rest of them with less trouble than I'd had.

When I pulled into the driveway Blase's Alfa was still there. The house was still shimmering in the sunlight, like a Mediterranean villa, I decided. I parked and dashed up the deck steps. Savannah shook her head as I passed her. "I take it you still don't want nothin' to eat?"

"Not at the moment, thanks!"

I fumbled for my door key. Again I locked the door behind me and sat to spread the snapshots on the table. I fanned them out like tarot cards. Clinton's painting in miniature. Five versions of Clinton's painting. Certain proof at last.

I would tell Alison early this afternoon when there was time to intrude. Alison spent her mornings working hard in conference, often with Randy, or on the telephone. Colin and I were able to finish our lessons easily by noon these days, so

226

it would be after lunch, and maybe at last someone would tell me why this odd thing was happening. And see about the locks.

Savannah said Alison had not wanted lunch, but she had not gone into town.

"Do you think she's napping?" I asked anxiously.

"Not her. Not in the summertime anyway. This summer leastways."

But Alison was not in her office. And not in the house, although I looked upstairs and down. Her bedroom door was open. The dressing room, too. I called, but no one was there. Colin was engrossed in the TV soap drama that bemused him. Savannah had said it was all right, she even liked it herself. Carol Burnett liked it and who could be more wholesome than Carol Burnett? She had about a dozen kids of her own.

So I wandered outdoors. Two cars were gone from the garages, but the Mercedes that Alison preferred to use was there. And so was Randy Paul's Lincoln, parked on the apron of the drive. They were probably checking inventory at the studio. I would have to wait.

It was a Van Gogh sky today. Arles in midsummer. I decided it was finally time to see the maze, and I ran across grass as richly green as any the Impressionists had captured. I entered the boxwood labyrinth, with an almost guilty sense of intruding, of betraying Colin who didn't want to come here himself, and wouldn't like it in the least if he knew I wanted to explore. "Just stay away from it," even Randy Paul had advised me, in the beginning, and once again when I mentioned Colin's really deep dislike of the place.

I followed lanes into blind alleys, backtracked, and tried to keep from giggling at my mistakes. I would have to persuade Colin that it was all in fun, nothing to be afraid of. Listening

227

to a bird caroling, I almost hugged myself to keep from shouting for the fun of it. Wishing I'd come around the next tricky corner and find Michael Caine bumbling along and Laurence Olivier smirking in the center of it all. *Sleuth* had been worth standing in line to see, and both actors were my favorites. I wound round and round, wanting to take off my shoes and let my foot and my heel sink into the deep, luxurious grass on this burnished, golden afternoon.

I eased triumphantly around the last lane into the heart of the compound and came to a standstill. A nude figure lay on a multicolored Guatemalan serape, or shawl—it was widespread and fringed—and for some seconds my eyes focused on the crimson fringe. Not on the deeply tanned woman who lay on her back, her green shadowed eyes closed. Her thick, dark lashes trembled, her wine-red lips were parted. The wine-red polish on her long nails made a pattern on Randy's too white body as she pressed it to her own. He was too intent to see that I had intruded, or to hear my shallow breathing. Alison was too transported. I melted backward around the bend of the boxwood lane and tiptoed away, dragging my lame foot, and then ran despite stabbing pains when I reached the driveway and hit the gravel too hard, pounding my way to the back deck. And beyond. I took the balcony stairs and ran along to my own windows, forgetting they were locked and I had only the key for the hall door.

I lay on the deck, getting my breath, and laughing with relief that I had got away undetected. But sobered when I thought of Colin. Undoubtedly he had blundered on a rendezvous in time past. And to him it would have been a betrayal of his beloved father, not a thing to laugh about.

Well, love in the afternoon or no love, the locks to my doors had to be changed. What to do about Colin was another matter—and beyond my ability to cope. Maybe someday he'd understand, and know that his father probably did

228

not care. Though I couldn't imagine not caring if one's mate sought elsewhere for intimate comfort. No matter what Jonathan had said that night in the library, his pride, at the least, must be wounded.

Dinner looked to be another of Savannah's culinary masterpieces, but the grilled sole which Randy boned at the serving cart as gracefully as if he were a ballet dancer was tasteless, for me. Even *zucchini fritti*, in Tuscan style, was no more than so much crisp paper to be chewed and swallowed. No wonder Randy can kick up his heels and flourish his hands, I was thinking sullenly. If Randy intended to hang around for the evening, too, I would have no chance to show my snapshots to Alison.

She was sparkling in a flowing pink chiffon hostess gown with a tea rose tucked in her dark hair and pale pink nails now. Scarlett O'Hara on Lake Michigan.

Randy, at least, took note of my lack of appetite and looked concerned. "Is anything wrong, Tyler?"

I said, "I would like to talk to Alison, just for a moment, but I don't want to intrude—"

"Then see me tomorrow," Alison said blithely, lifting a champagne glass and admiring its bubbles.

Colin poked at his salad. He seemed to have caught my mood instinctively, though he had no notion that I'd strayed off limits today.

"White wine for the common folk," Alison was saying, "champagne for me."

Randy's sandy brows lifted. He flicked me an apologetic glance. "Takes only a little of the stuff to make our *Mrs. Clinton* tiddly." It seemed that he bore down on her title, as well he might, lest she forget in her tiddliness.

"Why don't you two talk tonight?" he suggested. "I think I'd better get back to town early."

Alison's soft pink lips were turning into a pout, but his glance not only kept her silent, she rang for Savannah and asked for iced coffee.

"Well, Tyler, what's on your mind?" she asked, when we were alone in her office.

I brought out the snapshots and spread them on her desk. She looked puzzled, then she bent over them and concentrated for several minutes. At last she looked up and said, "Where did you get these?"

"I took them. Blase left a camera, don't you recall?"

She thought about it and remembered. "I understand, I guess. You wanted something to remember—when you leave —but why five shots in exactly the same position? I'm no photographer but—"

"The whole point is that the camera is in the same position but the painting is changed."

She paused only to light a cigarette, then she spoke briskly, "I want to see for myself."

We went downstairs. When she had studied the changes, she looked again at the snapshots and then at me. "First thing, we will have the locks changed. The second thing is that I suppose I had better admit to you that we've all been worried sick about Jonathan. He isn't well, Tyler; have you suspected that?"

I nodded.

"Did you know he was the one who must have thrown the green paint on his own canvas?"

"No, and I don't think—I don't see how—" *Must have,* she'd said. So even Alison wasn't certain.

Her voice was friendly. "Let's sit down, Tyler. It's hard to believe, I know that. But you never saw Jonathan when he was ill before. When he took the painting from the Modern

Art Museum—I mentioned that once—perhaps you've forgotten."

I hadn't forgotten. But that had been a drunken prank. Jonathan Clinton had not been drunk the day I arrived here.

"I thought you told me, or someone told me, maybe Savannah, that he actually didn't remove the painting—only had it in mind. And wanted to replace it. And was drinking at the time—"

Alison waved her hand as if to drive away smoke and also my words. "There's no point in bringing up ancient history. What we have to think about is here and now. Jonathan has been behaving very strangely—coming and going at all hours. And he didn't come to poor Mr. Paul's funeral. Don't you find *that* odd?"

I hesitated. "Alison, I don't think it's my place to decide whether it's odd or not."

"But you've got eyes, girl!" She almost snapped. "There might come a time when—" *When what?* I screamed in silence, but she didn't finish her thought. She lit one of her cigarettes, having an endless supply, I thought, but she hadn't brought an ashtray and I didn't have one handy. I'd taken them all back to the kitchen.

"I'll get something," I said. And fetched my soap dish. It was a beautiful porcelain shell and I hated to hand it over, which she must have perceived. She wrinkled her nose.

"I know it's a messy habit, but I don't indulge myself in many vices—you'll have to forgive me."

Oh, ho, I thought, saying, "Of course. But you will see to the locks? It gives me the creeps to think someone can come and go. Even if it's Jonathan—I mean, your husband—and this house does belong to him, so perhaps I shouldn't object."

"It's Agatha's house," Alison said. She gave her head a tiny shake of regret and bit her lip as if she had revealed more than intended. "Was, anyway. Nobody has a right to invade

231

anyone's privacy. Jonathan should be more aware of that than any of us—considering his great rage if he's ever intruded upon."

I wondered what she might say if I suggested that thanks to her deviousness, never explained, I had intruded upon him and he had not been in a rage, had made me welcome. But too much was going on around here for me to add to the confusion.

"*My* room he would, should feel free to invade, if only he would," she was saying, looking all pink and maidenly and wistful, but game. The suntanned chin managed a tremble. The green eyes looked at me from beneath the lowered heavy lashes, and she must have seen that I wasn't impressed.

She smoked in agitated little puffs for a time. And then tried a new approach, or maybe a new honesty. She leaned forward and spoke in a low voice, "Randy and I chose you for this job not only because you had the right background—art major, a fine scholastic record, and certainly a reason not to be—well, flighty, isn't the word I want—"

"A reason to stay put," I said it for her, and she nodded abstractedly.

"I—we both—look upon you as a person of integrity, with fairness, with open-minded judgment, not taking sides, not jumping to conclusions—"

I began to squirm. I had jumped to conclusions a dozen times daily, and probably all the wrong ones, but hear her out, keep the lip zipped, Tyler, and just maybe you'll get some of the long-wanted answers.

I was wrong about that, for certain. She talked on and on without saying anything. She seemed to grow aware that my attention was wandering. She stood up abruptly and said, "Tyler, let's go up to my office. I want to show you something."

We went back upstairs in silence. In her office she took a

black leather portfolio from the long drawer in her desk. Its gold initials were ADC. Alison Dent Clinton, I assumed—or Agatha Dornblaser Clinton. Alison looked up and caught my glance. "This was Agatha's," she affirmed. "It was too good to throw away—and we have—had—the same initials." Her lips twisted. "You know what they say, a change of the name and not of the letter—"

"—is a change for the worse and not for the better." The old rhyme that kids used to write in autograph books in my mother's or maybe it had been my grandmother's day. I knew the rhyme, but both of us left it unfinished. Alison slipped a piece of engraved stationery from the portfolio and held it out for me to read.

"It's a poem Jonathan copied. He does that from time to time. I'm not bothered about his copying it—but I want to know—I *need* to know if it seems to have any peculiar, that is, any particular meaning at this time. Tell me what you think." She waited.

The stationery was creamy and the handwriting looked to be Jonathan's, bold but legible:

> I promise nothing: friends will part;
> All things may end, for all began;
> And truth and singleness of heart
> Are mortal even as is man.
>
> But this unlucky love should last
> When answered passions thin to air;
> Eternal fate so deep has cast
> Its sure foundation of despair.

"Are *you* his unlucky lover, Tyler?" Alison demanded, green fire seeming to blaze from her steady eyes.

I winced. "It's just a beautiful poem, why do you want to cheapen it? *Love* not *lover*." I felt my skin crawl at the ugliness of the question and the suspicion that prompted it. And then I remembered that it was Jonathan's wife, even if she happened to be his erring wife; she *cared*, that was the main thing.

I said, "No, of course not. I'm sure no one is. He gave me—that is, he quoted another poem for me, a few weeks ago, and Mr. Paul told me what it was about. I was worried it might indicate his state of mind. *Mr. Clinton's* state of mind. The name of the poem was 'A Farewell to a Friend.' I hope he isn't thinking of, worrying about, dying—"

"He isn't!" Alison was almost scolding me. "Get that out of your head. He's thinking of love not dying!"

The silence rang with unfired shots, then she looked away and sighed. "It's better to get these matters out in the open, isn't it?"

"Depends, I guess." I stayed motionless for a few minutes. Then I said firmly, "I think I'll give him his painting back. Right now."

I was unprepared for Alison to spring at me, to grasp my shoulder and give me a shake, and hold on to my arm. Her grasp was surprisingly strong. "You will not!" she shouted. "You will not do anything so utterly stupid. You are a silly, silly girl! Don't you know—can't you see—how that would upset him totally?"

I said, "You're hurting my arm."

She dropped her hand and walked to the far end of the room where she stood by the Replogle globe and gave it a vicious spin. *Bet she wishes it were my head and she could bounce it like a volleyball,* I was thinking, not without sympathy.

I stood waiting for dismissal. Having a chill, but curiously empathetic about Alison. More than I had ever been. I liked her better, knowing she cared about her husband. If I were

234

married to—to a Clinton, wouldn't I be just as deeply anguished at infidelity—imagined or not?

"Blase might still have a key to your rooms, of course," Alison said in a perfectly normal voice. "But I don't think he'd ever touch one of Jonathan's paintings, however—but let's keep this to ourselves for the time being. I'll attend to the locks, first thing tomorrow. You aren't worried about tonight, are you? You could sleep upstairs—there's the guest room."

"I'll be fine," I said, and managed a smile, "now that help, so to say, is on the way."

"Blase and Randy are not too friendly," she remarked, surprising me again, just as I had reached the door.

"Well, that seems obvious." I kept my hand on the knob, wanting to escape any more heart-to-heart talk, not even wanting any answers now.

But Alison continued: "Randy has had to take over the galleries and that means he spends much more time with Jonathan. I suppose Blase feels shoved aside—he and his father, this summer, have actually avoided each other. And I don't know why. Jonathan has seen much more of Colin."

I said, "If it's all right with you, I think I'd better get to bed."

"Just one more thing, Tyler, did you know—has Savannah told you Stella is leaving?"

I nodded.

"We'll find her very hard to replace. But how she has managed to live with Miles all this time is beyond me."

Despite my urgency to get away, I lingered one more moment. "She's leaving Miles, too?"

"Looks that way." Alison suddenly pulled herself up to her full height and looked back in charge of things, no matter if the soft chiffon clung seductively to her shapely body. She slapped at her skirts as if to dispel any image of femininity.

She strode toward me and switched off the lights as she followed me through the door. "Another day, another dollar, as they say. We'll deal with whatever happens tomorrow. Have a good night's rest, my dear. And next time—if anything's troubling you—anything at all, come to me sooner, all right?"

She didn't wait for my answer, which was just as well. I had none.

27.

"*Well, she's* gone, I guess. Looks like, anyway. Just packed up and went." Savannah's face was alight with being the first to give the news this morning. "Looks like she left the telling to Mizz Alison. I put the note under Miles's door half an hour ago. He'll be fit to be tied once he wakes up and reads it. Well, ain't this the limit?" She stared at me and I tried to summon some degree of astonishment.

"It's the limit," I agreed. I wondered, without really caring, if Alison had Stella's farewell note in her pocket all the time we'd been talking last night. It wasn't my business. I hoped Stella had got her pictures before she left.

Before I had finished my first cup of coffee, the intercom had rung. Savannah listened to the message, emitting a series of noncommittal ums and yes, ma'ams, and a sure, sure, fine. When she hung up she told me I was wanted in the library, not the office, the library, got that right? And im-MEED-iately.

"On my way," I said. "What about Colin?"

"He's got the day off. I'll do somethin' about Colin. You git."

We both heard a car stop. "Well, here's Randy—to nobody's surprise. Git along, girl."

I detoured to fetch my sweater. The house was perpetually too cold these days, but no one else seemed to mind. By the time I reached the library, Randy was there. Alison was telling him that she had offered to threaten Miles by calling the police if he didn't behave himself, but Stella said that was the last thing she wanted.

"She's promised to send an address as soon as she knows where she'll be permanently." Alison was smiling. "I must say, when something you've worried about actually happens, it's a sort of relief."

"I know what you mean," Randy said very quickly, and changed the subject. "Tyler, the locksmith will be here today."

"Thanks."

Alison went on as if we had not spoken. "This way I can honestly tell Miles I don't know where she went. I probably won't hear for quite some time."

"Alison, please," Randy said, compelling her to look at him. "Let's get on with other matters. There's so much to be done. Have you told Tyler there'll be a press conference? She may want to attend."

"Well, as a matter of fact, I forgot about it."

"I can understand that, but perhaps Tyler won't mind pitching in to help hostess the event." He looked at me with one brow raised and I nodded, even if I didn't understand why a press conference. He soon filled me in. There would be a sort of preview of some of Jonathan's works. To start the

238

"How did she get to town?"

Randy cleared his throat. "I drove her. Dropped her at the station."

"Then she went north," Miles said thickly, his chest heaving. "Trains don't run south, late."

"It was the bus station," Randy said vaguely. "And yes, I gave her some extra money. She'll send it back. All she wanted was—a new life. Away from here."

I wondered why I got a strong impression Randy was improvising. Either he had taken Stella to a bus station or he had not. If Stella did not want Miles on her trail, well, he— Miles—must have known that. But I glanced moodily at the man and felt sad. My heart seemed pinched; that was a fancy way of putting it, but I turned away, not wanting to stare at the pitifully scarred muscular arms, the strong neck. Sometime after he'd been a man grown, he'd suffered hell itself. Only a woman who truly loved him would caress that body which might have been pitted, volcanic rock. Stella had never looked at him with tolerance, so far as I knew, let alone tenderness, double let alone love.

Miles had been trying to get his head together, it seemed. He looked ready to question Randy again, but he caught the unguarded look of sympathy in my eyes and he wanted no part of it. He made a low, almost growling sound. "You precious three, you make me puke!" His fiery glare swept us all into one heap of rubbish, it seemed. He worked his lips. *He's going to spit on us!* I thought, stepped back.

"That's right, baby, don't come near the freak! Keep your skirts clean!"

I ducked my head to hide tears. He was running back, crashingly, through Alison's office, hitting the walls as he went, surely. I had an almost irresistible urge to smash something myself. I clenched my fists at my sides and swallowed a body-shaking scream.

"Well, that's that," Alison said. "That wasn't so bad, now was it?"

I dashed blindly toward the door.

But Alison called out, "Tyler, just a minute, please." And she was my employer and I had to halt. I turned, looking resentful perhaps; it couldn't be helped.

Randy said, "Miles was burned saving Jonathan from a plane crash—did you know?"

"How would I know?" I asked, but without heat. Randy's back was not scarred. It was white, like a fish's belly, wasn't that the standard expression? He was looking at me in some bewilderment. Poor, fastidious Randy Paul taking what was offered him. Why blame him? In a swift, dangerously swift, change of mood, I grinned at him. I wanted to say, "It's probably the only outdoor exercise you get, right, Randy?"

He had no idea what thoughts were tumbling in my head, but he responded to the grin with enormous relief. "Tyler, I wanted to see those pictures you took—that was very smart of you, honey. I'm very proud of you—" He paused as if remembering that being too proud of anyone around here could be annoying to his hostess and my employer, Mrs. Alison Clinton. "Well, I hired you, didn't I?" he said. "I picked you out of a crowd."

"So you tell *me*," said Alison, eyes narrowed against the smoke she was exhaling.

"Well, let's go look at the pictures," I said, escaping at last, but with the two of them nearly at my heels. I was almost sorry I'd ever been so clever. As we reached my sitting room, Alison said, "There's one other thing that's been bothering me. Do you think Savannah has been giving me all the notes from Jonathan?"

Before I could speak, Randy put in, almost angrily, "Why would Tyler know that? For heaven's sake, Alison!"

"Well, *do* you?" Alison asked, unperturbed. "I wondered

if perhaps you might be keeping some of them yourself—as a souvenir—" she hastened to add, holding up her hand against Randy's beginning to sputter in outrage. "Strictly as a souvenir—as any girl might want—any girl who admires a great artist, as Tyler certainly does. As we all do."

"No, I haven't kept any notes. Nor seen any."

"Some are missing."

"Perhaps Savannah has forgotten and thrown them away."

"Perhaps. I'll ask her."

"Besides," I said, "I thought he was away." Both of them looked at me blankly for the moment. "I mean—the lights are out—and I assumed—well, that perhaps he'd gone sailing." "*So in the sunset think of me.*" But don't add that, I warned myself. Don't stir her up again. In the middle of many a fanciful night I had wondered if Jonathan Clinton, knowing he was very ill, might just sail away as Norman Lane, or whatever his name had been, the un-hero of *A Star Is Born*, the Fredric March one, not the sweaty one, with the curly hair and all the Ks in his name, and not even the British one, James Mason, but the real one. Norman Main. Maine? Gone into the sunset.

"Someone, of course, could sell them to a collector," Alison was saying in a hushed tone to Randy, but meant to be overheard, all right. A lump of rebellion rose like bile in my throat, keeping me from speaking, but Randy threw me an anxious glance again.

"I've heard there are ambitious fellows who scrounge around in the garbage of the famous," he said, wrinkling his nose. "Let's don't even *talk* about it." He strode across my sitting room to sweep the draperies back as far as they would go. Then he seated himself in my armchair and studied the painting before he looked at the snapshots. "Well done," he remarked. "Cunning." He seemed not to want to say more and Alison was equally silent.

243

I thought "cunning" was a regrettable choice if indeed Jonathan had changed the painting. I began to realize that despite its beauty the joy was gone for me. Part of it stemmed from the memory of Mr. Paul's last visit. I thought of asking Alison to move the canvas up to the main gallery. But the locksmith was coming and it would seem flighty of me, ridiculous, and I stayed quiet.

"You have the cosmopolitan eye," Randy told me. "Very good of you to spot this." He turned to study me. "I wonder if you've noticed anything changed about Jonathan?"

"I haven't seen him."

"But when you did—I understand you had an afternoon at his studio—did he seem erratic? Granted, you didn't know him before this summer."

"And don't know him now," I said firmly.

"He's going through a particularly difficult period, and I don't hold him entirely responsible for, well, running off the rails perhaps—just a little."

I didn't want to hear about it. I thought being blunt might put a quick end to the session. "Do you mean you think he's losing his mind?"

"Oh, no! No, nothing so drastic as all that. But very eccentric. When he's coming out of a slump and beginning to work again, he always tortures himself with self-doubts."

"Some of the best actors and actresses say they never get over stage fright."

"It's something like that."

"Trollope, or some other writer, always started a new book the same day he finished one." And then there was Hemingway, I thought, who hadn't come out of *his* slump.

Alison, moving restlessly around the room, said, "Why don't you keep at least one ashtray here, Tyler?"

"I will, I will." Jumping from tragedies to ashtrays and back again to watch Randy lacing his long fingers. He said

244

slowly, "It's not an easy spot for me to be in. My business depends on the success of the exhibition, and that depends on Jonathan."

How did I get to be a member of the team—nearly as cozy as Miles thinks we are! I yearned for them to be gone, but I had no clue as to how to be rid of them.

Then it seemed as if miraculously Savannah was rescuing me. She appeared at the door and beckoned to Alison. But what she said was, "There's a cop upstairs. Wants to see everybody."

28.

Miles had gone to the police to report a missing person.

"We all know him," the sergeant said. "Just wanted to get it straight. We don't want to interfere in any family quarrels, but you know how it is—"

Alison was at her best handling such a matter. Even Randy kept out of it while she led the officer to the back deck and we all sat down, except Savannah who fetched iced tea. It was a cool and pleasant morning. It would be warm later, but the sky was Rubens blue today, adorned with white, drifting clouds, *The Farm at Laeken*, painted in the early seventeenth century. A domestic scene with cows. a cart laden with vegetables, farm girls, birds, I was dreamy, until I remembered that probably now my promised job at the gallery was gone. Alison would not have minded my working for old Mr. Paul, but for Randy, even though she had Randy under her spell, a different matter entirely.

And it wouldn't be the same, in any case. But there were other galleries.

"Is there anything you can add, miss?" The policeman was speaking to me in a fatherly tone.

I said, "No, everyone knows Stella has been planning to leave for several days."

They laughed in chorus, and I realized I must have repeated what the others had said. I had been drifting, when I should have been paying attention. I sat up straight and thought about mentioning the snapshots. But my own films had got me into too much trouble already.

When the policeman had gone, Alison remarked that he had been as considerate as anyone could have asked. "They're a good bunch," she added. "I suspect that Jonathan has always remembered to be generous at Christmastime. They've had to bring Miles home often. They know the way."

No one alluded to the days of nearly seven years ago when policemen came and stayed to trample, question, and search. We moved back indoors. In departing, the policeman had said to let him know when we heard from Stella, or if Burton got out of hand.

"He didn't ask to see the head of the house," I said, thinking out loud.

Again everyone looked at me, and finally Alison said, "I truly think it's high time you had a day away from us, Tyler. Go somewhere and have fun—all on your own. Take any of the cars, or if you don't feel like driving, we'll call a cab."

"I'll be leaving before noon," Randy said, "if Tyler cares to wait—"

"No, go now," Alison said, speaking softly, with only gentle concern in the green eyes.

I went.

The taximan seemed glad to see me. He asked how I'd been making out, such a hot summer. We discussed the weather until we reached the edge of town, and I asked him if

247

he would stop at the Snap and Shutter for just a minute and wait for me.

I asked Mr. Trynne if Stella Burton had finally got her films. He leaned on the counter and rolled his gray eyes heavenward. "Didn't I tell you? Didn't I tell you? They all want their pictures in five minutes, less even. Then they forget all about them. *Her* bunch came in. They're still here. Do you want them?"

"You mean I can *have* them?"

"Well, if you pay for them, certainly. You both work at the same place, right?"

I said, "Um. How much are they?"

There were three packages. Luckily I had spare traveler's checks I'd been carrying in my wallet for two months now, nearly three months. "It's a nice day," Mr. Trynne said. "Enjoy yourself."

"I'll try."

Stella's packets seemed to burn like hot lead in my shoulder bag. I asked my driver to let me off at the depot. He said the next train would be nearly an hour from now. I said I had plenty to think about. "You know what time you're coming back?" he asked. "I could arrange to be here."

"No, I'm free as a bird today. And I may take the bus."

"What bus?" he asked blankly.

"The one that St—" I caught myself. "The bus that stops somewhere here in town," I corrected. "I don't know where because I've never taken it, but I've heard of others who have."

"Must be a ghost bus, little lady. Anyway I'll probably be here for most trains. And if I ain't, you still got my card?"

"Yes, of course, it's still in my wallet." I went inside the station to wait, feeling that he might never leave if I didn't get out of sight. I had plenty to think about. The obvious thing was that I had heard Randy wrong. He had taken Stella

248

to some other bus. There were plenty of towns along the North Shore, and there must be plenty of buses. No big deal.

In Chicago I walked through a dozen stores along the Magnificent Mile. I sat in a new hotel lobby and admired its splendid furnishings. I thought of trying to get a matinee ticket for a theater, but a movie was easier, and in the end I settled for popcorn, candy bar, and a film that told me more about the pores on Candice Bergen's face and the pimples on some actor's back than I really wanted to know. Randy Paul had no blemishes on his back at least. When I thought about it, if Randy and Alison were accustomed to making love in the maze on sunny days, he should have more tan. And if I intended to sit in a movie thinking about the house of Clinton, I was wasting everybody's time. I walked down Michigan Avenue to the Art Institute and went in to find the Clintons on permanent exhibition. They were in a second-floor wing, and I sat on a bench in the center of the vast room, feeling as awed as if I'd never before seen his work.

After I finally left the building I went to a restaurant, ordered coffee, asked for a lot of change, and tried to phone the travel writers' office in Washington, D.C. A very nice man told me he would do his best to locate my Aunt Lynne and tell her I would really like to know where to send a letter. He said someone in the organization probably knew where she was. He wanted to know if I had tried the Ritz in Madrid, or the Cadogan in London, or the Cancun Caribe? I laughed and said, "Mr. Fischer, the next person that tells me it's a small world is going to get a punch in the nose."

He said to hang in there and he'd put someone on her trail. Now that he thought about it, there was a junket to Red China she might be on. He could get a list.

I thanked him and went to look for a hotel. I chose one near the Chicago Tribune Tower which was large and pleasant, with a coffee shop that had reasonable prices. Alison had offered to let me use the Clinton place in town, but I had said I wasn't sure where I'd be and I just wanted to wander. Maybe go to Springfield and look at all the Lincoln memorials. I had two free nights and days.

I would give Stella's photographs to Miles when I got back, I decided, and after that I managed to keep the Clintons out of mind most of the time.

29.

So much for planning ahead. The first thing Savannah had to tell me on my first morning back was that Miles had disappeared. "He didn't come home two nights in a row. Randy Paul stayed over last night, slept in the back room here. Mizz Alison was so upset."

I said, "I don't see why she'd even be wondering about it. I'm sure he must have stayed away before, when he's drinking, and now that he's probably out looking for Stella—at least that's a perfectly legitimate excuse to go on a tear. I don't see how anybody could be surprised that she's gone—she kept telling us she was leaving. We all knew it."

"Something we didn't *all* know," Savannah said, in a husky voice. She'd remembered that Randy Paul was still sleeping nearby, and she made a motion for me to come closer and listen.

"All right," I played the game, "what didn't we know?"

"Stella wasn't his wife. Ain't his wife, wherever she be."

Now I sat and gaped while Savannah, speaking softly, filled in the scanty background as much as she knew. Alison had gone to turn off the air conditioning—anyway that was the reason she gave—when Miles failed to show up by midnight last night. I murmured that Miles often didn't show up by midnight, wasn't that right? Savannah said this was different and to hush if I wanted to hear about it. I subsided.

"She's his sister. Now how do you like them apples?"

"Is Alison certain? How could she be?"

"She poked in their papers—some of 'em leastways, just trying to find out something helpful." Here Savannah paused to look heavenward and angelic for a moment. "Not just being nosy as you and me would've been, right? Anyway, Stella's driver's license is made out to Stella Anna Burton, and so's her Social Security card, and her bank account."

"I've got all of those things," I said, "and it doesn't say married or unmarried."

"I got 'em, too." Savannah set her jaw and looked scornful before she continued. "Mine says Savannah Bertrand Hamilton. Not Savannah Louise Hamilton. A married woman uses her maiden name on them legal documents. You ought to know that."

"I don't think it's a law. It strikes me as very flimsy evidence—"

"How would a family album strike you, Tyler Ames? With pictures of you and your brother and your ma and pa?"

"Do you mean Alison went through all of Stella's things?"

Savannah nodded solemnly. "Felt she had to—in the circumstances."

I gulped in sudden horror. "My God, Savannah! They were there!"

"I tole you they were there, her 'n' him both, going through the works."

252

"I mean Stella's papers were there! Why?"

"Well, she left her purse—" Savannah's black eyes went round with shock as the realization sank in. "Oh, my God, you right. Oh, my Lord in heaven, we better find Blase. We better find somebody!"

"I don't think it's up to us," I said. "At least now." I hastened to add that I wasn't being one of those inhuman humans who stand by, or rather *don't* stand by but drive on, or lock their doors, or look the other way when someone needs help. "It would be different if Alison and Randy hadn't already looked and weren't taking an interest. You can call Blase, if you can find him. For some reason, I think he intended to let us know when he came back from—wherever he went. Stella planned to leave. She was talking about a new life. So perhaps she means just that. A new name, identity, everything. Maybe she was planning a full-blown case of amnesia. Did she leave her money behind?"

Savannah shook her head. "They didn't say."

"Were you *with* them?" I asked. "Or did they tell you all this?"

"Neither one." Savannah looked almost furtive. "I listened. I served coffee, and I didn't always leave *all the way*. Ordinary times I wouldn't be bothered, you see, but I figure with Miles gone and Blase who knows where and Himself probably up at that island, I better keep my eyes and ears open, no matter *who* is talking. That's one thing about being black. They don't see me. What I mean is—"

"I know what you mean," I said. "You're not talking about color, you're talking about being invisible—and you've got no idea how I wanted to be, just for a while."

"Being black isn't just for a while, and I *wouldn't* want to change either!"

"I know, I know, or I don't know, but we're getting off the track about Stella. If she took the money, maybe that's all she needed for that new life."

"We may never know, I guess. Less Miles finds out and decides to tell us." All of a sudden Savannah laughed. It wasn't her usual robust outburst that made you want to join her. It had a little meanness, just a touch. "Alison—Mizz Clinton—was just as surprised as you 'n' me about Stella and him being kin. Ain't got the least idea why, and it buggin' her. I guess she wonder what else Himself hasn't tole her."

I remembered Stella's packages of photographs in my purse. I would put them away unopened until Miles got back. He was the next of kin, as Savannah had unintentionally reminded me.

The intercom shrilled. Alison wanted me in her office. Savannah said, "Maybe you going to get the straight of it, now."

I said, "I doubt it, but if I do I'll share it with you. I hate secrets."

I hated the photographs lying in the clutter of my shoulder bag. But if anyone wanted to hide a dead body—my mind recoiled from the use of the phrase at this moment—my purse would be the place, my father had always said. And my mother had always added that a lit professor should be fired for promulgating clichés among the young. Then he had said anyone who used promulgating should be locked up. All this silliness brought me to Alison's door half smiling and forgetful of the present.

She said, "I take it from your expression that you haven't heard the latest."

I said, "Um." And raised a politely inquiring brow lest Savannah catch hell for gossiping.

"Stella's dead," Alison said.

I fell into a chair and waited.

She pushed her hair back from her forehead as if it would help her to think. "The police called me because Miles isn't here. Savannah tell you?"

I nodded.

"They are almost sure it's Stella. I have to—identify her, if she doesn't show up soon."

"Identify her," I repeated in a dazed way. I'd read a lot of thrillers, but I had encountered sudden death only twice in my life and there'd been no question of identity. "I guess that's routine," I said lamely, hoping to comfort Alison who looked stricken for once.

"Not in this case. She was run over by a subway train two nights ago—but her hair is red and I guess—what remains— could be Stella. Oh, Tyler, will you drive into town with me, please?"

I gripped the sides of the chair and wanted to shout, "Why me? Why not Randy? Savannah?" But reason returned. It would be easier for a virtual stranger to look upon poor Stella's body. I nodded reluctantly. "Are you going to try to find Mr. Clinton? Doesn't he have to know?"

"We talked about that—Randy and I—way into the night. He's still sleeping. I think it must have been nearly dawn when he got to bed. If Jonathan is working as hard as we suspect, we feel it is better to handle it all by ourselves. Jonathan has known Stella for twenty years—maybe more. It will be a blow, no matter when he hears about it. We can spare him a little more time. Anyway, that's what we decided." She gazed at me with tired, overbright eyes. She was running on nervous energy obviously. "Is there something you want to ask?"

"Did she fall—or do you think—do the police think—she jumped in front of the train?"

"Fell, beyond doubt. There was a rock concert letting out. A jam of people I hear. She may have been drinking, or stoned on pot, so they tell me." Alison looked at her watch. "We'd better get it over with. There's always a chance it isn't Stella, of course. There are a lot of redheaded women in the world, with good bodies, but a bus ticket to Detroit in her

255

pocket and the fact that Miles reported her missing somehow got them to wondering."

"Why Detroit?" I asked when we were on our way, with Alison driving the Mercedes expertly.

"No reason that I know of. And we don't have Miles to ask. Randy and I looked in the apartment, but there wasn't a clue."

I glanced at her profile. She was concentrating on the expressway traffic as we neared the city. *She's not going to tell me about what they did find.* Alison wore enormous sunglasses, but her mouth was pinched and the tendons in her slim neck tautly drawn. "If it *is* Stella," she said, "I guess that means we have another funeral on our hands. Or maybe just a simple burial. We should wait for Miles to let us know— what he wants—"

It was Stella, and we waited for Miles for three days. Then he was back, and—much as we had expected—was sleeping off a monumental hangover, Savannah reported. Stella was cremated and her ashes were buried somewhere on the estate. Miles said he was convinced Jonathan woud have wanted it that way.

When Randy seemed to squirm at the idea, Miles peered at him nearsightedly, and said, "Do you think I should go and *ask* Jonathan?"

"Go where?" Randy had returned blankly at first, and then added, "You mean all the way to Isle Royale?"

"Is that where he is?"

"How would I know?" Randy looked helplessly to Alison with a bewildered how-did-I-get-into-this-conversation expression. He lifted his shoulders and his sandy eyebrows in a gesture of complete puzzlement. "I thought—" He paused and glanced again at Alison. "Didn't you say he took the *Agatha Two?*" The *Agatha II* was Clinton's boat, the cabin cruiser, Savannah informed me in a low voice.

"No," Alison said, "I said the boat was getting repaired. Blase told me days ago." She looked disconsolate and almost too drained to speak. "Isle Royale is millions of miles away," she told Randy, or whoever wanted to listen. "I've only been there once and I hated it. It's almost total wilderness—the part Jonathan prefers, and Agatha was fond of it, too. For them it was a change, to be sure. You don't just get in your little boat and chug up there, Randy dear. It's in Lake Superior. The middle of nowhere."

"It's a national park," I said helpfully. "My Aunt Lynne has been there, too. She liked it." Then I gave Alison an apologetic smile. "I can see how lots of people wouldn't. You get there by boat or seaplane and there aren't any roads."

Alison shuddered. "And timber wolves; don't remind me."

"Moose, too," I said.

"The point is," Alison spoke again, sounding more cheerful, "it's really too far to try to reach someone when the matter isn't urgent. Getting Jonathan back to decide where Stella's ashes should be placed would hardly help anyone, including Stella, Miles."

He nodded, in agreement for once. "There can be a service when he comes back," I put in and immediately was sorry I was invading their territory again. But nobody seemed to object. Indeed Randy looked relieved and said that was a good idea. Miles said nothing but went out without banging the door behind him as he often did. Probably his head was aching dreadfully. His shoulders in the flannel shirt again had been uncharacteristically slumped. He'd worn a half-defiant, half-defeated look the brief time he'd been in the kitchen.

Colin, who probably had been listening in Stella's office, sidled up to me and slipped his hand in mine. "I never thought Miles really liked her so much," he whispered, and I remembered that Colin, at least, thought the deeply dejected man had lost a wife he was usually at odds with, not a sister, for whom he must have cared once.

257

"We've all got to get back to work," Alison said. "Colin, you can watch all the television you can stand today. I'll need Tyler and Savannah's help."

He ran off without a backward glance, while we waited for her orders.

"I'll have to think of something to distract Miles—get him out of the apartment," she began, but Randy, who had walked to the back door, said Miles was leaving on his own, in the jeep. Alison said crisply, "Then you girls can get right to it—I want you to clear out Stella's things before he gets back. You can box them and store them in the garage spare room. If Miles wants to go through them later, they're his, of course. But I think it will spare him pain if he doesn't have to attend to it himself." She frowned in concentration for a moment. "Am I forgetting anything, Randy?"

"No, but if the girls need help with the boxes—"

"I'm sure we won't," I said. And Alison nodded. "Stella never went in for many clothes," she commented. "Just pack away her personal things."

Randy suddenly intervened. "Alison, you'd better prepare them for a surprise. Both Tyler and Savannah are discreet— and there's not much point in trying to hide Stella's secret."

Savannah slid a glance at me and quickly looked at Randy again, waiting for him to continue.

Alison said, "They didn't use the same bedroom, you'll find. As a matter of fact, that will make your work easier. Stella's things are all in her own room."

That was all Alison intended to say. Randy opened his mouth and shut it again.

"Let's get moving," Savannah said. "There be boxes in the garage."

30.

The apartment smelled of whiskey but it was immaculate, or nearly so. I peeked into Miles's bedroom and saw that he must have slept on top of the spread. It was crumpled where he probably had flung himself. A damp bath towel lay on a chair, but nothing else seemed to be out of order. There were shelves filled with books and a typewriter on a desk with stacks of paper beside it.

It was early afternoon but all the shades were drawn. Savannah gave a quick tug, sending two of them snapping into their rollers, and turned on a floor lamp.

"Lord God, how I hate going through other people's things," she muttered.

"Why don't you sit down and let me get started?" I volunteered. "You don't get a chance to sit in the daytime very often. Not lately anyway. And I really don't mind. I didn't know Stella well. I'm sorry for her, and even sorrier for Miles, but it must be much harder on all the rest of you."

"Somethin' to that, all right," Savannah agreed, and lowered herself into an armchair. "Would it be out of order if I turned on the TV?" she asked. "Anything to get my mind off things."

"Please do."

"Yell when you're ready. I'll help haul the stuff."

I looked in some surprise at the loaded bookshelves which also lined the living room. But Miles usually had a paperback book stuffed into his hip pocket. Here were hardcovers ranging from Greek plays to Yale's Younger Poets in a series. Classics, biographies, art books, criticism, very few novels.

"Whut are you looking at?" Savannah asked. Then she peered at an object on a table. "Them's Colin's binoculars. He been asking every day have I seen 'em. Guess he forgot he left 'em here."

I put the binoculars, which were on a table by the window, into her lap before I headed for Stella's bedroom down a small hall. I opened the door and stood on the threshold. The room looked as if Stella had never left. Perfumes and colognes were lined on the dressing table. A silver-back comb and brush set with matching hand mirror, all monogrammed with Cs swirling. And a heap of lavender matches. Agatha Clinton. Agatha who had been dead for years when one of these had been dropped in the clearing on the day someone had tried to trip me.

Now Stella was dead and I would probably never know why she had hated me. I sighed and began packing the items from Stella's bureau drawers and her closets. Some of them were very old-fashioned, many were monogrammed, but all with the letter C. A marcasite hat pin, a lighter with a diamond C, and a brushed gold C on a brown leather bag, on two expensive evening bags. The tissue paper they lay in crackled with age. Obviously no one, not even Stella, had used them for years. Jonathan must have given her everything that had been in Agatha's wardrobe, or perhaps Alison had.

On a closet shelf, in a faded, pink-flowered, chintz-covered hatbox, under a knitted winter hat, I found an old candy box with papers in it. Papers which had been wrinkled and smoothed out. A pile of Clinton's notes, unmistakably.

"Ain't you about through?" Savannah called petulantly.

"Yes, in a minute!" I stuffed the papers in my skirt pocket. It was a khaki skirt and the pocket buttoned. The papers scarcely made a bulge in it. I hadn't the least notion why I decided to take them with me, but there'd been a fuss about missing notes already. And Savannah didn't need more trouble. Alison might begin to wonder what was taking so long.

"Come and help with these boxes!" I yelled, and we finished the job in half an hour. Savannah had clucked her tongue at all the bottles and monogrammed items on the bureau. I hadn't packed them, waiting to see if she thought we ought to leave them. She said, "They been here too long already," then brought paper toweling from the kitchen and put them in a box which she carefully marked, FACE STUFF.

"Well, let's go," she said, but something was wrong. Something was missing. I stood trying to think, but I couldn't bring it into focus.

In my own room later on I looked at one or two of the notes Stella had hoarded. One said, "Please don't burn the toast. Carbon may cause cancer." Another asked, "If soufflés don't travel any better than wine, why make them?" I smiled at Clinton's bluntness. I would return these to him if I had a chance and let him dispose of them, so that Savannah

261

wouldn't be blamed. Meanwhile, I put them in my Valentine box.

In the morning Alison phoned before seven-thirty. "Tyler, try to hurry through breakfast, please. The press conference is set for this morning, and I'd like you to help out, if you don't mind. Let Colin skip another day—he's already ahead of himself, isn't he?"

"Yes, he's fine."

Savannah was baking cookies and Colin was waiting to drop in the chocolate chips.

"You get any sleep last night?" she asked me. "Must have been plenty of racket going on."

"I didn't hear anything. I think I could have slept through doomsday."

"They brought in three more paintings from the studio."

"They? Jonathan and Miles?" Wanting to ask, And Blase, too?

"Randy and Miles. Okay, that's enough chips," this last to Colin, who put the bag down and said he wanted to see the paintings.

"You better keep out from underfoot!" Savannah yelled after him, but he was gone. "You got time for coffee and a roll," she told me. "Ain't nobody come yet."

I sat at the bar, wondering what was on her mind. She had a way of pursing her mouth when she wanted to ask something and hadn't decided whether to speak or not.

Finally she said, "All them old things up there—" Head inclined toward the back and the apartment above the garages.

"Monogrammed C," I helped her along.

"Jonathan gave 'em to her. She was awfully good to Mizz Clinton when she—Mizz Agatha—was took bad toward the end."

262

"Took bad?" I repeated in astonishment. "But she drowned!"

"She would've died anyway, Doc Gibson said. Maybe a year or two, maybe more. Maybe less. I've got to tell you somethin', Tyler. I think somebody ought to know. Somebody younger'n I am. Closer to the boy." Her voice had dropped to a hoarse whisper. She leaned across the counter and spoke directly to me. "There's been too much funny stuff going on and too many folks turning up missing, you know?"

I nodded. Her solemnity convinced me this was no time to protest that she was just as close to Colin as I was. "Stella was his—Clinton's—woman—what you want t'call it—mistress? way back when he was gone."

I swallowed hard, wondering if I really had heard the words. Savannah nodded somberly. "Anyway when I first come here that's how it had been, somewhere over there. Europe, wherever. I don't think it went on after he came home and I know it didn't after he married Alison. I'm sure of it— even if Mr. Clinton don't seem to have nobody now, not even his wife."

"Savannah, how do you know all this? Did Mrs. Agatha know?"

"No, I'm pretty sure of that. They took a lot of pains to keep it from her. Mr. Clinton met up with Miles and Stella in Paris, somewhere like that, and after Miles saved Mr Clinton's life, they came here to live. That's why I guess they made up that story about Stella being Miles's wife."

I asked again, "How did you know?"

"Blase told me once, after his mother died. He got drunk —that's not something he ever does, but he tied one on just before he left for Spain."

My next question stumped her: "Why didn't they marry— after Agatha was gone?"

"I don't really know. Either it had already wore itself out

263

—their carrying-on, what you want to call it—or Mr. Clinton might have took it into his head that Stella maybe had something to do with Mizz Agatha's fall. He nearly went out of his mind, I can tell you. He was ready to blame anybody, believe anybody. He really loved that woman even if she couldn't perform as a wife. We all did. I think he was still out of his head when he up and married Alison. *That* didn't last, I can tell you. That honeymoon was over and done with before the sheets got cold, you ask me."

I thought about it. I knew I should hurry but I couldn't bear to leave just yet. "How could Stella stay on—with the new wife here?"

"I don't suppose she would've if the marriage had took. And something else that was funny—queer funny—Stella took to religion again. She'd been born a Catholic and she went back to it. Started going to church and all. She kept on modeling naked when they asked her—the old man or Blase —that didn't mean nothin' to any of 'm—but I don't think she ever thought about another man. So that wasn't no problem, and I would bet my bottom dollar Alison never got wind of any of whut I been telling you. She wouldn't have kept Stella, you can bet on that, or Miles either. She would've *liked* to get rid of us all, make a clean sweep once she got that wedding ring, but she didn't dare fire any of us. Mr. Clinton wouldn't stand for it. She'd been an *employee* same as us— when Mizz Agatha was alive—and right up to the day they got married, her and him. And that's just about all she is now, except she *thinks* she's the boss."

Savannah glanced at the intercom which was ringing. "That'll be her—wanting you to show off what a nice home-folks household we got here." Her voice was heavy with sarcasm. "We was all here before Missy Alison got herself hired. She'd like to forget that."

264

"That's why you're all on a first-name basis," I mused out loud. "I had figured it was democracy."

"Democracy, hell," said Savannah. "You better scoot now."

As I reached the door, she called out, "Sometime—later on today—I got something more to say to you, Tyler. Might as well get it off my mind."

I said, "All right. I'll be back whenever I can get away."

The gallery was filled with smoke. Three men were making notes, and Randy rose to greet me as I came in and to introduce the visitors. His pale face seemed to blend with the haze. I decided he'd been working indoors so much he'd lost what little tan he'd had in June. Losing his father had made him more somber, though his manners were as courteous as ever. There were five newspapermen in all. Two were wandering at the L end of the room, studying a new work which hung there and talking in low tones. The low glass and chrome table was cluttered with coffee cups, cocktail glasses, pastries, crumbs, and tiny linen napkins embroidered with Agatha's monogram.

I realized that I hadn't caught anybody's name; I was still thinking of the revelations Savannah had thrown at my head, or so it felt. I needed time to think, but one of the men, a short, plump fellow with gold-rimmed glasses, was questioning me. "Could I see the photographs, Miss Ames?"

I looked at Alison. She said, "I told them about the changes in the painting. We brought it up for today—I hope you don't mind." *Windless Afternoon* indeed was hanging on the west wall of the room and I hadn't noticed it.

"I'll have to get them," I said. I was astonished that Alison had mentioned them and my reaction must have been obvious. She followed me into the hall to explain. She put her hand on my arm and I could feel the tension, even though she seemed perfectly poised. "Jonathan would be the last to object that his eccentricities be known. Anything that will get the public interested helps the exhibition. I sometimes think half his behavior is calculated to get attention."

"I'll get the pictures," I said. Her skin looked tightly drawn to the bone. Her green eyes were piercing.

She asked, "Are you making a judgment, Tyler? Disapproving?"

"No, not at all. It's just that—" I couldn't say it was beginning to be a burden, a Sisyphus chore, to try to sort out the puzzles of this household. Though no one had actually asked me to do so. Like the ancient Corinthian, rolling his enormous boulder up a mountain slope for eternity, each time I thought I had found an answer to a question, there was another puzzlement. "It's really nothing. I guess I'm tired today." She patted my arm and said, "They'll be gone soon."

When I came back it was even smokier. Words like "organic," "dynamic," "vaporous," and "cataclysmic" were floating as easily as Alison's smoke rings. The man in the gold-rimmed glasses studied the snapshots and made notes. One man was asking Randy about what celebrities were invited and could be expected. A tall, lanky fellow peered at objects in the room as if they had price tags.

Alison's eyes were watchful, but her manner combined both benevolence and a certain regality. As if she'd always been a hostess here, never a waitress, nor a secretary. Her personal bubble had been carefully built over the years and I saw it as an accomplishment, if only it didn't seem somehow as visible and tough as Plexiglas.

All five visitors, in turn, handled the photographs and compared them with the painting. One voiced a disappointment they all shared, that Jonathan himself was not here. "Will we have a chance to talk with him before the actual opening?" one asked. "His new use of black seems revolutionary." Another man said Clinton's style had changed but he couldn't quite grasp what was different.

266

A younger man taking notes said he was vague about the Modern Art museum story—"Would someone fill me in?"

Alison related the tale again, as if she had once memorized it. Pens scratched busily across paper pads.

"You were the one who first noticed the changes in this painting?" Gold-glasses asked me.

I nodded. A red-bearded man commented, "That was very observant. You're an art student?"

"Was. I'm a tutor now."

"We expect Miss Ames to work for us in the fall," Randy said.

Both Alison and I looked at him in surprise. Then she seemed to nod in approval. He shook his head slightly. "I can't get out of the habit of saying 'we.' I mean, *I* expect her, if she still wants to come."

This was an odd moment to be asking me, I thought, but I nodded. Alison said nothing. She was still wearing her plastic smile.

The red-bearded man had asked a question; apparently he was speaking to me, but I hadn't heard. I apologized and he repeated, "How did Mr. Clinton look when you saw him the other night?"

"I beg your pardon?" *How did he know?*

"Mrs. Clinton tells me you saw him here in the gallery. You were the last to see him, before he went north, is that right?"

I shot an appalled glance at Alison. She said, "Tyler is really very tired today. We've had so much extra work lately. Do you think we could let her leave now?"

Their feet shuffled, and the red-bearded one plainly showed his annoyance that his question would not be answered. I thought, for Jonathan's sake, a little dissembling was in order. "He looked well," I said, sounding casual but

267

positive, and Randy winked approval at me. Even Alison smiled and seemed to relax.

"Tyler, take the day off, please." Her eyes added, *You've earned it*. She whispered, "Jonathan told me—he didn't mean to frighten you."

I thanked her, but my plans were to take Colin to the library. I wanted to look up old newspapers. "Mr. Clinton is looking forward to the exhibition," I added one more lie, in departing. "We all are." That, at least, was true.

31.

Mrs. Murkell, the head librarian, told me they were sorry but there wasn't room to keep newspapers for long, and they didn't have microfilm equipment but were hoping for it.

I had given her the approximate dates I wanted and she said hesitantly, but bright-eyed with interest, "If it's about the accident on the Clinton estate—"

I nodded.

"Well, you can find it at the main library in Chicago. Didn't Mr. Burton tell you?"

"No, why on earth would he?"

"Well, he looked it up—I thought perhaps—"

I tried to concentrate. "Why would he want to look it up? Wasn't he here at the time?"

"He was in the veterans' hospital, having plastic surgery. Extensive surgery on his neck, hands, his arms, too, I believe. Poor man—he's been through such a lot." She looked to see if

269

our conversation was bothering anyone, but no one was near. "I read about his wife's death. I hope you'll tell him how sorry we all were and we hope he'll be back soon."

I wondered how she knew he was gone, had been gone, but I didn't want to question her. "He's back," I said, to put her mind at rest.

"I mean back here," she corrected me. "He uses the library a lot, you know. As a matter of fact, several of his requests have come in—we use the interlibrary loan system. You might tell him that the books are here."

What a day this has been! I thought, feeling almost dizzy with the surprises there'd been since morning. "I think I'm getting an information overload," I smiled at her. "All sorts of unexpected news today, but will you tell me what kind of books Miles asks for? That is, if it's not betraying a confidence—"

"Why, no. He's writing a biography of Mr. Clinton. I thought everyone knew that."

I stared at her. She said, "Excuse me." She lowered her head and a contact lens fell into her palm. Then she removed the other one. "My eyes get tired," she explained. "I'm trying to get accustomed to soft lenses, but I never last the whole day without going back to my specs." For the first time I realized that she didn't have foxy, overly curious eyes, and her smile was friendlier than I had recognized. The mote was in my own eye. Mrs. Murkell was a sort of public servant, doing her job and doing it well. My own blindness had made me view her as a stereotype, dreamed up from a dozen old movies, not as a real person. "I'll tell Miles," I promised her. "If you like, I can take the books to him."

"Thank you, but he reads them here. We have a room in the basement with a typewriter. He likes to work there. Or did. Maybe now he'll work at home. I don't suppose he'll keep the cat, do you?"

270

It was my turn to say, "Excuse me," and I followed it with an admission that I hadn't the faintest idea what she meant about the cat.

"Mrs. Burton's cat. He's allergic to it."

Stella's cat! That was what had been bothering me about the apartment. That was what was missing. Plaid, the cat. Had she taken it with her—when she left her purse and most of her belongings? And where was Plaid now?

I drove home slowly, worried that I might be guilty of "blind driving" because I was thinking so hard. At a stoplight when I'd failed to respond fast enough to the green, a man had shouted, "Lady driver!" at me and leaned on his horn.

But I made it back to the estate and parked the car in the garage. Savannah was alone in the kitchen. I was bursting to tell her about Miles and his writing, but she had been waiting all day to finish her talk with me. She had lemonade ready and we took our glasses to the deck.

"What I really want you to understand," she said, speaking barely above a whisper, "is that Herself"—a slight nod to indicate Alison was meant—"is not above lying when it suits her purposes."

"Well, neither am I," I said, remembering this morning and the reply I'd given the red-bearded newspaperman about Jonathan's health and how he'd "looked"—when I had seen only a shadow of a man, not the man himself.

"I'm talking about hurtful lies," Savannah continued. "Did she ever tell you Stella was a whatchacallit—a klepto—steals things?"

"Yes, is it—was it true?"

"Not at all."

"But Alison must have believed it was true—"

"I don't think so. I think she wanted to hurt Stella in Clinton's eyes. Everybody's eyes, for all I know. The Pauls, all of

271

them. Stella never cared much for possessions. You saw what little she had. All that old stuff of Mizz Agatha's, Clinton gave her that." She thought of something else and said, "She had them matches made herself. Mizz Agatha didn't favor purple."

"But why are you telling me, Savannah? You seem so—troubled, I guess."

"I may not be around too much longer. No, don't interrupt," as I raised a hand to protest. "If anything happens to the mister, I'm quitting."

"Your husband is ill?"

"I'm talking about Mr. Clinton. I don't like this business of him bein' away so long, and holin' up so long, all summer nearly. He don't look like himself and don't act like himself —except for a little while there. Time you went to see him and then he took Colin sailing. That was the way he used to be all the time."

"We all change, grow older and change, get tired; sorry if I sound like a broken record."

"What I want to say is I hope some way you can keep an eye on the boy. I know it won't be any picnic, but maybe you can figure out a way to keep in touch. I don't want to see her taking over that child when he comes into his money. Or anytime."

"He's not very fond of her," I said. "It seems more likely his brother would look out for him."

"I would've said the same thing, but Blase ain't been himself either, if you ask me. He's been peculiar this summer. Somethin' eatin' Blase, all right. I know a little bit about it, but not enough. And he lives reckless. Who knows what could happen to Blase?"

We sat in troubled silence for a few minutes, then I remembered at least one happy circumstance. "Randy Paul offered me the job his father suggested. I can probably man-

272

age to stay in touch with Colin through Randy. Savannah, this talk is getting me horribly depressed. Can't we think about something else? I know you care about Colin, almost as if he were one of your own, and so do I. We'll both keep an eye on him. Beebee, too. Everything will be all right."

"I wish a few folks would get themselves back here," she said, still gloomy, but beginning to sound just a bit more optimistic.

"Now let me tell you something amazing," I said, and related the librarian's story about Miles and his book. By the time I got through she was grinning again and deciding she might treat herself to a cold beer.

"Ain't that the berries! He couldn't be doin' half the drinkin' everybody thinks. Miles is a author! How about that! You think he's got us all in his book?"

"You, maybe. We can ask him next time he shows up." Then I remembered something else Mrs. Murkell had told me. "What do you suppose became of Stella's cat?" I asked.

Savannah had no answer except to point out that a cat, even one that had spent most of its life indoors, could usually make out for itself, find a cozy spot somewhere.

I wondered if perhaps Stella had taken Plaid somewhere to be put to sleep mercifully, by a vet, since she couldn't travel with her and couldn't be sure anyone here would look out for her. Or if somehow she'd found another home for her. Then I wondered if she'd taken pictures of Plaid to save as I had photographed my painting. I would take one quick look to see. It wouldn't be snooping exactly. If Stella had photographed her cat, I would feel better about it. The envelopes weren't sealed anyway. The outside package had one staple holding it, for convenience that was all, not for keeping the contents secret. Even so, I felt guilty of trespassing.

And all for nothing. No cat pictures. Stella had photographed trees and parked cars, it seemed. Then a photo

273

showed Randy coming out of the studio carrying a canvas. In another Randy was pushing a painting on a dolly. Randy's Lincoln Continental was photographed, too. Twice. Two pictures were too dark to be recognizable but I studied them anyway. And wished I hadn't. At first I thought they were of two swimmers lying on a midnight beach. But then I saw they weren't swimmers, at least when the photographs were snapped.

In another envelope most of the photographs seemed to be of Clinton's studio, and in one old Mr. Paul stood clutching at his chest as if in pain. He was on the very steps of the studio but turned away from it. One hand clawed at his coat as if he were trying to open it for air. The other hand was on the doorknob as if he had just pulled the door shut. So he had gotten inside, and Stella could have proved it. Why hadn't she said anything? Couldn't she have run to help him? She must have seen it in her viewfinder. But Stella had said nothing. And now she was past saying.

I shivered and put the photographs away. But not in my grandmother's Valentine box. In the bottom drawer of the bureau which I never used. For some dark reason I didn't want to examine, I thrust them under the extra blankets stored in the drawer. And hoped I could get them out of my mind as easily.

At dinner Alison was relaxed and beautiful in another billowy gauze hostess caftan. She said, "Good news, Tyler— Colin. I've heard from a friend of Jonathan's. He phoned from Benton Harbor, I think it was. He tells me he saw Jonathan and that my husband is taking advantage of the fine weather up north." She smiled. "He said Jonathan promises to be home before the snow flies—Randy is not to worry."

"I wish I could've gone," Colin said. "I'd like a wilderness, I think." Then he grinned at me. "But I wouldn't want to miss your last days here."

I squeezed his hand. I asked Alison, "Does the friend live in Benton Harbor?"

Alison looked puzzled. "I don't think so—I gathered he was on his way home—I didn't think to ask. Why?"

"Well, it's nothing much," I said. "I just thought I might ask if Jonathan took Plaid with him."

"Took *who?*" Her eyes widened.

Colin's knee nudged mine urgently. The message flashed from my nerve ends. Alison probably never even knew Stella kept a cat, and I was spilling the beans. I coughed into my napkin, to gain time.

My eyes watered and I sipped the water Colin handed me and managed to choke a bit more. "Not a who," I gasped out, "a cat, just a cat, that was wandering around. You know, Dick Whittington and all his cats—"

Alison looked at my wineglass and back at me and shook her head. "I'm more than ever convinced," she said, "that what I'd already planned is an excellent idea. I thought we'd all take a little break this weekend. Colin can go home with Savannah—"

"Oh, boy!" signified Colin's approval.

"And you can take another little holiday, Tyler, then we can all settle down for the big push. Wind up everything after we've had a rest. Does that sound good to you?"

I nodded, wondering where on earth to go.

Wherever it was I hoped I could be in charge of the air conditioning. Lately it had been much too cold here. For the past week I'd needed my sweater indoors. Even Savannah had complained, but the house remained below sixty degrees.

32.

Sunday was hot and hazy. The skies were overcast. I went back to bed in a motel room somewhere north of Highland Park and south of Waukegan, and heard slithering tires on pavement instead of waves lapping against rocks. It must have rained during the night, but I had slept well.

I had brought churchgoing clothes, a summer voile, bought on my trip to Chicago, green shoes, white gloves, and purse. The act of getting ready was so set a pattern from the past I felt as if I had returned to a normal world again. It was still early, so I sat down again to read from a paperback copy of *Richard III*. It had notes prepared by Elizabethan authorities, "the world's foremost," according to the back jacket. But the notes were on pages facing the text and made the going easy for any reader.

"Humpbacked" in Richard's time, or Shakespeare's time, had been "bunch-backed." I wondered what a stub-footed person would have been. There must have been plenty of maimed unfortunates bumbling around. I was lucky not only to be alive, but to be alive in a day of prosthesis. Let Richard, once an archvillain, now maybe a victim, go for today. I opened *The Kenneth Grahame Day Book,* an English edition, picked up secondhand. No! On the front flyleaf in my father's neat and tiny handwriting: "Cardiff, 15 March 1944." He'd been in England, waiting for D day, along with a lot of other American boys. I pressed the book to my lips momentarily.

Perversely, it seemed, the book fell open to September 13—Colin's birthday—but Grahame's notation had no particular meaning for my life. It was September 14 that caught my full attention:

"To-day, to him gazing south with a new-born need stirring in his heart, the unseen was everything, the unknown the only real fact of life."

Gazing north or south, east or west, I had a need stirring in me. I wanted to be loved and love back, and to be needed.

I put my books away, left the motel key on the bureau and a dollar for the maid, then put my packed overnight case in the back of the Mercedes, which Alison had insisted I take. I drove slowly to the nearest village. I would pick out a church by the spire I liked best this morning, not by denomination. I was a free agent. I wondered if all free agents dreaded eating Sunday dinner alone as much as I did.

In midafternoon I parked the Mercedes in its proper stall in the garage. As a free agent I could return to my own room whenever I liked, no matter that it was earlier than expected. No one's business but mine. At least I could fix my own supper and read while I ate, if I ate at all. Lunch, though in a pleasant restaurant, had been something to be endured in loneliness.

Even the birds seemed asleep as I crossed the driveway and

277

let myself into the kitchen with the key Savannah had lent me. The house, too, was awesomely still except for the gentle whirring of the refrigerator and the clock ticking.

I walked slowly to the stairs and took a step downward, but halted with my foot in midair. Someone was talking in a low, insistent tone. Was it above or below me? Impossible to tell in this stairwell. It was Randy Paul speaking. He was pleading with someone, "Don't even think of that. It's just not possible. And it's not necessary."

I held to the railing. If I could back up without a sound and ease into the kitchen, I could leave again, but I stood as if frozen. Because Alison's voice said, "I won't let you protect the girl if it turns out to be necessary that—"

That what? Randy had intruded with an ardent, "No, not the girl! I won't have it."

"You won't have *her*, either," Alison said. "Don't even think it."

"Oh, please," It was a very tired lover's voice, sounding on the edge of hopelessness.

I could have left now, but I stayed rigid. They were talking about me. It was my right to listen and beware.

"Well, the boy can be handled easily," Alison said.

Not by you, I thought rebelliously. *He doesn't like you very much.* And if Colin had recognized Randy in the maze, whenever he had stumbled upon that act of love, agonizing in his young eyes, he probably could not be "handled" by Randy, either. Colin had loved old Mr. Paul. He had seemed mostly indifferent to Randy, when I thought about it. If anything happened to Jonathan, if he was really as ill as he had looked that one afternoon, would Alison marry Randy? It seemed likely. As Jonathan's widow would she automatically be Colin's guardian? Or would his brother, who was of age, but was not married, be the one? My father's estate had not been large enough to cause any stir, but Jonathan's would be. And I had been the only survivor, except for my Aunt

278

Lynne, who was wealthier by far than her brother had ever been. She had inherited from her husband a comfortable amount, enough to make her independent, and her books sold well. I'd never had occasion to worry about wills and inheritances and guardians. I wondered why it bothered me so very much now as I backed away at last and moved quietly outdoors again, taking a seat on the deck. The sun had not come out but a breeze had cooled the air. A hint of autumn, though August had almost a week remaining.

After all Jonathan Clinton was very much alive and enjoying a wilderness. The last remark I'd overheard just before I moved away from the stairs had been an innocuous one. "I should have adopted him right at the beginning. Everything would have been better. I wasn't thinking—"

Randy had snorted at that. An Alison who wasn't thinking was indeed an odd concept. I'd almost smiled. If Alison cared enough about the boy to adopt him, maybe she cared much more than she seemed to. Lots of people can't show emotion easily. So Alison was one of them. If there were any way to tell Alison why Colin didn't like the maze—it would help her to get closer to him, perhaps. But there wasn't any way without getting involved. Embarrassingly involved.

It would even be embarrassing to be caught sitting here, I decided, but where to wander? It looked as if the rain would begin at almost any moment. I thought of Blase's cabin. He would not be there and he probably never bothered to lock his door. It had been swinging open the one time I saw it, and might be again. I wished I could change my clothes, but I didn't want to go back into the house for any reason. The voices might have been coming from the gallery, but they could have been in the lounge. I wouldn't run the risk.

The cabin door was ajar. I stepped into the anteroom and picked my way past the logs and abandoned blocks of marble and granite. And opened the inner door.

Blase Clinton, in wrinkled shorts, was sleeping on the couch where once the nude Stella lay. My gasp was just a sudden intake of breath but it was enough to waken him. He sat up instantly and blinked at me. And immediately looked relieved. I wondered who it was he'd feared it might be. He said, "Oh, it's you, Tyler. Welcome." And motioned to a swaybacked chair.

I sat gingerly, not wanting to linger now that the cabin wasn't unoccupied as I'd thought.

"What's on your mind?" he asked.

"Plaid," I said.

"Plaid's here, somewhere. I've been feeding her. Sometimes she prefers to catch her own dinner. I'd post a warning for the birds, if I knew their language."

His nose wrinkled. "I thought Stella had her trained but Plaid seems to think this whole place is a litter box. Shall we go outdoors?"

The smell of cat was overpowering, now that I was over my surprise at seeing him, and my worries about Plaid. "It's raining," I said. "Not hard, but too wet to sit in."

"I have a screened and roofed porch," he mentioned. "Follow me."

The porch was on the lake side but screened in copper mesh as well as trees and neglected shrubbery. The porch, too, was neglected, but the cat hadn't invaded it. The furniture was redwood, weathered and dusty. Last year's leaves were brittle in corners where they had blown through a torn screen or a door left open. A sketch pad lay beside a blackened coffeepot, and there were two chipped stoneware mugs —one with lipstick.

"Did you finish Stella's—the sculpture she was the model for?" I hadn't been aware of it indoors but I hadn't really looked.

He shrugged. "I'm not working at the moment." He was

wearing a bath towel around his neck. He had flicked it from the back of a straight chair as we came out. Now he used it to dust a redwood seat for me. He sat on the wide arm of a lounge chair and stared toward the lake.

"I didn't see your car," I said. "I wouldn't have intruded if I'd known you were here."

"Lent it," he said. For minutes more he sat without stirring, then he turned and looked at me quizzically. "Out of the rain? All the way up here?"

"Well, I was looking for the cat." I sighed. "And I didn't want to go in the house."

"Why not?" His navy eyes were almost black again. "Who is in the house, Tyler?"

"Alison has company," I evaded.

"Randy?"

"Yes."

"I hope they didn't embarrass you," he said evenly. "In other words, I hope they heard you coming."

"They didn't embarrass me," I said just as steadily as he had spoken. "And they didn't hear me coming, or going."

"But you know about them—you already knew." He was making a statement, not asking me.

"Same as Colin," I said. "I couldn't stay away from the maze."

"I hope you took it a bit better."

I shrugged. "It's not my business."

"Well, that's true, but Colin was hit pretty hard."

I said, "I'm glad he told you about it. That must have been some comfort to him. If you explained—how it is—" I was getting red and I hated myself for speaking so hesitantly. Old maid Tyler.

"It might have helped, if I'd been here at the time," Blase said. He wasn't laughing at me, not even smiling, that was something to be grateful for. "I was at school and Colin

281

brooded much too long before I found out what was bugging him. By then, he had gained a very bad impression of his stepmother."

"But not of Randy?" I had to ask.

Blase shook his head. His hair fell in ringlets, damp with perspiration from his nap. "I don't think Colin has the dimmest notion whose backside he saw. I think he just ran like hell."

"But didn't they—didn't Alison go after him, eventually anyway?"

"No." Blase smiled briefly. "Least said, soonest mended, isn't that from McGuffey's *Reader*? Well, anyway, that seems to be Alison's policy—but I truly doubt if she saw Colin. I believe we'd have heard."

The rain was ending and sunlight returned. He went out the screen door to study the sky. The sun caught his hair and turned it to gold. He needed a shave and he rubbed his chin as if the thought had occurred to him, too.

Plaid came around the corner of the porch and nuzzled against his bare shins. "Scat," he said. "Scat, scat, little cat." He came back indoors and shut the screen door, hooking it. "She'll find her way in, sooner or later."

I said, "There was a kid's book—something about 'scat, scat, little cat'—I used to read it to Sam until we both knew it backwards."

"Sam?"

"My brother, who died."

"Sorry, I wasn't thinking."

I said, "I'd better go, now the rain has stopped."

"Don't run away again." He put his hand on my good knee and added, "Stay and listen, please." Absently his fingers folded the sheer fabric of my skirt and pressed back a pleat in it. It was a gesture reminiscent of my father straightening a Sunday dress long ago, awkwardly, but with affection. If I breathed, the magic moment of past and present would vanish. I sat without moving.

But when Blase spoke it was not of love. It was of recklessness and indifference and of hate. "I believe Randy Paul killed the cats—Plaid's kittens."

I gasped and said, "Oh, no!" instinctively. "Randy is a gentle man."

As if he hadn't heard, Blase said, "He was the hit-and-run driver who damn near killed Picasso. He left the house that night no more than five minutes before I did. The dog was barely alive when I found him about a hundred yards down the road. Ravine Drive is not exactly a highway. There weren't any other cars."

"But the kittens!" I thought of their tumbling warmth and Colin's delight. "That wouldn't have been an accident."

"Randy can't stand a mess."

"But he doesn't even live here!"

"Not yet anyway," Blase said.

It was as if he were trying to convince himself as much as me.

"But he seems so courteous, so kind. He's been very kind to me—" I murmured in mild protest. I didn't feel ready to take up Randy's defense, but I couldn't believe he was heartless. "He's so clean—the way they used to say—squeaky clean. He's always so perfectly turned out, so tidy—"

"And *I'm* such a mess, right?" His smile was rueful and his eyes were almost hostile. "Cleanliness is next to godliness in your book, Tyler? Okay, let's forget about it."

"No, please," I said anxiously. "But couldn't Randy have thought it was just a bump, a clod of dirt, and if he was in a hurry, would he have stopped?"

"He did stop," Blase said, sounding almost hostile now. "He stopped and looked back. It wasn't dark yet. It was just about twilight, but it wasn't dark. I remember because Stella had just got a camera—I gave it to her—and she was fooling around with it. She was walking around the yard taking pictures, like a kid, and she just happened to snap poor old Picasso in what might have been his last moments. So she came running for me. Pure luck all around, but don't tell me it can't happen. It *did* happen. I was already in my car. I had a date in town—a date I never had again—" He grinned at me fleetingly. "The lady didn't think a dying dog was more important than she was, even though I called her from the vet's and told her to wait." He shook his head. "Women," he said, and I frowned at the generality, but kept quiet. I was thinking about the case he had presented. It explained why he didn't care much for Randy and made it obvious.

"Well, there you are!" I almost sang out in relief. "Maybe Randy had a date in town, too, and he saw that Stella was getting help. Maybe he even saw that you were on the way—"

"Defend him all you like," Blase said. His face closed now. "Let old Randy continue to be your knight in shining armor, clean threads, anyway, but he didn't know I was coming. And he was one hell of a lot closer to the body. *And* he was gone, long gone, when I got there."

"Did you ever mention it to him? Let him know?" I asked.

"No, not until now, I suppose you could say."

"I don't understand you at all!"

"Don't you report back to him any tidbit that might possibly be of any interest to him? Isn't that really why you're here? Randy hired you, is still hiring you, isn't he? And he put his poor old dad up to planning on hiring you for the fall, right? I guess you've got that job for certain now, is that correct?"

"Well, yes, but—"

Blase stood up. He said nothing. His eyes were unreadable.

"You're so wrong," I said bleakly. "You're so very wrong."

"Be careful on the path," he said. "It might be slippery when wet."

I was dismissed. With everything still mixed hopelessly. I limped toward the door, too distressed to think about trying to walk carefully. Possibly he took a moment's pity. He said, "Do be careful, Tyler, even if Stella isn't around to trip you up. She was sorry about that, you know. It was only an impulse, a meant-to-be-warning to slow down, and I am sure she was jealous of your friendship with Colin."

I halted and stared at him. He tried to smile. "Poor old Stella made plenty of mistakes. She was sure you were with Randy all the way, but she got around to believing you cared about Colin, too, after you got to know him. Even I believed that. Savannah must have told you about Stella and my father. She had a baby that died, but if it had lived he would have been our half brother." The navy eyes studied me. "Someone still seems worried that the child lived. Someone is still just a bit antsy that he might show up and claim a piece of the pie. Right?"

"You're so wrong!" I was nearly whimpering. I hated my trembling voice and shaking body. I longed for my cane, to lean on, to strike out with, but I had nothing, and no one, for support. I was back to that threadbare cliché, Square One. A stranger in a strange house. Watch and beware. And meanwhile get out of here.

He actually dared to offer to help me down the path. He added, "There's a dogwood cane around here somewhere. Will you take that, at least, if I can find it? I brought it home from Tennessee once."

"Better not tempt me," I muttered, and then I limped on my way.

33.

Tomorrow I would leave. I yearned to be gone tonight. I lay
awake thinking, how could I tell Alison? And then minutes
later I would summon back my courage and tell myself it was
only two weeks at the most until Colin would be in school
and the job would be properly finished as promised. I would
have kept my word and I could walk away—*not* limping, not
much at least—that was one promise I would keep. I would
never let myself get too tired or too upset to remember to
plant my feet one at a time, slowly but like any normal elderly person.

I was much, much stronger. It was only after a climb, and
when I was terribly upset, that I forgot. And I decided that I
never had been more disturbed in my whole life than in the
terrible moments when I found out what Blase Clinton really
thought of me. A hired spy, lowest of the low.

At least Colin didn't think so. Open-faced, trusting Colin,

his joy was bubbling over in the morning. When I arrived in the kitchen at breakfast time, everyone was smiling. Savannah and Colin grinned from ear to ear. "Let me tell her!" he begged, and Savannah nodded.

I had to laugh at his exuberance. Had to ask him to repeat what he'd just said. I surely hadn't heard it right. Jonathan was back and we were going sailing tomorrow. I glanced at the light over the door. It was a steady red.

"You're to wind up everything today, if you can, and take the rest of the week easy," Savannah confirmed. "Herself was here early. Ain't that good news?"

"Wonderful!" A last time to see Jonathan Clinton and to spend a glorious day with Colin away from this house which now seemed almost like a prison to me, or had last night.

"You're to leave early. Six o'clock. He's got a special place for y'all to picnic and explore, whatever you want to do. You can take your books, he said."

"*He* said? You talked to Jonathan himself?"

She shook her head. "Got a note. He typed it so's I could read it," she laughed. "It's all here and plain enough—you can read it for yourself. Deviled eggs, potato salad, ham and chicken samwiches—he likes a ham spread I make myself. Lemonade for Colin, you, too, or beer. He even asked if you preferred wine."

"Lemonade," I said. "It will be a splendid day." I hugged Colin. "Now let's get crackin', as Savannah says, and see if there's anything we need more work on."

"I got to get crackin', too," Savannah mocked me in good humor. "After I get all them eggs boiled."

In the late afternoon I pondered what to do about Stella's photographs. Miles was gone. I had phoned Mrs. Murkell, but he was not spending any time at the library and his books on interlibrary loan would have to be returned if he didn't show up soon. If I heard from him, would I please tell him? I assured her that someone would pass the message on. When I consulted Savannah about it, she had a practical solution. "Why don't you write it out and slip it under his door? He'll see it whenever he gets back. You could also try calling Griff's Tavern, or I will."

She called more than Griff's place but no one had seen Miles. I wrote the note and took it to his door, climbing the stairs with greater ease than before and congratulating myself that I wasn't even out of breath. I knocked in case he had returned, but no one answered. No sound from within. Something brushed my leg and I jumped, but it was only Plaid, still wandering, still looking for her lost mistress.

I picked up the cat and stroked it for a moment. If Randy Paul had drowned the kittens, it must have been on someone's orders, or by request. Maybe Stella had asked out of mistaken kindness, knowing she wouldn't be here to care for them. And maybe Blase had been as wrong about Randy as he was about me.

When I went back to the house I tried to ask Savannah about the litter, but she wore her closed look again. She scowled and said, "I ain't studying no kittens. I got no time to talk about nothing." She was baking in two ovens and she was out of sorts, that was for sure. But something else troubled me, and I dared her wrath to mention that the light had gone out. The red light over the door.

"So Himself went somewhere," she answered shortly. "Randy Paul was here. I reckon maybe they all took off. Probably got stuff to do at the gallery downtown, wouldn't they?"

It made sense, so why did I remain so ill at ease?

For the first time I felt estranged even from Savannah. Colin was the only one who hadn't taken on sudden stand-off attitudes, making me feel a blundering intruder asking unwelcome questions. But I wouldn't bother Colin today about anything. He was planning to go to bed early and be ready for his great outing.

I went back to my own quarters. *Windless Afternoon* was gone. I headed for the gallery to see if it was still there. The walls were bare. I felt mild resentment that they hadn't even told me they were removing the painting to the gallery in Chicago, and then I made a conscious effort to back away from a mire of self-pity. I would read Saki tonight. He would cheer up anyone.

I was getting bad nerves only because I had to make a change soon. That was it, and understandable, so why not settle down? Even at ten o'clock I was still edgy, apprehensive of small sounds, listening for sounds of cars or voices. Normal sounds. I turned on the television in the lounge but found only monster shows and reruns of ghouls and creepies, sons of apes or robots. "I'd almost give another toe for a rerun of *Random Harvest*—Ronald Colman and Greer Garson and their lovely love and reunion. Born too late," I said aloud. Indeed I almost yelled it, and though I was not to know until long later, a man in a tree house jumped and held his aching ear and cursed.

At ten past eleven I showered and dressed again in shorts, a cotton gauze top, and tennis socks and the beige shoes. I would go for a stroll outdoors where it was still summertime. It was moonlight, almost stage lighting, easy to see. I wondered if Plaid was out, too, but I didn't want to call her name and a cat probably didn't respond to a whistle. I would have welcomed her company, as Stella must have enjoyed it. Stella surely had been a very lonely woman these last years. And found it painful to see Colin growing into boyhood and school years, and to think of her lost son. No wonder she'd stayed clear of Colin.

I wandered carefully, avoiding steps, keeping in the moonlight. I needed time to think. To gather loose ends, set things in order before I left forever. I couldn't take the job at the Paul Galleries now. I could go back to Missouri, perhaps. Alison would be glad to give me a reference—the farther off the better, probably.

I could write to Colin sometimes. I could send him a special present for his birthday. Meanwhile I must do something with the photographs Stella had never picked up. They still lay in the bottom drawer of my bureau under the blankets. Maybe Savannah would hold them for Miles. The key that Mr. Paul had clutched in his dying hand was in my pile of Swiss handkerchiefs. I wondered why I had instinctively hidden it. But tomorrow I could give it to Jonathan and explain. Except that Colin missed nothing when he was present. It would be better to give Jonathan the key now.

I went back to pocket the key and headed for the studio, hoping the lights were on. It surely didn't matter this time of night whether the blinker was red or green. He wouldn't mind if I merely took a minute on the doorstep to give him his own property back and a quick word of explanation. I needn't linger.

I crossed the clearing, the outdoor living room, and was nearing the last two steps to the entrance when the door opened. A shadow fell across the clearing as a cloud obscured the moon and I called out, "Don't be alarmed, Mr. Clinton—Jonathan—it's only me, Tyler.

"Wait!" I called, as he seemed to be withdrawing, back into the hall. "I'll only take a minute. I have a key for you!"

He emerged again. He said, "A key?"

But it wasn't Jonathan who spoke. It was Randy Paul, in a yellow smock.

290

34.

"*Come in*, Tyler," Randy said. "What key are you talking about?"

I stared at the studio, unable to conceal my horrified astonishment. "Where's Jonathan? Isn't he here? Is he—ill?"

Food was stacked on a worktable. Trays of it. Spoiled food, toast, dried into tight brown curls, molded applesauce, moss-green sandwiches. So old there wasn't even any rotting smell —as if long ago Clinton had stopped eating. I saw two paint cans filled with debris, as if someone had started to clean up and then let it go. A pile of smocks was heaped on the Eames chair I'd sat in forever ago on a golden afternoon. A grocery bag held rubber gloves. It had fallen to one side and the red rubber gloves spilled out. On the stairs to the balcony bed-room were boxes never opened. Records and books, from the look of them.

"Seen enough?" Randy asked. His voice was strange, light

and excited. His head was cocked on one side. There was excitement leaping in his eyes, too.

"Enough?" I echoed. My heart was pounding and my knees felt watery. I thought I might pitch forward at any second, but I had never fainted, truly fainted, in my life.

"Well, let's say enough to draw any conclusions? That Jonathan isn't here, for one. For a start, say."

I put my fingers to my temples and pressed hard as if to make my head stop whirling. The spinning was all *in* my head. I was steady enough, but I couldn't think, couldn't take in what I was seeing or thought I saw. Maybe I'd gone slightly mad.

"You should sit down, Tyler. You look pale."

He picked up the heap of dirty smocks and dropped them behind the Chinese screen, then dusted his palms. "Well, with Stella gone—who's to clean?" he said cheerfully.

I sat slumped in the chair he'd emptied and shut my eyes.

"It must have been the dreadful shock," I murmured. "For him to see this place. Why didn't Alison send Savannah, or me, to help clean? Alice could slick it up in a minute. Well, I'm rambling but—"

"You *are* rambling, honey. And not thinking at all. There hasn't been time for anything but work, work, work." Why did he sound so queer, almost exhilarated, almost as if he held back a fit of giggling? Why were the amber eyes so brilliant? Why was he wearing Jonathan's smock! And there was fresh paint on the canvas on the working easel nearest the table. Damp brushes upended in a jar. A sticky palette.

"Now listen, honey, tell me about this key. Jonathan gave you a key?"

I shook my head dumbly.

He came to stand over me. Then he leaned forward and slapped my face. "Sorry, honey, but I thought you were about to pass out. Give me the key, dear. Right now." His hand was raised to slap again. I gave him the key.

He turned it over in his fingers, looking surprised, even disbelieving. "Have you used it before?"

"Never." I thought if he called me honey one more time I would summon strength to slap *him*. Or I would scream and scream. "You let me in. I never used it."

He glanced at his watch and I looked more carefully at the worktable; the far end held a typewriter with a half-typed message rolled on the platen. Papers were heaped beside it; some were crumpled and had fallen to the floor.

"Go ahead and look," he told me. "Enjoy my selection."

I stumbled toward the machine, nearly pitching full length in my haste, and caught the edge of the table, leaning on my hands to bend over the machine and read:

> The sand's are number'd that
> make up my life
> Here I must stay, and
> here my life must end.

But someone had typed the last line in capitals, more or less: "hERE mY LIFe must ENd."

Randy was shaking his head. For once his neat hair had fallen out of place. A lank strand lay across his pale forehead. He brushed it back. "I never was a typist. I don't suppose you'd care to dash it off for me? But typing aside, how do you like it for a farewell to the masses? Credible? Shakespeare's finest. Just the thing Jonathan would choose for his curtain line?"

I moaned. My right hand slid on the table surface and I picked up one of the half-crunched messages: "Savannah, have Colin ready for sailing early. Six, no later. And leave the hamper at the back door." There were other versions. I reached for other pages and read with sickening understanding. Leave the hamper. Alison would be in town. Tyler and Colin would be sailing.

293

Alison would be in town! She had probably gone already. Oh, God! Savannah, too. Everybody was gone. And who could tell where Miles might be? Even if Blase remained at the cabin there was no hope he could hear sounds from the studio. And he'd never invade his father's private place. Not if I screamed my head off. I must have opened my mouth. A damp hand closed over my lips.

The amber eyes were reproachful. He said slyly, "I wish we had time to play, honey—there's never enough time in this world. Remember that moment on the bluff? I almost had you then. And you'd have loved it, dear. I'm an expert swordsman, darling."

My widening eyes must have told him I remembered with terror.

He said, "Shhhh! If Miles hadn't gone whistling up to the cabin, there'd have been plenty of time. But how could I know which way he was headed? And now I have to work. Sorry, darling, but out you go."

He reached for a jersey rag with his left hand. He opened a small bottle with his teeth and tipped some of the liquid into the cloth. Then he put it over my face as his hand slid away. The whole world slid, too.

The man in the tree house flicked a tiny beam on his watch. The girl had been gone two hours now.

He was feeling rotten. He'd guessed wrong. Dead wrong and that bothered him deeply. Stella might be alive if he hadn't been blinded by his own rage. He used to trust his instincts. He would have trusted the girl, but Blase was right. He hunkered down and slowed his breathing. Someone was coming out of the house and gliding down the steps, crossing the driveway, light-footed as a ghost, skimming soundlessly up the path to the studio. But wait—the figure stopped and listened.

The man in the tree house listened, too. A hoot owl way off above the trees, toward the cabin. The figure stayed motionless. So did the man. He didn't dare answer the hoot owl. Give the all clear. Nothing was clear, and he was too damned close to the woman on the path.

He waited, easily twisted almost double. He seemed to be jointless and he liked to keep himself that way although once upon a time it had been no effort. He was getting a little old for crawling around in trees and dumbwaiters, but he could do it. He thought maybe hate helped.

Eventually the woman down below seemed satisfied she was hearing night birds, nothing more. She went up to the studio door, tapped it four times briskly, quietly, and it opened for her.

The man waited a minute more, then stretched full length and answered the hoot owl just once.

One mournful hoot meant be on the alert, be ready, just in case, further message coming. Not all clear. Not by a long shot.

He landed on the ground soundlessly and moved swiftly to the dumbwaiter, the outside contraption he'd helped design himself, to haul food in, paint supplies, even small canvases. He'd ridden up and down in it for years, just for the hell of it, never dreaming that someday it might come in desperately handy as a listening post, and a lookout.

He fitted himself inside, thanking heaven and hell both, whichever might be on the job, that Randy hadn't sent for any snacks this time. He hated sitting on chicken sandwiches. He wondered if the silly bastard had used the waiter at all, had noticed how easy it rode these days, with oiled ease. No noise at all. The tiniest of creaks from the wood protesting his weight, but no more than the wind sighing might make, an old building settling, a squirrel in the rafters.

35.

My arms ached. Not my leg, my knee, nor my missing toes, but my arms and shoulders ached horribly. I couldn't move them. Couldn't move my legs. I was paralyzed. I opened my eyes. Let me be in post-op. Let there be nurses, intravenous bottles, doctors hovering.

I was lying on the floor of Jonathan Clinton's studio. It took me minutes or hours to decide. I seemed to be trussed up like a turkey for roasting on a spit, but I was tied, not paralyzed, and my tears were for joy and thankfulness. Rope bound my hands behind my back, my knees and ankles were tied. I tried to look down at my feet but I couldn't lift my head far enough. The floor was cold and hard but I was alive.

Randy Paul was standing at the easel, in Jonathan's yellow smock, holding Jonathan's brush, wearing surgeon's colorless gloves—not the red ones I had seen—how many hours or days ago?—spilling out of the grocery bag. I was used to coming awake slowly and remembering odd circumstances, pieces of the past. It would all seep back. I could wait.

"Where is he?" I tried to ask, after a while, but my mouth was gagged. A piece of cloth was tied behind my head and the knot hurt. My hair was caught in it, but hurting meant living. I gurgled and Randy at last looked my way. "Awake, are we? Comfy?"

Younger by years than Vincent Price but he had the Price voice, the Price audacity and cheerfulness in outrageous times. The determined courtesy.

I groaned and he sighed but put down his brush and came to stand over me again, trying to read my eyes. "Clinton?" I tried a nod and failing that, a confirming blink.

"Dead, darling. Gone to coral. Five fathoms deep or whatever. Drowned, days ago."

Tears filled my stinging closed lids, ran down my face, and threatened to choke me.

"Weep not, Tyler, for he is dead. Gone to hell and chances are is already improving the place. Painting scenery, no doubt. Sorry, love, I haven't much time."

He went away again and began to hum as he worked.

I began to choke again. Was it possible to drown in your own tears? I twisted my chin and sucked against the cloth, inhaled noisily, and moaned.

"If you can promise to stop that dreary sound, I'll loosen the gag," he said. "There's nobody to hear you, dear. Colin is way up the other side of the house and sound asleep with a touch of phenobarbital to keep him dreaming." He winked at me. "Colin's even dressed and in his sleeping bag. He won't even know he's gone until he's *gone*, understand?"

I nodded as violently as possible, and he at last jerked the rag free, taking part of my hair with the loosened knot. My eyes streamed with tears but it didn't matter, reflex action.

297

My mind was clear. I could breathe again and I could think. "If you c-could j-just l-let m-me s-sit up," I pleaded wanly, kitten weak, and wished I hadn't thought of kittens. "P-please, R-Randy."

He hoisted me roughly against the wall and I thought, *Now we are getting somewhere.* Then I looked down. My shoes and tennis socks were gone. My prosthesis was gone. The stump of my left foot was bare and anger stirred deep within me. I could fight the monster somehow, cunning would save me. There was no one else.

I had automatically shut my eyes when I saw the bare stump. Now I felt a soft tickling movement. Randy had bent over and was drawing a line of yellow down my leg, making a sort of daisy on my partial foot. I bit my lips to keep from screaming and miraculously a voice said icily, "I think you had better stop that nonsense at once."

Alison! I breathed, "Oh, thank you, God!" And then hope died. I saw Alison's eyes. Narrowed, thoughtful, malicious.

She said, "It's twenty past three already. Why in God's name did you bring her here?" And a second later she added, "Or can I guess, lover?"

"She walked in," Randy protested. "She had a key."

Alison's nostrils flared. "If you're lying to me—"

But the threat was never finished. He reached in his smock pocket and handed her the key.

She studied it before she questioned me. "Where did you get this goddamned key, Tyler?" Her foot nudged my leg. She ran the toe of her sneakers across my ankle and gave a little kick at the stump which nearly sent me into the black void again. I took minutes to rally and she was aware that I was not faking the pain. She glanced at her watch. I saw that she was dressed in slacks and a windbreaker, with a scarf at her neck, ready for sailing. I hadn't realized how small she was until now, seeing her compact, put together for business and travel, no high heels, no flowing caftans. I could have overcome her easily in the old days. But not now. And not tied. "Tyler, you're not listening," she complained. "I asked you where you got this key? Jonathan?"

"I don't have to tell you," I said.

"How would it be if I kicked this stump, really kicked it? Stepped on it? Jumped up and down?"

I shivered uncontrollably. "Bad," I managed to whisper. "Bad. I would pass out and you'd get no answer then."

"I'll get an answer, you silly little bitch." She smiled at me evilly. A bit of tobacco clung to her perfectly painted lips. "Do you really think anyone can stop me now?"

No one could. But Randy said, "Oh, Alison, knock it off, please. None of the heavy stuff, we agreed on that, remember?"

None of the heavy stuff. But Jonathan had drowned— how? And Colin and I were headed for a supposed sailing date with the dead man. Alison studied him, biting her lip, then moved away. She went to the kitchenette and poured herself a drink, coming back to stand in the doorway to drink it. Straight whiskey without water. She drank it all and poured another.

Randy asked, "Why don't you lay off until tomorrow?"

"Why don't you shut up?"

"Alison, it's not good for you to—"

"You damned pantywaist, don't try to tell me anything!"

She came closer to me again. I wanted to shut my eyes but I felt mesmerized. "If you tell me where you got the key, Tyler, I will cover your stump. How's that?"

"Okay," I yielded. I was prepared to shout it out anyway because an absurd idea had suddenly occurred to me. Maybe, just maybe, Randy didn't know that his father had seen the studio. Must have known Jonathan was gone, may have

299

guessed Jonathan was dead, and knew that someone else was copying his painting. Undoubtedly shrewd old Mr. Paul had known his son could copy. And maybe that had killed him.

"It was your father's key," I said, directly to Randy, trying to ignore Alison, though I was dreadfully aware of her. At least she had thrown one of Jonathan's old smocks over my feet. "I'm not getting soft," she told me. "I keep my word."

Honor among murderers, as well as thieves? No matter. I was looking at Randy, who seemed stunned. He said, "I don't understand." Alison said, "What does it matter? He's dead."

"That's probably why he's dead," I said softly to Randy, and my cheek stung from the slap Alison delivered. "He saw this place! He was no dummy—he could tell a real Jonathan Clinton from a fake!"

Alison looked around wildly and said, "Where's that chloroform bottle? Oh, the devil with it. Why put her out of her misery? Or you either," she added, seeing Randy slump into a chair. "The old man was on his last legs anyway. Same as Jonathan, right? Same as Agatha—" She caught her lip with her teeth as if she hadn't meant to put that last name in the list. He stared at her with glazed, stricken eyes. "Agatha, too?" She was headed back for the kitchen area.

She poured herself another drink and downed it before leaving the drainboard in the kitchen where the bottle stood. She brought the bottle with her and refilled her glass. "All we did, my dear Randy, was help some sick old people into eternity. Just a gentle little push, that's all. They were all headed there anyway. We just hurried them along." She hiccuped, and Randy recoiled as if he were suddenly seeing her clearly for the first time.

He held up his hands and stared at them. They were trembling. "It all started, all of it," he was either talking to himself or—perhaps appealingly—to me, "the day I killed, or nearly killed, that damn dog when it ran in front of me.

That's when it started. That's when I went wrong and couldn't go back and ever get right again."

"But the dog didn't die," I reminded him.

"Well, I didn't know that. And it was that week we stole the first Clinton and sold it. After that it was easy."

"Easy *money*," Alison said, sipping her drink now, much more slowly. "I don't know why you're bothering to tell her all this. She's not going to be around to use any information packed into her pretty little head, but talk if it makes you feel better. Bigger—" she snorted. "Maybe it makes you feel more manly. Brag about your wicked, wicked ways. But don't try to tell her you were any good in bed because you weren't, you were lousy."

Randy slumped deeper into the chair and looked, if possible, even sicker. *Let them talk*, I thought frantically. *Let them talk and talk, it doesn't matter what they say, or if they argue, maybe daylight will come, maybe Miles will come home. Even Blase. But at daylight Colin would be up, expecting to go sailing.* I huddled against the wall, feeling that my brain was like a man-made rat in a labyrinth, searching endlessly and no way out.

"It's four o'cock—o'clock," Alison said, slurring her words, but just a little. Shaking her head to clear it. "I think we'd better move up our schedule. Just in case— I don't think Miles is coming back, ever. I think he took off for good. He didn't leave anything worth having anyway. I checked that out. I don't expect to ever see old Miles again unless he just happens to be sober enough to read a paper or see a TV when news of the accident gets out. And even then I doubt he'd show up for the funeral—especially when there isn't going to be one."

"You said a service. It would look funny without a service," Randy said bleakly.

It was impossible that I was sitting here listening to talk

about Colin's memorial service. They weren't talking about mine. Nobody would bother about mine. My Aunt Lynne might not even hear that I was gone—not for years and years, if ever.

"Blase will see to a service," I heard myself saying, as if I were a stranger, getting involved in somebody's business— uninvited. *But I am a stranger*, I wanted to shriek. *What am I doing here anyway?* Hollering would only get me gagged again. Even chloroformed, because Alison had that bottle in her hands now and was asking Randy to get a move on. She poked around on the worktable and found another cloth, a paint rag, and wrapped it around the bottle. "Take both of these and give the kid one quick sniff—enough but not too much. He'll be easier to handle if he's still breathing until you get the boat out far enough." She glanced at me. "Same for her. Knock her out now."

I opened my mouth fast and I screamed, "Blase! Blase, help me!" before Alison slapped me hard again. Randy's shaking hand was pouring liquid into the cloth, but she told him to hold it a minute. "I want her to know where her precious Blase is right about now." She looked at her watch again. "He's over the North Atlantic, honey-child, precious lamb, so yell your pretty head off. I don't think he can hear you in a seven forty-seven. He's on his way back to Spain, Tyler darling. He has a girl there. Doesn't that just about break your heart?"

"When," I gasped, "when did he leave?"

"What does it matter, he's gone."

Randy looked at me and stayed his hand for a moment.

Randy was my only hope. Oh, I had no hope, I knew that, but my whole body begged to be alive. It was really true—it was better to be alive, lucky, whatever the words were. The smell of the chloroform was making me dizzy. Looking sorry for me, and maybe for himself, Randy held the rag away, held it behind his back for the moment. Alison was wandering elsewhere in the room, looking for cigarettes. And Randy had enough wits to call out, "For God's sake, don't light one in here even if you find any. Wait till you get outdoors."

"Just shut up," she snapped back at him.

I rolled my eyes wildly. Trying desperately to use a brain I was sure had shriveled to prune size. Randy was the weak one, but what could that help? If she drank enough, would she pass out? Not likely. She would only feel more powerful, nastier. She was muttering to herself, beside herself because there weren't any cigarettes in sight. "I'll try his bed—he must smoke at night—used to, anyway. We had a few nights, anyway. And those few, let me tell you, Randy dear, were worth more than all your puny efforts. You could've taken lessons." She had a really mean laugh. Randy squirmed and tried not to look at me.

Something light, but not hurtful, fell on my forehead. I shook it off. Was Alison throwing things at me from the balcony? I twisted my head as far as it would go. A small pebble lay beside me. And it couldn't have come from the balcony. She'd gone out of sight, into a bathroom perhaps. I turned my eyes in the other direction and saw movement, just a slit in the paneling, a mouse perhaps. Nothing helpful. Randy was talking to himself. "This rag is filthy. Sorry, Tyler, but you won't smell it long."

Play on Randy's fastidious nature. Do anything to delay, delay. I whispered hoarsely; all my saliva seemed to have dried up and gone forever; it was hard to get a sound out, but it was even harder to do nothing, to give up and let Alison win. "Randy, other rags, piles of them—get a towel— kitchen, bathroom, please, Randy."

He looked at me doubtfully. He seemed drugged by despair.

I tried to smile, but winced. "Randy, please, a clean towel. Just a clean towel?"

His nostrils twisted to show distaste—maybe for smokers

—maybe for dirt—maybe for murder. Whatever it was, he delayed. He said, "I'll see what I can find."

He came back all too soon with a clean washcloth, and Alison came down the stairs, still muttering. Her search had been fruitless. She poked in a cupboard, opened and slammed drawers shut.

"The Slough of Despond," I said giddily. "Yeah, though I walk through the valley of the shadow . . . I shall fear no evil. . . ."

Allison yelled, "Will you shut her up? I can't stand that idiotic muttering. Can't you do anything right?"

I whispered, "Randy, please, can't you spare Colin? Isn't there any way? He's so young. He—he likes you." God would forgive the monstrous lie. "He told me so. He loved your dad—" The ring of truth there was unmistakable and Randy heard it. "And your father loved him. It would hurt your father terribly if you—if you—" But I couldn't say it. Alison had come back and was peering at us suspiciously. "What are you two plotting? Wasting time, that's all it is." Randy brought the chloroform-soaked rag nearer again, but his hand was shaking so hard he nearly dropped it.

"Give me that thing," Alison said. "Good-bye, Tyler."

I went spinning into the dark.

One long, mournful hoot from the tree house brought the runner down the path from the clearing. His feet seemed scarcely to touch the earth. He had been waiting a long, long time. Centuries. He had been cursing but he had also, from time to time, been chuckling. Now his feet flew in terror at the signal.

The man dropped down from the platform. He was taller, thinner than the runner and obviously in charge of guerrillas anytime, anywhere. He put his finger to his lips until they had reached the back deck where the lanky woman waited, huddled in a shawl, but ready.

"You okay?" the runner whispered. She nodded. "Don't worry," and showed him a switchblade. "Borrowed it, and the know-how, if I need it."

"Where are they?" the runner asked. "The kids."

"Where they sposed to be. We got to get moving."

"Let's go," the tall man ordered. The trio silently moved around the house to the rocks beneath the cantilevered gallery.

The moon disappeared in a bank of clouds. When it shone forth again, the trio had vanished.

36.

Incredibly I awoke and I was still in the studio, still tied, violently nauseated; I turned my head sideways and was horribly sick, but I couldn't lift my hands to wipe my face.

Alison, of all people, was wiping up the mess with a cold dishcloth. "I should have known that bastard couldn't even handle chloroform and do it right," she was saying. "I thought he'd killed you and now you're back with the living too soon. I just hope he doesn't give Colin too much until we get to the boat."

So it wasn't all a nightmare I had dreamed. It was all real and my nausea rose in waves. I choked again and Alison slapped at me with the dishcloth.

My bones felt as if they were nailed to the floor. Pain rode in cresting waves, broke and began again. Alison said, "I wonder if it's safe to smoke. I'm dying for a cigarette. That bastard should've been back five minutes ago." She went to the entryway and peered out. Then she came back and stood restlessly in the center of the room; she appeared to be thinking hard, as if she were a hostess, worrying about last-minute details for a party.

I found that if I took deep, slow breaths, the pain was less and the nausea receded.

"It'll be light any minute now," Alison remarked, ever so casually. "You know I should be very angry with you. You were supposed to be our objective observer. The sweet young thing, a stranger to our household, who would sit at the inquest, crying softly and trying to comfort me. And then take the stand and tell all about Jonathan's strange behavior all summer—his attack on you in the woods. His splashing green paint all over his own best work."

"It wasn't his best," I protested weakly, too far gone to care. "*Windless Afternoon* is his masterpiece."

She looked almost pleased with me. "Well, I agree with you there. And we had that for you to point out the changes. Thank God, you already told the press about them."

"Randy made them?" I asked, my head aching as if it were on fire, as if a million needles were pricking my scalp.

"Randy did it all. There's an old secret staircase, leads to the gallery. Agatha left it—she was going to tell Colin all about it someday. Well, she never got the chance. But she told me. She trusted me—right up till the end." Alison wore a satisfied smirk. "Even Jonathan trusted me, but not Stella. That's why Stella had to die."

"I trusted you, too," I said, as if it mattered. "More or less." It was some comfort to know that Blase did not and Savannah did not, at least. Maybe someday they would put their heads together and catch up with this villainous woman and her cool, cool smile.

I thought of Stella's photographs under the blankets in the bottom bureau drawer. Maybe Savannah would find them and start to wondering. It would be too late to help Colin or me, but maybe someday justice would be done.

There was something else Alison had said just now that troubled me. A tag end—even if nothing would matter much longer now. "You said—the attack in the woods—Mr. Clinton would never—"

She smiled ever so sweetly. "No, of course not. Randy gave that performance. He wouldn't have gone all the way. You'd have liked that, wouldn't you? You're such a silly little fool. Too clever for your own good, agreed? We would have painted half your *Windless Afternoon* black, or red, if it had taken that to make you see the changes. But you were so smart. You took photographs. That was something even we hadn't thought of. It helped enormously."

She smiled again. "They're priceless, as evidence. As good as you would have been, sobbing in guilt that we let Colin go sailing with a man no longer accountable for his behavior—that was the way we had it planned."

"It was a good plan," I said thickly. My throat was dry. "Why did you kill Jonathan? He was ill. He would probably die soon."

"He was going to change his will and he made the mistake of telling his dear friend, Mr. Paul. Randy found out about it. We couldn't let him change the will. He leaves everything to me until Colin is twenty-one. He made that will on our honeymoon—well, to be truthful, the day before our honeymoon."

"So Colin can never be twenty-one," I said dreamily. There was no way out. Randy was a pasteboard man. Even if he took pity on the boy, he had no extra strength of his own. He was a puppet, with Alison pulling the strings. I was getting too sleepy. She waved the rag toward me, but not close enough yet, and smiled and smiled.

She wanted to tell her story to an attentive listener. That

was it. She put the rag down, stepped closer, and kicked at my stump still covered as it was. "Would a good sharp slap open your big brown eyes?" she asked thoughtfully.

I nodded and then quickly shook my head. I forced my heavy lids open. "I can hear you. Tell me, please, why Stella?"

"She intended to call in the police if I wouldn't pay and pay plenty. Stella got religion for a while I understand, but toward the end Stella got greedy. She smoked too much, got careless. And she assured me she had proof."

"Proof? That Randy drowned Jonathan somehow?" Why wouldn't she go away and let me sleep?

I felt a stinging slap on my cheek. My eyes flew open again.

Alison said, "It will be much better if you can walk or hobble to the boat. Randy has Jonathan's sneakers. It makes sense that Colin be carried in his sleeping bag. He's already dressed."

"S-slept in his clothes, poor tyke," I murmured. "S-so ready for his wonderful day."

"You bleeding hearts make me puke," Alison said, without any particular emphasis, as if she were saying it looked like rain. "Stella didn't know a goddamn thing about Jonathan— or anything else, if you ask me. She was bluffing. She knew some of the paintings were missing but not anything more. Anyway, good riddance." Her voice sharpened. "It's about time you got back!" She was speaking to a puffing Randy who had a boy in a hooded sleeping bag over his shoulder.

"This damn kid weighs twice as much as anyone could've guessed."

"And you have rubber bands for muscles," Alison snapped. She slid an evil wink at me. "Everywhere, that is, and no balls."

Randy let the bag slip to the floor but broke its fall so that the boy inside would not awake, nor be hurt. His face was almost yellow with agony. His shoulders sagged with more than weariness. He was heartsick and I had even worse news for him. Alison was telling him to hurry up and get his second wind. "Get her shoes on! She has to walk—we need the prints."

"I can't." I moaned. "I simply can't force my shoe on—my foot's swollen." I thrust it toward Alison. "See for yourself, you were so smart!"

Her kicks had bruised my injury without breaking the skin, sutured expertly months and months ago, and without causing any swelling, but I put all my hopes in her thinking it was impossible for me to slip into my shoe again.

She said briskly, "Oh, what the hell's the difference—this is all nonsense about footprints—you won't be found soon enough to matter."

I was racking my softened brains to think of anything to delay her. She was thinking of details. "You didn't turn on a light in the house?" she asked Randy, who shook his head. "No need to. The boy was sound asleep. I listened to his breathing—one little pill did the trick."

One little pill! I shouted, "One little pill didn't help your father, Randy! She poisoned him with the sherry, too, did she tell you that?"

I had hit home! He stared at me, as Alison, too startled to speak for a moment, gave me the chance to remind him, "She had two pillboxes—remember? One was poisoned. Her handy-dandy sherry wasn't enough maybe—she couldn't take a chance."

"Shut your stupid face!" she shrieked at me. "Randy, don't listen to her—she's a babbling idiot!"

But Randy gave her a shove that sent her reeling backward and shocked her into silence for another moment. He put his hand under my chin and forced my face up roughly, holding my chin in a savage grip. "All right, Tyler, tell me again. What sherry, what pills?"

310

I said very slowly and clearly, as if I were speaking to a bewildered child. "I think your friend killed your father when he might have died anyway from the shock of seeing this place. She didn't know he had a key. So she must have poisoned his heart pills, in one of the cases, the one I took from his poor old hand. And then she pretended to find the good one—the nitro, whatever, that might have eased his pain. She's a monster, can't you see that?"

"Are you going to listen to this drivel all night?" Alison was raging now, but Randy still held my chin as if his hand were a vise. I slid a glance at Alison. She was rubbing her elbow where she'd struck it when Randy shoved her so unexpectedly. Thinking only of her own small wounds, I decided, but I was wrong. She was also thinking of Stella. And so, suddenly, did I. "Stella had pictures to prove Mr. Paul was here—he died on the steps on his way out. He knew something—he told me that!"

Alison stared at me. "I thought Stella had the other box. I thought that was her 'proof,' but I couldn't find it anywhere."

Randy turned heavy, dull eyes toward Alison. "You told me Stella killed Agatha—not—not my poor old dad." Randy was confused and exhausted, a broken man, but how could he help Colin and me, even if I could win him to our side?

"Stella didn't kill anybody," I said. "Not even herself. She was a good Catholic in her last years—maybe a little greedy, but she didn't commit suicide. You pushed her, Randy?"

He nodded, but his mind was elsewhere. "Alison! You killed an old man who was probably dying anyway—like Jonathan." Randy turned to me. "Jonathan had a brain tumor, you know. He was dying, too."

I curled my bruised lip. "Another one of her stories?" But it could be true, all too true. His behavior had been all too erratic.

Alison drew up her shoulders and said flatly, "The sun will

be up any minute. On schedule. As things ought to be. As things will be from now on. No more crackpots to deal with, Randy. You ought to be glad of that. No more moving things at night. You can get some sleep."

Eternal sleep, I thought suddenly. That was what she had in mind for all of us. I inched myself across the floor and put a hand inside the sleeping bag to see if Colin's face was cool or flushed and prayed that he would sleep his way into eternity.

"What the hell do you think you're doing?" Alison demanded, seeing my slow movement.

"Just let me touch him once, please. I promise I won't wake him— My God, Alison, I don't want him to wake up to this!"

No mistaking the truth in my appeal. She said, "Oh, for God's sake, pat the kid and let's get moving. You're such an asshole, Randy, you always were. We should have been out of here an hour ago."

I reached gently inside the sleeping bag to touch the small face. A little hand touched mine and squeezed one finger warningly. I swallowed a gasp, but it could have been a sob. They didn't seem surprised. I swallowed back another sound that was almost a squeal of hope. Alison was right in her mutterings. It was getting light—light enough for me to see that the little hand was black! If Beebee was here, could Savannah be far behind?

37.

"*While we* get to the boat, you can tell me where the snapshots are," Alison said with enormous calm.

I said, "Never," and tried to duck her slap.

"We can untie her hands at least," Randy said. "Let her last moments be comfortable." The look in his eyes was kindness itself. Gentleness laced with insanity. I doubted that Randy could remember his own name by now.

"What did you do with Jonathan?" I whispered, as he worked to loosen the ropes knotted tightly at my wrists.

"Dumped him where he won't be found."

"How can you be sure of that?"

"They never found Agatha, did they?" Alison joined in, looking mildly amused and ever so smug.

Randy shot her a wild glance. His eyes were like marbles rolling.

"Sure I gave her a shove. She was dying, too. All we ever did was help a few oldsters into—whatever there is."

"Oh, God, Alison, why? She was a nice woman. I—we—liked her."

"I wanted her husband and her money. I'll settle for half. The money." Her green eyes smiled at me. "She trusted me. There was nothing difficult about it."

"Not all the way," a voice said. "The trust part. She didn't tell you about the hidey-hole for the boys, now did she, love?"

Alison took one disbelieving look at the man in the doorway and shrieked, "You're dead!"

"Tired, but not dead," Jonathan said, and he winked at me. "Rub your hands hard. It will help. Sorry we couldn't get here a bit sooner."

I felt as if my voice crawled across my tongue and the word dropped off. "We?"

"Several of us. Me, for one," said another male voice. I was caught up in strong brown arms. I was kissed hard and hungrily and at last tenderly. My foot was cradled in a sculptor's gentle fingers. "No harm that I can see. How does it feel?" he asked. The navy blue eyes were black with anger, but sparkling, too, with hope—with love?

"Never better," I said. "Oh, Blase, is it really you?"

"It is really I," he said lightly. Then his voice broke. "I love you, Tyler. My God, how I've wanted to say that! To yell it!"

"Me, too," said a smaller voice, and Beebee slid his hand in mine.

Jonathan Clinton, tall, lean, lithe, with his eyes as vivid a blue as ever and roguish now, stepped over Alison's body which lay in a real or pretend faint, no one seemed to care which. "About my brain tumor," he said affably, "though no one has asked, I may as well tell you the Mayo brothers couldn't find it. I need to watch my blood pressure, that's about it."

314

"You were drowned," I said weakly, held close and warm in Blase's arms, hearing his heartbeat, hearing my own.

"It's very difficult to drown successfully with two magicians at hand," Jonathan said. He looked at Blase and over his shoulder at Miles, who stood scowling at the still prostrate body of Alison.

"I wish she'd wake up so I could kill her," Miles said. "She was actually responsible for having my little sister done in, though this birdbrain here was the instrument."

Randy Paul sat as still and unhearing as a blunt instrument. He was worlds away and might never come back fully. Time would tell.

Savannah came in and toyed with her switchblade. "I might just give her a prick to see if she's fallen into a trance, you think? I didn't get to use this damn thing."

My fingers traced Blase's dark golden eyebrows, outlined his lips, as they had in dreams. "Where were you all this time—oh, my God!" I sat up. *"Where is Colin?"*

Everyone laughed. Everyone except Randy. A little bit of spittle was running down his chin. Except Alison who lay without moving.

"Dr. Gibson is on his way, with the police. They'll deal with her," Jonathan said, stepping over the body again.

"Where is Colin?" I demanded.

"You'll never believe, unless you see for yourself," Blase said. "I'll fetch you to Colin, beloved, for one quick look, and then I've got other plans."

He carried me. Not an easy trip. Not a short one. "We may as well take the long way," he said, "or you'll be up all night asking questions."

So we went by way of the sealed-off cellar room which Agatha had planned for her boys, knowing boys liked a hiding place. Only Jonathan and Blase had been told. Colin was to know later. But Miles had found the spot and later Stella had spied on her brother and found it also though only Stella knew that. I decided it was lucky I had collected the photos that would have told Alison there was a room she hadn't found in all her prowling, handily concealed behind rocks, so cleverly hidden no one would ever guess it was here. A room where Jonathan had dried out and rested after Blase and Miles had helped him from the deep water and where the three of them had stored whatever stolen and sold paintings they'd been able to trace and buy back. A room with its own air conditioning and lighting system. "I helped a little with the plans," Blase said. "It would have pleased Houdini, I think."

"It's lovely, I'm sure," I said, fighting my claustrophobia. "But why did you wait so long to confront Alison and Randy?"

"We had plenty of suspicions but damn little proof of anything but stealing. Alison convinced my father that Stella had murdered my mother. But he didn't stay convinced. Dad and I faked our falling out this summer to make it easier to fool Alison. We've all been watching closely. Miles and I were never far away when poor old goof-off Randy thought he was sending Dad to Davy Jones's locker for keeps—" Blase stopped when he saw me shudder. "We wouldn't have let anything happen to him, Tyler."

I asked again, "But where is Colin?" And Blase insisted on carrying me upstairs and to the second-floor storeroom, but no Colin. "Here's where we put him but he had other ideas. Luckily Savannah figured out his thinking and located him."

I said, "Hurry, please. I want to see for myself." So he carried me to the guest bedroom, with the canopied bed.

Again no Colin.

"I don't want to stay here," I said, dizzy with love and lingering chloroform, "it's too damn fancy."

"For you and me, yes, but look who likes it—"

He pulled up the dust ruffle and knelt to show me a sleeping Colin and a striped kitten, the runt of the litter. "I was

316

wrong about Randy drowning the cats. Colin hid them in his clearing."

Colin opened one eye just as Blase kissed me and I kissed him back joyfully.

"Oh, Tyler," Colin complained, "You going to get mushy, too?"

"What do you mean 'too'?"

"Even Baretta got all mushy last night."

"I plan to get all mushy tonight," I told him.

"Tyler, can we get on our way now that you've actually seen the monster?"

I took one more look at Colin. "What am I going to do about you? Too big for ring bearer and too short for best man?"

"No problem," Blase said. "We'll elope."

"Okay," Colin said. "Can I bring the cat?"